Books by Gena Showalter
available from Inkyard Press and Harlequin TEEN
(each series lists titles in reading order)

The Forest of Good and Evil

The Evil Queen

The Everlife Novels

Firstlife
Lifeblood
Everlife

The White Rabbit Chronicles

Alice in Zombieland
Through the Zombie Glass
The Queen of Zombie Hearts
A Mad Zombie Party

The Intertwined Novels

Intertwined
Unraveled
Twisted

GENA SHOWALTER

THE EVIL QUEEN

ink
yard
press

ISBN-13: 978-1-335-54224-3

The Evil Queen

I dedicate this book to my nephew and niece:
Nathan Hurt and Meagan Hurt.

I treasure, adore and love you. If ever you doubt it, just remember
I did some public speaking for you, and only whined about it a little
beforehand…and during…and after. And every day since.

You are both so incredibly talented, beautiful inside and out,
and bright, shining stars—and I just want to make sure
you never forget that I did, in fact, stand in front of
a room full of people and make words.

Love,

Aunt Gena

The Azul
Dynasty

Enchantia

Provence of
Fleur

The
Enchantian
Forest

A TALE AS OLD AS TIME

*Why do we love fairy tales? Oh, let me count
the reasons. Magic. Inspiration. Adventure.*

True love.

But there are reasons to hate these stories, as well.
Murder. Betrayal. Heartbreak. Some characters live,
some die, but all suffer in one way or another.

I do. I suffer. My name is Everly Morrow,
and I am the star of "Little Snow White." Except, I'm not
the heroine foolish enough to eat a poisonous apple.
I'm the villain. The Evil Queen.

You think you understand what drives me. You think
I'm cruel and heartless. You think you know the truth
about good and evil. You think wrong.

Hidden inside every fairy tale is a prophecy of events
to come, and I play my part to perfection. Not that
anyone understands my endgame—yet.

But you will. Soon. I will set the record straight.

Fair warning, my darklings.
This tale isn't for the faint of heart.

Mirror, mirror on the wall,
who will perish when I call?

FROM THE
ANNALS OF ENCHANTIA

THE REIGN OF GOOD AND EVIL

O nce upon a time in the magical land of Enchantia, a queen sat in her turret, dreaming of a new life. One of hope and fulfilment rather than dread and emptiness.

She was not alone. Whether a royal or a peasant, a newly married woman had twelve months to conceive a child. If the clock ran out, a husband had the right to end the union—with the wife's beheading.

The queen had been married for eleven months, had seduced her husband time and time again…to no avail.

Desperate to survive, she joined forces with four other women trapped in similar situations. Another queen, a princess, a witch and an oracle. The five females scoured the endless *Annals of Enchantia*…and learned of the mystical Tree of New Beginnings.

Owned by a cruel king, the tree possessed a trunk both towering and broad, its ebony-black limbs displaying snow-white leaves and bloodred apples. A mesmerizing triad of colors.

The king guarded his treasured possession mercilessly. Eons had passed since the consumption of an apple. A shame, for legend claimed the apples restored lost power, strengthened magic, healed physical injuries and aided a woman's quest to conceive.

The legend provided warnings, as well. Apple babies—forever known as *bonum et malum*—would wield more power and magic than any of their peers…

But they would also suffer a tragic end.

The hopeful mothers-to-be chose to believe the blessings and dismiss the curse. Risking everything, they stole and ate one apple apiece. Except for the second queen. She ate *two* apples, just to be doubly sure.

Nine months later, on the same day, each woman gave birth to a healthy, beautiful baby girl. Actually, Queen Doubly Sure gave birth to *two* healthy, beautiful baby girls.

The new mothers rejoiced…until the oracle spoke a prophecy of doom and darkness, claiming the six newborns would one day play a part in "Snow White and the Evil Queen," the fairy tale a road map for their fates.

First, though, they had to escape the cruel king.

When he learned what had happened, he ordered the executions of the mothers *and* their children.

One of the queens ran away…and died at the hands of a dangerous sorcerer. The oracle and the witch went into hiding… only to be found and killed. Thankfully, their daughters survived.

Terrified, the princess and the other queen enacted a desperate plan to secret their girls to the mortal world, where the king would never think to search.

But there was one thing that they did not yet comprehend. Evil never came dressed as a devil; evil came disguised as a dream, as tempting as the shiny red apples they'd once consumed.

If they weren't careful, they *would* succumb…

PROLOGUE

A brief glimpse into the future
The Enchantian Forest

"Well, well, well." Overcome by dark delight, I unveiled my coldest, wickedest smile. "Hello, my darklings."

Standing before me, bound by thorny vines, were my greatest enemies—Snow White, Prince Charming and three of the seven dwarfs, or *protectors*. Above us, golden sunlight filtered through a canopy made of ivory leaves. Around us, majestic trees teemed with fruit and flowers.

The loveliest war zone I'd ever seen.

Radiating her patented mix of shock and fury, Snow White bucked and strained for freedom. I didn't want to brag, but I was the one who had introduced her to that fury. Before me, she'd been all sunshine and roses. *You're welcome.*

One by one, the protectors bowed their heads, ashamed. *Too little, too late.* All the while, Prince Charming held my gaze, unafraid of my wrath. But then, he was a warrior to his core, forged in fire, then honed and sharpened like a blade, one strike at a time.

Shivers careened down my spine as I breathed in the sugar and spice of his scent. *Focus*. "Dear, sweet Prince Charming. Mere hours ago, you wished to prove your love for me." Would he prevail at long last, or let me down once again? "Behold. This is your chance. Side with me, and lose her. Or, side with her, and lose me. What you cannot do? Side with us both."

Snow White had wounded me so deeply, so profoundly, I would never recover. But I could be comforted by Prince Charming—if he did as I asked.

The fact that he didn't respond right away...

I bit my tongue until I tasted blood. *Calm. Steady*. Whatever his decision, I would survive.

Finally, he said, "I love you, Everly, and I choose you." His ragged voice teased my ears. "I will *always* choose you."

Joy began to stir to life. I'd actually *won*?

Then he added, "But I will not let you kill her."

My lungs deflated, leaving me breathless and dizzy. "You love me, so you protect her? Good one. For your next trick, pull a rabbit out of your invisible hat."

He lifted his chin. "I will be your sword, and I will be your shield. I will protect you until I take my last breath...even when *you* are your own worst adversary."

A lie! No adversary was worse than his precious Snow White.

I longed to shout curses at him. But I couldn't reveal my true feelings without also revealing my vulnerabilities. Vulnerabilities could be exploited. So I blanked my expression. Or tried to. My muscles refused to obey my mind, my pain simply too great.

Very well. My illusion magic wasn't second nature, but I could wield it when needed, as long as I remained linked to someone else and syphoned enough of their power.

Since I had tapped into an amazing power source only minutes ago, I had this in the bag.

Streams of heat and energy flowed into my every cell, and I moaned. Had strength ever been this intoxicating? I wanted more, more, *more*. More strength meant I could safeguard who and what I loved.

A truth I'd learned: love without strength equaled misery.

Strength equaled security.

Or maybe I should cut ties with those loved ones instead. No ties, no heartache. I would be bulletproof.

With a twirl of my finger, I unleashed a tendril of magic to craft an illusion of calm. Excellent. After faking a yawn, I buffed the metal claws that adorned my fingers. "Why am I not surprised you claim to want me while defending her? Oh, yes. Because you *always* defend her."

Eyes hauntingly beautiful as they filled with torment, he said, "Do you not see the irony, sweetling? You plan to commit the same crimes as the one you loathe."

How dare he! I would *never* be like Snow White. "This just in," I said, mimicking a prime-time anchorman. "Prince Charming could have enjoyed a happily-ever-after with the Evil Queen, the best thing to ever happen to him. Alas. The fool tossed her aside, and she moved on."

"*You* are the best thing to ever happen to him?" Snow White laughed. "Poor, poor Prince Charming."

Do not react. "Yes. Poor, poor Prince Charming. A supervillain in denial."

Without missing a beat, he said, "Every hero is a villain, and every villain is a hero. It just depends on who you ask."

He wasn't wrong. I was a villain to many and a hero to... myself. Prince Charming and Snow White were heroes to the world, but villains to me.

I had a brand-new "no mercy" policy for my villains.

"She struck at you, and we *will* punish her for it—calmly,

rationally," he added. "Otherwise, we merely perpetuate the cycle of violence."

My heart leaped. We would strike at Snow White together? "Tell me how we'll punish her."

"We will lock her in the tower, to suffer as you suffered."

I waited for him to elaborate, to mention the whipping I'd suffered, too. The forced marriage to an old man. The insults lobbed at me, and the common kindnesses I'd been denied. But he didn't. Of course he didn't.

"We both know you'll fill her cell with luxuries, then free her far too soon." *Not. Good. Enough.* I doubted any sentence but death would be good enough. "Face it. You are blind to her many, many, *many* faults."

"How can you… You can't…" Snow White peered at Prince Charming, the fury melting from her countenance, leaving only raw despondency. "She killed our king and hopes to break our bond. You *cannot* support her."

"I can. I will." He held my stare, unwavering. "I will do *anything* for Everly—except help her destroy herself."

I thrilled, and then I cursed. *Enough!* If anyone had the power to sway me from the proper path, it was this boy and his black-magic voice. But I couldn't let him do it. Not this time. Pretty words meant nothing without consequent action.

"You have made your choice," I told him, "and I have made mine. Our course is set."

"That is true, though it will not end the way you hope." Snow White's fury returned in a flash, her gaze spilling fire at me. "Prophecy says I will come back to life and slay you. Prophecy is *never* wrong."

Prophecy was fairy tale, and fairy tale was prophecy. While some parts were literal, other parts were symbolic. Oh, how I prayed my death and her victory were symbolic.

"You will *not* harm Everly," Prince Charming snapped, causing Snow White to flinch.

I kissed the tip of my middle finger and blew in her direction. Once, I'd admired this girl, and yes, okay, I'd envied her, too. Such strength! Now? Pure, unadulterated rage blistered me inside and out whenever I thought of her.

"Why don't we liven up this party?" I twirled my finger, unleashing another tendril of magic.

No need to look over my shoulder to know vines had grown together to construct a regal throne, different flowers blooming over the seat, creating a colorful bouquet.

Head high, I swished the tail of my gown aside and eased down.

Creatures hid in nearby shadows, watching as the prophecy unfolded. I welcomed our audience, calling, "Come one, come all. Look. See. Learn what happens when you betray the Queen of Evil…"

One by one, the creatures moved into sunlight, forming a circle around us. Trolls and chimera, unicorns and griffins, nymphs and centaurs. What a fearsome sight they made.

How much more fearsome was *I*?

Incalculably. I almost fluffed my hair.

As the creatures twittered with excitement, Snow White shrank back. Prince Charming raised his chin higher, refusing to back down, no matter the odds stacked against him. The protectors struggled against their bonds, determined to aid their royal charges.

Drumming metal claws against the arms of the throne, I announced, "Today I am your judge, jury and executioner. Spoiler alert. You're all guilty, and you're all going to die. But we shouldn't let the outcome taint our enjoyment. There's fun to be had—for me. Shall we begin?"

Stubborn to his core, the prince took a step in my direction. An action he surely regretted when the vines jerked him back in place, their sharp thorns cutting into his wrists, streams of his blood dripping to the ground. "This isn't you. Grief has hidden your joy, but we can find it again."

Hardly. "I was born to be the Evil Queen. The monster other monsters fear. Selected by Fate. Joy is the carrot forever dangled out of my reach."

He shook his head, a lock of midnight hair falling over his forehead. "Fate might have predicted our course, and the corresponding outcomes, but we decide what parts of the fairy tale are literal and what parts are symbolic. We still have freedom of choice, and I am thankful for that. You are the one I crave more than breath, Everly."

Perhaps. *No ties.* "You may call me Your Majesty." A howling wind blew past us, leaves rattling and branches clapping, an eerie ballad I enjoyed. "Or Stepmother Dearest."

"I'm sorry you were forced to wed my father." Once again, he took a step forward. Once again, the vines stopped him. But all the while, his eyes implored me. "Words cannot adequately express my remorse."

Another gust of wind, the scent of cinnamon, nutmeg and cloves—*his* scent—filling my nose, stronger than before. Awareness heated my blood and fractured my defenses.

Well, why not? He was my most wicked fantasy come to startling life.

"Let me think about whether or not I care what you feel." I drummed my claws with more force. "Still thinking…no. I don't care."

He radiated abject disappointment. *Too bad, so sad.*

Determined, I returned my gaze to Snow White, who regarded me with haughty disdain. "Come closer, child."

I made the vines push her forward. And okay, okay. Maybe I was showing off. But only a bit! I had a link to never-ending power; she did not.

"Let's forget the atrocities you've committed this day." *Do not choke on your hatred. Exhibit control.* "You are also accused of selfishness, greed and rampant stupidity. Opening argument?"

"*You* are guilty of being a plague upon humanity." She struggled for freedom, a little crazed. "One day, one day soon, I will burn you alive, just as our fairy tale suggests."

I canted my head and met Prince Charming's gaze. "Any admonishments for *her*?"

"Right now, you are my primary concern." He searched my eyes. Hoping to find a hint of the optimistic girl he'd first met? "You have never enjoyed harming others. Don't start now."

"Don't do this. Don't do that," I mocked. Inside, I commanded, *Don't soften.* "You're no fun anymore."

But then, I wasn't fun anymore, either. Once, I'd been an innocent who'd thought I could have anything I wanted as long as I worked hard enough. Once, I'd chosen to believe the best of people. Once...but no longer. You could work yourself to death and gain nothing. And people, well, they would always put themselves first, no matter how many others got hurt in the process.

To survive, I had to do the same. I had to be tougher, smarter, stronger.

Everything always came back to strength.

Finally, one of the protectors decided to speak up. The one I hated almost as much as Snow White. "If you do this," she said, "if you step off this emotional cliff, you *will* fall."

"I guess you would know," I snapped. "All of you fail to comprehend a single glaring fact." I motioned to Snow White. "I will eagerly walk into a sword as long as I can impale her, too."

The members of my audience regarded me with horror and awe—the perfect combination.

I stood and sauntered toward Prince Charming, the hem of my gown swishing at my feet. "Evil isn't born, it's made. One thought and action at a time." I paused for effect. "Take a good look at what you've made."

Snow White spit curses at me.

When I stopped a few feet away, Prince Charming swept his gaze over me, slowly, leisurely, devouring me one tasty bite at a time—and I liked it.

"I'm looking," he rasped. His irises flamed, every muscle in his body knotting with sudden tension. "Never want to stop."

New shivers almost knocked me down. *Hide your vulnerabilities. Grin.* Better. I traced a fingertip along the dark stubble that shadowed his jaw, then glided around him, scrutinizing him the way he'd so often scrutinized me. Could I truly destroy this beautiful warrior?

He turned with me, twisting the vines that bound him. *Fraying* the vines. Soon, he would gain his freedom.

"Want to know the difference between us?" I asked, unconcerned. "I admit I'm bad. You pretend you're good."

The vines fell away, and he walked me backward. Soon was now. Got it. My heart raced. Eventually, a tree trunk halted my retreat.

Prince Charming reached up, bracketing my temples with his hands, caging me in. At six-foot-four, he loomed over me, his gloriously broad shoulders seeming to surround me...and I loved it.

When I inhaled, he exhaled and vice versa. We breathed for each other, agonizing awareness sizzling between us.

"Once, I hurt you when I should have safeguarded you. Something I will forever regret. But I have learned from my mistakes." He moved one of those big, calloused hands to my jaw and traced my cheekbone with his thumb. "Your happiness is *my* happiness."

Pull away. Pull away now! But my limbs had frozen and refused to obey my mind. I stood there, floundering, trapped by my own weaknesses. For him. For what he made me feel.

And he wasn't done! "Marry me, Everly. Become my wife. Let's make each other smile and laugh for eternity."

I gulped. Technically, I *could* wed him. My so-called husband was dead. But...

No! "You can't be serious," I said, my heart racing faster, thudding against my ribs.

"This madness must cease." Snow White yanked at her bonds. "Has she ensorcelled you?"

The protectors issued protests of their own, until my tree limbs stuffed their mouths full of leaves.

"Your thoughts and opinions are unwelcome," Prince Charming told Snow White. His gaze never released mine. Those exquisite eyes, framed by the longest, thickest black lashes, created a beautiful portrait of fierce adoration. "Say yes, Everly."

Must stay strong. If I weakened, the vulnerability he oh so easily cultivated would cost me everything—again. I'd lost too much already. "I say...no. My vengeance will not be denied."

I twirled my finger, new vines wrenching Prince Charming back in line. Much better. I returned to my throne and sat with far less grace than before.

"Do I have your full attention?" I asked.

He remained unperturbed. "You've had my full attention since the moment we met."

Ignore the pleasure of his words. Forge ahead.

"I declare everyone is guilty as charged." I extended my arm to the side and slowly opened my fist. At the same time, a tree branch stretched out...out...to place a white apple in my palm. Prophecy proclaimed I would kill Snow White with poisoned fruit—for a time, at least—so I would. Only, hers would not be a restful sleep. "Now, for the sentencing portion of the trial."

Just as the Apple of New Beginnings had once granted me life, the Apple of Life and Death would grant me peace.

"One bite," I said, "and you will sleep for eternity."

Still not good enough. I raked my claws over my forearm. Skin tore, my venomous blood welling. I painted each claw crimson before I sank the metal tips into the apple.

In seconds, one half of the fruit turned red.

Fear shook Snow White when I added, "You will willingly eat this poisonous, poisonous apple, Princess, or you will watch me force-feed it to your friends. Decide."

Prince Charming jerked as if I'd struck him.

Realization: yes, I could destroy him, as long as I destroyed Snow White, too. I might feel guilty for it, but I wouldn't be swayed from my course. Not again. *This is justified.*

She paled, her mouth floundering open and closed. "I won't... you can't..."

She would. I could.

Sounding resigned, Prince Charming said, "This is what you need, Everly? This will help you heal from the damage we've caused?"

The questions surprised me.

"Without a doubt," I replied. Except, deep in my bones, I knew I *couldn't* heal. Some wounds were permanent.

"Very well. For you, my queen, I will do anything. Even this." Somehow, he freed himself a second time, shot across the distance in a blink and snatched the apple from my grip.

No! "Don't you dare—" Too late.

With his gaze still locked on mine, he bit into the poisoned fruit.

1

Listen well, and I'll tell you a story.
But take note, my darklings, it's a wee bit gory.

PRESENT DAY
MORTAL WORLD

Students surrounded me, each one parked at a desk, listening as a guest professor explained quantum theory and Schrödinger's cat.

As he paced in front of the chalkboard, he said, "If we sealed a cat and a vial of poison inside a box, we could consider the cat both dead *and* alive. A fascinating paradox."

One student muttered something about the "tomcat" in his pants, and the kids closest to him snickered. Someone else joked about watching kitty porn, earning outright laughs, while a third boy claimed he'd put his tomcat in the wrong kitten's litter box last night.

We were all (supposedly) gifted students who'd tested (remarkably) high in the sciences. I had to wonder about the validity of our scores.

The visiting professor seemed to fight a smile before saying, "That's inappropriate. Let's remain on topic."

Underneath my desktop, I stealthily opened and closed a small compact mirror. No one looked my way. Not even Peter Kinds, the boy sitting at my right—my first, only and former boyfriend. We'd dated all summer, only to break up a week ago, the first day of our senior year. Although…

If no one at school knows I dated him, did I ever really date him?

Peter had demanded we keep our relationship a secret because we didn't need "the whole school knowing our business." Lie! I'd done an autopsy of our relationship. He'd wanted to be with me, yes, but he'd wanted the approval of our peers even more.

I wasn't popular. He was. I wasn't well liked. I suspected I gave off some kind of a toxic vibe. I had one friend—my twin sister, Hartly—but she was better than a legion of admirers. She only ever saw the best in me. Meanwhile Peter, a football god, was universally adored.

Once, I'd adored him, too.

Open.

Close.

When he discovered my love for fiction, he'd decided to play the part of hero. Kind of. He'd brought me flowers, serenaded me outside my bedroom window, and delivered food from my favorite vegan restaurant. On the flip side, he'd refused to drive me to school, walk me to class, or sit beside me at lunch. Until we returned home, he wouldn't even acknowledge my presence.

If only I could kick my own butt for crushing on a shallow POS.

The worst part? I couldn't blame him. Facts were facts, and I was grade-A weird. A girl obsessed with mirrors and prone to daily delusions.

Open.

Close.

Open.

Don't look down. Don't you dare.

People assumed I was vain. I wasn't. For years, Mom had touted the dangers and absurdity of valuing appearance over inner substance. *You have a pretty face. So what? You are not the architect of your DNA.*

I agreed 100 percent. Or rather, 90 percent. Okay, maybe closer to 80 percent. Loving yourself wasn't a bad thing. But I didn't stare into a mirror for hours at a time because I admired the view. Sometimes I thought I kinda sorta saw…someone else. A sweetheart I'd nicknamed Angel. She had pale white skin and long, dark hair. She always wore a ball gown, a thousand pounds of jewelry and a genuinely happy smile.

For the past couple of months, I'd watched her life unfold in the glass. She gave baskets of food to the poor, visited orphanages and tirelessly cared for the sick.

Too good to be true?

If I *was* delusional, I'd deal. I didn't want to take meds because I didn't want to lose Angel. I liked keeping up with her activities—liked *her.* Though we'd never interacted, she had the number two spot on my roster of friends.

How sad was that?

Open. What would one glance hurt?

No, no. Resist! I could lose track of my surroundings.

Close.

At least I wasn't alone in my weirdness. Hartly drew animals in droves and had legit conversations with our dog, Thor, as if he spoke back. Mom obsessed about every version of "Snow White" in existence, and my stepdad, Nicolas, liked to dress up in wizard robes and attend sci-fi conventions.

"Focus, Miss Morrow."

I jolted, tightening my hold on the compact. "Uh…"

Mr. Wong—our regular physics teacher—peered at me from

behind his desk. A total professional, he wore a white button-down and khaki slacks.

In ripped jeans, combat boots and a black T-shirt that read An Apple A Day Will Keep People Away—If You Throw It Hard Enough, I looked better suited for a comfy night in.

Mr. Wong had never before singled me out. Few ever had. Most people were afraid of me from moment one. The more they got to know me, the more the fear grew, no matter how nice I was. I'd never understood it, but I had accepted my inability to change it. What had changed?

"Are you giving our guest your full attention?" he asked.

"No, sir. I'm not." According to Mom, lies were the language of villains, and truth was the language of heroes. So, I always opted for honesty. "You don't need to worry. I've got the gist. But let's be honest, I'm never going to use this information in real life."

Desks squeaked and clothing rustled as students turned to face me. Even Peter, whose gaze I avoided…whose gaze I felt like a live wire. Whispers erupted.

Word about my "misbehavior" would spread through South Central High like an STD. This was a small school in small-town Oklahoma, where everyone's life was fodder for debate.

Mr. Wong flung an "I'm so sorry" glance at the visiting professor. "What do you plan to do with your *real* life, Miss Morrow?"

"I'll double major in business and economics, and start my own company." I know, I know, I made it sound like I'd snap my fingers and poof, I'd have a billion-dollar empire. I understood I'd have to work for it, that there would be ups and downs.

Hartly would get a degree in veterinary studies, and her practice would be next door to my office.

"What kind of company?" Mr. Wong asked.

I had yet to commit to a single idea. If I focused on the economics side of my degree, I could offer risk and reward assessments. I'd get to tell people everything they were doing wrong—and get paid for it. Fun!

Over the summer, I'd taken every workshop and class available online and at a nearby community college.

Plain and simple, I needed to be my own boss. That way, no one could fire me, dock my pay or demand I do something I didn't want to do. I would be in total control. The one responsible for my success or failure.

Before Mom had married Nicolas, she'd been dependent on the goodwill of her bosses. How many times had she sobbed because of something they'd done or said? How many times had she gotten fired unexpectedly, and we'd ended up on the streets?

Never again would we suffer in such a way. One way or another, I would provide for my family. Yes, Nicolas supported us right now. But what would happen if he fell out of love with Mom or died?

Better to be self-reliant.

"Does it matter?" I would not discuss my plans with someone I didn't know. Playing dumb, I fluffed my hair and added, "I'm a premillionaire." *Open, close.*

"Physics teaches us to think, Miss Morrow." The visiting professor motioned to the formulas he'd written on the chalkboard. "Physics makes the impossible possible, and helps us find solutions for the smallest and biggest problems. Please, tell us how that isn't helpful in real life."

Ready to shed all this unwanted interest, I said, "Please, tell me about the moral and ethical ramifications of Schrödinger's cat. I mean, an animal might or might not have been murdered, dying a torturous death, simply to satisfy and dissatisfy one person's curiosity about a question he both could and could not answer. In this case, curiosity literally did and did not kill the cat, but neither outcome justifies the means he employed to both discover and not discover the answer."

Gasps and giggles abounded, and he pursed his lips.

To my relief, the end-of-day bell rang, putting an end to our debate. Kids gathered their belongings and stood. I did the same, stuffing the compact into my back pocket.

What was Angel doing right this moment? Saving someone from misery, no doubt. Dang, I missed her.

To my surprise, Peter approached, his gaze riveted on my birthmark—about the size of a quarter and shaped like an apple, the bright red mark occupied the center of my wrist. Hartly had one on the back of her neck.

Mom often called us her sweet *bonum et malum*. She'd said the phrase meant "apple babies." And maybe it did, where she was from. But I'd done a little research and discovered the phrase was Latin and literally translated to "good and evil."

Once, Peter had loved tracing the mark with his fingertips.

"What?" I snapped now, as prickly as a rosebush.

He paled, then stormed out of the classroom without saying a word. Like everyone else, Peter was afraid of me. He'd once told me, *You scare me, but I like it.*

"Today's homework is on my desk," Mr. Wong called, and groans of disappointment sounded. "And, Miss Morrow? Think about what was said today."

"I will…and I won't." I hurried over, swiped up the assignment and darted out the door.

Students flooded the hallway where myriad blue and gold posters decorated the walls, praising the mighty Sabercats. Lockers swung open and slammed shut. Hundreds of conversations took place at once, excitement palpable as kids grabbed their bags and raced to the parking lot, ready to enjoy the weekend.

"Everly. Wait up."

Ugh. I recognized that "my kingdom, my peasants" tone. It belonged to one of Hartly's legion of friends. The girl most likely to win prom queen.

Yesterday, Prom Queen had posted, oh, about a thousand pictures of her and Peter with the caption "Best boyfriend ever!" I'd wanted to bleach my eyes and scrub my brain with sandpaper.

Peter had moved on with lightning speed, and he had no problem going public with *their* relationship. What a shocker.

Sighing, I turned. "Yeah?"

PQ stood next to Peter, her back pressed against the bank of lockers. A dark braid hung over one shoulder, and a flirty baby-doll dress clung to her hourglass figure. Yellow ribbons criss-crossed down her lightly tanned calves, ending in a pair of ballet flats.

My former boyfriend flicked me an uncomfortable glance before getting very busy, very fast, stuffing books into his backpack.

Ignore the hurt. The way he treated me proved *his* worth, not mine.

PQ took a moment to gather her courage before crossing the distance, giving me a thorough once-over and grimacing as if she'd spied something distasteful. Whatever. Her opinion meant nothing to me. Less than nothing.

Toying with her braid, she said, "I'm having a snookball party tonight. Do me a favor and tell Hartly...even though she'll insist you tag along. Are you house-trained?"

I'd heard of snookball and wanted to play so bad. Participants kicked a soccer ball–sized "cue ball" across an inflated billiards table, sinking other balls into one of four corner pockets. Like pool on steroids, with people acting as the cues.

I loved games, sports and mechanical puzzles. Actually, I loved winning. The rush! The high! But because I was the world's sorest loser, no one ever wanted to play with me.

At PQ's, no one would want to play with me anyway.

Just like that, my excitement dulled.

"Hello." PQ snapped her fingers in front of my face. "Anyone home?"

I chomped my teeth at her, earning a gasp. "Implying I'm a

dog isn't an insult. Dogs are one hundred percent adorable one hundred percent of the time." Dogs *loved* me. If LOVED stood for Let's Organize a Violent End, Dangit.

Sometimes I wondered if they sensed something was terribly wrong with me.

Was something terribly wrong with me?

"Whatever. Will you give her the message or not?" PQ demanded.

"I both will and won't give Harts the message." Fingers crossed I irritated PQ as much as Mr. Wong had irritated me. "You won't know until we do or do not arrive at your house." Hartly loved parties and people, and yes, she would insist I attend, just as PQ had predicted. I wouldn't have the strength to decline, because *I* loved making my twin happy. "If I *do* show up, I won't pee on your rug…more than a couple dozen times. Probably."

She scowled and muttered, "My boyfriend is off-limits to you. Go near him, and I'll make you regret it."

"Oh, no. Not that. Anything but that." I faked a shudder. Why issue the warning, unless she'd learned about my summer romance? And how did my twin tolerate this girl? How did she see the best in others, while I only ever noticed their faults?

As if my day hadn't been bad enough, Peter sauntered over, all swagger and superiority, and slung an arm over PQ's shoulders. He was an inch taller than me, with hair the color of dark honey, tanned skin and hazel eyes framed by stubby lashes. As handsome as he was smooth.

Once he'd told me, *When you walk into a room, you're the only girl I see.*

Warning bells had clanged inside my head—*too smooth, too practiced.* Though I'd questioned his sincerity, I'd ignored my instincts. In the end, I'd suffered for my stupidity, my heart taking an emotional beating.

"You ready to go, babe?" Peter asked her.

Babe?! "Aw," I said in a sing-song voice. "A generic endearment for your generic girlfriend. How adorable." As much as I despised the way he'd treated me, I couldn't regret the emotional scars he'd left behind. They made me stronger.

He flicked me a glance, his eyes projecting a mix of anger, confusion and...longing? Did he want me still? Was it wrong to hope that he did...so I could watch him choke on his misery?

"Better *babe* than *mistake*," PQ said with a smirk.

I pressed my tongue to the roof of my mouth, struggling to maintain a neutral expression. Any hint of vulnerability would cause her to strike. "Enjoy my castoffs with my compliments—and condolences." I blew the happy couple a kiss, then strolled away, my head high, my shoulders squared.

Her outraged hiss trailed me. Did Peter's gaze do the same? I thought I felt the heat of it.

I turned a corner, then another. The hallway crowd had thinned, providing an open path to my twin. My world righted itself, and I grinned.

Wearing a pink fit-and-flare dress she'd sewn herself, Hartly stood in front of our locker, fiddling with the combination. (We shared everything but taste in boys.)

Two jocks moseyed past her, elbowing each other in the chest. The taller one—so cute and muscular with deep brown skin—called out, "Uh. Hey, Hartly. Hi. Hello."

His pale, redheaded friend ribbed him about his awkwardness.

Hartly smiled and waved. "Hey, Thomas. Great job on your oral report. I learned so much!"

Thomas—the tall one—puffed up his chest as if he'd just conquered the world.

Another day, another kid with a crush. Totally understandable. Hartly didn't just see the best in people. She always supported and never judged.

No wonder she was my lifeline.

We were two halves of a whole, yet we didn't look like sisters, much less twins. Her hair was black; mine was silvery-white. Her eyes were baby blue; mine were gunmetal gray and rimmed with gold. Her flawless skin had a dusky golden tint; I was ghostly pale, with a smattering of freckles across my nose. She was short and curvy; I was tallish and slender.

Our personalities were just as different. She was sweeter than sugar. I was…not.

Once, I'd overheard a private conversation between Mom and Nicolas. She'd likened us to seasons. *Hartly is summer, warm and inviting. Others can bask in her light, then walk away with a smile. Everly is winter, cold and driven. She's fun, but she's treacherous, too. Rouse her fury, and you will suffer.*

I agreed. Hurt a member of my family, and I would go nuclear.

I sidled up to Hartly and took over the lock. Using our secret twin-language, Isnenglisnish, I said, "Fisnorgisnet thisne cisnombisninatisnion isnagaisnin?" *Forget the combination again?*

We placed *I-S-N* before vowels, one per syllable. So far, no one had decoded our words.

She replied, "Isnif yisnou isnopisnen thisnat stisnupisnid thisning isnas isneasy isnas pisnie isnaftisner isni hisnave strisnugglisned fisnor isnan isnetisnernisnity—"

Click. The lock released, and the door swung open.

I laughed as I translated. *If you open that stupid thing as easy as pie after I've struggled for an eternity—*

"Isni isnam gisnoisning tisno scrisneam," she finished with a laugh of her own. *I am going to scream.*

She reached for her books, only to pause and wince. Pain glazed her eyes and tension pulled at her mouth.

My chest clenched. "Another headache?" About the time I'd started seeing Angel in mirrors, Hartly had started having migraines.

I'd been keeping track of timing and intensity. The last one had been so bad, she'd yanked at hanks of hair while banging her head against a wall.

"This one isn't as severe as the others." She smiled and bumped her shoulder against mine. "Plisneasisne, disnon't wisnorrisny isnabisnout misne." *Please, don't worry about me.*

Not worry about the most important person in my life? Try again.

"Maybe it's time to tell Mom." Maybe medication would help.

"No!" she shouted, then sagged. After confiscating my book and homework, then stuffing the items inside my backpack, she said more quietly, "Sorry. I didn't mean to bellow. But you *know* Mom will think I'm dying."

Yeah. Freak-out was Mom's default setting. She found hidden signs in everything, and all those signs pointed to the tragic death of her girls. The common cold = perishing in our sickbed. Tired = falling asleep and never waking up. Riding in a car = expiring in a crash. Without exception, the slightest change in our lives sent her into a tailspin of panic. The very reason I hadn't mentioned my mirror Angel.

"Hey." Hartly gave my shoulder another nudge, saying, "What is red, blue and yellow all over?" A pause. Then, "Colors."

I snorted. Telling ridiculous anti-jokes had become our thing, helping to take the sting out of a bad situation. "What did the vampire say to the werewolf? Nothing. Both creatures are fictional."

As she laughed, frantic yelps erupted at the end of the hall. A bucking, bleating minigoat raced rounded the corner, with a clear destination in mind: Hartly.

She crouched down, opening her arms in welcome. As much as she loved animals, they loved her back. Stray cats and dogs gravitated to her, no matter where she happened to be. A parking lot, restaurant, even the grocery store. At home, a substantial number of birds tended to congregate outside our bedroom window.

"Look at you," she said, nuzzling the minigoat's fur. "So stinking cute!"

I wasn't surprised when the creature purposely bumped into my leg, pushing me away. I let him. He'd distracted Hartly from her headache, so I owed him.

Thomas and his friend—I didn't remember his name, so I decided to call him Red—came rushing back to ask if Hartly needed help. When she oh so sweetly declined, the guys stuck around to flirt, even singing, "Hartly Had a Little Lamb."

"Any idea where this sweetie came from?" she asked.

"No, but I think *you* came straight from heaven." Thomas grinned.

She smiled at him. That was when Red swatted her on the butt.

She gasped with surprise, clearly uncomfortable.

Fury straightened my spine with a jolt. What he'd done was *not* okay.

The goat agreed. With a bleat, he kicked Red in the shin.

Over the years, Mom had tasked me with one job, only one. *Protect Hartly at all costs.*

Of course, she also liked to say, *Whatever the question, violence is not the answer.*

Even as my mind shouted, *Stop! The reward doesn't outweigh the risk,* I crashed my fist into Red's nose. Tit for tat. Or smack for smack.

Cartilage snapped, blood pouring over his lips and chin as he stumbled backward.

Thomas moved between us and stretched out his arms to keep us apart.

Guilt prickled the back of my neck, my shoulders slumping. I'd both failed and aided my girls today.

"You brog by dose!" Bombs of rage exploded in Red's eyes. He tried to skirt around his friend.

I guess he had no fear of me.

I ignored little tremors of dismay and braced for a fight. Thanks to Nicolas, I'd had a crap-ton of self-defense lessons. A round of practice might do me some good.

"Come closer, and I'll break something else," I said, just before I unveiled my most maniacal smile.

Red went still. Thomas backed up a step.

"Miss Morrow!" The swift *click-clack* of high heels sounded down the hall. Then the principal came marching around the corner. "What did you do? And why is there a goat in my building?"

I looked to Hartly and muttered, "Iisni isnam tisno bisne thisne scisnapegisnoat, it sisneems." *I am to be the scapegoat, it seems.*

Guaranteed, Red and I would get suspended for our smacks. No big deal, right? More time at home meant more time with Angel. More time to read and practice doing a market analysis.

I tried not to smile as I went to face my "punishment."

2

Innocence, heartache and treachery, oh, my.
What is truth, and what is lie?

Looking back, I could pinpoint specific moments that forever altered the course of my life, shaping the girl I had become.

Most recently, the instant I'd realized Peter was embarrassed by me.

The first time I'd seen Angel.

The day Mom married Nicolas.

In the beginning, I'd wanted him gone. He had the weirdest vernacular, like someone who'd grown up in a fantasy novel.

Son of a troll!

May your magic be strong and your heart be true.

A halfpence of gold for your thoughts.

However, I'd soon grown to love him. He put a much-needed sparkle in Mom's eyes, never experienced irrational fear or anger around me like so many others, and always treated our family with kindness and respect.

Something else I liked about him. He had an award-winning poker face. The only time you could glean any type of emotion from him? When he looked at Aubrey Morrow. Well, Aubrey Soren now. He radiated adoration.

Today, as I sat at the rose-veined marble counter in the kitchen, I experienced another life-altering moment.

Hartly sat beside me. I did my homework, while she discussed proper table manners with Thor, a black-and-white Pomeranian with a lion cut and a propensity for yipping.

Mom bustled from one state-of-the-art appliance to another, preparing dinner. On the cabinets, Nicolas had painted quotes from "Snow White and the Evil Queen," some long-lost version of "Little Snow White," the one Mom had heard as a child.

A seedling of envy bloomed deep in her soul, her every thought like water, helping it grow.

One drop of poison will kill her strongest foe...and the last remnant of goodness that burns in her heart.

For she had forgotten a simple truth. Character meant more than beauty, always.

With Mom's cascade of black hair, ocean-water eyes and golden brown skin, she was an older version of Hartly. I figured I'd taken after our father. Not that I'd ever seen a picture of him. Or knew anything about him.

I thought his name might be Edwin or Stephan—the only two names I'd ever overheard Mom whisper to Nicolas. Only once had Hartly and I gathered enough courage to ask about our father, but Mom had burst into tears, so we'd ended the conversation without receiving a single answer.

I'd often wondered if our father had abused her. Then again, she also refused to speak of her parents. And her childhood. And her homeland. We figured she'd come from overseas and English was her second language. She had a crisp, overly formal accent, like Nicolas, and sometimes referred to people as "mortals."

"Everly, dear. You have been here for half an hour, yet you've said nothing about your after-school fisticuffs." Mom wiped her floury hands on the pink apron that shielded her yellow sundress. Like my twin, she enjoyed sewing her own clothes. Because *every lady should know how to sew, knit, swim, banter with kings and peasants alike, dance with grace and dignity, and defend herself from unscrupulous rogues.*

I sucked at sewing and knitting but rocked at everything else. Go me! "Mom, you should be cheering. I only fisticuffed the boy once."

From his perch on Hartly's lap, Thor barked at me. Translation: *Let me at her! I'll show her a proper fisticuff!*

Or maybe: *Bacon!* Hard to tell.

"Shhh. Enough of that. Sleep," Hartly said, scratching behind his ears. Within seconds, Thor closed his eyes and drifted off. My sister didn't just draw animals, she somehow calmed—and commanded?—them.

"The new school year has *just* begun." Chopping up a potato and some thyme for a vegetable potpie, Mom added, "How are you already in trouble? Why did you hit him?"

I detected a tinge of disappointment in her voice—and fear? Did she think I would strike at her? *Ignore the hurt.* But, but... how could she ever believe such a thing? "I was protecting Hartly from a bully, just as you requested. He smacked her butt, so I smacked his face."

"Were his actions inappropriate? Yes. Were yours? Yes. You protected your sister from a bully by *being* a bully."

Hartly opened her mouth, intending to defend me, I was sure.

I reached over and squeezed her hand. *No worries. I've got this.* "Sometimes words aren't enough, Mom."

She floundered for a response, and I sighed.

I'd confounded her, as usual. We were just so different. Chocolate versus vanilla. Or arsenic versus vanilla.

Eventually, she settled on, "The principal telephoned. You are suspended for two weeks."

"Knew it," I muttered.

"You can turn in all homework assignments when you return and take makeup tests if your teachers are agreeable, but you will not be allowed to do extra credit. If you get in trouble again—do not get into trouble again."

"That's fair. As long as my victim is suspended for the same amount of time, since he is also an offender." Trying not to grin, I pushed Mr. Wong's worksheet aside. No hurry now.

"Are you sassing me, young lady?"

I pinched my index finger and thumb together, saying, "Just a bit."

Hartly hid a grin behind her hand. "Remind me to teach you the art of evasion."

"Why evade when you can Hulk-smash?" I responded.

"This is serious business, girls." Mom wagged a wooden spoon in our direction, then stirred the pot of simmering vegetable stock. "The victim's parents decided not to lodge a formal complaint with the police. For now. What if they change their minds? What if you are taken away from me again?"

Uh…again? To my knowledge, no one had ever separated me from my family. "What do you mean, 'again'?"

Tremors racked her small frame, the color fading from her cheeks. "When you girls were only a few months old, I was deemed…unfit. The two of you were placed in a temporary foster home."

What? My heart thudded as I asked Hartly, "Do you remember this?"

"No!" she burst out, waking Thor. He began to squirm, so she placed him on the floor.

"Why were you deemed unfit?" Seeking comfort in the familiar, I shifted atop the bar stool to slide the compact out my pocket. Opened, closed. "And why are you just now telling us?"

Voice feather-soft, she said, "No one enjoys reliving the worst moments of their life."

My chest tightened, a sharp pang shooting through me.

"Let's discuss the past no longer." She turned away—to wipe away a tear? *Pang, pang.* "You will use this time to contemplate the consequences of your actions. The hurt you've caused others...the disappointment you've caused me."

PANG. Open, close. "I'm sorry, Mom." I hated disappointing her more than anything else in the world.

Over the years, as she'd worked herself to the bone, she'd done everything in her power to ensure we had good food, nice clothes and a roof over our heads. Until Nicolas, no one had pitched in to help her. My father, whoever he was, had never given her a dime.

I would be forever in her debt. And I *would* repay her, just as soon as I started my company. Money was power, and power was security.

Security was everything.

"What if the boy had fought back?" She stirred the broth again, splattering droplets over the stove top. "You could have *died*. You still could! What if you're bleeding internally?"

See? Irrational fear. "Spoiler alert. Nine out of ten doctors agree—none of us are getting out of here alive. But I'm not going anytime soon, and I promise I'm not bleeding internally."

Mom slanted me *the look*. A regal expression that projected a thousand reprisals, deeper disappointment and more gut-wrenching fear. I shrank into my seat.

"You take death so lightly," she said. "I know you think my

concerns are unfounded, but I see the whole picture. You do not."

"What is the whole picture, then?" The scent of leek and fennel made my mouth water. Because of Hartly's affinity for animals, we'd all become hardcore vegans. The diet suited me well.

"To begin with, you are a prin—" She pressed her lips together. "You are destined for—" Again, she pressed her lips together, going quiet.

I was what? A principled girl? "*Please* tell me you didn't visit another psychic."

She'd always referred to psychics as "oracles," and more than once she'd forked over huge hunks of cash for "a way to change fate itself." A couple of times, she'd even paid a "witch" for a "protection spell."

The first time, she'd been so excited, muttering, *At home, readings and spells are too expensive, even for royalty, a true sacrifice necessary. Here, readings and spells are so cheap. I must only part with stacks of green paper. I don't understand why every peasant from every land doesn't seek mystical aid.*

The last time, she'd wilted, saying, *Oracles are descended from the fae and cannot lie. But...I think this one did. She knew nothing about the fairy tale.*

She'd been talking to herself, unaware that I'd been absorbing every word and worried about her mental health.

"You are destined for..." Once again, the color in Mom's cheeks faded. For a brief moment, she met my gaze. The fear had returned and redoubled, causing a small corner of my heart to wither. "You are my daughter, Everly, and I will love you forever, no matter what you do. I just hope you've learned a valuable truth this day. Revenge is poison—for you. Revenge is evil."

All my life I'd heard a million variations of *evil is this*, and *evil is that*. The one I'd internalized: *evil is knowing what's right and doing what's wrong anyway.*

———

Now shame coursed through me in one sizzling wave after another.

And Mom wasn't even done! "Evil wears many faces. Today it wore yours, eh?"

A new pang cut through my chest, courtesy of an invisible dagger.

"I did my best to provide you with a normal childhood, and safeguard you from others," she said. "Must I now safeguard others from you?"

The invisible dagger twisted. "No. I'll do better. I'll *be* better."

This time, Hartly reached over to squeeze *my* hand, a simple touch that conveyed an avalanche of love and support. I'd always looked out for her physically, yes, but she'd always looked out for me emotionally.

"I'm glad you'll do better," Mom said, "but you are not going to enjoy your suspension from school. You will spend the next two weeks doing everyone's chores. You will clean the house from top to bottom, do all the dishes, dust every surface, mow the yard and pull weeds in the garden."

"Okay. Yes, I will." I traced my thumb over the rim of the compact. "Like a true Disney princess, I'll do everything with a smile and a song."

Hartly put the few drama classes she'd taken to good use, pretending I'd stabbed her in the heart. "If you start singing, Thor will start howling and the neighbors will call the cops, claiming someone is being murdered."

Mom bobbed her head in agreement, until she noticed the compact I'd inadvertently lifted. She stilled, frowned.

"Okay, no singing," I said, hoping to get her mind back on track.

Hartly blew me a kiss. "This is for your own good, Everly." To Mom, she said, "I have an idea. A friend of mine is hosting a party later tonight. Forget the chores. As part of Everly's punishment, you should make her go with me."

I groaned. "I'd rather do the chores."

"Will the friend's parents be home?" Mom asked.

"Probably not," I piped up. "I bet kids will be pounding beers, doing drugs and having sex."

Mom arched a brow, all *Sherlock Holmes just found a clue*. "Do *you* plan to drink or do drugs, Everly?"

"No," I grumbled. I'd gotten drunk once in my life. Over the summer, I'd gone to a party and had too many shots. I'd hated the loss of control.

Before Mom rendered her verdict, hinges squeaked as a door snicked shut. Nicolas entered the kitchen, wearing his usual suit and tie, a briefcase in hand.

Mom brightened at the sight of him. "May your star shine bright, my love." Her standard greeting.

"May your star shine brighter, Princess." He lifted her hand and kissed her knuckles, before facing us and nodding. "Hello, girls."

"Hello," we said in unison.

Nicolas was tall, lean and golden from head to toe, with model-handsome looks that often left my mom sighing dreamily. Once I'd heard her say, *Appearance never matters, but oh, Nicolas's face…his body…they certainly do not hurt*.

Nicolas came from money. A lot of money. He didn't have to work, but work he did, using his wealth to help others, running a shelter for refugees and immigrants. A place of hope. And yet, peopled tended to fear or hate him from moment one, too.

Except Mom. She'd all but melted at moment one. Maybe that was why he enjoyed pampering her so much. Last year, he'd bought her this two-story farmhouse. Outside, blue shutters framed stained glass windows; inside, designer curtains accented every pane. Fancy wainscoting and gold-leaf paint adorned… everything. There was a crystal chandelier in each room, even the bathrooms. At the bottom of a winding staircase, carved lions stood sentry.

"How was your day?" Mom asked.

For a moment, he projected irritation, and I had to do a double take. That was a first. His day must have sucked the big one.

Mom framed his face with her hands. "Tell me what's wrong, love."

He brushed the tip of his nose against the tip of hers. "One of my projects met with…obstacles. Nothing I cannot handle. Now, tell me what has caused *your* strain, and I will move heaven and earth to fix it."

How I envied their connection. They built each other up, never tore each other down.

After Mom explained the situation at school, Nicolas said, "We want the suspension lifted? Done. I will visit—"

"No, no." Mom shook her head. "We're upset because Everly broke a boy's nose, and violence is never the answer."

"Right. Yes. Of course." He nodded, as if he'd known her meaning all along. "But she showed great restraint, did she not? The boy walked away. He did not have to be carried. Let us celebrate the victories, however they come."

Dang, I loved this man.

He wasn't just good for her. He was good for me. Every time he'd taught me self-defense, he'd focused on dirty, underhanded moves guaranteed to put an opponent in the hospital. (Mom had no idea.)

"Go wash up, love." She waved her husband away. "Dinner will be ready in half an hour."

"For Aubrey Standard Time, I must add an hour." He kissed her brow, ruffled Hartly's hair, then tweaked my nose.

Hartly laughed. "He's got you there, Mom. If you wore a watch, it would only ever need to read *Late*."

"I am not that bad," she said.

She was worse. "May I be excused until dinner, Mom?" Anything to escape her verdict about PQ's party. Besides, I was ready to spend quality time with Angel.

"No, you may not." She wagged a carrot in my direction. "You're going to sit there and think about your actions."

Fine. I'd just sneak a quick peek at my compact.

In stealth mode, I hid the mirror under the counter again, leaned to the side and adjusted the angle of my wrist. Finally, I had a clear view of the glass.

I didn't see Angel.

I saw my mother.

Horror stabbed me, and I had to swallow a cry. She looked haggard and sickly, as if she had one foot in the grave. Her dark hair hung in matted tangles, and her usually tanned skin was pale and waxen. Blood dripped from her nose, and a blue tinge shaded her chapped lips. She'd lost weight, pounds her small bone structure had needed.

In real life, Thor barked and raced around my chair, foam collecting at the corners of his mouth. I barely heard him, my ears roaring with distress.

Features taut with concern, Hartly gripped my shoulder and gave me a little shake. "What's wrong? Are you okay?"

Nicolas returned in a rush, as if he'd sensed something amiss.

Breathe, just breathe. Real-life Mom stood on the other side of the counter, just as before, just as *beautiful* as before. But she'd grown pale, a sheen of sweat slicking her brow.

Frowning, she peered at her trembling hands before clutching the counter as if she feared she would fall.

"Mom, are *you* okay?" I demanded.

"A moment of weakness," she muttered. "I'm fine. Or I will *be* fine."

Is she dying?

My stomach churned. Our roles had just reversed. Something strange had happened, and I'd imagined *her* at death's door, while she'd denied anything was wrong.

I thought I understood the paradox of Schrödinger's cat a bit better now. Not knowing what had happened, I could both believe I'd seen my mother in the glass, and that I hadn't seen her in the glass. The choice belonged to me.

What am I going to believe?

Better question: *What am I going to do about it?*

3

In this tale of vengeance and woe,
foe may be friend and friend may be foe.

Dinner passed without a hitch, life returning to normal. Well, our version of normal, anyway.

Between a lively chat about what we'd call milk if we couldn't actually call it *milk*—I'd gone with udder juice—and which fictional characters we loved in books but might dislike in real life, Hartly tried to convince Mom I needed to attend PQ's snookball party. Thankfully, a verdict still had not been rendered.

After dinner, Mom and Nicolas retired to their bedroom—I did not want to know why—and I got busy on the dishes.

Hartly helped out, drying after I washed.

"Go to the party without me?" I pleaded when we finished. "Peter will be there, and I'd rather not see him." Although, it might be kind of nice to show up and ruin his evening.

I smiled. *It's the little things in life.*

No, no. I preferred to stay in tonight. "Besides, everyone at school hates me." People hated what they feared, I guessed.

"They don't hate you," she said, Thor dancing at her feet. "They just don't know you. If you'd drop your force field, even for a second, they'd grow to love you."

"Doubtful. Underneath layers of vengeful crankiness are more layers of vengeful crankiness." Maybe people sensed my negativity, and that was why they feared me on sight?

"At least you have layers!"

"Ha! If my layers are a raindrop, yours are an ocean." Underneath her smiles and sweetness was a wild ferocity I admired. If someone hurt an animal or a child, she unleashed the kraken.

"Please, Everly. Please, please, please." She smashed her hands together, forming a steeple. "Go to the party. I'll owe you so big. I'll even play snookball with you, and I won't tease you when you lose. Not at first, anyway. In case I wasn't clear, you're gonna lose."

How could I resist her? "Fine. If Mom agrees, I'll go to the stupid party. But only because you won my lottery for a butt kickin'."

With a squeal of happiness, she threw her arms around me. "Thank you, thank you! You're the best!"

I decided not to tell her about the image I'd seen in the compact, not until I knew what had happened. Had I hallucinated? Could I blame an overactive imagination? A medical condition, perhaps? Had I lost touch with reality for a split second? Deep down, I still felt like me.

Was Mom sick? Was I? I felt normal.

Normal…

I gave you a normal childhood. As normal as possible, anyway.

What did Mom consider an *abnormal* childhood? Was she *going* to get sick?

Foreboding wrapped me in a cloak of ice. I wished I knew more about her. Where she came from, the identity of her parents, the identity of my father or any genetic medical conditions in our family line.

"You'll have fun." Hartly hopped up and down and clapped. "I'll make sure of it."

"Why do you like Prom Queen and her pack of wildebeests, anyway? They are emotional bullies, cruel to anyone they deem unworthy."

"Well, you know how wounded animals growl and snap at anyone who approaches? I've noticed the same behavior in humans. People who hurt deep inside often lash out at others, creating a toxic cycle. I just want to love them and help them heal."

Or maybe they used their internal hurts as an excuse? "That is very kind of you. And another layer."

Hartly kissed my cheek. "I'll talk to Mom, change, and we'll head out."

"So certain she'll say yes?"

"Name one time she's ever told me no," she said, her eyes gleaming with merriment.

Good point.

Hartly dashed off to our bedroom, our sanctuary. The cathedral ceiling boasted a mural of sunshine and clouds. We'd even adhered glow-in-the-dark stars. The walls were painted in different shades of green and brown to resemble a summer forest. A cluster of small potted lemon trees provided a clean, citrusy fragrance, adding to the outdoorsy effect.

Footsteps sounded. Mom stepped into the kitchen while cinching the tie on her robe. Oh, good gracious, she had bedhead.

"I have made a decision," she said. "You may attend the party, but you must guard Hartly with your life. As part of your punishment, you are not to have any fun. That's an order."

Ah. The real reason Mom had relented. To enlist my protection services.

I offered a jaunty salute. "I won't let anyone peer pressure me into laughing, Mom. Not even Hartly, who promised me *tons* of fun. You have my word."

Hartly joined us. She wore a pink T-shirt with lace trim, a pair of shorts and tennis shoes decorated with hearts. Around her neck, a small apple dangled from a silver chain. The only piece of jewelry she owned.

Mom had often said, *Greed is the beating heart of evil. Do not feed it, and it will not grow.*

"Be careful, girls," Mom said now, already wringing her hands with worry.

We muttered assurances and kissed her goodbye. As I walked away, she clung to my hand until the very last second.

Hartly and I piled into our fully loaded SUV, with Hartly behind the wheel. I never drove, too afraid I'd see Angel in one of the mirrors and lose track of the road. Not that my sister knew the reason I refused.

I should tell her, even though I didn't know what, exactly, was going on, but I didn't want the one person who loved me unconditionally, who never feared me, who only ever saw the best in me, to start wondering about my sanity.

"Why did the boy cry?" Hartly asked as we motored down the road. "Because water leaked from his tear ducts."

Good one. "What do you call a fly with no wings? A fly with no wings."

She chuckled as she pulled into PQ's neighborhood, where a multitude of vehicles littered the streets. Thankfully, acres of land separated the houses, so there was plenty of space to park.

We emerged into cool night air fragrant with magnolias and car exhaust. I looked to the stars, the jewelry of the sky. Pinpricks of light scattered across the inky blackness; the beauty took my breath away. I frowned. Or maybe homesickness was responsible for my breathlessness? I felt the burn of it deep in my bones. Weird!

"Come on." My sister urged me forward.

In PQ's front yard, crowds of kids milled around a row of tiki torches.

Hartly had a smile and word of encouragement for everyone, while the forced interactions frayed my nerves. I quickened my pace, all but dragging her into the backyard.

Cheers resounded around the inflated pool table, where Peter and another boy were playing snookball. I stutter-stepped at the sight of him, my pulse points hammering.

"Hartly!" PQ and three others rushed over to hug my sister, each girl accompanied by the sharp, pungent odor of alcohol. "I'm so glad you came."

She returned the hugs, offering each girl a compliment.

"Oh, you two look so pretty!" Then "Your hair is gorgeous. You've got to teach me how to create those curls." And "Do you even have pores? Your skin is flawless!"

She threw her arm around my waist, adding, "You guys know my twin, Everly. The most amazing person in the whole world. I took a poll. It's official."

PQ's bright glow of happiness dimmed, and monotone greetings rang out.

"Wow, I can really feel the love." I kissed Hartly's cheek, and told her, "You promised me fun, but Mom made me promise not to have any. So, I'm going to get something to drink and see if I can find trouble instead." In actuality, I didn't want her worrying about my ever-darkening mood. And though I'd played with the idea of ruining the party, I decided I'd keep myself entertained some other way. I'd hate ruining Hartly's fun in the process.

"You don't want to play snookball with me?" Hartly asked with a pout.

"And embarrass you in front of your friends? Nah."

PQ made a shook motion. Slurring her words, she said, "Drinks are in back." I'd go out on a limb and guess her parents *weren't* here.

I met her stare. "What *is* your name? No. Never mind. I still don't care."

As she sputtered, I made my way to the back of the yard, where a foldable table displayed cans of pop and beer, as well as bottles of tequila and vodka. I overheard Hartly tell PQ, "Be nice to her, and she'll be nice to you. Be mean to her, and we can't be friends. It's that simple."

No, no, no. I didn't want her giving up her friends on my behalf.

And, ugh, I really didn't want to be here. I received sneers, leers and one-bird salutes, every breeze laden with a whispered insult. Why was no one else treated this way? How did I unearth everyone's inner creeper?

A usually shy boy stepped in front of me and grabbed his crotch. "Go ahead. Shout into my megaphone."

His friends guffawed.

I winced as if embarrassed for him, saying, "Sorry, but it looks like you only brought your *mini*phone." At least I'd get to leave these meat clowns in my rearview as soon as I graduated. Then I'd start and finish college, and finally open my business.

I imagined rolling in my piles of money, and laughed.

A new round of cheers rang out, some of the kids chanting Peter's name. Fingers crossed he'd gotten a busted nut!

After selecting a bottle of cranberry juice, I found an abandoned corner bathed in shadows and stood sentry near Hartly. When a bunny braved the crowd to approach her, she picked up the little fluff nugget and nuzzled his fur. I smiled, my heart warming. PQ and the others cooed.

A hand shot from the darkness, snaked around my wrist and yanked me deeper into the shadows. I gasped, readying my fist.

Peter stepped into a beam of moonlight, and my surprise morphed into fury.

"What are you doing?" I demanded.

"I need to talk to you." He framed my face with his hands.

"I miss you. I miss what you make me feel. I made a mistake when I let you go."

You've got to be kidding me. "You have a girlfriend," I snapped, wrenching free. His willingness to cheat on PQ—whether I liked her or not—disgusted me.

I couldn't believe I'd wasted my first kiss on this POS. Part of me wanted to kiss someone else, anyone else, right here, right now. That way, Peter wouldn't be my *last* kiss, as well. But no one at this party tempted me to forget my brand-new rule: a guy had to like me to date me.

"Please, Everly." Eyes wild, even feverish, he backed me into the fence. "I'm desperate for you."

My heart raced. Many South Central seniors congregated nearby, yet I'd never felt more isolated. "Let me go, Peter. Now."

"Please," he repeated, gripping my waist. "I need it. I need you."

"Need?" I scoffed. "You *need* to back off."

Despite a new round of protests, he pressed his mouth against mine. Instant shock. My thoughts tangled as I turned my face away and balled my hand, planning to disable him with one of Nicolas's dirty tricks. But I hesitated.

Violence, twice in one day? The risk—Mom's wrath. But the reward...

This would stop. I wanted this to stop.

Decision made. I swung, hammering my fist into his cheek. As his head whipped to the side, pain surged through my knuckles. I didn't care. I struck again. The bridge of his nose cracked, blood spurting. Just like Red, he howled, agonized.

I shouldn't feel a rush of satisfaction right now. Should I? That would be...wrong?

No! Defending yourself was never wrong. *See Everly bask in satisfaction.*

"For the record," I said, unveiling my most menacing grin for the second time that day. "I could have ripped off your balls and stuffed them down your throat. Come near me again, and I will." Though I wanted to kick him, I walked away as if I hadn't a care.

I grimaced when I spotted a smear of blood on my hand. My *trembling* hand. If Hartly saw me like this, she'd worry. Drawing in a shaky breath, I cast her a parting glance—she was still holding the bunny and laughing with PQ. As stealthily as possible, I worked my way through the crowd and entered the house, a spacious two-story with brick walls and fancy furniture.

A line stretched in front of the guest bathroom. Unwilling to wait, I climbed the stairs. A tabby cat jumped onto a side table and hissed when I passed.

"You hate me. I get it," I muttered, moving on. At last, I found a second bathroom, this one connected to the master bedroom, where a couple was making out on the bed. My poor eyes!

I sealed myself in the bathroom, scrubbed my hands with soap, then splashed ice-cold water on my overheated face. Droplets cleaved to my lashes as I peered at my reflection, seeking comfort in the glass, a glimpse of Angel. Something!

My eyes… I frowned. My eyes were lighter than usual, metallic and glittering wildly.

"What is *wrong* with you?" I whispered, reaching out to trace my finger around my reflection's face.

In seconds, tingling heat ignited in my fingertips and spread up my arms. My jaw dropped. Ripples appeared in the glass, and I blinked, trying to focus.

No way I was seeing what I thought I was seeing. No way my reflection had changed so drastically, so fast.

Plaited snow-white hair twined around a crown of bloodred crystal roses. Thick slashes of kohl rimmed my eyelids, creating a smoky come-hither look. No sign of my freckles, my pale skin seemingly dusted with diamond powder. I—she—wore a skintight black corset embroidered with red roses, a perfect match to the crown. A deep V displayed her cleavage to its best advantage.

I frowned, but my reflection grinned with cold calculation. This was no Angel.

"You want to know what's wrong?" she asked. Another shock. A voice had never before come from the glass. And this was not just any voice, but mine. "Look. See."

My chest clenched, flattening my lungs. New ripples appeared in the glass, a scene taking shape, like a movie playing on a TV screen, only brighter, more intense—more *real*—and chillingly familiar. I saw what looked to be Nicolas and Mom's bedroom. Same chandelier. Same four-poster bed with a wispy, white canopy. Same nightstand, with the same three vases filled with dried roses. Same plush rug with a tree of life pattern. Same bay window with lace curtains.

Cannot compute.

Mom trembled as she cinched her robe and faced a girl I'd never met.

The stranger seemed close to my age, with wavy brown hair, rich brown eyes and lovely brown skin. Multiple diamond chokers circled her neck. A golden breastplate carved with strange symbols protected her torso, metal cuffs adorned her wrists, and a thick leather belt looped around her hips, with a bejeweled dagger sheathed on each side. Underneath a mesh skirt was a pair of leather tights. On her feet, fur-lined boots.

Who was she? Just a figment of my imagination?

"—is dead, and the prophecy is demanding its due," the girl was saying. "You and the princesses must return. I'll give you a week to get your affairs in order. Be ready." She waved her hand and vanished. Just. Like. That.

My heart leaped into my throat, a terrible chill invading my bones. That had *not* just happened. Right?

In the mirror, Mom whirled on Nicolas, appearing both horrified and terrified. "Learning I can take my girls home should be the happiest day of my life. But you...you..." A sob burst from her, and she wrapped her arms around her middle. "You are a *monster.*"

Features twisting with regret and shame, he reached for her. "Give me a chance to explain, Princess."

She bounded out of range. "No! Don't touch me. Don't you dare. You need to leave. I don't want you near my daughters. We will return to Enchantia without you."

Enchantia?

Shocker of shockers, panic set his eyes ablaze. "Despite my origins, I have never hurt you. I have only ever protected you and our family. From the very beginning, I wanted to tell the princesses about their parentage, their homeland, their exalted stations and their prophecy. You didn't, so I kept quiet. Now they are using magic, Aubrey. I sensed it earlier today. You did, too. Don't deny it. Everly needs to learn how to control her magic. She needs my help."

Breathe, just breathe. In, out. Had he just referred to me and my sister as *literal* princesses?

"No," Mom repeated. Disgust darkened her features. "You aren't just sorcerian. You are the overlord."

Sorcerian…overlord? What the what?

He made no denials, just took a step closer. "Listen to me. Please. Everly is a danger to you, and to Hartly."

Me, a danger to my family? *Never.*

"You're wrong," Mom croaked. "The girls cannot wield magic here. Or anywhere! No witch has ever bestowed a power upon them."

His hard tone jagged at the edges, he said, "You ate of the Tree of New Beginnings, did you not?"

She bristled. "You can't prove that. No one can."

"My statement stands. The girls desperately need guidance. Especially Everly. Stronger magic requires more power—power she will syphon from *you.*"

In, out. Bestow power? Magic? Syphon? Why me especially, and not Hartly, too? What was the Tree of New Beginnings?

"If she *does* syphon from me," Mom said, "my magic will replenish. But she won't. *You* are sorcerian, Everly is not. For all I know, *you* are the one syphoning my power."

He went still. "She's begun syphoning from you already, then?"

"No, no, of course not." Her gaze darted here, there, anywhere but Nicolas. "I'm done talking with you. Leave."

He scrubbed a hand over his face, the muscles in his biceps bulging. "You are right, my secret is out. Before I came here, I had two goals. Acquire more power and assume the role of the overlord. Then I met you, and those goals changed. I wanted only to make you happy. So, I need you to forget my past and listen in order to save your life. There *is* a sorcerer in Everly's bloodline. And like all sorcerian children, she can and will steal power from family first, then others. *If* the family is not prepared."

"No," Mom insisted. "Sorcerers trick. They lie."

He ran his tongue over his pearly whites. "You and Hartly will leave. I will stay here and watch over Everly. I will explain what is happening and teach her how to survive without harming others. You will return only when the witch does. Once we are in Enchantia, I will acquire an altilium for Everly so that she syphons only from its members."

Uh, what the heck was an *altilium*?

As if Mom heard my thoughts, she said, "You want Everly to abduct magic wielders and syphon their magic continually? Never!" Mom tripped to the door. "Even if I believed you, your suggestion is despicable. You *are* a monster. The worst! I'm better off without you."

He flinched but didn't try to change her mind. Meanwhile, my head spun. None of this made sense. No way this conversation was actually transpiring back at home. Or had transpired. Or would transpire.

Oh, crap. So many options.

Tears streamed down Mom's cheeks. Head high, she stalked to the closet and fished out a travel bag. "Pack your things. Leave. *Now*."

Nicolas evinced no reaction, his expression blanking. For once, I had no trouble reading his poker face. Fisted hands gave him away. "Very well. I will leave, but I will also take measures to help Everly. Maybe then you'll admit not all sorcerers are villains."

"Everly?" Hartly's voice seeped through the bathroom door, jolting me back to reality. "Are you in there?"

The bedroom disappeared, my reflection peering back at me. My *normal* reflection.

Blood whooshed out of my head, and dizziness whooshed in. "Come back." Leaning forward, I banged on the glass. If the mirror could show me a problem, the mirror could show me a freaking solution.

Just one more peek…

"Show me," I commanded. Then I waited, tense. Tenser. "Please," I beseeched. But again, nothing happened.

Dang it! How had I galvanized the mirror the first time, if not by voice? *Think, think! Had* I galvanized the mirror, or had I hallucinated, as I'd previously feared?

Nicolas's claims drifted through my mind. *Using magic…no idea how to control it…a danger.*

A humorless laugh escaped me. *Magic was a fantasy*, not a reality. Right?

Knock, knock. "Everly," Hartly said and moaned. "I need your help. Something happened. Something's wrong."

What! I pulled my gaze from the pale, shaky girl projecting all kinds of strain from the glass and tripped to the door.

4

Who will survive, and who will fall?
Who will shatter like a porcelain doll?

I whisked Hartly to our SUV, throwing elbows and glaring at anyone foolish enough to approach us. Everyone slinked away.

My sister's ocean water blues were as wide as saucers, and her cheeks were as pale as snow. Sweat beaded on her brow and upper lip. Dried blood caked her nostrils.

"I'm going to drive." No need to dig the car key from her pocket; we had a keyless ignition. And no way I'd make her drive in this condition. I'd be extra careful, and I wouldn't glance in the mirrors unless absolutely necessary.

She muttered a halfhearted protest but allowed me to buckle her into the passenger seat.

"Hey," I said, settling behind the wheel. "Guess who I saw today? Everyone I looked at."

The barest smile bloomed, her color brightening. "What did

the maid say when she couldn't find her broom? *Where's my broom?*"

I chuckled, both amused and relieved. With the mood somewhat lightened, I lapsed into silence, giving her time to breathe. One minute passed. Two. Three.

The side mirror called to me, whispery soft and seductive. *Look...see...*

No. Focus! Should I tell Hartly what I'd seen? What if I'd somehow tapped into a real-life fight between our parents? She had a right to know, but oh, I despised the thought of upsetting her more.

Still, I would do it, I would tell her...after she shared her troubles with me.

Patience had never been a tool in my arsenal. I eased onto a main roadway, merging with traffic, and quietly prompted, "Tell me what happened."

Another minute passed before she sighed and said, "I was standing outside when I got super weak. Blood poured from my nose, and my knees buckled, but I knew I'd be okay if I found you."

Me, a cure-all? I clutched the steering wheel so tightly, my knuckles bleached. "Maybe you caught Mom's bug?"

"Maybe," she said, but she didn't sound convinced.

"How did you find me?"

"The cat—" She nibbled on her bottom lip. "I have a confession to make. Something very strange. I should have told you sooner, but I didn't want you upset."

Uh-oh. "Strange how?"

"My headaches aren't really headaches. Not the way you think. I've been hearing voices. So many voices. At first, I thought I was having some kind of psychotic break. Then I wondered if I could be a mutant or something, with an ability to hear other people's thoughts. But no. Ever, I hear *animal* thoughts."

I had no idea how to respond, every new thought setting off

a land mine of emotion. Mutants, another surreal possibility to explain the unexplainable, and just as unlikely as magic.

As if we were part of an infomercial, Hartly added, "But wait, there's more. I can also lull animals to sleep."

"I... You..."

Groaning, she covered her face with her hands. "You think I'm losing my mind. You think I need medical help."

"Wrong! You surprised me, that's all. I just need time to process." *Could* I process this, on top of everything else?

Yes, of course. My sister didn't have an overactive imagination, and she didn't lie for attention. So, let's say Hartly *could* hear animal thoughts and lull the creatures to sleep. Let's say I *hadn't* imagined the things I'd seen in the mirror. What were the odds that something strange and random would happen to us at the same time? Not good. There had to be a connection. Something *deliberate*.

To figure this out, we needed to shine light on every available piece of the puzzle. My turn had come. "All right, I have a confession of my own." I donned my big girl panties and detailed the fight I'd witnessed in the mirror.

Hartly listened, rapt, her jaw nearly unhinging. "Magic... you, me...the timing... What are the odds?"

"My thoughts exactly."

She palmed her cell phone, typed, then released a *pft* of air. "A search for *Enchantia* gives a list of fictional books and a video game." Grimace. "We're going to have to suck it up and talk to Mom, aren't we?"

"Yeah. We are." Maybe Mom had answers. "Whatever she says, we'll be okay. As long as we're together."

We reached the house without incident, and I heaved a sigh of relief. Then I parked in the four-car garage and noted the absence of Nicolas's truck. My blood flashed cold.

Where had he gone, and why?

You know why...

Nope. No way. Only a coincidence. Yet tremors rocked me as we entered the house. Mom was pacing in the living room, her face red and putty and stained with tears.

I stopped abruptly, ready to vomit. She wore the same nightgown I'd seen in the mirror...in the *vision. Magic. Mutant.*

Thor perched on the arm of the couch. He growled at me before jumping down to wind around my sister's ankles.

"Momma?" Hartly whimpered, dismayed, and rushed over to enfold Mom in her embrace.

What a lovely picture they presented, alike in so many ways. Not just physically, with their dark hair and electric blues, but personality-wise, too. So kind. So caring.

I was the oddball in every way.

"Where's Nicolas?" I croaked.

Mom shifted, putting her body between me and my twin as if we needed to be shielded from each other. But why would—

Realization struck, and I stiffened. No, not as if we needed to be shielded from each other. As if *Hartly* needed to be shielded from *me.* Fear crackled in Mom's eyes. The same fear she'd projected at Nicolas.

Everly is a danger to you, to Hartly.

Part of her must believe what Nicolas said. Would I get the boot, too? Thorns seemed to sprout in my throat and leak acid.

"He's gone," Mom said, then tried to soften the blow with an "everything will be okay" half smile that didn't quite work. "I'm sorry, girls, but he's never coming back."

Hartly and I shared a spooked look. Mom had just verified part of my mirror vision.

Thor growled, and my sister wagged a finger at him.

"No, Thor. You're wrong," she said. "Everly would never hurt me."

"Hurt you?" Mom shifted, shielding more of Hartly's body. "You wouldn't hurt us, would you, Everly?"

"No! Never! How can you ask such a terrible question?"

"Yeah, Mom. How?" Hartly demanded.

"Let's talk in the morning, all right? I just... I can't do this right now." She kissed Hartly's cheek, nodded at me, then strode from the room.

Hartly lifted Thor to her chest and cooed until he quieted. "I'll take him out back and let him burn off some excess energy." Meaning, *converse* with him? "Join us?"

"Not tonight." I planned to park in front of a mirror and speak with that strange version of myself. I—she—might know how to mend the rift between my parents. For the sake of their hearts, but also for the sake of our survival.

Bottom line: we needed Nicolas's income. And yeah, I hated reducing a marriage to a business transaction, especially when I loved my stepdad, but Mom had struggled so hard in the past to support us on her own, and I couldn't bear for her to lose all we had now. Even if she found the kind of job she'd done in the past and Hartly and I got after-school jobs, we wouldn't make enough to cover our bills.

See? It was always best to acquire your own money than to rely on the generosity of someone else.

I might need to forgo a degree, rethink my field of commerce, and start my company sooner rather than later. Once I had a personal store of resources to care for my family, all would be well.

"I love you, Ever."

"I love you, too, Harts."

We headed in opposite directions. A sense of unease hit me when I shut myself in our private bathroom. Frowning, I positioned myself in front of the mirror. *Inhale, exhale.* I met my reflection's gaze, hoping against hope, but nothing happened.

"Hey. Hi. Hello. Yo," I said. "Come out, come out, wherever you are."

Nothing.

Fighting a tide of disappointment, I waited...still waiting... Still nothing. Argh! What was I doing wrong?

I would try again in the morning, I decided, after I'd gotten some rest. I would try again and again and again, until I succeeded. For me, failure would never be an option.

I tossed and turned all night, too keyed up to sleep. As soon as the first rays of sunlight filtered through my bedroom curtains, signaling Mirror o'clock, I hopped to my feet and stumbled into the bathroom, ready, willing and (hopefully) able to summon...conjure...another vision.

But nervousness went head-to-head with excitement as I sealed myself inside, igniting electric shock waves under my skin. I decided to wait until I calmed.

Avoiding my reflection, I brushed my teeth and showered, hot water sluicing away the last vestiges of exhaustion. After drying my hair, I dressed in my most comfortable clothes: a longish white tank, black yoga pants and fuzzy house-boots.

From start to finish, the mirror called to me.

Look. See...

My palms sweated and my mouth dried when I positioned myself in front of the glass. Calm wasn't on today's menu, it seemed. Very well. I would proceed anyway.

Slowly, I lifted my gaze, hoping, hoping...

Nope. A normal reflection stared back at me. Well, as normal as could be with my hollow-eyed gaze. I wasn't even gifted with a glimpse of Angel.

"Please," I whispered. "Show me what I want—what I need—to see."

An eternity passed, impatience simmering in my veins...no, boiling. Again, nothing. Disappointment raked me.

This was unacceptable. As my summertime professor used to say, *Follow the train of logic.* What had I done to spur the visions of Angel? Not a danged thing. What had I done to spur the vision of my parents? Washed my hands, splashed my face, asked a question and banged on the glass.

Right! "Mirror," I said, tapping my reflection. "Show me what I need to see."

My fingertips heated, and ripples danced over the glass. I gasped. I'd done it? Seriously?

My thoughts grew dim as an image crystalized—a massive fortress seated atop a snowcapped mountain, with a stone tower on each side, and a roof hidden inside cloud sheets. Winged men and women soared here, there, everywhere, and I could only gape. Their feathers…not even a peacock's tail could compare.

Had I found heaven? Was I watching real-life angels?

The view zoomed closer to the fortress. Fast, faster. I would swear I felt an icy wind combing through my hair and smelled the earth every time I inhaled. Faster still. Through a stone wall…inside the fortress…down a hall and into a chamber double the size of my classrooms at school.

The sheer magnificence stole my breath. A crystal chandelier bore a thousand candles flickering with light and heat. Lifelike marble dragons flanked the sides of a flaming hearth. Every chair and sofa boasted shiny golden fabric, the perfect match for the gilded floor. A wall of windows overlooked one side of the mountain, where those winged creatures danced through the clouds.

Two girls dressed in fancy gowns sat at a small table, sipping tea. Tension crackled between them.

The first girl possessed a delicate yet edgy beauty, with white-and-black hair, tanned and freckled skin and bicolored eyes— the left blue, the right gray. There was something about her, a niggling familiarity I couldn't shake.

The second girl made me grin. My sweet Angel, with her long dark hair, white skin even paler than mine, and eyes the color of frosted shamrocks.

On the other side of the room I found… *Well, hello there.* A boy so hot he basically melted my brain. He wasn't classically handsome or without flaws; he was better. He was strength made flesh.

I don't care about appearance. Nope. Not me. My pulse points didn't get the memo; they fluttered. He had tousled dark hair of the deepest jet, brown skin and a face surely chiseled from granite, with broad cheekbones, a slightly crooked nose (from a break?) and a square jaw dusted with a dark stubble. His lips were red, plump and lush, and the softest thing about him. His eyes... *Melting faster.* Eyes the same frosted shamrocks as Angel's glittered with affection as he helped an old man walk across the room and ease into the seat next to Angel.

Were Hot Stuff and Angel related?

The more I watched him, the more a strange and undeniable sense of connection bloomed. He was older than me, but not by much. A long-sleeved white tunic and black leather pants displayed a lean body jam-packed with muscle. A strip of fur draped across his wide shoulders, two straps crisscrossing over his torso to anchor swords to his back.

Would he fear and hate me at first sight like so many others? Would he leer? What was his name? Where was he from, and what was he like?

Was he single?

He said something to Angel, and I lamented the lack of volume. What I wouldn't give to hear his voice. Before stalking from the room, he offered the second girl a terse nod.

Between one blink and the next, the scene blanked, my reflection coming back into focus. "What? No! I wasn't done. Show me more." I banged on the mirror, astonished by the intensity of my dismay...and just as astonished by the intensity of my relief when the boy returned.

For some reason, the vision didn't pick up where it had left off. I would have figured out why, no problem, if my brain hadn't melted all over again. He stood beside a bed, shirtless, a massive tree-of-life tattoo on magnificent display. The image covered his chest and his back, with branches running the length of his arms. His hair was unkempt, his pants unfastened.

So. Many. Muscles. Was I drooling? Small white scars bisected his pectorals and—

Sweet mercy! He had pierced nipples.

When he pulled a white shirt over his head, I almost booed and threw popcorn at him.

A girl with shoulder-length sable hair lay atop the mattress, buried under a mound of covers. Pale skin, smoky eyes and red, red lips made her look like a supermodel.

When he turned to go, she lunged, latching on to his wrist and attempting to pull him into bed. Well, *back* into bed, I was sure. So. He did have a girlfriend.

Or not. Reminding me of a fiction hero in need of a heroine's gentle taming, he scowled and snapped something that made her tear up and retreat.

Oookay, there went my fascination with him. I refused to be impressed by a potential hump-her-and-dump-her offender.

Freed from her clasp, he took a step toward the door, paused, then closed his eyes, as if praying for divine intervention. He looked tormented. I shouldn't care, but the pangs started cutting through my chest again. Maybe I would—

His image flickered before vanishing for good.

With a screech, I smacked the glass. "Show me more of him—I mean, show me how to help Mom and Nicolas."

My reflection stared back. Frustration and disappointment clawed at me. Just beyond the bathroom door, Thor was barking up a storm. Farther away—the kitchen, perhaps—I detected the sound of shattering glass.

"Everly?" Hartly called.

Leaving the bathroom required an iron will, the mirror calling to me once again. *Look. See.*

I tried!

Thor went from barking to growling as I maneuvered around

him—and drew up short. Hartly sat at the edge of my bed, her dark hair anchored in a ponytail, her face freshly scrubbed. Worry marred her expression as she stood.

"What did the teenage girl say the morning after her parents split?" Chin quivering, she delivered the punchline. "Oh, crap, my parents split."

The pangs sharpened. "What did one sister say to the other? If there's breath, there's hope." I just needed to decipher all the gibberish I'd overheard at the party. Reverting to Isnenglisnish, I said, "Whisnatisnevisner hisnappisnens, wisne wisnill isnalwisnays hisnave isneach isnothisner."

Her features softened, and she offered me a small smile. "Yisnou isnare risnight."

We made our way to the kitchen, where Mom was sweeping up pieces of broken glass. Her eyes were still swollen and rimmed with red, her cheeks even more ashen. Had she lost weight overnight? A summer dress sagged over her seemingly emaciated frame.

Everly is a danger to you.

I tried not to panic. "Are you all right?" A question we'd all had to ask way too many times lately.

"Still fighting that bug, I think." Avoiding my gaze, she motioned to the dining table. "Sit down, girls. There are things I must confess."

Hartly and I shared a wide-eyed look before we sat across from each other. Between us, Mom plopped into a chair without a shred of grace, very unlike her.

How quickly life could change. Yesterday, we'd been happy. Today? A storm cloud of depression hung over us.

Wringing her hands, Mom said, "The two of you have always wondered about your heritage, where I come from, and why I am the way I am. There's no easy way to tell you the truth, so I'm just going to blurt out everything, then answer your questions."

"We love you, Mom." Hartly offered her most encouraging smile, though it didn't quite reach her eyes. "No matter what."

"Love you no matter what," I echoed. *Keep an open mind, whatever she says.*

"Here goes." Looking like she would shatter at any second, Mom began. "I hail from the magical land of Enchantia. I am a princess and the first, only and former wife of Prince Edwin Morrow. You are princesses, too. Princess Hartly and Princess Everly."

Open mind. Nicolas had mentioned Enchantia, as well. Yet, I couldn't... I didn't... *Head spinning...*

"We are daughters of a prince," Hartly said, awed, accepting Mom's word without reservation. And why wouldn't she? Mom detested lies. "Prince Edwin."

Edwin. Our father. Aaaand the pangs sharpened.

Mom said, "All the creatures and beings of myth and legend live in Enchantia."

"Creatures? *Beings?*" *Open mind, open mind.* "We need examples."

She nibbled on her bottom lip. "There are the magic wielders. Witches. Oracles. Fairies. Warlocks. Sorcerers. The water dwellers. Mermaids. Sirens. Shifters. The forest imps. Satyrs. Unicorns. Nymphs. Dragons. Elves. Goblins. Trolls. And so many more, far too many to list." A dreamy smile appeared, there and gone. "But I digress. Edwin's older brother—King Stephan Morrow—tried to murder you and another newborn, his own daughter, your cousin." Her gaze slid to me at last, only to dart away. "Princess Truly Morrow."

"Our uncle tried to *murder* us?" I gasped out. "Why? Please tell me Truly survived."

"She did, yes." Dread emanated from Mom. "As for...your uncle. He did it because of the Tree of New Beginnings."

"I don't understand. Explain." I didn't mean to snap an order, but my impatience had reared its ugly head.

She reached out to tap my birthmark. "The Tree of New Beginnings is found in the Kingdom of Airaria. Its mystical apples contain power beyond imagining. And not just antioxidants humans love so much, but power King Stephan hoped to hoard. He appointed himself the tree's guardian and killed anyone who showed an interest in his apples. With the help of four other women—one of whom was Truly's mother, Queen Violet—I used illusion magic to render myself invisible, then stole a basket of apples. Nine months later, we all gave birth."

So our births were somehow tied to a magic tree?

Mom shifted nervously before continuing. "Oracles are descended from the fae. Or fairies. They see into the future. Physically, they cannot lie. Their prophecies are known as fairy tales, part symbolism, part puzzle, all open for interpretation. Or *mis*interpretation. The day of your birth, an oracle claimed your fates were tied to a certain fairy tale."

Fairy tales doubling as prophecies... *Open. Freaking. Mind.* Still, suspicions danced in my head, and all I could do was inwardly cry, *No, no, no.* I knew of only one fairy tale with a girl and her magic mirror. The one Mom obsessed over.

I comprehended the instant Hartly made the connection. Eyes widening, she said, "Are you trying to say we are living embodiments of the characters in Snow White?"

A pause. A firm nod. Again, Mom slid her tear-glistened gaze to me. "Were the Brothers Grimm oracles? I do not know. But they wrote two versions of 'Little Snow White.' Combined, those tales are the closest incarnation to the story told in Enchantia."

Open mind! Don't panic.

But what if I was supposed to be...

The Evil Queen.

My heart shuddered as if I'd been shocked with paddles. I refused to accept that I was some incarnation of evil. I was bad, but I wasn't *that* bad.

Hartly could absolutely pass for Snow White. All fairy-tale princesses enchanted animals, right?

I'd read both versions of the tale. In one, the Evil Queen was Snow White's birth mother. In the other, she was Snow White's stepmother.

See! I wasn't the Evil Queen. I wasn't a mother or a stepmother. Unless motherhood was merely symbolic of a familial connection.

Crap.

In both versions, the Evil Queen was vain, with a selfish, greedy heart. She ordered the Huntsman to escort the girl to a nearby forest, savagely murder her, and bring back her liver and lungs—for dinner. She used magic to disguise herself as a hag, not once, not twice, but thrice, attempting to murder the surprisingly un-killable SW each time. First with a corset, then a comb and finally the infamous apple.

While I could communicate with mirrors, I couldn't craft illusions. I wasn't vain, and I had no plans to marry an old fart of a king.

"In the Enchantian version—'Snow White and the Evil Queen'—the mother versus stepmother issue is never clarified," Mom said, "and both Snow White and the Evil Queen have a fairy godmother."

My mind returned to the group of people I'd seen in the mirror. Angel. The girl I'd both recognized and not recognized. The boy who'd set my blood aflame. My connection to them. Were they part of the tale? Why else would I have *needed* to see them?

"Who is supposed to be whom?" Hartly asked.

"The oracle did not say, but I can guess." Mom reached over and patted my sister's hand, saying, "The wild beasts refused to harm her."

When she glanced at me, her blue eyes shadowed with fear, and I knew. With every fiber of my being, I knew. She, too, suspected me of being the Evil Queen.

———

Knife. Through. The. Heart. I blinked to hide a sudden prickle of tears. I would not cry. This was a happy day. The day we learned about our dad. "Tell us about our father, Prince Edwin. Is he alive? Is he kind?"

A choking sound escaped her, and I almost withdrew the question. "He is... I'm so sorry, darlings, but he is dead. He lost his life protecting...you...from King Stephan."

The knife wedged ever deeper into my heart and then twisted. For so long, I'd thought the worst about our father. Abuser. Deadbeat. Villain. All along, he'd been a hero, sacrificing his life to save his babies.

"Do you have photos of him?" I asked softly.

"No. I am so sorry," she repeated.

So, not only would I never meet him or speak with him, I would never know what he'd looked like. Or what he thought of his grown-up daughters. I would always wonder whether he would have been proud of me, or disappointed.

Tears prickled anew, but again I blinked them away. I had to be strong for Hartly. "And the king?" I asked. Our uncle. "What happened to him?"

"According to the witch who visited me, he was murdered just this week, drained of his magic and power."

Magic. Power. Another dead family member I'd never get to meet. Needing a moment to process, I faced the wall of windows that overlooked our backyard. More birds than usual congregated there, picking seeds from the grass. A scissor-tailed flycatcher landed on the highest arch of a wrought-iron trellis. Hummingbirds sipped sugar water from containers Mom filled daily.

"I will tell you whatever you want to know about your... about Edwin, I promise. First, I must tell you everything else." With her gaze, Mom *begged* us to agree. I wasn't the only one hurting, I realized. She still grieved for her lost love. "If you do not understand *why*, you will not understand *who*."

Though confused, I nodded.

72

"King Stephan was a handsome man. Though he could freeze you with a glance, he could charm you with a smile. Queen Violet was his fourth wife. Though he'd killed the first three, she fell in love with him." Mom offered me a sad smile. "You look so much like them."

I looked like an aunt with no blood tie to me, and the man who'd murdered my father? Wonderful.

"After Stephan killed Edwin," she continued, "Violet and I realized we were next. We fled, hoping to raise our daughters in the mortal world, but Stephan's army caught us, injuring Violet in the process. She couldn't walk, but I knew I couldn't stay. I used my illusion magic to escape with you. Leaving Violet and Truly behind…it was the most difficult thing I've ever done. If I could have carried a third infant, I would have."

"Do you know what happened to Violet and Truly after you left?" Hartly asked.

"For some reason, Stephan decided not to kill them. I don't know why, only that mother and daughter still live."

I shared another look with Hartly. Though only seconds passed, we had a conversation with our eyes. A perk of twinhood, I supposed.

Me: *Do we think she's delusional?*

Hartly: *No way. I'm sold. We aren't mutants. We're magic!*

Me: *I have a bad feeling about this.*

Hartly: *Just remember. We'll be okay, as long as we're together.*

The same words I'd given her, time and time again.

"When we first arrived, I had a bag overflowing with the most beautiful jewels." Mom smiled dreamily. "Diamonds, sapphires, rubies and emeralds, all as big as a fist. Within days, however, most of them were stolen. I had no money, no job and no understanding of this strange world. It wasn't long before authorities deemed me unfit and took you girls away. As soon as I got you back, I ran, deciding to raise you as mortals, so that you would not be treated the way I was."

"I'm sorry, Mom." Hartly flattened a palm over her heart. "I'm sorry you suffered."

"Thank you, my sweet." Staring down, Mom gripped the edge of the table. "Last night, an Enchantian witch visited me. She told me King Stephan is dead and no longer a threat. We have one week to do whatever is needed for travel, then she will return to escort us home."

The witch. The one I'd seen in the mirror. No doubt about it; Hartly was right. *Mom* was right. We did use magic. *Reeling...*

Brow scrunched, Hartly said, "Why do we need her?"

"She is able to use magic here, but I am not," Mom replied. "And magic is needed to shift the invisible curtain between our worlds."

Invisible curtain? I squirmed in my chair. "If we decide to go, we'll take Nicolas with us, yes?"

Mom winced. "No, honey. We will go, and he will stay. The witch...she told me some truths about him. Terrible things I didn't know. He is not the man we thought he was."

How much to reveal about what I knew, and how much to hide? "He's from Enchantia, too?"

"He is." A sob bubbled from her, but she sobered quickly. "I was so happy to come across another Enchantian. He recognized me, you see. Princess Aubrey Morrow of Airaria. With him, I didn't have to hide who or what I was, and I reveled in the freedom."

She'd mentioned Airaria before. Our kingdom. I wanted to visit, but I didn't want to say goodbye to everything familiar. Something Mom had been forced to do once before, I realized. She'd left the only home she'd ever known, traded riches for poverty, abandoned family and friends, all to save two infants.

If I turned out to be the Evil Queen, I also turned her sacrifice into a punishment without reward.

"What's so bad about Nicolas?" I asked, my tone sharper than I'd intended. Mom had tossed him aside because he was "sorcerian," whatever that meant. If Hartly and I were somehow sorcerian, too, as he'd seemed to hint, I had to wonder if Mom would toss *us* aside one day.

She sniffled. "I will speak of him no more today. Let us focus on the good news. We can go home!"

All right. She'd left me with no other choice. To get the answers I wanted, I'd have to push. "What is a sorcerian?"

Her gaze snapped back to me. Looking like a caged animal, she said, "How do you know that term?"

"You tell me, and I'll tell you."

Breath wheezed from her. "The sorcerian have magical abilities, like witches, but only if they steal—or drain—power from other magical beings. It's called syphoning."

Reeling again. "I don't understand."

She thought for a moment. "Imagine power as a piece of string, and I hold one end of it. But a sorcerer comes along and picks up the other end. Now we both hold a piece of the string, so we both wield the magical ability, my power arcing between us, fueling us both, only at a much weaker capacity. If the sorcerer pulls the string, taking more and more of its length, he can ultimately pluck my end from my grasp, killing me and stealing my magical ability forever. The problem is, he cannot use that ability again unless and until he picks up someone else's string."

In other words, sorcerian were thieves.

Mom scanned my face with ruthless determination, giving me a glimpse of the royal she used to be. "Now. Tell me where you heard that term, Everly."

Deep breath in, out.

Hartly nodded encouragingly. "Disno isnit. Tisnell hisner."

Lifting my chin, squaring my shoulders—bracing—I said, "I see things…in mirrors."

"Mirrors." Panic marred Mom's expression. "Tell me. Tell me every detail. Leave nothing out."

My heart raced faster than ever. "For months, I've seen a dark-haired girl go about her day. She feeds the homeless, plays with orphans, always smiles and laughs. Last night, I saw and heard you and Nicolas arguing. The witch had just come and gone, had told you that Nicolas was a—the—sorcerian overlord. You kicked him out."

A strangled noise left Mom. "That is seer magic."

Seer magic. Some dormant instinct stretched, awakening inside me. *Yes. That's it.*

"Your father possessed seer magic, as well." She pressed a hand against her throat. "The prophecy...the Evil Queen..."

"I am *not* the Evil Queen." I would never kill someone just because they were dubbed the fairest of all.

Mom pinned me with a hard stare. "Show me your ability. Now."

5

*Put your heart back together, my sweet.
It's time to rise up, there are answers to seek.*

The look Mom sometimes gave me—anger, disappointment and fear, as if she suspected I would hack her into a million pieces while she slept. Yeah, that one. Suddenly I was on the receiving end of its country cousin, pure unadulterated terror.

Mom led the charge to the guest bathroom, where we could fit comfortably.

Maybe I should refuse to do this. Did I really want to prove I had the same ability as the Evil Queen?

At my side, Mom rested a hand on my shoulder. Tremors shook us both. I kept my gaze downcast. Hartly remained in the open door, chewing her bottom lip, as Mom often did. Thor sat at her feet, on guard.

Did *he* sense that I was the Evil Queen?

Stalling, I said, "I have more questions about the fairy tale."

"And I'm happy to answer them. *After.* Go ahead, honey." Mom gave my shoulder an encouraging squeeze. "No matter what happens, I love you. I will *always* love you."

Would she? *Only one way to find out...*

I did it, I lifted my gaze and reached for the glass, saying, "Mirror, show me Enchantia. Show me what I need to see."

A bolt of electricity zapped me, and I gasped. Next, the tips of my fingers heated, hot, so hot. Needle pricks tormented my nape.

Ripples moved through the glass, distorting our reflections.

"What's happening?" Mom demanded.

"Ripples...never felt this much power before," I replied, almost drunk on it. Had I somehow plugged into an ocean of strength? So good!

"I see nothing. *So dizzy.*" Mom tightened her grip on me as if fighting to stay upright. "Keep going, honey."

No way. I would check on Mom. Any second...trying...

The ripples accelerated, mesmerizing me, until I *couldn't* avert my gaze. Then everything else faded from my awareness, forgotten, a map of Enchantia taking shape. My heart knew it, even if my mind still didn't understand it.

I counted four distinct regions, with two up top and two down below, and several large bodies of water. Separating each parcel of land was a massive forest in the shape of a dragon.

I felt a strange tingle of kinship with the forest. Like the sense of connection I'd felt with Hot Stuff.

Now details crystalized whenever I focused on a specific location, as if I'd moved a magnifying glass over the map. Even better, bits and pieces of information flowed straight into my brain.

Icy mountains with village valleys—*the Empire of Sevón.*

Sand dunes crested by a glittering night sky—*the Kingdom of Airaria.*

Flatlands carpeted by a dazzling array of flowers—*the Provence of Fleur.*

Bodies of water and island clusters, laid out in a fishy pattern— *the Azul Dynasty.*

The dragon-shaped woodlands—*the Enchantian Forest, also known as the Forest of Good and Evil.*

There, the magnifying glass revealed rocky hills, wildflower meadows and honeysuckle glades. A babbling brook ran through misshapen thickets, tangled vines and spindly trees that swayed in a gentle wind. Colorful flower petals glistened as if brushed with stardust. Ghostly shadows sneaked here and there, twining with mist and moonlight. The effect was haunting and exquisite, and more vivid than reality.

Awe hummed in my veins. I'd lived my life in a dream and had only now woken up.

What intrigued me most? A spellbinding azure glow enveloped the trees.

What *was* that? It called to me. *You are mine, and I am yours…*

I breathed deep, an earthy aroma teasing my nostrils— wildflowers, cinnamon, nutmeg and a dash of honey. My head fogged, goose bumps spreading over my limbs.

Unacceptable reaction. Instinct warned, *The most beautiful things are the deadliest.*

Then suddenly, the view switched, revealing a mining town directly beneath the mountaintop fortress. The one I'd seen last night. People of all shapes, sizes and heritages worked alongside creatures of myth and legend. Some of those creatures had horns, others had wings. Some were half human, half animal. Most pushed wheelbarrows filled with gold, diamonds, crystals and stones out of the surrounding caves.

A memory prodded me. A time Mom had read her daughters stories—about these very beings. Light bulb! In her own way, Mom had tried to prepare us for the return home.

I doubted anything could have prepared me.

Tents and tables littered the ice-covered streets, vendors hawking clothes, jewels and food. The aroma of fresh baked breads joined the deluge, and my mouth watered. Dozens of firepits crackled with blue flames, dark smoke curling up, up.

Hungry for knowledge, I returned my gaze to the creatures. Once again, knowledge flowed straight into my brain.

Those with the upper half of a human and lower half of a goat—*satyrs*.

Those with pointy ears and rainbow-colored hair—*elves*.

The winged ones wearing a multitude of necklaces and bracelets—*avian*.

Not angels? Really?

Every woman wore a gown, some plain and functional, others fancy and ornamental. Most of the men wore loose-fitting tunics and leather pants. A few rocked a loincloth.

A recurrent *clang* drew my attention to…a blacksmith. He drove a sledgehammer into a sword, then moved to plunge the blade into a cauldron of water. I marveled. He was human up top and horse down below—*centaur*.

Each new sight dazzled me.

Zooming forward once again, past the tents, down a row of stone buildings. Closing in on… Angel!

She stood underneath an awning, partially masked by shadows, and spoke with Miss Familiar Unfamiliar. One stepped closer, and the other followed suit. They leaned in…and kissed as if the world would end tomorrow.

Ahhh. Yesterday's tension made sense.

What a lovely couple, I wished them all the best. But as I watched them—like a total creeper—a kernel of envy snuck up on me. These girls were lost in each other, the rest of the world forgotten. Something I'd never experienced with Peter. Or anyone!

Would I ever?

"Go away." Male voice, harsh tone. No room for argument.

I exhaled a happy breath. I had volume once again. Whatever

the reason—I'd improved, or accessed more of my magic—I wholeheartedly approved.

I shifted to look at the speaker, the avian who stood sentry at the end of the alley. He held a wicker basket, and oh, wow—Wonder of Wonders. He was drop-dead gorgeous, with dark hair, dark brown skin and whiskey-colored eyes. Massive wings the same color as a morning sky rose over his shoulders. He wore more necklaces and bracelets than the other avian, and I wondered if the jewelry was purely decorative or had a deeper meaning.

"This is wrong. We must stop," Angel said between panting breaths, reclaiming my attention. "You're engaged, and every time we do this, I hate myself a little more."

With a groan, the other girl wrenched away. "You're right. I know you're right." Sunlight washed over her, highlighting details I'd missed before. Her hair was the same silver white as mine, as well as the same jet-black as Hartly's. Her gray eye had a golden trim, like mine, and her blue eye rivaled the ocean, like Hartly's. She had my freckles, and Hartly's bronze tint.

Familiar but not familiar… Realization struck, nearly knocking me down. She was Princess Truly Morrow, my cousin. My family! My heart swelled with love for her.

"I didn't choose him, Farrah, and he didn't choose me," she said. "Our parents arranged the marriage."

Farrah. Finally, I knew Angel's real name.

The fact that Queen Violet hoped to marry Truly off to someone she didn't love made my hackles rise. If ever Mom tried to arrange a marriage for me, I would blow a gasket. *Give me love, or give me spinsterhood.* I wanted what Mom and Nicolas had. Joy. Communion. Contentment. Like two puzzle pieces that fit together seamlessly.

Correction: I wanted what Mom and Nicolas had once had. Did true love never last? And why would Aunt Violet keep Truly from Farrah? Did the queen not know her daughter was gay—bi? Something else?—or did she not accept it?

Truly toyed with a lock of Farrah's hair. "I don't know if I can go through with the marriage. I want you, only you."

The avian glanced over his shoulder, calling, "Time's up, Princess."

I thought he addressed Truly, but Farrah piped up, saying, "Thank you, Saxon. You are a wonderful friend."

"This, I know," he responded, his gruff tone laced with affection.

"I wish...so many things." Truly caressed Farrah's jawline before severing contact and righting her clothing. As she backed away, the hem of her dress swayed around her ankles.

Clearly, both girls came from money. Farrah wore a finely made hooded cloak, fur-trimmed gloves, and a blue-and-yellow gown embroidered with images of the sun. Truly wore a similar ensemble in pink and white, only she had a crossbow strapped to her back.

"Come on. Let's go save your father," my cousin said. "Everything else can be settled later."

"Thank you." Tears gathered in Farrah's eyes as she approached Saxon. Her chin wobbled.

"You should tell your family about your feelings for the girl," he said, handing her the basket. "The king will be upset, but only temporarily. Your brother will support you, overjoyed you are happy."

Panic glazed her delicate features. "I can't tell them, I just... can't. I'm not ready."

"Not ready," Truly echoed. She pasted on a brittle smile, and I ached for her. She'd taken the words as a personal rejection, hadn't she?

The trio abandoned the alley and marched into town, following an icy path. People stopped to bow, smile and wave, even the ones carrying bags of grain or leading animals.

Farrah passed out cookies, earning squeals of thanks.

Golden sunshine spotlighted the buildings that lined both sides of the road, made of limestone and roofed by a spectacular array of amethyst, rose quartz and agate.

"Magnificent," I breathed. Such splendor. *Like a fairy tale come to life.* But why had I *needed* to see this? And why did I feel tapping on my shoulder?

Just as soon as I noticed that tapping, I forgot it as more questions flooded in. Would Truly like me? Would Farrah?

I desperately craved their friendship.

The threesome crested and descended a hill, then entered a shop at the end of the row. A bell tinkled, announcing their presence.

"Ophelia?" Farrah called. "Noel?"

Ivy had grown over the floorboards and walls. Candles flickered here and there, light and shadows twining, illuminating the herbs that hung from hooks in the ceiling. Jars filled with *things* lined various shelves. Oh, good gracious. An eyeball floated to the surface of one and peered right at me.

In back, a sign read Magics, Foretellings and More. Cleaning a long wooden counter was a teenage girl dressed to kill in golden armor, dark leather and an array of glittering jewelry.

I stiffened. She wasn't just any girl. She was a witch. *The* witch. The one who'd (inadvertently?) pitted my mother against Nicolas and planned to take us back to Enchantia.

Wait. She resided in Sevón, rather than Airaria? But why was Truly, an Airarian princess, in Sevón?

Farrah executed a flawless curtsey, saying, "Good morn, Ophelia."

"Good morn, Princess Farrah. Princess Truly. Saxon." The witch—Ophelia—continued wiping the counter. "You're here to speak with Noel, I'm sure, but she's with a customer."

Saxon remained behind the princesses, a tower of menace and might. He didn't respond to the witch, or even acknowledge her presence. Instead, he scanned the shop for any possible threat to his charges. I liked his dedication. Nothing swayed him from his task.

"Actually, you might have the answers I seek." Farrah withdrew a small bag of coins, or maybe jewels, the pieces clinking together. "In her last vision, Noel told us my father could be saved, but only after the harvest moon. Well, the harvest moon has come and gone."

"You wish to know if Noel has had any other visions?"

So, oracles had visions separate from the prophecies/fairy tales. Good to know.

"I do," Farrah said. "Hours ago, my father's heart stopped. If not for our healers, he would have died. One day, one day soon, I fear their magic will not be enough."

Sympathy welled. Poor Farrah.

Ophelia extended her hand, palm up, a silent demand for payment.

I had to admire her business acumen.

As soon as Farrah tossed the bag, the witch announced, "Yes, Noel has had another vision. In it, your brother journeyed through the Enchantian Forest, risking life and limb to find the Apple of Life and Death."

The princess blinked rapidly as if trying to jump-start her brain. "What is the Apple of Life and Death? Why have I never heard of it?"

Ophelia smiled, a little sly. "You ask the wrong question. You, who cannot live, until you die."

I jolted, as if hit by lightning. Had I just heard a bit of prophecy?

"What is the *right* question, then?" Truly all but vibrated with irritation. "And what does that even mean? *Cannot live until you die,*" she mocked. "You make no sense. Not that you ever do."

The tapping on my shoulder started up again but didn't last long.

The witch quirked a dark brow. "Not every death signifies the end of a life. Sometimes death heralds a new beginning."

Ooh la la. Mom had mentioned the *Tree* of New Beginnings. Any connection between the two?

Behind the counter, an older man in the midst of a grumbling tirade brushed aside a beaded partition and marched toward us. Noticing Farrah and Truly, he ended the mantrum midsentence and gawked.

"Your majesties," he said, reaching out to take their hands.

Saxon lunged before contact was made, pushing the man away.

Realizing he'd angered the royal bodyguard, the man muttered an apology and raced from the shop.

Farrah heaved a sigh. "Must you be so forceful with my subjects?"

"Yes, Princess," the avian replied. "I must."

"He meant no harm."

"How do you know?"

The beads were swept aside a second time, ending their conversation. A pretty teenager with fire engine–red hair, pinkish skin and purple eyes emerged. This must be Noel. She wore the same type of armor as the witch, and just as many jewels. While Ophelia hit *badass* status, this girl appeared more delicate, even fragile, but also like chaos walking, as if she'd dressed in the dark...while in a hurry...as alien ships bombed her house.

"Hello, Great Oracle." Farrah executed another flawless curtsy, bowing her head in deference. "We long to purchase a few moments of your valuable time."

Excitement spiked. A real, honest to goodness oracle, who might or might not have answers about Snow White and the Evil Queen. I wanted to speak with her, too.

"Oh, goodie. Prince Roth is here, too. Shhh." Noel pressed a finger to her lips, then loudly proclaimed, "No one mention how much I want to chain him inside my lady dungeon and have my wicked way with him. Even though he's meant for— Cookie!"

As she'd spoken, Ophelia had waved a hand and produced a platter of cookies.

Noel swiped a treat, reminding me of Thor when he caught a glimpse of a squirrel.

Roth... a name found inside the word *brother*. The Brothers Grimm—bROTHers. Coincidence?

"The strange way you speak." Truly frowned. "Where do you hear these things?"

"Only everywhere," Ophelia said on behalf of her friend.

The bell over the door tinkled, and the *thump, thump* of footsteps sounded. As the newcomer stalked around the shelves, breathing got a whole lot harder, my heart sprinting.

This *is Prince Roth?* Hot Stuff, the darkly hypnotic boy I'd seen bang and bail.

Just as before, the sight of him arrested me. My instincts shouted, *Dangerous!*

Oh, yes. Dangerous to my peace of mind.

He scowled at Farrah, fury pulsing from him. "You disregarded my orders. *Again.*"

Oh, sweet goodness. His voice! Deep and growly. As smooth as butter and as rich as chocolate.

"I gave you one order, only one," he said. "If you ventured from the palace, you were to take Vikander. So, why is the fairy at the palace while you traipse about the village?"

Guilt darkened her expression, but she rallied swiftly, lifting her head high. "I never meant to worry you, and I'm sorry I did. But Vikander hovers, and I—I'm an independent woman well able to take care of myself."

Or maybe this Vikander guy would have stopped her from getting busy with Truly? Just a guess.

"Vikander protects you in ways others cannot," Roth said.

"Saxon protects me, too," she said, lifting her chin another notch. "Truly protects me."

"Saxon coddles you, and Truly—" He ran his tongue over

straight, white teeth and massaged the back of his neck. "We teeter at the edge of war with Azul. I have meetings scheduled with Fleur, the outcome critical. Spies abound. If you were hurt, if you were taken captive to force my hand, if I were to lose you and Father... I need to know you're safe, Farrah."

Once again, sympathy welled. While his expression evinced zero emotion, his tone conveyed incredible pain. No doubt he'd already lost someone he loved, maybe even multiple someones.

Noel fake-coughed, gaining everyone's attention. "You wish to learn more about the Apple of Life and Death, and how to save the King of Sevón, yes? Or perhaps you wish to buy a spell from Ophelia?"

Roth went still, not even daring to breathe. "*More* about it? Oracle, I know *nothing* about it. Are you saying I can save my father if I find this apple?"

"Yes. I am, and you *can*."

Why the emphasis on *can*?

"Tell me where to find it, then," he commanded.

"Far, far away," she replied, "but oh so close. You must search the forest, high and low."

A muscle jumped beneath his eye. "A search takes time. Time my father might not have. Time I cannot spare. I have trade meetings with Fleur's representatives, and I must escort Princess Truly back to Airaria—" he balled his hands "—for a *brief* visit with her mother, to pay respects to her father. And buy a spell from Ophelia? No. She demands a sacrifice. The price is too steep."

Ophelia spread her arms as if she were the last sane person in a world gone wrong. "If you won't make a sacrifice for me, why should I make a sacrifice for you to use my magic?"

"What do you actually sacrifice? You weaken when you cast a spell, yes," Truly said, "but your power always replenishes itself."

Ophelia narrowed her eyes. "Do not act as if you know the trials of a witch."

Noel scratched her head, as if confused. To the witch, she said, "Did I pre-remember the conversation I had with Roth about the apple?"

"You did," the witch replied, her anger draining. "If Prince Roth wants answers, he'll pay double the usual cost. I post-remembered we raised our rates. And, Prince? My spell might be the most expensive commodity in Enchantia, but there's a reason. I'm that good."

Truly mumbled something that sounded like "Greedy wenches." Maybe *wretches*?

"I'll pay for information only. You will speak." Roth tossed a second bag of coins to Ophelia, then waved his hand, a royal decree for the oracle to continue. "The sooner the better."

"Let's go back and I'll—" A sudden, strange calm fell over Noel. The whites of her eyes expanded, spreading over her irises. Creep city! Voice monotone, she said, "No, your father will not die while you are away. The opposite is true. Go to your meetings, escort Truly and search for the apple in the heart of the forest. Only then will the King of Sevón have a chance to heal. But take heed, dear Prince. The apple metes life and death with equal measure. Make the right choices, bask in the rewards."

Fascinating. A vision in action, one both detailed and vague. What choices were right, and what choices were wrong?

"How will I know the difference?" Roth asked, his tone gentle. I didn't know him well, or at all, but I suspected he would prefer to snap and shout.

"Your heart will know," Noel replied. "Listen to it. Listen well. The heart wants what the heart wants, and no other will do."

Everyone waited for her to say more, but the milky film dissipated in her eyes and she smiled. "What'd I miss?"

Ophelia patted the top of her head. "I'll explain later."

"I'll go on this journey with you," Farrah told Roth, resolute. "I'll help you find the apple."

The prince shook his head, a lock of dark hair falling over his brow. "No, sister. I need you home, caring for Father. Safe." Looking to Noel, he said, "What can you tell me about my negotiations with Fleur? We need their crops. What should I offer in—" He stiffened and withdrew a sword, his gaze darting left, right. "Someone's watching us."

Uh-oh. He sensed me. Did the others?

"Put the sword away before she decides not to come." Noel winked—at me. "Hello, Your Majesty. We are going to become the *best* of friends. Well, maybe not the best. You're going to hate me, but only for a time. But after that… No, still not the best." She frowned and tapped her chin, then brightened. "We're going to be such mediocre friends! *Bonum et malum*, united forever in life and in death!"

I opened and closed my mouth. How was this possible?

Bonum et malum—good and evil. United. Had her mother eaten a forbidden apple, too? Was she the strongest oracle in the land, just like Hartly and I were the strongest…princesses? Mortal magic wielders? A type of witch?

Roth's gaze zipped past me, then returned. I reared back, snared by the mesmerizing haze of those green, green eyes. He stared hard, awareness boring into my soul.

His image began to wink in and out, like a wire had frayed. I banged on the glass, not ready to lose the connection. I needed to know more, *everything*.

But my actions had no effect. Roth and Truly vanished, my flushed, sweat-dampened reflection staring back at me. My eyes glowed metallic silver, and it was eerie AF.

My attention moved to Mom. Through the mirror, in slow motion, I watched her collapse against me. Impact shoved me down. I pinwheeled my arms as I fell, trying to grab the counter. No luck. I ended up on the floor, the rest of the world rushing back into focus.

Hartly was screaming. Thor was barking.

Mom lay beside me, unconscious, her face bloody. She looked like the woman I'd seen in my yesterday's vision. Thinner, sickly, with yellowed skin, lifeless hair and blue-tinted lips.

"Mom!" I scrambled to my knees. "What's wrong with her?" I felt for a pulse. Yes! It was reedy, but there.

"I don't know, I don't know," Hartly cried. "Before she fell, she clutched her heart. You have to help her!"

"Call 9-1-1."

"Already did. They're on the way," she said between sobs, then crumpled at my other side.

Fighting hysteria, I patted Mom's cheek. "Mom! Aubrey!" Tears scalded my eyes, obscuring my vision. I patted her cheek with more force.

Finally, she came around, moaning and blinking open her eyes. When she managed to focus her gaze, she looked between Hartly and me, realization dawning. "Listen. Must explain." Her beautiful blue irises grew dimmer by the second. "Mother, aunt...father, sorcerer...sister, cousin. Love, hate. Will be...whatever heart...desires."

"Shhh, shhh," I said, fat tears streaming down my cheeks. I clasped her hand. So cold, so weak. "Save your strength, okay? Help is on the way."

"Love..." A long stream of breath seeped from her parted lips, her body going lax.

"No!" Hartly and I shouted in unison.

Again, I felt for a pulse. This time, I couldn't find one.

Frantic, not knowing what else to do, I cuddled Mom's wrist, flattened my hands above her heart and pressed. Once, twice. Ten. Twenty. "I won't let you die. I won't, I won't."

I loved her, needed her, and any moment she would jerk awake. Paramedics would arrive and whisk her to a hospital, where she would receive expert medical care. She would recover. We would have a long, happy life together. We would return to Enchantia, a family united, and Mom would regain everything she'd lost. But minute after minute passed with no improvement.

Sweat poured from me, my muscles quivering. *Can't stop, won't stop.*

"Harder," Hartly pleaded. *"Make her live."*

I pushed so hard I felt Mom's sternum crack. I whimpered, my tears dripping on her brow, collecting in the corner of her eye as if she, too, were crying.

Finally, the paramedics arrived. Someone forced me aside. Hartly picked up Thor and gathered me close. We trembled against each other.

Mom was lifted onto a gurney, a clear mask strapped to the lower half of her face. Someone straddled her waist, picking up where I'd left off, administering CPR. One, two, three…

Though the group worked feverishly, Mom never opened her eyes, never took another breath. Aubrey Morrow died, a piece of my heart dying with her.

6

Dry your tears and march ahead.
You can rest when you are dead.

Thunder crashed and lightning flashed, lighting up the sky. Hail beat against the roof of our house, an end-of-summer storm bringing freezing rain and wild winds.

I felt like the one being pummeled. Raw inside. Hollowed out as if the best parts of me had been removed, only scar tissue and a sickly layer of guilt remained. I kept replaying things Mom had told me over the years.

Hope is like a seedling. In darkness it dies, in light it thrives.

How easy it is to love the lovable. The true test of strength is loving the unlovable.

A dirty dollar bill isn't worth any less than a clean one. Every life has value.

I desperately needed light, my hope withering.

Mirrors continued to call to me. *One more peek. Look, see.*

Learn. I had a lot of questions. Why had Mom died? Where was Nicolas, and what was he doing? Would I ever see Truly and Farrah again? What about Roth? How could I help Hartly? She'd grown despondent.

What should I do next? Every day, I communed with a mirror for one hour. Problem was, I continued to see the freaky version of myself, and all she ever did was study me, silently, creeping me out.

Desperate for a light bulb moment, I shuffled through the house, grazing my fingertips over Mom's favorite paintings. An apple orchard. A crown made from browned apple cores. A glass coffin, with Snow White sleeping inside.

My ears twitched as a soft moan drifted through the house. Soft, yes, but it crashed through my calm like a wrecking ball. I rushed into the living room, where Hartly slept fitfully on the couch. How innocent she appeared, curled in a ball with a pillow clutched to her chest, Thor resting beside her.

Ever since our return from the hospital—where Mom had been declared DOA—Hartly had camped here, dozing on and off as if awaiting our parents' arrival, so they could wake her from this nightmare.

Barbed wire wrapped around my heart and squeezed. If I broke down, I sensed I would be like Humpty Dumpty; all the king's horses and all the king's men would fail to put Everly Morrow back together again.

Every day, Hartly weakened a little more…and I strengthened. Physically, at least. Mentally and emotionally, I teetered at the razor's edge of misery.

Careful not to jostle my precious sister, I settled at her side. Thor growled at me, his new normal, but Hartly didn't rouse. Ignoring the dog, I checked her temperature. Hot, but not frightfully so. I tucked an afghan around her shoulders. One of the many blankets Mom had knitted throughout the years.

I cleared my throat to dissolve a lump of grief. "Can you believe Peter came knocking on our door this morning? I didn't answer." I smoothed a damp lock of hair behind her ear and cringed. Bruises marred the flesh under her eyes. Her skin was ashen, her lips chapped, and she'd lost weight. Too much, too fast. "What is wrong with you, Harts?"

I'd forced her to visit a clinic early this morning. The doctor diagnosed situational depression and gave her a prescription to help her sleep. I didn't have a medical degree, but I wasn't convinced. What if she'd contracted whatever killed Mom?

What *had* killed Mom? A virus? Heart attack?

Everly is a danger to you.

I knocked at my temples to dislodge Nicolas's voice. Angrier by the second, I whipped out my cell phone and typed, Where are you? TELL ME! Please come home!

I'd texted him a thousand times but hadn't received a single response. Did he know what had happened? Did he not know we missed him? Could the sorcerer not sense that we *needed* him?

What if something terrible had happened to him?

The hospital kept calling, hoping to speak with someone about releasing Mom's body, and the results of the autopsy. A memorial service had to be planned and paid for by someone with money. I didn't qualify on either count.

I wasn't sure how much time we had until Social Services showed up.

"What can I do to help you, Harts?" *Could* I help her? How were we supposed to go on without our mother?

Some fairy tales ended with a happily-ever-after. Why hadn't ours? Honestly, I wasn't sure I would ever be happy again.

What message had Mom tried to convey with her final words? *Mother, aunt. Father, sorcerer. Sister, cousin. Love, hate. Will be whatever heart desires.*

Hartly gave another moan, and I lifted her limp hand to my cheek. I couldn't lose her, too. I would rather die. "I'm here. Whatever you need, I'll do."

No response.

Leaning over, I plucked a fresh rag and a bottle of icy water from the coffee table. I kept all kinds of supplies close, just in case. After soaking the rag, I returned the bottle without its cap—where had that little bugger gone?—then dabbed at her feverish skin.

I slid my gaze over the living room. How many times had I watched Mom bustle around in here? How many times had she smiled as we knitted? How many times had she paced while giving us a lecture?

On the walls, next to her paintings, were pictures of her. Bookshelves contained a bazillion variations of "Little Snow White." An array of vases overflowed with dried flowers, emitting a sweet fragrance. All gifts from Nicolas.

Pretties for my pretty, he'd said.

I didn't want to remember. I didn't want to forget. I wanted to destroy the vases and books. I wanted to protect every item with bubble wrap.

"I need you to get better, Harts," I said. "*Please*, get better. You are my life. Enchantia is real, and the witch—an actual, honest to goodness *witch*—might come to retrieve us in seventy-two hours, so we have a major decision to make. Do we go without Mom? Or do we stay here, the only home we've ever known? Without Nicolas, we'll probably end up in foster care and lose everything we've ever known anyway."

Silence. I sighed.

"Enchantia it is, then." Farrah had mentioned magical healers. Maybe they could aid Hartly. "We can meet Aunt Violet and Truly and tour the land. From what I can tell, there are four territories. Airaria is a desert paradise. Sevón is a mining town, with mountains and avian. The Province of Fleur is a wonderland of flowers. And the Azul Dynasty is all water and islands. I'm so curious about them."

Silence.

"There's this avian, a protector to the max," I said. "You could date him, and I could date...oh, I don't know...just spit-balling off the top of my head, with no one specific in mind...a prince." I had zero desire to date right now but wanted to give Hartly hope about *something*.

"You'll flip when you see Truly," I continued. "She's an Everly-Hartly hybrid, and she has a secret girlfriend named Far-rah. *Princess* Farrah. Apparently, we Morrow girls like to go for the gold. Well, except for me. With Peter, I went for rusted tin."

Amid my chatter, Hartly blinked open her eyes. Relief bathed me, only to rinse away a second later. If eyes were the window to the soul, her soul had become an ocean of pain.

To be fair, I could be seeing my own reflection. *Never experienced such grief.*

Happy smile. Pretend all is well. "Why is six afraid of seven? It's not. Numbers aren't capable of feeling emotion."

Though her eyes remained bleak, she managed a small, half-hearted smile. "What did the small cat say to the big cat? Meow." Her voice was raspy from disuse. "I'm sorry I've been so out of it. I'm trying to rally, I promise, but I'm just so tired." Frowning, she canted her head to the side. "The birds say he's coming."

"Who's coming? What birds?" There were no birds in the house. And the ones outside had scattered just before the storm hit.

"Ever since Mom—" Her chin trembled. "The voices have been muted. Now, I'm hearing them again."

Happy smile.

The front door burst open and crashed against the wall, and I nearly jumped out of my skin. An icy breeze blustered through the living room, my neatly stacked washrags tumbling off the coffee table. A bottle of Tylenol followed. The capless water tipped over, liquid glugging to the floor.

Breath sharpened like a blade, lodging in my throat. Nicolas stood there, panting, rain and hail hammering at the porch.

Strain enveloped his red-rimmed eyes. His golden hair and dark suit were drenched. Somehow, that wetness made him appear more menacing than ever, like he was an extension of the shadows and a living embodiment of the storm. Fury in human form.

In seconds, I underwent a complete cycle of all-consuming emotion. Relief, joy, anxiety, confusion, more anger. My stepdad had returned healthy and whole. Why had he stayed away? Why hadn't he texted or called?

As I stood, lightning streaked the sky, bathing him in bright light. Raindrops clung to his lashes. Or tears? Both?

He slitted his lids, pure malevolence emanating from him. When he noticed Hartly, who was struggling to sit up, the malevolence magnified. I shrank back, every heartbeat like a cannon blast.

This was Nicolas, my stepdad. I had nothing to fear.

Everly is a danger to you, and to Hartly. Stronger magic requires more power—power she'll syphon from you.

Had I syphoned from my mother every time I'd peered into a mirror? My sister?

A storm began to rage inside *me*. Hartly's color had improved for the first time in days. Because I hadn't sought another vision?

No. I couldn't have syphoned from her. I didn't know how.

Well, I didn't know how to breathe, either, but still I managed to do it multiple times a minute.

I sucked in a breath—proving it—then shook my head. I would *never* hurt my loved ones.

"Where have you been?" I shouted, almost choking on the words. "We needed you. *Mom* needed you. She's…she died, and you weren't here, and…and…"

Voice frayed at the edges, he said, "I was taking steps to save your mother and help you. I never thought…" His fury doubled. Tripled.

I will help her acquire an altilium.

Pure aggression, he took a step toward me. "Have you been using your magic, Everly?"

The accusation in his tone frightened me, and I considered lying. But no. No way would I dishonor Mom by speaking what she'd dubbed the language of evil. "Not today. But yesterday? The day before? Yes. I tried and failed."

Another step. "What magical ability do you possess?"

Gulp. "Mom called it seer magic."

Flinch. "Just like your father, then."

"You knew Prince Edwin?" I asked.

He paused, a strange gleam flashing over his expression, there and gone. "Edwin was entitled, like most Enchantian royals, but not cruel. He communed with animals, like Hartly."

So Edwin had communed with mirrors *and* animals?

"On the other hand, the king, Edwin's brother, was the cruelest man I've ever met. I admired him greatly. Just…stay here." He kicked the door shut, then stalked to the office located in back of the house, leaving puddles of water in his wake.

My stomach churned, and I sat back down to rest my head on Hartly's shoulder. Thor jumped between us, nudging me out of the way.

"He means well," she whispered.

Who? Nicolas or Thor?

Our stepdad returned with a sheet of paper in hand. Expression as blank as ever—which now frightened me more than the fury—he planted himself in the center of the room. "Your mother wrote a letter and made me vow to read it to you if ever something happened to her. So I'm going to read it, and then we're going to talk."

At the same time, I reached for Hartly and she reached for me. We clung to each other.

"'To my greatest loves,'" he began. Immediately, my broken heart erupted like a volcano, scalding lava pouring through the many cracks.

"What you are about to hear will shock and hurt you, and I'm sorry for that. But I'll never be sorry for safeguarding your happiness. Had you known the truth, you would have worried and wondered what-if, and wanted what you couldn't have—yet. A way back. Worse, mortals would doubt you and lock you away. I planned to tell you about your origins only if and when we returned home. Or if I died."

He paused, giving us a moment to absorb and calm. Though I doubted anything would ever calm me again.

He read.

"I married Prince Edwin of Airaria around the same time Lady Violet married his brother, the ever cruel and maddened King Stephan. According to Enchantian law, a wife has one year to conceive a child. If she fails, the husband is allowed to kill her. With time running out, Violet and I worked with another queen, a witch and an oracle to acquire apples from the Tree of New Beginnings. Within a month, we all conceived. Later we each gave birth to a healthy baby girl. Except for Violet, who gave birth to twins. Hartly, my love, your father is Prince Edwin. My darling Everly, your father is…not. I love you like a daughter, but I am your aunt. Your mother is Queen Violet, and your father is King Stephan. Hartly isn't your sister, but your cousin. Truly isn't your cousin, but your twin."

Every sentence hit me like a bomb blast. Blood rushed from my head and rang in my ears. Dizziness had me swaying on the couch. I was… I wasn't… I couldn't…

A cruel king.

Father.

Maddened. Murderous. Evil.

Dead.

Had he regretted what he'd done to his brother, or what he'd wanted to do to six innocent infants?

Far too soon, Nicolas resumed his task.

"Hartly, Edwin died protecting us from Stephan's sword. He distracted the king, allowing me to hide us both inside an illusion. I hid the twins and Violet, too. We planned to take you all to the mortal world, but we were caught, and Violet was injured. I could only carry Hartly and one other child. Violet had less than a second to decide which twin to place in my hands. Oh, how she sobbed, reminding me of a wounded animal. As soon as I had Everly in hand, I ran, leaving Violet and Truly behind. It remains one of the most difficult things I've ever done."

Less than a second to decide… Violet's choice. More bomb blasts. More roaring and dizziness, terrible pangs bombarding my heart and mind. The worst I'd ever experienced.

Hartly placed Thor in her lap and scooted closer to me. "You are my sister, my twin, and I love you. Always. I don't care about semantics."

"I love you, too," I croaked, then motioned to Nicolas. "Let's hear the rest." Before I broke down. *No breaking down. Must stay strong.*

He gave a clipped nod and resumed reading.

"I debated keeping your girls in the mortal world forever to circumvent the prophecy. A young girl tormented by someone she loves. A lethal plot by an evil queen. A kingdom forever stained by evil. A poisonous apple. Death in flames. What is literal, and what is symbolic? Then I wondered if trying to circumvent the prophecy is what causes it to come true. You must prepare for the worst, which means you must consult oracles and witches, which means you must return to Enchantia. If ever King Stephan dies, a witch will come here and escort you home. Do not worry. You need do nothing. An oracle will know your location and tell the witch."

You were right, Mom. The witch came.
Nicolas continued,

"When she arrives, say yes. Go to Enchantia. Get to know Queen Violet and Princess Truly. Learn about the prophecy. Study magic. Practice using it. Fight for better. Maybe one day, you'll even change the law.'"

He flipped up his gaze and glared at me. "'Do *not* practice using magic. There are things you must learn first.'"
Everly is a danger to you. I nodded, dazed, those pangs growing stronger.
He cleared his throat and pulled the letter taut.

"I pray you'll forgive me one day. I love and adore you both, and I value every moment we've spent together. I'm so proud of the kind girls you are, and the strong women you're becoming. I hope you live without regret. Create your own destiny one decision, one action at a time. Fall in love with someone who sees your incredible worth. When you reach the end of your wonderful, exciting lives, I hope you look back and smile because you did everything you wanted, loved with your whole heart, helped others and eschewed evil. From the bottom of my heart,
Mom."

My lungs constricted, and I struggled to breathe.
Hartly cuddled Thor against her chest. "I don't want to wait. I want to see Mom's homeland."

Nicolas shook his head. "Moving between dimensions requires power we do not have."

"Dimensions?" There were *more* worlds out there?

"Countless," he said. "They are like building blocks, stacked side by side and one atop the other, each one separated by a mystical curtain." He folded the letter, saying, "Now, for the hard part."

What! "That wasn't the hard part?"

He pinned me with a glare. "Your mother denied it, but you are a sorceress, Everly. You might be *the* sorceress. The overlord. The most formidable of our kind, stronger even than me."

"No thanks. I'll pass."

"Only fools ignore such a glorious birthright. Perhaps you require more information. Perhaps you *want* to kill others?"

"No!" I gave my head a violent shake. "Mom told me a little about syphoning."

He blinked, surprised. "There is much I do not know about you, but one fact is true. A sorcerian steals other people's magic by draining them to death, and we never have a preternatural ability of our own. You are different, probably because you are *bonum et malum.* I'm willing to bet you require more power than most. Which means you will syphon and kill more people than most."

Too much to process. I rubbed my aching temples. "You're wrong. I'm not sorcerian."

He arched a brow, all, *Oh really?* "Do people fear and despise you for seemingly no reason? Do people inexplicably weaken around you? Do you sometimes enjoy the harm you cause others?"

I flicked my tongue over an incisor. "You know I do."

"If the glass slipper fits," he muttered. "Sorcerers are natural born predators. We make ourselves stronger by weakening our prey, stealing power—the battery—to wield magic that isn't ours. People sense it."

I rubbed my temples harder. Only minutes ago, I'd been 100 percent certain I wasn't dangerous. Now, that certainty dipped to 90— 85— 70 percent. If Mom *had* died because of me...

Tears scalded my eyes, and shudders racked my body.

"Now that Aubrey is gone, Hartly is your next source." He scrubbed his face, wiping away even a micro-hint of emotion. "Being around you is life threatening for her. So, I will take her away, and you will stay here. You will not leave this house. Understand? If you leave, you could harm someone else. Is that what you want?"

"No," I whispered.

"Someone *else*? A-are you trying to say Everly killed Mom?" Hartly gasped out, making the connection, too.

He said nothing, and his expression never wavered. Answer enough. I curled into myself, fighting a sob.

"I don't believe you." She patted my back. "I know you didn't do it, Ever."

Her support meant everything.

"In three days, the witch will return," he said. "We will travel to Enchantia—together—and I will teach you how to control your magic. The little bit— *witch* will try to leave me behind, but you won't let her. You need me, for you can trust no one else, Ever. Others will only ever want to destroy you."

"Teach me today," I said. *Please.* "Help me build an altilium."

He sucked in a breath. "How do you know— Never mind. There isn't enough time for an altilium, especially now that you've begun syphoning from Hartly. By the way, take more of her power, and you will kill her."

7

Fee-fie-fo-fum,
I smell the blood of a broken one.

You will kill her.
    Kill. Her.
Kill.

As Nicolas's words reverberated inside my head, upending my entire world, he stalked to the couch, snatched Hartly around the waist and lifted her like a sack of potatoes. She held on to Thor, even as she thrashed against our stepfather's rigid hold.

"I'm taking you somewhere safe," he told her. "We will return in time to greet the witch."

"No!" she bellowed. "I refuse to leave Everly."

The lava-filled cracks in my heart expanded. My lifeline was being taken from me, and it was too much to bear. Any second, *I* would die. Surely.

Merciless, Nicolas strode to the door...*past* the door, entering the storm. Better to be battered by hail than to remain close to me?

With her free hand, Hartly reached for me. Pain and panic glazed her eyes. "Don't let him do this. Please, Everly!"

Protests screaming inside my head, I sprinted to the door. Then I stopped. What if I *had* killed my mother? What if I'd hurt my sister?

I needed answers. But to get answers, I needed to use my magic despite Nicolas's warning. Therefore, I needed Hartly out of the danger zone.

I watched, dying inside, as Nicolas stuffed her and Thor into his truck. Icy rain misted over my skin, freezing the blood in my veins.

He climbed behind the wheel. Seconds later, the truck sped away, its tires burning rubber. The heart-lava spread to the rest of me, turning my organs to ash.

Mom had known about sorcerers, and she'd kicked Nicolas to the curb. I knew nothing about sorcerers, yet I'd just allowed the top dog to cart my sister, my reason for breathing, away. Dang, dang, dang. Had I made a terrible mistake?

Eyes blurring, I shut the door. An eerie silence crept through the house, making my heartbeat seem thunderous.

I swallowed a sob. Breaking down still wasn't an option. Too much to do, too little time. So, I gathered my emotional pain— the anguish, regret and sadness, all the mental poison—stuffed it deep inside my heart, then built a wall around it.

A strange, wonderful numbness settled over me, and I laughed without humor. I was now the human equivalent of Schröding-er's cat: both alive *and* dead.

Well, no matter. There was work to do. I jutted my chin, rolled my shoulders, and I stalked into the guest bathroom, with its papered walls, stainless steel sink atop a barrel converted into a vanity, and large mirror with a gilt frame.

My eyes were bloodshot, swollen and glazed with grief. Guess

I hadn't gotten rid of *all* my emotional pain. My pale cheeks had hollowed, like Hartly's, and bite marks littered my lips

"Hartly is gone, so I can't syphon from her," I told my reflection. *If* I even needed to syphon. Which I didn't. Heck, I'd do this Evil Queen style and prove it. Two birds, one stone.

Waving a hand, I said, "Mirror, mirror, on the wall. Who is the fairest—" Ugh. No. Why waste magic with such a stupid request, even when attempting an experiment? "Scratch that. Talk to me. Tell me all."

The ends of my fingers burned white-hot, while flames flickered inside my chest, an inferno quickly spreading. I hissed.

When ripples appeared in the glass, I almost cheered.

See, Nicolas? I had my own supply of power. I was about to have another vision, and I hadn't needed *anyone's* help.

Except, he'd already acknowledged this possibility, hadn't he? I could have charged my battery, storing power I'd stolen. But I'd never wielded a second ability; and, if I *had* syphoned from my mother, I would have access to her illusion magic. Right?

What if I'd never *needed* to syphon, but I'd done it anyway, either unconsciously or instinctively, to keep my personal battery charged?

As grief tried to fight its way free of its cage, I forced my mind to blank with brutal precision. Perfect timing. An image appeared in the glass, the weird version of me. My greedy gaze drank her in. She had changed, the hair framing her face now a stunning jet-black. The rest of the strands remained white, with bloodred rose petals twined throughout. Thicker slashes of kohl outlined her eyelids, more dramatic than ever before. She wore a corset top bedazzled with diamonds, the center V deep enough to showcase her navel tattoo—an apple.

I didn't have a navel tattoo. Or any tattoo, for that matter.

The corners of her crimson lips lifted in a slow smile. "Are you sure you don't want to know the fairest of them all? Spoiler alert. It's me!"

I swallowed a groan. "You only care about outer beauty?"

"Who said anything about outward appearance?"

What had she meant, then?

Doesn't matter. I won't get hung up on unimportant details this time. "Who are you?"

"That should be obvious. I'm you. The *best* of you." She fluffed her hair, bracelets clinking; metal links branched from one of those bracelets, stretching over the back of her hand, along each finger and ending in detachable claws, forming a lethal yet delicate gauntlet. "If you want me to get technical—"

"I do."

"I'm an eternal extension of your magical sixth sense. I am a new beginning, and my roots run deep. I am a tree in a forest of thousands. I see and hear what others do not."

Translation: gibberish, gibberish, gibberish.

Overwhelmed, I focused on one point at a time. "Eternal extension, huh? I guess that makes you—"

"Foreverly," we said in unison.

I scowled. She grinned.

"What is Hartly's role in 'Snow White and the Evil Queen'?" I asked. First things first.

"I don't know. Some things, even I cannot see. The ebb and flow of free will causes certain things to blur."

So...we weren't bound by the dictates of the prophecy, as Mom had believed? Our fate wasn't already decided? Our choices would dictate which character we played?

The double meaning of *character* struck me as important, but my mind was a mess, intelligence currently beyond me. "Am I dangerous to Hartly?"

She tilted her head to the side, her gaze far away. "You want to know if you will kill her. The answer is simple. You will, and you will not."

Ugh. "Don't you dare Schrödinger's cat me. Will I or won't I harm her? Am I a sorceress?" Wait. I should probably rephrase for accuracy. "Am I the sorcerian overlord? Is Hartly safe with Nicolas?"

"You won't," she said, and relief nearly felled me. Then she added, "And you will. You *are* a sorceress...and you are not a sorceress. Do you *want* to be the overlord? Nicolas is...Nicolas."

"I want straight answers."

"Exactly what I've offered, yet I haven't heard a single *thank you*."

Why had I ever enjoyed puzzles? Stomach filling with acid, I grated, "Did I drain my mother to death? Did I make Hartly sick?" Again, grief tried to fight free of its cage. I had to reinforce the brick wall—with another brick wall.

Foreverly tilted her head, her study of me intensifying. "Will you believe me one way or the other?"

"I...won't." I didn't know her, not really, no matter who she claimed to be, or how much she looked like me. "I guess our conversation is futile, then." Not just futile, but a waste of power and magic.

How much fuel did my battery possess anyway? And how had I stored power when I didn't freaking know how to store power? Instinctively? Now my stomach churned, as if trying to turn the acid into butter. Did I wield my power—or Mom's?

Voice low and raspy, Foreverly said, "You're right. Why *tell* you when I can *show* you? Come. Visit Enchantia ahead of schedule. Learn about yourself and do recon on Nicolas."

I... She... *Yes!* I needed to learn more about the man who'd said I could trust no one else. The man my mother had kicked out of our house. "How can I travel without a witch?" Didn't I need Ophelia to shift the curtain or whatever?

"You are rooted in Enchantia. Unlike others, you may return anytime you desire." She stepped closer and reached out... out...her hand slipped past the mirror. Or the doorway. Portal? Considering the things I'd smelled... "Come, my darkling. See. Learn."

I reared back, my whole world suddenly knocked off its axis. But awe soon overtook me, and I returned to my post. Fear of the unknown would not dictate my reaction.

Think this through. My reflection could be tangible and intangible, real and not real. If I accepted her hand, I could travel to Enchantia, as promised, or end up in some sort of hell.

"Come," she repeated. "You know you want to."

What I knew beyond a doubt? Everything and nothing. But… I shouldn't do this. I'd done zero planning or prep. For all I knew, *she* was the Evil Queen, I was Snow White and *this* was how she first tricked me.

"Greatness awaits you," she said, pure temptation. "Research Nicolas. Meet Queen Violet and Princess Truly. Meet Prince Roth." She wiggled her brows. "Tour Airaria. Taste the full force of your magic. Or spend the next three days agonizing about what is truth and what is lie. Lady's choice."

Lives were at stake. Caution mattered. I shook my head, locks of hair slapping my cheeks.

"Very well." With a pout, she withdrew her hand. "If you change your mind, you know where to find me. Or simply walk through a full-length mirror. Your heart will find its way home."

Instead of crafting a well-thought-out plan, I paced in the living room, trying to elude my frustration. A whirlwind of what could have and should have been battered my mind.

Eventually I made my way to the bathroom, where I showered and washed my hair. After a quick blow-dry, I plaited the top half into an elaborate braid-crown, because why not, and left the bottom half loose. Just like Foreverly.

Hoping for a better outcome, I began to pace all over again… and encountered another whirlwind.

Okay, I needed to tackle this a different way. Over the summer, I'd completed multiple risk/reward assessments for an econ class. What better time to put those skills to use?

The issue: What would happen if I journeyed to Enchantia without my stepdad and Hartly?

The rewards: possibly gain answers about Nicolas. Meet Truly, Violet and Farrah. Fine, and Roth! Learn more about magic. *Use* magic. Have an adventure. Take my rightful place as a princess of a mystical kingdom sooner rather than later. A new and better distraction from my pain.

The risks: this whole thing could be a trick. Possible run-ins with mythological monsters. The fish out of water experience, being unprepared and helpless. Getting lost or trapped. Not finding my people. Accidentally syphoning from others, or worse. Unknown hazards.

How hazardous could a world…realm…whatever really be, with a name like Enchantia?

More risks: I was (and was not) a sorceress, part of the sorcerian. Would all Enchantians despise me, the way Mom had despised Nicolas?

I snorted. So what if they did? Everyone hated me on sight here, too. Besides, Mom hadn't known about Nicolas until she'd been told. No one would know who or what I was.

Could I trust Foreverly? *Should* I trust Foreverly? Could I afford to miss an opportunity to learn about myself and my world without Nicolas's interference?

A girl on a mission, I ransacked Mom's closet for anything remotely Enchantian. In back, I discovered a box labeled My Old Life. *Don't cry, don't cry, don't cry.*

Trembling, I lifted the lid. A cloud of dust plumed around me, and I coughed. Inside, I found clothes and a pair of leather wrist cuffs. Each cuff had a tiny metal hook; one pull uncoiled a long length of garrote wire.

Aubrey Morrow…badass?

Ignore the pang. Among the garments, I discovered a finely made corset and petticoat, a royal blue cloak with pockets, and a matching royal blue dress with detachable sleeves, delicate golden threads, crystals and pearls sewn throughout. I'd never handled anything so soft. I bet Mom had stunned in the outfit.

She isn't your mother, but your aunt.

Pang. I added another layer of brick around my heart and gave the structure a mental kick. Holding steady. Excellent.

At the bottom of the box, I found a jagged meteorite, a pair of bejeweled daggers and a signet ring with diamonds and sapphires arranged in a starburst pattern. *So beautiful.*

How had she saved these items from the thief? Or had she collected them from other displaced Enchantians throughout the years?

Enchantians... I needed to speak with other Enchantians.

To learn more about sorcerers in general, and Nicolas in particular, I *had* to journey to Enchantia. If I strengthened, magically speaking, even better. I could search for a way to protect myself and Hartly from any threat.

Decided, I marched around the house, cramming supplies into a backpack. Items I might not be able to find elsewhere. Multiple compacts. A toothbrush and toothpaste. A box of tampons. A bottle of painkillers. A canteen of water, complete with a filter cap. Canned vegan soups with easy pop-tops. Energy bars. A thin fleece blanket. Clothes—white T-shirts, faux-leather pants, socks, a couple of bra and panty sets. Lastly, I sealed a copy of "Little Snow White" inside a plastic bag, along with an ink pen for note taking, matches and another compact, then stuffed the treasures in the cloak's pockets.

Though I planned to return before Ophelia's arrival, I wrote a note for Hartly, just in case I failed. I let her know I'd discovered another way into Enchantia, that I had questions about Nicolas and myself.

I ended with *How do you know I'm missing you? Because we aren't together.*

Do. Not. Cry. I donned Mom's gown, the top too loose, the

bottom too short. Oh, well. Better to blend in with the proper fabrics and styles than stand out in my jeans. For all I knew, mortals…kind of mortals, whatever…were burned at the stake.

A light floral scent drifted from the garments. *Mom's* scent. I stilled, closed my burning eyes and breathed deeply, savoring. For a moment, I thought I felt her arms wrap around me.

As much as I wanted to stay right here and bask, fanciful musings were a waste of time. I hurried on to my next tasks, donning combat boots, then tying two pairs of laces together and threading the loops. If one pair broke, I could use the other.

Next, I stuffed the meteorite in my pocket, hung Mom's ring from a necklace, and secured her cuffs around my wrists. The daggers I anchored to a belt of braided gold thread. With nothing left to do, I settled the backpack in place and hid everything under the cloak.

Showtime.

Adrenaline drove me forward, giving my feet wings. Keeping my head down, I approached the full-length mirror in Mom's walk-in closet and wondered where returning to a fairy tale world fit within "Little Snow White." The time SW ran from the Evil Queen, perhaps?

Not that I believed I was SW or anything. I still thought Hartly had a better shot. And what about Truly?

Were our roles already decided? Or did our choices shape us, as Noel and Ophelia had hinted?

Problem: EQ and SW despised each other. If I *was* fated to be EQ—even though I wasn't—neither Hartly nor Truly qualified as SW. EQ ordered SW's murder, and I would never, ever purposely harm my sisters.

Enough stalling. I could stand here all day, asking countless questions, or I could hunt for the answers.

My knees quaked, but I did it. I flipped up my gaze, a little disappointed to greet a normal reflection. Though grief stricken and shell shocked, I possessed a glow of excitement.

"Foreverly," I rasped with a wave of my hand. "I'm ready to go to Enchantia."

8

A welcome home, the stuff of dreams.
Of course, nothing is ever as it seems.

Warmth pooled in my fingertips, then sped through the rest of me, effervescent and wondrous. Familiar. The mirror seemed to melt before my eyes, becoming a *Stargate*-like portal.

Tremors consumed me, my mind spinning. Standing there, wearing my fancy dress, my veins alive with magic, destiny waiting on the other side of the glass, I was following Mom's example, leaving everything I'd ever known in order to keep my loved one safe.

Pride blended with sadness, washing through me. An odd combination, but these were odd circumstances. The end of an era, and the beginning of a new life.

"Down the rabbit hole we go," I muttered. My knees quaked more forcefully as I stepped forward, entering the cascade of melted glass. A cocoon of heat enfolded me, just before my

world blackened. My ears twitched, a cacophony of noise erupting. Glugging liquid. Various volumes of static. Bumblebee-like
buzzing.

Something cold and heavy seemed to snap around my ankles,
yanking me down, down into a deeper, darker abyss. *Too dark!
Can't see.* I flailed, panicked, no end in sight.

Suddenly, a cornucopia of white lights exploded in every direction, chasing away the darkness. *Too bright!*

Can't take much more.

In an instant, the sensation of falling ceased. Not that it mattered. I was left feeling like I flew, ran and stood all at once.
The glugging dwindled, and the cocoon of heat evaporated. The
lights dimmed. My head swam. I was dazed and possibly drunk,
even though I hadn't consumed a drop of alcohol.

A new kaleidoscope of sounds erupted—shuffling footsteps,
murmuring voices, whistling winds and flapping material. The
temperature dropped, chilling me to the bone. Wind kicked up,
every blast hitting me like a thousand needles pricks.

The darkness remained. I blinked, rubbed my eyes, but still
couldn't see. Deep breath in, out. I caught the scent of jasmine.
In, out. Calm settled over me, a murky film seeming to peel
away from my eyes.

I gaped as a whole new world took shape. Above me, two
full moons shone bright and golden. The eyes of the sky, windows to its soul. Shimmering emerald and amethyst mist coiled
around a cluster of stars.

I'd done it? I'd reached Enchantia?

Everly Morrow for the win!

A comet blazed past, a trail of fire in its wake. Laughing, I
reached up. Sparkles rained down, shockingly cool.

Before me stretched an endless sea of white sand. People wearing headscarves, loose-fitting tunics and long, sleeveless robes
slugged across the dunes, sifting through the grains to find...
what were those things? Blue pearls?

I bent down to sink my fingers into the sand. Oh, how interesting. The grains were dry, but soft as silk. I plucked the first stone I came across. Not a blue pearl, after all, but an iridescent meteorite an inch or so bigger than Mom's.

My heart must have steered me to Airaria: Why not directly in front of Queen Violet?

As I straightened, I added the meteorite to the goodies in my pockets. The fragments must be valuable; people scrambled about to gather them. People who'd stopped what they were doing to stare at me.

Not knowing what else to do, I waved. "Hello."

Sensing movement behind me, I spun—

And came face-to-face with my reflection. Silver eyed and rosy cheeked, brimming with more excitement, more grief.

The mirror fell to the side, revealing the girl who'd held it, and I huffed with surprise.

"You're Noel," I said, giddy. "An oracle."

"The one and only." She smiled, her incredible purple eyes a wonderland of secrets and wisdom. "You're going to be so happy, Everly. Joyous beyond your wildest imaginings. *If* you get stronger. Unfortunately, the only way to turn a lump of coal into a diamond is to apply heat and pressure. The only way to help a tree bear more fruit is to prune unnecessary branches. To soar, a butterfly must fight free of the chrysalis. The only way—"

"I get it," I interjected. "You're telling me what happens next is going to hurt." The fact that she knew my name, the day I would arrive and the manner upon I would land, well, her power must be incredible.

"So smart!" She patted the top of my head. "I only wish you'd dressed for the job you're going to want, not the job you've already got. Presentation matters!"

Uh...how was I supposed to respond to that? "What job am I going to want?"

"Queen of Hearts, yo? Wife, mother, obsession? Weapon?

Shield? Alluring? Choices abound." She winked at me. "Violet is in a snit, and the storm will only worsen. Go. Find shelter, then meet your mother. I'll quill you in for an appointment tomorrow, when we patch up your wounds. Now, I must go. I promised Ophelia I'd meet her for transport home."

"Wounds? What wounds?"

She waved my question away. "Oh! I almost forgot. I need to quill you in for five minutes from now, too. When I come a-knocking, answer. It's only polite." With a little wave, she rushed away, leaving me more confused than ever.

"Please stay," I called. "I have more questions. Do you know anything about Nicolas Soren? What about the sorcerian?" I chased after her, only to stop. She'd vanished into the night.

As predicted, the storm worsened, the winds growing violent, soon hiding her footprints. I winced when grains pelted my cheeks.

Find shelter, Noel had said. *Ten-four.*

I drew the hood of Mom's cloak up. To the left, a wall of storm clouds loomed, land and sky practically woven together. To the right, a single tent withstood the gale force, creating an oasis as bright and golden as the moonbeams.

The wind kicked up another notch, the bulk of scavengers darting off, avoiding the tent. Why?

Perhaps the queen waited inside? Only one way to find out.

I trudged forward, flinging sand with every step and fighting nerves. Soon I would interact with other Enchantians.

Mom should be here. She should—

I scrubbed the thought from my mind before it could elicit an emotional response and refocused. What had Noel said? *You're going to be so happy.*

Oracles were descended from fairies, and fairies couldn't lie. She'd foreseen my happiness, but only if I got stronger.

Well, sign me up for an extra helping of strength!

I reached my destination, surprised to find the entrance of

the tent unguarded. As quietly as possible, I palmed my daggers, just in case, and slipped inside. My lungs rejoiced, the cloth blocking the winds.

I wiped the grit from my eyes, and the view crystalized. A scream lodged in my throat. Three horned, tusked brutes stood around a table soaked with crimson paint. They were eating—

I gagged. A human. They were eating a human. He lay on his back, his chest cracked open, his organs exposed. Sushi redefined. The crimson wasn't paint, but blood.

A *splish-splash* sound assaulted my ears as the diners reached *inside* the man's body to select an entrée.

What *were* these things?

A whimper joined the deluge of noise, but it wasn't mine. I pressed a hand against my belly. The man was still alive.

Head spinning. I couldn't leave him to suffer like this. I had to— Never mind. One of the brutes ripped out his heart, laughing with glee before devouring the still-beating organ.

Was this normal in Enchantia? Or just in Airaria? Did Queen Violet condone it?

Was I next?

Go, go, go! I spun but didn't manage to take a single step. A larger male with tusks and horns stepped in my path, and I had to crane my head up to meet eyes as lovely as the star-filled sky outside.

Those eyes mesmerized me. Until I remembered the feast behind me, and panic surged anew. He was shirtless, displaying a barrel of a chest, a wealth of scars, tattoos and piercings. He had a prominent brow, beaked nose and pointy chin, every feature exaggerated to an extreme, making his face both nightmarishly grotesque and insanely beautiful.

Beak flipped back the hood of my cloak, his reflexes supernaturally fast. The panic sharpened, robbing me of wits. One strike from this brute and I'd be a goner.

He looked me over and nodded as if he'd just made a monumental decision. "I've always preferred the ugly ones, and you are uglier than most. You will spend the night here."

Ugly? Me? Wait. What! Spend the night? I'd rather die.

You just might.

The other creatures laughed at his words. I made the mistake of glancing over my shoulder. Blood stained their teeth, and tissue clung to their gums.

The second the wires in my brain fired up again, I moved away from Beak. Plagued by tremors, I told him, "No, thanks. Mistake. Leaving."

He crossed his arms, refusing to budge. All right. I brought out my secret weapon—my maniacal smile.

He did a double-take, then reached out to grab a fistful of my hair. Strands pulled, stinging my scalp, and I cried out.

"I wasn't asking for permission, female."

Fury torched my panic. My thoughts aligned. I had trained in self-defense for a reason.

Violence is not the answer.

Sometimes it is, Mom.

Like a spring, I jumped up, using his thigh as a step stool. With one hand, I grabbed hold of a tusk. With the other, I punched his nose. Jab, jab. Cartilage snapped and blood spurted.

He howled as he stumbled back. I released him and dropped to my feet, then shot outside, entering the storm. Lesson learned. I never should have come to Enchantia on my own. I would find Noel's mirror and return home. When Ophelia returned, I might even tell her to hit the bricks. Introduce Hartly to cannibalistic brutes? No!

The only point in my favor? The gusty, dusty winds hid me from my pursuers. *If* they'd given chase. Had they? Ugh! I couldn't see. My eyes felt like they were being scrubbed with a scouring pad. Every breath sandpapered my throat.

As I ran up a sand dune, the apple-shaped birthmark on my wrist heated, jolting me. *That's new.*

—Knock, knock. Who's there? It's me! Your friendly, neighborhood oracle. Testing, testing, one, two, three.

The distinct female voice filled my head, and I cringed. Noel. No, no. Only a delusion.

—I am Noel the Great and Mighty, not a delusion.—

Struggling to make sense of such an ability, I replied, *Can you speak to everyone like this?*

—Not usually, but we are apples plucked from the same tree and our roots run deep. Now, turn here. Or let the trolls catch up with you. Oh! I should probably tell you they're fanged and venomized. One bite, and your brain will rot, you'll turn into a rage-goblin and die in agony.—

Apples. Deep roots. Trolls. Uncertain but out of options, I followed her directions, heading for the wall of clouds. My heart raced faster than my feet. Almost there…so close… I labored against the gale force, certain I would blow away at any moment.

Why help me? I asked. I'd offered no payment.

—One day, you'll return the favor. Destiny awaits.—

Destiny…a worry for later. Finally, blessedly, I slipped past the cool mist. Unfortunately, the winds didn't die down, and the sands didn't calm. I came upon another tent.

Noel twittered with excitement. *—Go ahead. Enter and be amazed.—*

Truth or lie? Good or bad? *Let's find out.* Almost completely blinded, I patted the cloth until I found the opening. I stumbled inside, crashing to my knees. No winds, clean air. Relief!

Once again, I rubbed the grit from my eyes and surveyed my new surroundings. My jaw almost unhinged, *Enter and be amazed?* Try flabbergasted, delighted and thrilled. Familiar faces greeted me, and I knew. *This.* This was the reason my heart had led me here.

Roth stood in the center of the spacious enclosure. Gashes and bruises marred his face. He pressed a booted foot into a fallen troll's windpipe and a blood-spattered sword between its legs.

Someone had cut off the troll's hands. Both appendages rested beside his body, the fingers flared and curled, revealing a set of claws.

At the far right, Truly huddled atop a pallet of furs. Tears streaked her face. One of her eyes was swollen and discolored, and her bottom lip was split. Blood caked her chin.

Fury razed my delight, a fire-breathing monster beneath the surface of my skin. Someone had hurt my twin. Someone would pay.

A boy with shimmering dark brown skin, long black hair and lavender eyes cooed words of comfort while gently petting her hair. Was he the one her mother expected her to marry?

The winged boy—Saxon—stood next to the couple, glaring bloody murder at the troll. On the couple's other side was a boy I'd never met. He reminded me of a living sunbeam, golden from head to toe. Scales decorated his arms, a small fin protruding from each elbow.

At any other time, those details would have fascinated me. Now? I was too busy contemplating the troll's murder. I didn't know Truly, and she didn't know me, but I already loved her and wanted her protected always. Maybe it was the twin thing. Maybe it was the deep roots and apple thing Noel had mentioned. Whatever that meant.

Roth glanced up, and I must have been a frightful sight— *uglier than most*—because he did a double take. "You."

Me? He recognized me?

The distraction cost us both.

The troll—I'd call him Stumpy—bucked, kicking the prince's ankles together. As Roth toppled, the troll leaped on top of him.

Time slowed to a crawl. Stumpy used his bloody arms as hammers and whaled on Roth. Rather than shield his face, Roth swung his sword. The next time Stumpy struck, flesh met metal. Metal won, shearing off another layer of the fiend's arm.

A hiss of pain, a growl of rage. Roth worked his legs between their bodies and shoved. The troll fell back but recovered quickly and hurled his body at the prince, teeth bared and ready to tear into his trachea.

Heart pounding, I lurched forward. Roth's guards lurched forward, too. No way any of us would reach him in time.

He managed to block, but the battle raged on.

One of Nicolas's first lessons echoed inside my head. *Draw a weapon only if you're ready to use it.*

Was I ready to use my daggers?

Beyond. As fast as my reflexes would allow, I tossed one. My tremors screwed with my aim, but I still hit my mark, the blade embedding in Stumpy's temple. He jolted, slumped over and crashed to the ground.

Realization. I had killed the troll.

I had *killed*, period. But...

I felt no guilt. Roth would live to see another day. I did feel remorse and wanted to vomit. How many people would mourn Stumpy's loss? Had I taken him from a sibling? Loving parents?

Roth climbed to his feet, the scowl he gave me all, *Why are you still here?* It reminded me of the one he'd given the girlfriend—ex? One-night stand?—who'd lain naked in his bed.

I looked back over my shoulder, wondering if someone else had maybe, hopefully entered the tent. Nope. Just me.

Cloaked in darkness and danger, Roth advanced, grating, "Tell me who you are and what you're doing in my tent. Refuse, and you won't like what happens next."

9

You can rest awhile, or you can fret.
Either way, your future is set.

I held my ground when Roth stopped a whisper away, consuming my personal space. This wasn't the welcome of my dreams, but it wasn't straight out of a nightmare, either, so I considered it a win.

And even though I was out of my element and in the line of fire, I enjoyed a major fangirl moment. Prince Roth, in the flesh! I almost said, *You rocked my favorite vision. Autograph my chest?*

The scent of cinnamon, nutmeg and cloves filled my nose and fogged my head. Like Christmas, only X-rated, starring a young, muscular and hotter–than-the-sun Santa.

Don't hate me on sight. Or leer. Or lie. And please, please do not fear me.

At six–four or five, Roth towered over me. He had broad shoulders and a gloriously powerful build. This close, I could see the tiniest flecks of amber in his pale green eyes. Eyes framed by a fan of long, spiky lashes. His cheekbones were sharper than I'd realized, his unshaven jaw harder.

"You have five seconds," he snapped.

All that anger... Why was he hotter than ever? Why, why?

"Hold that thought," I said, catching Truly's stare. "The troll is the one who hurt you, right, not these guys?" If they had, I'd have to take them out. Could I? What magic did these people wield?

A sense of connection burgeoned inside me as Truly met my gaze. Did she feel it, too? *Please, feel it!*

"Yes, the troll is responsible," she said. "He attacked while my...friends were erecting this tent. But he didn't bite me, I swear!"

Relieved, I returned my focus to Roth, who had yet to look away. Firelight loved his dark skin, giving him an almost otherworldly aura.

"What would you have done if we *had* hurt her?" he asked, and I thought I detected incredulity.

I arched a brow, all *take a guess*, and his anger evaporated. More shocking, he exhibited no trace of fear. Instead, he appeared...admiring?

Ribbons of pleasure danced inside me. "You asked who I am." Had Queen Violet told Truly about her long-lost twin? Watching her with laser focus, I said, "My name is Everly."

Not a single flicker of recognition. Dang it! What was I supposed to say now? *Hey, girl. Guess what? Your mother never mentioned me, but surprise! We are twins separated at birth. Honest!*

No, I would wait, I decided, and speak with Violet first. Then we would tell Truly together.

Would Violet like me? She had to like me. Our people had to like me.

Dude. I had *people*. Mom would—

As new pangs rent my chest, I stacked more bricks around my heart and blanked my mind.

If Violet doubted my identity, I'd...what? *Another worry for later.*

"Something you should know, Everly." Roth's deep baritone set off a series of nervous flutters deep in my gut. "If you act against me and mine, you will regret it."

He was so protective. So fierce! Offering a jaunty salute, I replied, "Right back at you, cuteness."

Baffled expression. Slight twitching at the corners of his lips.

As Saxon and Scales carted Stumpy out of the tent, I shouted, "My dagger!" I dashed over to pluck the blade from the troll's temple, then returned to Roth.

The flutters started up again. "I'm here because I had a gang of trolls on my tail and a lungful of sand. When I saw your tent, I darted inside." I kept Noel's aid to myself. I couldn't mention her without throwing in details about the *bonum et malum*, roots, new beginnings and seer magic. Until my chat with Queen Violet, I would hold all my secrets close. "Storm hack. If you want to keep people out, post guards at the door."

"And let those guards be pelted by sand? No." Staring at my lower half, he said, "You have a tail?"

What? "No!" I pinched the bridge of my nose. "A tail. Someone who's following you."

"What did the gang of trolls want?" He explored every inch of me with his gaze slowly, his irises heating. "You aren't their usual fare."

Was I *his* usual fare, even though I looked nothing like the stunner I'd seen in his bed? Because dang. That heat! After three months together, Peter had never come close to liquifying my brain and my bones. Roth continued to do it.

Not that it mattered. I wasn't here to score a date. And I wasn't his usual fare.

"I think they wanted me for the same reason Stumpy wanted

her?" I pointed to Truly, then shrugged. "Or maybe I'm just everyone's fare, usual or not?"

The corners of his lips twitched a second time. "Do you know who I am?"

"I do." I couldn't bring myself to lie. Besides, I'd bet royals were known by one and all. "You are Prince Roth...something or other. The mansel in distress I rescued from a troll."

A rusty sound escaped him. A chuckle, maybe. "You rescued me from nothing. I had the situation under control. But you are right. I am Prince Roth. Something or other."

He frowned. Disappointed? Because I hadn't known his last name, or because I *had* known his first name, like I was some kind of royal groupie who'd sought him out for a sandstorm quickie? News flash. I had royal blood, too.

"Nice to meet you. Maybe you could back off now and offer me a refreshing beverage? And yes, you were definitely, one hundred percent in distress. Unless you *wanted* the troll to use your neck as a snack pack?"

His guards snickered, reminding me of their presence. Oops. I'd lost track of the world. In this strange land, I needed to have better spatial awareness.

Roth crossed his arms over his chest, his tunic taut over his biceps. "Doubting the word of a royal is a crime."

"Crime," the other three boys echoed. Trying not to laugh?

"To receive forgiveness, you must pay the doubter's tax," Roth told me.

Doubter's tax? He was joking, right? Considering I knew zero-point nil about this world, I couldn't be sure. Wringing my hands together, I asked, "What am I expected to pay, exactly?"

"Yes, Roth," the guy with dark glittering skin said. "What must she pay?"

He threw his buddy a *shut it fast* glance. "This one time only, I will forget what's owed to me, *if* you convince me you mean us no harm."

In economic terms, this was an incentive for Roth, and an opportunity cost for me, the benefit I would forfeit in order to gain something else. Basically, I could purchase shelter by sharing my personal information.

Would Roth kick me out if I remained mute? Beyond the tent, the wind howled, louder and louder.

"How about I make dinner, and you ask me questions?" I could more easily evade his questions if he was distracted by food, and maybe even ask questions of my own.

"You *doubt* I can prepare my own meal?" He tsked.

Great! Had the doubter's tax just doubled?

As I carefully considered my response, I slid my tongue over my lips. Roth stiffened and scowled. Silent now, he strode past the firepit and the pallet of furs to sit at a small metal table, where he ran a rag along the length of his sword, removing Stumpy's blood. Up and down. *Up, down.*

Uh, what just happened? "I'm sure you're a perfectly adequate chef," I said. "But I have precooked cans of soup. Just open, heat and serve for a bona fide two-star dining experience."

The dark one laughed. "You carry precooked soup and eat stars?"

"You mean you *don't?*" I winced as if embarrassed for him, then untied my cloak and let my backpack drop to the ground, ten thousand pounds of metal clinking together. My shoulders all but wept with relief. "I didn't mean *literal* stars. I— Never mind." We had a language barrier. Noted.

"We've already eaten. But thank you," Saxon said, unerringly polite.

Careful. You shouldn't know his name.

"We wouldn't eat your soup anyway." Roth never glanced my way. *Up, down. Up, down.* He appeared utterly absorbed in his task, yet his tense body language suggested he remained aware of everyone and everything. "We don't know you, don't trust you. Perhaps you plan to poison us."

Disappointment skewered me. He *was* fearful, just like everyone else. "True," I said and sighed, "Ask your questions, then, and I'll try to prove myself. But maybe oversee a round of introductions first, like a good host?"

Silence reigned, the others looking to Roth for a response.

He set the rag on the table, placed the sword beside it, and finally met my gaze. Those shamrock eyes were no longer frosted—they smoldered with determination, making me shiver. "I am Prince Roth *Charmaine* from the Empire of Sevón."

Aw, had I hurt the big bad prince's ego? Wait, wait, wait. "Your last name is *Charmaine*?" As in *charming*. As in *Prince Charming*. No way. Just no way. He could *not* be Snow White's love interest. But…maybe? He had the title, the face and the body. Would he soon have a fated crush on a dead chick?

I don't care. I don't. I had no romantic interest in him. He was cute. But so what? I'd seen cuter. Probably. Somewhere.

Maybe he crushed on Snow White before she died. I mean, the fairy tale didn't specify when he first beheld the girl, only that he saw her lying inside a glass coffin and he had to get him a little some-some of *that*.

What if he had a huge crush on Truly? That might explain his continued terseness toward her.

Was I fated to become her greatest enemy?

Never! As I'd been told, death didn't always equate to death in prophecies. Maybe the Evil Queen didn't try to kill SW. Maybe the Evil Queen helped her achieve a new beginning.

Now that I was the Evil Queen, I would fight the possibility *forever*.

"Everyone else got names?" I asked.

Roth waved to the stunner with dark, glittery skin. "Meet Vikander Romanova from the House of…Love."

Why the pause? And why did the others snicker? Whatever. I was happy to meet the infamous Vikander, the one Farrah had wanted to avoid.

Yeah, he *must* be Truly's fiancé.

"There are three things you should know about me straight-away," Vikander said, all raw sensuality and potent allure. "I'm good with my hands, I'm good with my mouth, but I'm not very good at resisting temptation."

Truly rolled her eyes. "Actually, there's a fourth. He has zero boundaries."

"Ah. The resident flirt. Good to know. But what creature of myth are you, Viks?" I asked, then cringed. Inquiring about someone's species was probably a major no-no, and definitely rude.

Okay, I'd have to take a gamble and admit *something* personal about myself. Risk versus reward. Maybe these guys loved mortals. Maybe they hated mortals. Either way, they couldn't help but notice my oddities. Better to explain my origins now, in a welcome environment, than later, while accusations were hurled.

I braced and said, "Please forgive my ignorance. I come from...the mortal world."

Instant curiosity, everyone leaning in closer to study the new animal at the zoo. But no fear, no malice. Thank goodness!

They hurled questions at me.

Roth: "How did you get here? *Why* did you come here?"

Vikander: "How did you afford a witch's services? Actually, how did you contact a witch in the first place?"

Truly: "Tell me everything! I've always wanted to visit the mortal world all my life. It calls to me."

Or maybe *I* had been the one calling to her? Twins were two halves of a whole, after all. "I'll answer everyone's questions. Later." Much later. "Have you met any other mortals?"

"Long ago, there were wars between our worlds. Since then, most royals pay a witch to collect a mortal tutor for their chil-dren. A know-your-enemy strategy. Not that I consider you an enemy," she assured me. Her bicolored eyes brightened. "Do giant metal birds really carry people inside their bellies?"

Metal—? Ah. Okay. "They do. They're known as airplanes." I waved at Vikander. "Your turn. You never finished telling me what you are."

He gave a half smile and said, "I am fae. The most magnificent in all the land, obviously. Have you looked at me? Go ahead, you know you want to…"

"He's good at everything, except modesty," Roth said. Harsh words layered with affection. "And that's because he's *exceptional* at modesty."

Vikander grinned a wicked grin. "By the way, mortal. If you hoped to seduce the prince, you should have worn a better dress. Or no dress."

"Thanks for the tip," I replied, my tone as dry as the sand outside. How many girls had tried to win the prince by showing up unannounced and naked? "Though I prefer my usual method of just breathing." What? Confidence mattered.

Another rusty noise escaped Roth as he rubbed a hand over his mouth. Yeah, definitely a laugh.

The others gaped at him, making me think he rarely displayed mirth. I fought the urge to preen.

"I am Saxon. An avian, or bird shifter." He bowed his gorgeous head, exuding an air of determination, suspicion and kindness. An odd combination. "I am from the Skylair Clan, and one of Roth's generals."

Shifter as in *shape*-shifter? So cool! "Your wings are gorgeous. Will I creep you out if I ask to touch your feathers?"

The room got real quiet, real fast. Truly's cheeks reddened. Vikander and the guy with scales sniggered. Saxon scrubbed the back of his neck as if he didn't quite know what to say. Roth frowned.

"What?" I demanded. What blunder had I made?

"Asking to touch an avian's wings is the equivalent asking to stroke a male's…you know." Truly's scandalized tone caused *my* cheeks to redden.

"Seriously?" I groaned. "Never mind. Forget I asked."

Just like that, everyone exploded into fits of laughter.

"I'm Princess Truly Morrow, by the way." She smiled and winced, the wound in her lip paining her.

Great! Now I wanted to kill the troll all over again. Which wasn't as evil queenish as it sounded, because I would derive no joy from the action. Well, not *tons* of joy, just some. Or lots. But *lots* wasn't *tons*.

Roth motioned to the golden boy with scales and elbow fins. "This is Reese Acquta of Seaspray, a land within the Azul Dynasty."

Reese stepped forward and bowed, all calm dignity and quiet strength.

"He is one of the mer-folk," Roth continued. "A siren. Because his voice is enchanted, Reese has taken a vow of silence."

I thought…yes! I could *feeel* magic pouring off him. It seemed to brush against my skin, tingling. Eager to learn and brimming with curiosity, I asked, "Do you have a tail whenever you're in water?" Wait. Crap. Vow of silence. I looked to Roth. "How does he breathe out of water…and *in* the water?"

Reese turned his head one way, then the other, baring his neck to reveal three lines of raised skin on each side.

I swallowed a squeal of wonder. Gills?

"Most of the mer-folk are shape-shifters, but a rare few are not," Roth explained. "Reese is not. And we love and accept him just as he is."

Had other shape-shifters *not* loved and accepted him? I pressed my lips together, certain I'd reached the group's limit on too-personal questions.

"Well, it's nice to meet you guys." I waved, which wasn't lame *at all*.

Saxon snapped his majestic wings close to his sides, total warrior-angel chic, and said, "Time will tell."

I hiked my thumb in his direction while peering at Roth, "Is he always so warm and inviting to strangers?"

"No, but you caught him on a good day."

I snorted, and Roth's green, green eyes shimmered with a new round of amusement. Gossamer shivers slipped through me, rolling along each of my limbs.

"Your turn, Everly..." He waited, clearly hoping I would reveal my last name.

"Just Everly," I said.

He slitted his eyelids. "Tell us *something* about you, Just Everly."

His hard tone told me more than his words. *Do it or leave.* Fine! Incentive to let me stay, coming in three, two, one. "I need to speak with Queen Violet. She knew my...mother. The two were friends before Mom traveled to the mortal world. But my mom...she...she died." *More bricks, more bricks!* "I'm here to relay the news to...the queen."

Reactions varied, running the gamut. Everything from curiosity to sympathy.

"I'm so sorry about your mother," Truly said, and she seemed genuinely upset on my behalf.

"As am I," Roth intoned.

Light bulb moment! "Anyone willing to escort me to the palace after the storm passes? In return, I'll tell you stories about the mortal world." Good ones, too. I'd make Scheherazade proud, à la Arabian Nights. *Without* revealing anything else about myself.

Truly opened her mouth to agree, I was sure, but Roth silenced her with an imperious hand gesture.

He studied me all over again, his expression eventually softening, eliciting an odd sensation low in my belly. "Yes, sweetling. We will take you to the palace. That's where we were headed before the storm hit. But once there, you will be on your own. We cannot stay long."

That's right. He had a meeting with someone from Fleur, and then he had to find the Apple of Life and Death to save his dad.

Unless he'd met with the Fleurian—Fleuridian?—representative before this? To ask, I'd have to admit I'd mirror-spied. No, thanks. No telling how these people would react. But oh, how I hated the thought of parting with Truly so soon after meeting her.

And had the prince just called me *sweetling*?

He must have. Why else would I be shivering?

"Thank you," I said, then looked to Truly. "After I meet with Queen Violet, maybe I can catch up with you guys and tag along on your journey? I'll entertain you with even better stories." About me! By then, she'd know we were sisters.

A round of blinking ensued. Couldn't make sense of me, huh? Understandable. We'd just met, and I was coming on strong. But come on! Cut me some slack. I wanted to be her best friend, like, yesterday, and tell her all about her wonderful aunt Aubrey and incredible cousin Hartly. I wanted to hear tales about her childhood.

"I warn you, Everly," she said, ignoring my question. "My mother has changed. She is not the woman your mother probably described to you. Darkness has taken root in her heart. She hurts everyone she encounters. I alone am the exception."

Taken root. A reference to the apples Violet once consumed?

"I'm not concerned." I would be her second exception. And there was no reason to repeat my request to join these people later. I'd just show up, all *Was just in the neighborhood.*

"Very brave," she said with a small smile.

"Or very foolish," Roth grated.

After flipping him off with my expression, one I'd perfected over the years, I made my way to Truly's pallet. When no objections arose, I eased beside her. Then, to keep my end of the bargain, I launched into a description of TVs and cars.

The moment she relaxed, I attempted a subtle interrogation about Queen Violet—what darkness?—as well as our father, the king, and Truly's reasons for sticking with an entourage from

Sevón. She evaded most of the queries with a masterful skill I envied, though she *did* admit someone had murdered King Stephan a week ago, and she didn't mourn his loss. Apparently, he'd been universally despised.

I know the feeling.

The guys never relaxed. They watched me, ready to act if I lashed out.

"Here." Roth thrust a goblet of wine in my direction.

I meant to take a sip, just one, just to be polite, but I ended up draining every drop, the sweetness teasing my tongue.

Soon *I* relaxed, my lids going heavy. Darkness encroached upon my mind, dizziness hot on its heels, fatigue barreling through me like a freight train in hyperdrive.

A yawn nearly cracked my jaw. Lack of sleep had finally caught up with me, and I had to pay the toll.

"How far is the palace from here?" Were my words slurred?

"We're close," Truly replied. "Just a short ride away. We would have traveled on, despite the storm, and spent the night there, but centaurs moved in after the king's death, and I never feel safe when they are near."

Another yawn, my head drooping forward. *Stay awake. Fight!* Now wasn't the time to rest. I coveted more time with Truly and didn't trust the others to stay put. I had a feeling they'd ditch me the moment I fell asleep.

Plus, I needed to figure out where this group fit in the fairy tale. And they must fit, since they played a part in Truly's life. And... and...I had questions about Nicolas. Right! The reason I'd come here early. I should ask about the sorcerian, and tell these people all my secrets—

Would Ophelia return, as promised?

What the what? *Zip your lips. Say nothing.* I planned to save my questions for Violet, remember? She wouldn't draw the wrong conclusions. She would love me.

"You will sleep now." Roth's voice penetrated the dizziness. I think he traced his knuckles along my jaw.

I smiled. He wasn't afraid of me after all.

Another trace of his knuckles, the silken touch sending my thoughts deeper into the darkness.

I obeyed, helpless to do otherwise, and drifted off...

I dreamed of my mother's demise...of a faceless Snow White sprawled dead at my feet...of apples rotting around me, smothering me...of Roth holding me, offering comfort...of Hartly and Truly shouting curses at me, blaming me for their pain and suffering, hating me, fearing me.

An anguished cry shocked me awake. Had a wounded animal invaded my bedroom?

No, not my bedroom. Roth and Truly's tent. Before I even opened my eyes, an internal alarm clanged, letting me know something was very, very wrong. What, what?

The wall around my heart! Some of the bricks had crumbled, allowing streams of grief to flood me. I hurried to rebuild before I started sobbing and never stopped. There. Better. Little by little, tension seeped from my body.

I panted as I took stock. I lay on the pallet, covered by my cloak. Around me, air seemed to fizz like champagne, dust motes sparkling like glitter. I breathed deeply, drinking in the world's sweetest perfume: jasmine, honeysuckle and cinnamon.

Cinnamon. Roth's scent! He must be nearby.

I breathed faster, sucking in more of that scent, and scanned the rest of the sunlit tent. A few feet away, the prince was crouching beside my backpack, rummaging through my things.

"Hey!" The word emerged as a ragged sigh. I eased up and grimaced, a sharp pain lancing my temples. Ugh. I guess my low tolerance for alcohol had gotten the best of me. "What are you doing?"

He glanced over his shoulder, utterly unabashed, and oh, wow,

I didn't think I'd ever seen a more breathtaking sight. Morning light bathed him, paying homage, softening the roughness of his features while also revealing a detail I'd previously missed. A faint scar that slashed from his temple to the edge of his jaw. A mark of strength. He'd survived whatever had harmed him.

Handsome before, devastating now.

I searched his face for fear, hate, or a leer…no, no and no. The worst of my irritation dulled.

"I'm making sure you have nothing nefarious in here," he said, "that you do not hope to turn us into unwitting collaborators of an unscrupulous plan."

Oh, his voice! It was even better than I remembered, the rich timbre the audible equivalent of warm milk and honey sprinkled with crack. My lids turned heavy, hooding my eyes, and my chest tightened.

"What is this?" he asked, holding up the box of tampons.

Heat infused my cheeks. I—

Screamed. A spider-scorpion thing skittered across the sand mere inches from the pallet. With arachnids, my first instinct had always been *burn everything*!

Roth unsheathed a sword and rushed to my side, ready to take on an army. His posture said, *I will kill*. His expression said, *I will like it*. I had no doubt he would emerge the victor in any fight, no matter the odds stacked against him.

"What's wrong?" he demanded. "What happened?"

"A spider…thing." A full body shudder rocked me. "The monstrous creature disappeared under the tent."

At first, he gave no reaction. Then he laughed with less rust than before. Heat spread over the rest of my face, and not from embarrassment. Roth didn't wear amusement comfortably, but he wore it beautifully.

"This isn't funny, Chuckles. My heart has yet to calm."

"A tigress when facing a troll. A kitten when facing a spider thing," he said. "Who knew the little sweetling could be so adorable?"

How many other girls had he referred to as *sweetling*?

"You should be nice to me. This tigress doesn't scratch, she bites." And she might have rabies. I rescanned the tent to make sure there were no more arachnids, realized we were alone, and tensed. "Where are the others?" Translation: tell me where Truly is before I flip out!

"They are shopping for supplies while I act as your escort. We met with the queen earlier this morning."

But...but... I hadn't gotten to say goodbye or confirm my plan to meet up later. "Shouldn't Truly stay here with her mother?" And her twin!

A muscle jumped under his eye, a reaction I'd seen during his conversation with Noel. "She is betrothed to a warrior from Sevón, so in Sevón she lives."

Before, I'd wondered if he had a crush on her. Now, I wondered if he disliked her. He projected animosity and resentment, not attraction.

I opened up to tell him Truly didn't want the warrior— Vikander? She wanted Farrah. Anything to help her. *Zip it, Morrow.* My twin's secrets were not mine to share.

"Back to your unlawful search of my bag," I said. "I understand your reasoning, and if you'd asked, I would have granted permission. Now, I'm just annoyed." Another pain lanced through my head, ruining my stern expression, no doubt.

Roth crouched in front of me, my breath hitching as he traced his knuckles along my jaw. His body radiated heat like a furnace. Mmm. Heat. He made me feel feverish.

"Your pain will fade, Everly." His voice was deeper, huskier. Richer.

Miracle of miracles, my pain *did* fade. He must have the magic touch.

Magic...

I gulped. Was his touch *literally* magic? I wanted to ask but bit my tongue. No more rude, probing questions, unless I wanted to answer rude, probing questions in return.

The air charged with awareness as we stared at each other. I fought the urge to lean against him, wanting to feel his strong arms wrap around me. Would I experience the same comfort I'd found in my dream?

I'd never relied on Peter for comfort. *Peter who?* Why rely on someone who wouldn't stick around?

Roth looked away first, breaking the spell, and stood. All business, he said, "In Airaria, women and children should never travel without a guard. Scavengers kill strangers for their finds, trolls and centaurs roam free, and slavers prowl for fresh meat."

Nothing like the mystical homeland Mom had described. How had the kingdom fallen into such terrible disrepair? "Thank you, Roth. Prince Roth. Your Majesty. Whatever! I appreciate your assistance."

Terse nod. "In five minutes, I will return." He said no more, just strode from the tent.

With a grimace, I stood up. My balance teetered, my legs unsteady. On the table was a metal bowl and a metal cup, both filled with water. On the other side of the tent I found a metal screen hiding a metal bucket. The bathroom? Peachy. At least the bucket was clean. But why so much metal?

What to do first? More than anything, I wanted to palm a compact and speak with Foreverly. After a successful night in Enchantia, some of my distrust had eased. She might have warnings I'd need to heed to make this day even better. But first, I had other pressing needs and little time to spare.

I used the bucket, which was just as awful as expected. Then I washed up as thoroughly as possible and brushed my hair and teeth. I wanted to look (and smell) my best for Violet. My hope? She fell in love instantly. However, if she needed to get to know me first, fine.

And dang it, I still didn't know what Truly had meant. What darkness had taken root in the queen's soul? Aubrey had described Violet as a valiant young mother forced to make an agonizing choice about which daughter to keep and endanger and which daughter to send away and save.

So why had she chosen to save me and not Truly? How had she protected my twin from King Stephan?

After changing into clean undergarments, a plain white T-shirt and the faux-leather pants, I ate an energy bar, drained a cup of water, then anchored the backpack in place and secured my cloak.

Finally! I could summon Foreverly. I palmed a compact, noting my over-bright eyes and rosy cheeks. With a wave of my hand, my alter ego appeared, as freaky as ever.

"Am I syphoning from someone?" I asked quietly. Maybe I'd inadvertently stored power?

"You are—"

Movement to my left. Crap! I snapped the compact closed before she could finish her sentence. Roth strode into the tent, the sight of him like a punch in the gut.

"What's wrong? What happened?" I demanded.

He'd been squeaky clean before. Now blood splattered his cheek, dirt streaked his clothes and bruises ringed the underside of his eyes. He radiated aggression and brimmed with savagery...and I liked it.

Okay, clearly I had a thing for fighters.

He waved my words away. "Had a minor disagreement with a group of trolls."

No need to ask if he'd won; satisfaction oozed from him, making me want to rub against him and purr. "How many?" I asked.

"Only three. Also a handful of scavengers. And two centaurs." He gave me a once-over, a little slower this time, his gaze *hotter*.

His pupils expanded, dominating his irises. A half smile teased the corners of his mouth.

Magnificent boy.

"Pants," he mused. "On a female."

Had I committed a major fashion faux pas? "If you tell me you can't bear to look at me…"

"I would be lying," he muttered.

Pleasure seared me, sending my heart on a wild roller coaster ride. I might be in over my head with this boy.

Was I complaining? No way. I liked it—liked him. "Were the trolls looking for Stumpy?" Had they found his body and sought revenge?

He ignored the question, saying, "Trolls can see in the dark, and they enjoy chasing their prey. If not for the storm last night, they would have caught you."

"What should I do if I come across another bloodthirsty one, then?"

"They fear fire. If you can, burn them. If you get bitten, burn *yourself*. Their venom is mystical, and turns even the kindest, gentlest person into a murderous beast…before they die as blood leaks from every orifice."

I gulped. "Is no one immune?"

"Only venomous insects and animals and shape-shifters." He stepped closer to me. Trying it intimidate me? Too bad, so sad. I liked his nearness and loved his heat. "You don't have to worry, though." He reached up to adjust the his rim my cloak. "Get fanged while you're with me, and I will kill you straightaway."

No wonder Truly had rushed to assure everyone she hadn't been bitten. "Thanks. I guess."

"You chose a bad time to visit Enchantia. The whole realm is in a state of unrest. Truly's father just died. Two other kings, a queen, three princes and two princesses recently passed. My father is dying. Never in our history have there been so many royal deaths so close together. New leaders are unsure how to deal with each other. Citizens are rioting."

I wasn't just a visitor; I'd be staying. Maybe. Probably. Everything depended on Violet's reaction to me.

As I stood there, peering up at Roth, I remembered his determination to save his father and patted his shoulders. I shot for comfort but managed only awkward. "Fate shouldn't get to kick out the old to usher in the new. The changing of the guard should be done by our choice, at our pace. But it never is. We can only accept that these things happen, and hope better things await us."

He frowned and tilted his head, lost in thought for a moment. "While you are in the palace, remain on guard. Trust no one, especially the queen. Rumors suggest she's the one who murdered King Stephan."

Whoa. My *mother* killed my father? Wasn't like I could really blame her, though. He'd tried to kill three newborns, and he *had* murdered his own brother. "I'll be careful," I promised.

Roth looked unconvinced but nodded anyway. "Afterward, you are not to search for us. Do you understand?"

Oh, no, no, no. The big bad prince would not be ordering around the brand-new princess. "Sorry, but finding you afterward is as good as done." I might even have a royal escort by then.

He did the whole eye-slitting thing, clearly unused to being defied. "Why do you wish to join us?"

"Princess Truly," I corrected. "I want to join Princess Truly."

"I don't care. You are not to come looking for us," he reiterated. "We will be traveling through the Enchantian Forest, a land ruled by Allura, the Empress of Nymphs. Once you enter her territory, you are subject to her whims. There is no one more temperamental."

Allura.

Noel had called one of the jobs I was supposed to want "alluring." Any connection?

"Every day I have to handle a she-beast," I said. "Myself! I think I can deal with some empress. Plus, I'm willing to risk anything to…work for Truly. You know, be her personal guard or something. Maybe I heard she has a great benefits package."

His expression lit with intrigue, and I wondered if his mind had gone to the gutter—because mine certainly had. "I'll come back for you. I'll hire you for a position on my…staff."

I chuckled, blushed and groaned, in that order. Oh, yeah. His mind had definitely gone to the gutter. Deciding not to comment on the double entendre, I simply asked, "Why?"

He hiked a shoulder. "I'm a prince. I do what I want."

"Yes, but why do you *want* to return for me? Why do you want to hire me?"

"I'm a prince," he repeated. "I do not need to explain myself."

I rolled my eyes, and the corners of his mouth started twitching, just the way I liked.

"You will enjoy working for me, sweetling. I offer an even better benefits package than Truly."

When I did not offer immediate assurances, his features did that hardening thing, a quiet ferocity coming over him.

"What do you know about magic?" he asked.

"Not much, and definitely not as much as I'd like."

"Many wield it. Some good, some bad." His voice tightened, every word sharpened into a blade. "Among the bad are sorcerers. They can kill you in a thousand different ways. Or worse."

My good mood withered fast. Like Mom, he hated the sorcerian, and there'd be no changing his mind. Disdain stamped every line of his face.

He flicked his tongue over an incisor. "Sometimes, the only way to distinguish a magic wielder from a mortal is this." He tapped my wrist cuffs. "Do you know the significance of them?"

"Um. They're pretty? They belonged to my mother." The

pangs returned, ripping through my chest. *More bricks, coming up.* "I found them in her things."

"She wielded magic?"

"She did, yes," I rasped. "When she lived in Enchantia. Not the mortal world."

He nodded as if I'd just recited common knowledge. "Hands are a conduit for magic, and movement releases power. That's why your enemies will try to remove your hands. The cuffs provide a small barrier between flesh and blade."

Fascinating. My gaze dipped to his wrists. Sure enough, he wore a pair of silver cuffs. "What magical ability do *you* possess?" *No personal questions, remember?* Wait, why had I enacted such a rule?

"I'll consider telling you mine if you tell me yours."

That. That was why. "No, thank you."

He cupped my face, his gaze dropping to my lips. His thumb followed, tracing over the center seam. "Tell me," he repeated softly.

Such a gentle entreaty, as gentle as his touch, yet every point of contact proved electric. Goose bumps spread over me, spurring an avalanche of sensation. Tingles. Heat.

Enough. He belongs to SW. Whomever she happened to be. "How do you know I wield magic?"

"If your mother was a magus—a natural born magic wielder—then you are, too."

Was she? Was I? "If she *wasn't* a magus?"

Shrug. "Then someone paid witches to bestow a magical ability upon her. Something only royals can afford."

So much to learn! "I...no, I won't share what I can do." I'd be better served shoring up my defenses, just in case.

"Are you certain?" His husky voice tempted. His touch beguiled. He moved a hand into my hair and sifted a lock between his fingers. "Like moonlight," he whispered.

Resist his appeal! "I'm sure." I didn't know him, didn't trust him. *Focus on the conversation, not the touch.* "What magic does Queen Violet wield?"

He could have refused to answer. Instead, he told me, "She can control air. Winds."

Winds...like the ones last night? Hadn't Noel mentioned Violet's connection to the storm? "Is she a magus?"

"No." His expression hardened. He dropped his arms, releasing me, and stepped back. "I meant what I said. Do not follow us. It's too dangerous."

Okay, time to bring out the big guns. I unleashed my most maniacal smile.

He burst out laughing, the sound pure, smoky seduction, no hint of rust. "This is your attempt to intimidate me?"

"I..." No one had ever reacted this way, and I floundered.

He chucked me under the chin. "You, sweetling, are adorable."

Adorable? *Adorable?* I was hard-core and a total mess. But I had far more important issues to deal with than Roth's opinion of me. Like researching Nicolas and spending more time with Truly.

Truly, who might resent me when she learned my true identity. Right now, she was the sole heir to Violet's throne. My presence threatened her future.

While I liked the idea of being queen—fine!—loved the idea, I loved the idea of my twin's happiness even more.

I could live in the palace and work for her, just like I'd teased Roth. But what was I qualified to do in Enchantia?

Need a snarky comeback? I'm your gal! Hire me, Princess Everly Morrow, and I'll reduce your foes to tears. But wait, there's more! Call now, and I'll throw in a second snarky comeback FREE.

"Now you are pensive and sad," Roth said, pulling me from my thoughts. "This, I do not like. Come."

He took my hand and led me into a stormless morning. Vivid

stars still glowed in the bright morning sky. The scent of jasmine thickened, coating the cool breeze.

"Should you leave the tent unattended?" I asked. "Aren't you worried a scavenger will steal your stuff?"

"The tent is a rental, the furnishings inconsequential."

"Well. Do you realize you spoke to me like a dog? 'Come,'" I said, mimicking him. "I think you meant 'Pretty please follow me, Everly, oh glorious one.'"

He glanced my way, one corner of his mouth lifted. "Glorious one?"

I shrugged and tried not to be mesmerized by his presence, his sheer magnificence. This boy was my opponent. I wanted to join him after I met with Violet; he wanted me to stay behind. We were players in a zero-sum game, and only one of us could win. Remaining nonmesmerized mattered.

"Just repeating what your eyes are telling me," I told him with a smirk.

Slowly, languidly, that corner of his mouth lifted a little more, more, and I really wanted to be Snow White. The other side did the same. He displayed a heart-stopping, bone-melting, full-on megawatt smile, Prince Charming to the max. "I'm glad I dr— returned to help you."

Suddenly, breathing was a little more difficult. What had he stopped himself from saying?

"*Glorious one* certainly fits," he said.

"It does? I mean, of course it does." *Ignore the twinge of excitement.*

His hand flexed against mine, and he quickened our pace, effectively ending the conversation.

So, I ventured down another path. "Why *did* you decide to return to help me all on your own?" We crested a sand dune, my boots flinging sand at his feet. No one else was out. There were footprints, though—right next to marks. "You're a prince. Shouldn't your guards be here protecting you?"

"I've spent my life learning to defend an entire kingdom. I think I can handle a morning troll."

Dang it! His smugness made him cuter.

"As for my reasons," he said. "I'm a prince."

"Blah, blah, blah," I muttered, earning one of those rare chuckles.

We reached a wall of shimmering mist, cool to the touch and charged. Magical? Roth didn't hesitate, just marched forward, dragging me behind him.

He palmed a sword with his free hand. "Get ready," he said.

"For what?"

"You'll see."

We exited the mist and entered a whole new world.

10

The worst is done.
Let's have some fun.

Roth watched me as I gawked.

A great crowd stretched before us, people and creatures milling together in a courtyard desert market, almost everyone dressed in a rainbow of colors, with jewel-tone scarves, bright tunics, braided belts and sandals made of rope.

Sellers peddled everything from meteorites, fried meats, fruits, weapons and cloth. A vast number of aromas would have overwhelmed my senses, if I hadn't sifted through them, pinpointing individual notes. Leather. Poultry. Basil. Lemon. Roses. Copper. Sweat. Some kind of musk.

Two centaurs galloped between vendors, laughing as they brandished spears, sending people running. Protests rang out, a cacophony of voices creating a soundtrack of chaos. Emaciated children covered in sand raced about, stealing food. Armed guards gave chase. Trolls roamed in packs. Mothers gathered their children close. Fathers retained a tight grip on dagger hilts.

The palace loomed in the distance, an elaborate structure with ivory walls, golden pillars and bulbous peaks. Mom used to live there, had probably visited this very market and met some of these same people.

Heartbeat, pang, heartbeat. Thoughts of her brought pain, despite the cage I'd built. To maintain my calm, I had to perform a total factory shutdown inside my mind.

"Your Highness." An older man with a thick white beard and bright blue skin approached us, leading a gorgeous pink unicorn. *Enchantia—the Candy Land of Nightmares.*

The newcomer handed the reins to Roth, bowed low and darted off, there and gone.

I did something I'd never done before: I hopped up and down and clapped. "I love her! What's her name? Pepto? Fancy?" I petted her beautiful face. Her soft fur possessed a sweet woodsy scent I'd forever call "Horsey Heaven." "Princess Rose Petal?"

The prince gave me a strange look. "Her name is One Unicorn Rental, Return in One Hour."

"Oh." How underwhelming. "I guess we'll call her Ourrioh for short."

He laughed. "The unicorn's name disappoints you?"

"Well, yeah. This beautiful baby has got to be the champagne of unicorns, and you're treating her like beer."

"I have no idea what that means." He stretched his hand and lifted me in front of him, his biceps flexing. "Your bill increases. You owe me a confusion tax."

I straddled our sweet Ourrioh and twisted to stick out my tongue, earning another laugh. The merriment came so easily now. Such a small thing, such a big difference.

He gently nudged me into the proper position. With his chin resting on top of my head, and his arm around my waist, he eased the unicorn forward. "Tell me what you see when you study the village."

Honestly? "Chaos. Fear. Poverty. Cruelty." Violet couldn't be satisfied with this. She had to want better. I wanted better for her, and I was willing to work for it, to fight.

"I'm not often astonished, but you've managed to get me there." He tightened his hold. "I thought you'd focus on the revelry and excitement."

As we passed, everyone paused to bow. The few who dared to glance up projected a whole lotta fear—fear directed at me. Ugh. Well, why not? Back to business as usual. Did the prince wonder why everyone continued to regard me as a flesh-eating bacteria? And why wasn't Roth frightened of me?

Wait. Was that...? Ourrioh trotted closer, and I sucked in a breath. It was! Stumpy's head swung on a pike, a warning to anyone who thought to strike at Prince Charmaine and his charges.

A normal girl would have been disgusted, right? She wouldn't like the one responsible a thousand times more. Well, screw normal. I liked Roth more and admired his show of strength, especially as apprehension got the best of me. Soon, we would reach the palace, and I would come face-to-face with my birth mother.

I focused on my breathing...*in, out*...and the people, beings, around us. "Very few shoppers are wearing wrist cuffs."

"The magi dwindle. There are still witches, oracles and sorcerers—though the sorcerian are nearly extinct—but they cloak themselves with magic when they venture out. Many citizens kill the sorcerian on sight." The last time he'd mentioned sorcerers, his voice had tightened. Now his voice oozed fury. "The witches and oracles simply refuse to work on off hours outside their shops."

My apprehension increased by leaps and bounds. I was glad I'd never mentioned Nicolas, my connection to him or my own tie to the sorcerian. "Why are sorcerian killed on sight?"

"They syphon power and magic from others."

"Yes, I know that part. Mom told me. But what if a sorcerer *isn't* syphoning? I'm certain they do not steal from everyone they meet."

"Sorcerers are *always* syphoning."

I wasn't. Was I? "Where do the sorcerian live?"

"The Enchantian Forest. They've been in hiding for years, without an overlord."

I went still. Roth had just given me an in. With a little finagling, I could ask personal questions without revealing any personal information. "Who is the overlord, and what happened to him?"

"No one knows. But I hope he died screaming for mercy he never received."

Churning faster. "You have a history with him, then?"

He stiffened and lapsed into silence. I debated the wisdom of pushing. One thing I knew: his animosity extended to all sorcerian, no matter who they were or what they were doing. He must not know Truly had ties to the sorcerian.

Faster still. "What's his name?"

"Nicolas Soren."

Breath clanged in my lungs before seeping from my mouth. I needed to go home. I needed to go home *now*. I'd find my sister and *take* her from Nicolas.

And possibly drain her?

Hot tears gathered in my eyes, obscuring my vision. But the sting did not compare with the sting in my heart. Harts might be safer with the overlord than with me.

Maybe I needed to refocus my mission objective, then. Instead of delving into Nicolas's past, I would figure out how to keep Hartly—and others—safe from me.

Roth steered Ourrioh along a bridge made of meteorites and crystals...through another sheet of shimmering mist...and for the second time that day, I entered a whole new world. A second courtyard, this one private and walled.

Such grandeur! I couldn't look away. On the ground, a mosaic of tiles created a red-carpet-type effect. Trees bloomed throughout, their limbs heavy with lemons, pears and plums, the scents blending into a sublime perfume. Purple orchids grew from the sand, their petals emitting golden embers of light.

Armed guards lined the perimeter. When Roth came into view, the men bowed their heads in deference. They, too, exuded fear, but every bit of it was directed at the prince.

That *is real power.* Guaranteed no one ever smacked Roth's butt, or made lewd gestures or carried his screaming sister away.

I felt myself dividing. One part of me hated their fear, as usual—no one should have to live that way—but the other part of me began to understand its value. Others feared him, but they also respected his strength. I was feared but never respected. That had to change.

Roth dismounted and helped me do the same, a guard rushing over to take Ourrioh's reins. Without a word, the prince led me forward through a huge open archway dripping with sharp-edged crystals.

Head high. Shoulders back. Spine straight. *I'm a princess; I must act like one.*

We reached a third courtyard, the floor of this one tiled with a beautiful tree of life mosaic, the walls overflowing with flowering vines. A towering set of double doors waited up ahead, with four guards standing at each side.

Two of those guards leaped into action, shoving the doors open to ensure we never slowed our gait. As we passed, one said, "Welcome back, Your Majesty."

I was not acknowledged.

In the foyer, I gawked all over again. My new default setting, I supposed. The wide, spacious room was comprised of gold, gold and more gold. A ceiling mural featured another tree of life. A diamond chandelier hung from the center, every gemstone shaped like an apple. A staircase rose from both sides, a marble waterfall between them, also shaped like a tree of life.

"Take us to see the queen," Roth said, using a stern tone that sent two men scurrying to obey.

We passed a maid with small, delicate horns. *Do not stare. Rude.* She wore a serviceable brown dress with a midcalf hem, revealing legs covered in brown fur, and hooves instead of feet.

Like the others, she never glanced my way. But she curtsied to Roth, saying, "May your star always shine."

Hearing the words Mom and Nicolas used to speak to each other, I tripped over my own feet. Grief seared and strangled me, the brick wall threatening to topple, but I hurried to refortify it.

Little reminders of a past I'd loved were the best and the worst.

Roth kept me upright, never missing a beat. "The Airarian greeting upsets you?" he asked quietly.

"My mother used to speak those same words."

"Ah. I understand." To distract me (most likely), he bumped my shoulder. "In Sevón we say 'May you find gold.'"

I latched on to the distraction, grateful. "And Fleur?"

"May your roses forever bloom."

"Azul?"

"May you always be wet."

Again, I tripped over my own feet. This time, he snickered.

"Teasing, only teasing," he said. "In Azul, they say 'May the water wash you.'"

We strode upstairs and down a hall, bypassing several closed doors. Armed guards stood at the final entrance, barring us with crisscrossed spears. I dubbed them Frick and Frack.

"The girl is a stranger," Frick said, motioning to my daggers. Then, a familiar leer overtook his features. "She can have no weapons here. Though I accept—"

"She is with me," Roth interjected, his tone hard enough to cut glass. "Stand aside."

Frack was too busy staring at my chest to respond.

Though I hated parting with Mom's daggers, even for a few minutes, I had a single objective: get to the queen. So, I handed the blades to the prince.

Frick and Frack retracted their spears. As we passed Roth punched one, then the other, and they huffed for breath.

"Respect her or pay the price," he snapped.

"Yeah," I reiterated, fighting a grin. "Respect me or pay."

We entered a massive throne room, complete with marble columns and mirrored walls—*don't look!* Flecks of different-colored light spilled through a domed ceiling made from the most beautiful stained-glass panels in history. Other shards of light flickered from a diamond chandelier and blazing sconces. On the floor, a dizzying array of tiles in the same starburst pattern as Mom's ring. I twisted it absently.

"Your prince?" Roth asked quietly, nodding at my hand.

My cheeks heated. "Sorry, I'm too amazed to explain."

A crowd of people and mythological beings gathered before a dais, everyone dressed in formal attire. Women wore flimsy, floaty gowns made of beaded scarves, while men wore ankle-length jackets and billowy trousers that cinched at the ankles.

In the center of the dais, a throne of clouds backlit by a *Stargate*-type portal showcased a close-up view of the stars.

Where was Violet? I began to pant with nerves, inhaling a torrent of candle wax, jasmine and clashing perfumes. "Be honest. Do I look okay?" I whispered to Roth. I was extremely underdressed. What if I embarrassed the queen? "Should I leave, buy an appropriate dress and come back another day?"

"You look…" Dark heat filled his eyes as he slid his gaze over me. "I would change nothing."

What the…? Feminine power went straight to my head, strange urges bombarding me. *Step closer. Rub against him. Trace your hands up his muscular chest. Play with the ends of his hair. Run his bottom lip between your teeth.*

Resist! If the prophecy was accurate, he already had a soul mate teed up. A girl he would love wholeheartedly, who would love him back just as fiercely.

Using that logic, I could safely remove Truly's name from the list of candidates for Snow White.

"What thoughts tumble through your mind, hmm?" Roth asked me.

Before I had a chance to respond, or act on my silly impulses, the crowd noticed him. Instant silence. Lots of bowing. Roth didn't seem to notice or care. Some people watched him with awe and admiration, others with resentment and fear.

I received cursory glances, my usual sneers and leers, but also confusion. I knew what everyone wondered: Why is *he* with *her*?

Ugh. I'd never before lacked confidence. If anything, I had an overabundance. *Know your worth, and others will, too.* But I couldn't help but wonder, again, if Violet would hate me on sight, as so many others did.

Did I really want to know if this particular cat was dead or alive?

"Who dares to disturb our festivities?" A lone woman crossed the dais to ease atop the throne, all grace and dignity. She wore a pale pink corset overlaid with pearls, crystals and diamonds, material cut from both sides to spotlight a trim waist. Billowy pink scarves flowed from a belt of lace, creating a peekaboo skirt.

This. This was Queen Violet. My mother.

One second, just one, and my world remade itself. One second, and I fell deeply in love.

While my mane of hair was as white as snow...snow white... hers possessed a yellow tint. My eyes—slate gray. Hers—navy blue. We were both tallish and slender, but she had more noticeable curves.

To call her *beautiful* or *exquisite* would be the understatement of the century. This woman epitomized *fairest of them all*.

Roth led me forward, the crowd parting, creating a path for us, and oh, crap, nervousness destroyed my joy with a sneaky uppercut. I wanted to vomit. I wanted to run. We stopped at the dais steps, my heart thundering.

Rigid as steel, Queen Violet perused me up and down. "I know who you are."

Did she? No hint of giddiness came over her features. What did? Fear.

But there was no need to panic. I could win her over. I could prove myself worthy of her trust. "I have information you need," I announced. *Among other things.*

"I will listen, but only when we are alone." She turned her enigmatic gaze to Roth. "Go. You should be at my daughter's side."

He is.

He faced me, lifting my hand to his mouth and kissing my knuckles. His lips...so incredibly soft. Everywhere he touched, I tingled.

"Ask me to stay," he said for my ears only, "and I will."

I was tempted. Oh, was I tempted. But I didn't know why he'd *want* to stay. We weren't friends. He knew next to nothing about me and might stroke out when he learned he'd unwittingly aided the sorcerian stepdaughter of Nicolas Soren.

Better to part sooner rather than later. "You should go. Your friends are waiting."

He searched my eyes before offering a clipped nod. Releasing my hand, he said, "What the lady doesn't want, the lady doesn't get."

I mourned the loss of contact. A too-strong reaction to a guy I'd just met.

He made a big show of hanging my daggers from my belt loops, turned on his heel and strode away. Realization. Not once had he deigned to speak with Violet.

Part of me wanted to chase after him, call him back, something! He was familiar in an unfamiliar world, and dang it, I missed him already. Why did I miss him? I shouldn't.

"Out," Violet called. "All of you. Now!"

Would she draw me into her arms as soon as we were alone? Maybe explain she'd had to keep me a secret from her kingdom because...reasons.

No one moved fast enough for her liking. She waved her hand, and a violent wind swept through the room. People were knocked into each other and the walls, leaving specks of blood on the diamond studs. Curses and gasps arose, the throng racing to exit.

The incredible display of power boggled my mind. Pride flared—*that's my mother!*—right alongside envy. *Want, gimme!*

Though I wasn't hit by the initial air blast, I had to dig in my heels to withstand the residual blowback.

When the doors closed, only five guards remained behind. The most trusted? Two stood on the dais, three moved below it. Those three edged closer to me while also blocking the only exits.

Instinct suspected I'd been purposely boxed in.

Calm. Steady. My mother would never harm me.

"I do not want you here, girl," she announced. "You are not welcome."

But...but...she didn't understand, didn't comprehend who I was, no matter what she'd claimed. So I would spell it out for her. "I am your daughter. Princess Everly Morrow, twin to Princess Truly, raised by Princess Aubrey." The brick wall held steady. "I'm sorry to tell you this, but she Aubrey is dead."

The guards' shocked inhales chafed me inside and out.

"I have one daughter, only one," Violet stated. "I *want* no other."

No. No! Giving me up had been utter agony. Aubrey had said so. Now Violet couldn't tolerate the sight of me? No again. Her reaction made no sense, and I refused to accept it as final.

Maybe she doubted my identity. Maybe she required proof. "I have Aubrey's ring." I lifted the chain from underneath my shirt.

More fear flashed over her expression, then fury. Then guilt. Lastly...hatred? There was no excitement to welcome a long-lost daughter. No thrill to have her family complete. No happiness or hint of joy. No love.

"My darling Truly is all that is good and right," she said. "You are...not. I sense evil inside you."

Her words cut like swords. Like Mom, she had pegged me as the Evil Queen. Unlike Mom, she would rather deny my existence than admit our connection.

Shame and helplessness beat through me. Because I could offer no evidence to the contrary.

With my heart in my throat, I said, "Give me a chance. I can be good, too. I can grow on you." *Like a fungus.* I laughed without humor. *Begging now? Pathetic!*

"You should not have come here." The fury had returned, seething in her voice, I knew beyond a doubt. There would be no changing her mind.

Bile blistered my throat. I struggled to breathe. The wall around my heart just...shattered, dark emotion pouring out. All the pain. All the anguish. Only a raw wound remained.

What made me so disposable that my own mother didn't want me? What made me so unworthy? *Never good enough.*

Tears gathered, but I blinked until they receded. Reveal a weakness? I'd rather die. "I—I'll go," I whispered.

"You think to leave, to plot and scheme against me? Perhaps you hope to steal my crown." Violet white-knuckled the arms of the throne. "That, I will *never* allow."

"So you'll keep me here? Locked away?" I palmed my daggers, even as one of the tears escaped, sliding down my cheek. "I'm leaving this palace one way or another."

A shadow passed through her eyes, there and gone, as if she'd summoned a vile wind inside *herself.* "I remember cursing my husband for his seer magic. *Evil* magic. He learned of my plans to flee and stopped me. I seized the opportunity to save one daughter, only one. I agonized over who to pass to Aubrey, finally deciding to keep the quiet one. She could be hidden, you could not. I grieved for you, but finally, blessedly, I let go." She stood, her movements as fluid as molten gold. "To ensure the king spared Truly, I made a deal with a devil. But I worried day and night. How long until Stephan changed his mind and struck us down? For years, I saved every jewel, every coin, and sold everything I valued. Last week, I had enough. I paid witches to transfer his power to me. I smiled as he died. And now, you have come back, threatening to ruin everything I've fought to build."

Emotion clogged my throat. "I only wished to meet my mother. To love her." *To be loved by her in return.*

"Liar! You think I haven't pondered the prophecy and figured out who is who?" she spat. A great wind kicked up, blowing her hair around her face. "I have. I know. You are an extension of Stephan, the Queen of Evil, and I will *die* before I let you win."

I stumbled back. *Bleeding inside. Dying?* She'd compared me to a murderer of innocents. Someone despised, unloved and unwanted.

This woman...she might have loved me once, but no longer, and never again. She didn't just hate me; she blamed me for any evil to come.

"Seize her!" she shouted now.

All five guards sprinted my way. *Seize* me? I sputtered. She couldn't be serious. But a guard reached me and swung a sword... hilt to bash me —to kill me.

Neurons started firing in my brain again. I dove and rolled across the floor, bypassing my attacker without injury. As I straightened, my birthmark heated, and Noel's voice filled my head.

—*Here's hoping I timed this right. Are you currently in danger?*—

Yes! If the guards caught me, I would die here, alone and forgotten.

—*How exciting. For me! I'm getting good at sensing danger and reaching out. Let's take a moment to consider the impressiveness of my skill.—*

Another guard reached me. I ducked and dodged and evaded. I needed to make arrangements, just in case.

Noel, I need you to hear my next words. Do not let Ophelia take Nicolas and Hartly to Airaria. Okay? All right? Promise me.

—You have my word. The witch will never take Hartly and Nicolas to Airaria. She will never take Hartly to Airaria, period. Now, use your magic, escape the palace and kick-start your job interview.—

One worry alleviated, at least. *I would love to escape. Tell me how—never mind.* I could walk through a mirror. Duh! Simple, easy. *If* I could wield my magic under pressure and *if* I reached that wall of mirrors in time.

As the guards herded me *away* from my destination, Noel twittered happily. *—There's the girl I pre-know and pre-love.—*

Left with no other choice, I charged toward two of my opponents, dropped and slid closer on my knees. If you couldn't outrun them, hobble them. With my daggers, I jabbed kneecaps and severed Achilles tendons. Howls of pain. Blood.

No mercy.

I took a boot to the side, and my lungs hemorrhaged air. Stars winked through my vision. Another kick left me wheezing, but I rolled with it and kicked back, my boot slamming into the underside of my opponent's chin. *Pop.* Bone cracked.

With an open path, I ran. Closer to the mirror... Argh! Another guard jumped in my path.

—Go ahead. Use her magic.—

Whose? Foreverly's? How?

—I say the name, and you waste precious seconds questioning and doubting me. Been there, seen that. So figure it out and use her freaking magic.— Irritation and impatience dripped from the oracle's tone.

A spear whizzed past my shoulder. The vibrations rattled me, and I paused, shocked. How close I'd come to death.

Back in motion. Running, spinning to dodge, running again,

faster and faster…almost there… The mirrors beckoned. Literally! Foreverly consumed the glass, reaching for me.

"Hurry," she commanded.

Trying! I zigzagged.

—*Do you want to live, or do you want to die? Asking for a friend. Use. Her. Magic.*—

Her who? What else could I do, what other magic could I wield? *Think!*

Someone snagged the hem of my cloak, yanking me backward. As I fell, I kicked. My boots met his snack basket. Score one, Everly.

Freed once more, I surged forward. Faster… *Come on, come on.*

Another guard jumped into my path. Obstacle. I stabbed him in the thigh, warm blood gushing over my hand. He toppled and writhed in pain. I wanted to weep. I'd just hurt someone, maybe fatally.

Another worry for later.

Thoughts whirling. The only other ability I possessed—the maybe-maybe not syphoning of other people's power. My eyes widened. Yeah. That. That was what Noel had meant.

I needed to syphon. But how? If ever I'd drained anyone—*don't think about Mom, not now*—the mechanics of it eluded me; I'd done it automatically, subconsciously.

Another spear. This one grazed my biceps, cutting skin and muscle. Pain singed me, and I cried out.

"Hurry," Violet shouted. "End her!" She waved her hand, unleashing a savage wind, knocking down her own men.

I managed to dive away. Another spear sliced me, cutting into my side. More pain, another cry.

—*As soon as you finish playing tag with the royal guards, I'll send someone to patch you up. Noel, signing off to get poop done. By the way, mortal vernacular is atrocious. Tootles.*—

On my own? But…but…

The doors swung open and the rest of Violet's armed force

began filing into the room to surround me, blocking Foreverly. I whimpered. Trapped?

Violet stalked closer, menace in every step. Her men parted. Suddenly, I had a straight shot. If hands were conduits for magic... *Here goes nothing.* I stretched out my arm. My fingertips heated, tingles hurrying toward my elbow, my shoulder.

The queen frowned and slowed. Was I doing it, syphoning? If so, I should be able to summon gale-force winds.

Use her ability, Noel had said. *Her.* Maybe she *had* meant the evil queen. Just not me or Foreverly—not today, at least. I had to try.

Pushing through the pain, I waved my free hand toward the guards who obstructed the mirrored wall. A strong gust of wind sent them staggering to the side.

Yes, I had syphoned.

I was a sorceress, no question.

Though I hadn't exhibited the same forceful intensity as the queen, I'd exhibited enough. A new path opened up.

"No," Violet shouted as I hobbled forward. "Do not allow her to—no!"

Finally, I reached my destination. I didn't know if anyone would or could follow me, but I extended my arm and clasped Foreverly's hand.

As Violet screeched, "Fetch my centaurs. They'll find her, one way or another," the throne room vanished, a familiar warmth and darkness washing over me.

Where would my heart lead me this time?

11

For all the warnings you failed to heed,
prick your heart and let it bleed.

Pain consumed me inside and out. Physical. Emotional. I had no defenses, every inch of me raw and agonized.

My birth mother had ordered centaurs to find and kill me, and I'd effectively proven Nicolas's suspicions. I was a sorceress, and I had drained Aubrey to death.

Everly is a danger to you.

I didn't have the strength to build another wall around my heart, and I didn't have time to mourn. What I did have? An unshakable desire to survive. I turned and slammed my fist into the glass I'd just exited. Shards tinkled to the ground. New pains burned my knuckles, warm blood trickling, but no one would follow me through.

Where was I? I tried to focus, but my vision remained blurred, so I listened instead. No voices. Birds, a rush of water.

Cool, crisp air caressed my face. Already on my knees, I burrowed my hands into warm earth, not wet enough to be classified as mud, but not dry enough to be sand. Had I left Airaria?

Inhale. I detected pine, wildflowers and honeysuckle, but no jasmine, Violet's scent.

Hate jasmine!

I rubbed my eyes until the blur faded, then looked around. A multitude of trees, some with black bark, others covered with glowing lichens or dotted with green slime. Still others had gnarled limbs dripping with ripe red apples.

Noticing a familiar blue glow ghosting through the shadows, I sagged with relief. I'd reached the Enchantian Forest, the same spot I'd seen in a vision.

But why had my heart led me here, and who had left a full-length mirror out in the open? Noel?

Whatever. I had a decision to make. Hole up where I was or try to move on without bleeding out. Both options had risks and rewards. I just had to—

A strong arm slid under my knees and another pressed against my lower back, lifting me up. Fear and fury collided, reducing me to a short-fused bomb. I erupted, struggling for freedom. But I was weak, and the gash in my side opened up, spilling more of my blood. Once again, my vision hazed.

Still I thrashed. I might go down, but I'd never go down easy.

"Whoever you are, you have five seconds to put me down." Unless this was the person Noel had sent to patch me up?

Crickets sang and locusts buzzed. Snakes hissed. But my captor remained silent.

His arms…what were those jagged, scratchy protrusions? Other details filtered into my awareness. He projected zero heat, smelled like maple and held my body away from his. I felt like I was floating.

Without a word, he passed me off to someone who smelled

like smoke. The new person carried me a short distance before passing me off to another. This guy smelled like pine.

I concentrated on my breathing until the haze faded, revealing—

Branches? My jaw dropped. *Trees* were carrying me, not people. I didn't… I couldn't… The trees weren't walking around, using their roots as legs, but they *were* leaning, leaning to "hand" me off. A vine curled around my shoulder and side, applying pressure to my wounds to slow the flow of blood.

During the next handoff, a velvet soft leaf caressed my cheek with…affection? Were trees sentient? Being commanded by the nymph, Allura, perhaps? Maybe they were under a witch's spell.

Decision time. I could continue to resist without results, or I could conserve what little energy I had, attacking only if provoked.

Talk about a no-brainer.

I relaxed into the limbs. "Be gentler, okay?" *Expecting trees to talk back?* I kind of…did. Because, why not?

And maybe they *could* talk back. Whispers drifted on the breeze, though they were too gossamer to decipher. However, I knew the trees had understood me. The handoffs *did* soften.

Minutes later—an eternity—I was eased onto a bed of moss, next to a pond so clear I had a perfect view of the gemstones scattered across the bottom. Sapphires, rubies and emeralds, oh, my.

A short distance away, a lovely girl emerged from a tangle of shadows. She had curly brown hair, rich brown eyes and flawless brown skin, all familiar to me. Ophelia, the witch who'd visited Aubrey.

She approached, fearless, saying, "I am Ophelia de Luc, and you are Everly Morrow, princess extraordinaire. Noel has told me much about you."

In person, she pulsed with divine power. All I could think: *I can steal it, the way I stole from Violet…* Anything to better protect myself.

Hurt someone who'd come here to help me? No!

"Go ahead. Try to syphon my power, like a true sorcerian." She spit the last word like a curse. "I really want to hate you."

"I do want to syphon from you," I admitted, and she blinked with surprise. "Don't hurt me, and I won't hurt you."

"Why don't I believe you? Oh, yes. I remember. Because your kind has slaughtered mine for centuries, performing countless witch-sacrifices to steal our abilities. I've lost family, friends."

"I'm sorry. I am. But I am not responsible."

"You're right. Which is why you are the only sorceress in existence who need not fear me. As Noel has told me repeatedly, our fate is tied to yours."

Good to know.

"Let's get down to business, shall we?" Ophelia spread her arms wide. "I will aid you...for a price."

"If your fate is truly tied to mine, my acceptance of your aid is payment enough."

She chuckled. "Smart girl. Unfortunately for you, I will spite myself to spite others. If you want my services, you'll pay for them, just like everyone else. Only fools work for free."

Agreed. I pushed anyway. "Consider this a taste test of sorts, so I know if you're worth the hassle in the future."

Another chuckle. "How about this? I'll patch you up *and* answer any questions you have without charging you double. A two for one special."

"What do you want from me? I have zero money." I had one jewel, but there was no way I'd give up Aubrey's ring.

I miss you, Momma. One day, I might use that ring to prove my existence to the citizens of Airaria. I might *take* the crown from Violet.

A tendril of satisfaction unfurled deep inside me. Destroy the mother who'd tried to murder me? Lay siege to the very thing she'd striven to deny me?

Maybe I *was* destined to become the Evil Queen, because a

secret part of me *thrilled* over the idea. That part of me even admired EQ.

She had her faults, yes. She obsessed over beauty, and had tried to murder her daughter/stepdaughter, but she'd had a goal, and she'd stuck with it. Honestly, if she'd used her wits and power for something less nefarious, she might have been touted as a great role model.

Another option: I wasn't the Evil Queen—*Violet* was.

I hadn't grown up around her, so our connection had a very stepmother/stepdaughter feel. But that would make me Snow White. Roth's love interest…and a class dum-dum who fell for an evil woman's tricks not once, not twice, but thrice.

But how would my seer magic fit in such a scenario? In no version did Snow White commune with mirrors.

Symbolism, maybe? The Evil Queen's vanity destroyed her, the mirror acting as Snow White's greatest weapon.

A possibility, yes, so why did I feel like I was grasping at straws? And what of Hartly? Truly? Up for grabs: the Huntsman, the Seven Dwarfs, the deer the Huntsman killed, the blade he used and the apple.

The Huntsman betrayed the Evil Queen and protected Snow White. Only one person would struggle against a betrayal of Violet—Truly. Hartly would struggle against a betrayal to me.

The Seven Dwarfs protected Snow White. Hartly would die for me if necessary.

Maybe I *was* Snow White.

"Pay attention. You're fading in and out," Ophelia said, yanking me back into the present. "You asked about payment. Easy. I want your firstborn."

"What!"

My shout echoed through the trees, a school of birds taking flight.

"I tease, I tease," she said with a grin. "As if I'd want your squalling brat. If ever you are crowned queen, you will give safe harbor to Noel and to me. No matter the kingdom, and no questions asked."

Let's face it. I might not ever rule a kingdom. But even still, unease slithered through me. Why? Did it matter? The witch's aid might be the difference between life and death.

"Give me a sample of the kind of answers you're offering," I said.

She thought for a moment. "You probably wonder how I found Princess Aubrey in the mortal world. The answer is Noel. The answer is always Noel. She sees far, and she sees wide. Timing matters. Long ago, seeds were planted. Now the harvest has come."

"Actually, I didn't wonder. I knew." I remembered Ophelia talking to Mom the night she and Nicolas fought. I could put two and two together.

She cracked the bones in her hands, as if preparing for a fight. "Very well. I will tell you all about Nicolas Soren."

Well. Like a good salesman, she'd just reeled me in hook, line and sinker.

Could I trust her? I didn't even trust Noel, not 100 percent, and she'd saved my life. Both girls were mysteries to me.

Black dots wove through my vision, and I decided I *had* to trust her. I might not survive otherwise. "For safe passage in my kingdom, you will patch me up, vow not to harm my sisters *and* answer all of my questions honestly. If you later betray me, I will..." What? Nothing sounded violent enough. I let her imagination fill in the blank.

"Deal," she said, no hesitation, and I knew I'd somehow been played.

"Then do your worst, witch."

She shrugged. "I came prepared to do my best, but I'll do as Her Highness desires."

"No, no. I'll take your best," I rushed out.

Chuckling, she crouched beside me. As she ripped through my T-shirt, cool air left me shivering.

Disney met horror as birds flew over, hovering around her, with different items dangling from their beaks. Thorns, vines, rags.

Ophelia claimed the rags and washed blood and debris from my wounds. I jerked and twisted when she shoved a thorn beside every gash. White-hot licks of fire shot down my sides. Too much! My back arched, a scream tearing from my throat. But within seconds, a strange and wondrous numbness flowed through me, as if the thorns leaked medicine.

I winked in and out of focus as she sewed me up, using a thin length of vine as thread.

"Thank you," I murmured when she finished. Now for my questions. No time to waste.

"As for the information I owe you... I know I will never bring Nicolas back to Enchantia," she said, settling on her haunches. "He is pure evil. Dangerous. Dastardly. Self-serving. Trust him, and you will suffer for it."

And I'd left my favorite person in all the world in his care.

Part of me still wanted to believe he was a good man. The way he'd loved my mother... There was light in him, I knew it. "Do you still plan to bring my sister Hartly here?"

"For the good of the kingdoms, I must. There is a task only she can complete."

I waited for her to say more. "What task?"

"A taming of the beasts, as it were."

Animals, then. Hartly's specialty. "Earlier, I told Noel to stop you from escorting Hartly to Airaria." When she laughed, I scrunched my brow with confusion. "What?"

"Never would I take Hartly to Airaria, a cesspool of crime. What Noel promised for a price, we had already planned to do for free."

I ground my teeth—beaten at my own game! "Will you move

up your timeline and go get her now?" I was torn in two over this, too. Part of me wanted Harts to stay in the mortal world, where she'd never have to face Violet or hungry trolls. The other part of me wanted her far away from Nicolas until I'd learned more. "Hartly's safety means more to me than anything." There was no price I wouldn't pay.

"Her safety *is* a priority," Ophelia said. "I will fetch her at the proper time, no sooner, no later. Our futures are at stake, too. But you may rest easy. Nicolas will not harm her, because he believes he can use her later. That is the sorcerian way."

Well, three cheers for the sorcerian way, then. "How does he plan to use her later?"

"She is a powerful princess. *Bonum et malum.* Like us. Perhaps a future queen and lawmaker. What's *not* to use?"

Supposition rather than a concrete answer. "Why do you and Noel have to be so cryptic all the time?" I grumbled.

"When you do not work for answers, you dismiss the truth."

Well. She wasn't wrong.

My temples began to throb. I reached up to rub them. When my wounds tingled, nothing more, my spirits buoyed. If only I could snap my fingers and recover my energy just as easily.

"You are ill prepared for the journey ahead," Ophelia said. "You should work *with* your fairy tale and stop fighting it."

I lumbered to an upright position. "What do you know about the prophecy, exactly? Do you play a part? Am I the Queen of Evil? Snow White?"

The witch tilted her head. "You think *I* decide the answer?"

Did *I*? Did Fate? Getting nowhere fast, I changed the direction of the conversation. "How long can a sorceress borrow someone else's magical ability?" When would I lose Violet's ability to summon wind? Wait. "Can I wield multiple abilities at once?" What if I couldn't commune with mirrors until I ditched Violet's ability?

Ophelia sighed. "You wield the ability only as long as you

remain linked to its owner—in life or in death. In the first instance, you borrow, and the victim replenishes. In the second, you steal and kill. Yes, you can wield multiple abilities at once, as long as you have enough power." A scowl darkened her features. "I cannot believe I'm instructing a sorceress."

The disgust in her tone roused a tide of shame deep, deep inside me. How could no one see a very real truth? I couldn't help what I was.

Anger followed the shame. How dare anyone make me feel bad about being me? I wasn't perfect, but I had a lot of love to give.

"You're free to go," I grated. "I'm done with the Q and A." I'd get answers another way.

She nodded, relieved. "You'll be safe from centaurs and other predators. For a time."

Trepidation turned my blood to ice, but I said, "Thank you. For everything." Despite the flare of anger, I appreciated what she'd done for me.

"Remember your gratitude when next we meet." She smiled as she stood and waved. "See you at the wedding!"

Wedding?

Poof! She vanished in a cloud of glitter.

I tried to stand, but dizziness kept me down. The same sensation I'd battled after Roth had given me that goblet of sweetened wine.

I was drunk without consuming a drop of alcohol?

No, no. I'd been drugged, then and now. The wine. The thorns. My fury boiled over.

Why would Roth do such a terrible thing? Just to search my bag uninterrupted? Well, he'd failed. I'd caught him red-handed.

As sleep came and conquered, I slumped over with a final thought: *the prince will be paying a bad-decision tax.*

Dappled sunlight warmed my face. I fluttered open my eyelids and frowned. I was outside? With a grimace, I eased upright.

Pain stabbed my arm, only to fade within seconds, my wounds mostly healed. The stitches had even dissolved, as if by magic.

As I scanned the surrounding trees and pond, memories flooded me, and I relived the agony of Violet's rejection. Forget my physical injuries. The emotional ones ripped me apart.

What had turned the queen into a cold, callous woman willing to harm her own daughter? The years spent with Stephan, worrying about her fate? The ceremony she'd mentioned, where she'd stolen his magic?

For that matter, how had a non-sorcerer stolen magic?

I swallowed a whimper. Mom had said evil possessed many faces. Now? I knew beyond a doubt Violet wore one of them.

Had I not syphoned her power, I would have died. The ability everyone despised had saved my life and made me one of the most hated beings in Enchantia.

Truly had ties to the sorcerian, too, but seemed universally beloved. Did no one know the truth about her origins? Had she never syphoned power? Did she even *need* to? We had different hair and eye color, different body types. Why not different magical abilities, as well? As if one twin was born with a disease, and the other was born healthy.

The analogy made me cringe. Had she ever hurt another person the way I had hurt—

Stop! My eyes burned, and my chin wobbled. *Follow that thought to its conclusion and suffer.*

To distract myself, I scanned my surroundings. A carpet of glittery blue grass created a breathtaking illusion, trees and plants seeming to grow from ocean waves. Massive oaks, gorgeous wisteria. Luscious pink flowers the size of a fist, with jagged-edged petals; one flower swallowed a hummingbird. Breakfast served.

A woodpecker *knock, knock, knock*ed on wood while a family of horned squirrels raced along tree limbs. A creature that looked like a monkey-raccoon hybrid—moncoon? Raconkey?—approached the lake, noticed me, then fled at the speed of light.

Butterflies flittered from bush to bush, leaving trails of spar-kling dust in their wake. Birds and crickets chirped as two Thumbelina-type creatures waged epic battle midair, brandish-ing little sticks like swords. Adorable!

The scent of wildflowers, honeysuckle and exotic spices in-toxicated my senses as a blue squirrel jumped on the limb closest to me and held out his arms, seeking pets. Yeah, right. I'd get bit, guaranteed, and probably die in agonizing pain, my loved ones unaware of what had happened to me. Or best-case sce-nario, I'd develop a case of uncontrollable diarrhea.

Considering my luck, I'd suffer both best and worst.

You'll be safe from centaurs and other predators. For a time.

"Sorry, squirrel," I said. "But you need to get lost."

He slinked away, dejected, and guilt nearly choked me. *I know the feeling, little man.*

"You're better off without me," I called. Nicolas was right. I was dangerous to one, to all. I had killed my mother, a woman who'd done nothing but love and protect me. I'd reduced her to a lifeless husk.

When Hartly learned the truth, she would hate me.

A tear streaked down my cheek, followed by another and an-other, little trails of lava. A sob escaped, too stout to be denied. Suddenly, my entire body was heaving.

I curled into a fetal ball, tide after tide of despair, grief and sorrow crashing over me, into me, fracturing a heart I doubted I'd ever be able to mend.

I'd known that eventually I would crack. Humpty Dumpty style, but crying wasn't going to bring back Mom. Crying changed nothing. I had to pick up the pieces of my heart, build another wall and go on.

And I would. The decision solidified inside me. I would fight for better and make Aubrey proud. I would do what she'd always wanted and guard Hartly with my life. Even if Hartly didn't want me beside her.

Look. See.

The desire to speak with Foreverly barraged me. Trembling, I withdrew a compact and flipped open the lid. Cringe! My eyes were red and swollen, all grief, no excitement, my cheeks pink and wet.

Waving my hand over the glass, I said, "Show me Hartly." Nothing. Wave. "Show me Nicolas." Again, nothing. Wave. "Foreverly?" Nope. Not her, either. Frustration smacked me.

Noel? I called inside my head.

Silence.

I must be out of power, and un-linked to a battery. Sighing, I dug a protein bar and the canteen from my backpack. After I ate, I brushed my teeth, then stripped to my underwear and dove into the lake. Cool water cleaned away dirt, grit and blood. And it felt good, far better than I deserved.

Mid-swim, a young woman stepped from a tree. Like, she legit *ghosted* through the freaking bark, catching me off guard. Her skin and hair blended perfectly with the forest.

Foe? My daggers were too far away. A mistake on my part, one I would never make again.

She placed a wicker basket next to my bag, curtsied and grinned. Grinned. At me! She had no fear. "Compliments of Allura."

Allura. The temperamental being Roth had warned me about. Treading water, I said, "Thank you. But, uh…"

Giggle, giggle. "You wish to know what I am?" she asked, and I nodded. "I am a nymph, and a servant of Allura."

Once-forgotten memories surfaced, all the tales Mom used to tell Hartly and me before bed. Forest nymphs lived for fun and games and were extremely curious. Their male counterparts were goblins, beings able to morph into dark mist.

"Allura doesn't know me," I said. "Why would she help me?"

"Perhaps she needs a friend? Perhaps you remind her of someone? Perhaps you have something she wants?"

As she spoke, my arms acted of their own accord, lifting, my fingers pointed toward the nymph. The tips heated, and strength flooded me. What the—

My visitor gasped and paled, peering at me with the fear I'd originally expected, before backing away from me and running.

"Wait," I called, but she'd already vanished through a tree. "I'm sorry!"

I'd syphoned from her. Even though I had no familiar connection with her, no link of any kind. And I needed a link, right? Nicolas had said as much. Unless...

Bonum et malum...the strongest of my kind...

Maybe I *didn't* need a link. Or I was already linked to the forest and its inhabitants, since I had roots in the Tree of New Beginnings?

I had so much more to learn.

Heart leaping, I emerged from the water. Brighter rays of sunlight filtered through the overhead umbrella, beaming on a two-headed snake, watching me, rapt. Any other time, I would have screamed. After being stabbed? Two-headed snake, shmoo-headed snake.

I dug into the nymph's basket. Gorgeous black boots with lace ties, the perfect size. A black dress made from dried rose petals, shed snakeskins and soft, luxurious pelts I prayed were fake, or that they'd come from animals that had died of natural causes. A satchel of fruit and nuts. A jug of wine. A handful of glimmering gemstones. So pretty.

The kindness only reignited my guilt and rallied my suspicions. "Thank you, Allura," I whispered. "I'm sorry I syphoned from your representative. I didn't know what I was doing. But, uh, are you, like, my fairy godmother, here to prepare me for the ball or something?"

No answer, only a stronger gust of whistling wind.

Tremors reignited. I changed into dry underwear I'd brought

from home, donned Allura's beautiful ensemble, then plaited my hair and stuffed any remaining items in my backpack.

By the time I finished, a sense of foreboding had gobbled me whole, stronger than ever before. Frowning, I withdrew the compact. I had power now; I should be able to see something.

Peering into the glass, I said, "Mirror?"

Foreverly appeared in a flash, her silver eyes wild, her cheeks pale. She shouted one word. "Run!"

12

Run, run, they're on your trail.
If you get caught, you will face hell.

I sprinted through the forest for minutes, hours, an eternity, tree limbs slapping my cheeks, the pack thudding against my back. The soup cans bruised my muscles and nearly cracked my bones. Adrenaline helped dull the pain, but even still my inhalations doubled as a punch to the lungs.

Fear became my closest companion, Violet's centaurs hot on my trail.

Wanted: Everly Morrow, both dead and alive.

I laughed without humor, my brain unable to compute the fact that the terrible sound came from me.

Can't stop, can't slow. The scent of dirt, pine and horse clung to my nose, a constant reminder I was being hunted.

As I ran, a thousand noises vied for my attention. Wails in the distance. Howls. Roars. Singing—both bird and human. Or *in*human, like the call of a whale. The soft melodies made my head spin. I felt drunk and high. Was I?

What did I know about these plants and their spores? Nothing, that's what.

I rounded a large tree trunk. In the timespan of a heartbeat, I seemed to step through a door, leaving a sauna and entering a winter wonderland, overly warm air suddenly freezing cold.

But the freezing cold didn't last, either, the alteration happening again and again, until I felt like I'd entered a maze. Every invisible doorway led to a new paradise or hellscape.

I rounded another tree and passed a horrifying quagmire, where thorny vines *moved*, shooting out to capture and kill animals. Trapped within were countless skeletons and carcasses in various stages of decay.

Next, I passed a slushy marsh. Then a flower glade, where stalks nipped me hard enough to draw blood.

A new surge of dizziness. I entered a rainstorm, droplets of water nailing me. My injuries had mostly healed, but all this exertion had left me weak and achy. How long could I maintain this pace?

A creature—a minotaur—stepped into my path, and I reared back. He had the head and tail of a bull, and the body of a man, a leather loincloth his only clothing.

He pointed to the right. "Allura say go there, be safe."

Truth? Lie? With no time for a risk/reward analysis, I followed his suggestion, surging down a path full of briars. *Ow, ow, ow.* Those briars sliced and diced my feet as if I'd tussled with the inside of a blender.

With pain came a flare of mental clarity. I wondered if I was living a snippet of the fairy tale right this second, watching it unfold. The time the Evil Queen ordered the Huntsman to escort Snow White to the forest and kill her.

That would mean I *was* Snow White and Violet *was* the Evil Queen.

Here, now, the idea struck me as *wrong*. Why, why?

I came upon a tree covered in a thick, sticky web, a spider-scorpion dangling from one of the limbs, his beady gaze glued to me. Acting on instinct, I waved my hand, intending to use Violet's magic and blow down the entire tree. Nope. Major fail. Either I'd lost the ability, or I hadn't syphoned enough from the nymph.

As soon as I found a safe haven, I would syphon from someone else, just a little, just enough, and summon Foreverly. Maybe I'd go home to the mortal world. Screw the kingdoms and the forest. Screw the fairy tale and fate.

Leave, like a coward, letting Violet win? No!

I wanted to claim my freaking birthright. I wanted Hartly and Truly safe, forever. I wanted to stay, to find a way to use my magic in peace, without harming anyone. I wanted happiness, acceptance and security, just like everyone else in the world. But to obtain any of these things, I needed power.

I quickened my pace when I heard the *click-clack* of horse hooves coming in hot behind me.

My limbs shook as I followed a stream of azure light—straight through another invisible doorway! This one led to a land with pink *everything*.

Hours passed, maybe minutes, my adrenaline ebbing. I grew lethargic, my brain broadcasting a very clear message. *Ready or not, you're going to rest.*

Soon. Must find a place to hide. When a shadow fell over me, I chanced a glance up. An open view of the sky revealed a huge creature with the head of a lion, the body of a goat and the tail of a serpent.

I gasped, *"Chimera."*

If I was being chased by a chimera, I was as good as dead. According to Mom's bedtime stories, the fire-breathing monsters would rather perish than give up a hunt.

I continued to follow the azure light, *faster*, panting, my nose and lungs burning. My fatigue worsened, my eyelids almost too heavy to hold up. I circled the drain of exhaustion. I needed to be—

There! A small cave, partially hidden by rosebushes.

Relief. But still my mind whirled. Risk: staying in one location increased the likelihood of capture. Reward: my pursuers might pass me and lose my trail, giving me a chance to rest, eat, recharge and speak with Foreverly.

Rewards won by a landslide. I braved the thorns, scrambling into the cave. Well, more like a shallow cubbyhole.

To my surprise and delight, pink vines grew over the opening, hiding me in a shroud of darkness.

In the ensuing quiet, my panting breaths became as loud as bomb blasts. My feet throbbed. Actually, every inch of me throbbed. My nerves continued to fray as I waited...waited... no hint of hoofbeats.

I was safe—for now.

"Thank you, Allura," I whispered, my relief redoubling.

I drank from my canteen and ate a protein bar, hoping to rebuild my strength, but I remained weak, cold sneaking over my limbs. Oh, how I missed the warmth of Roth's tent...and his body.

With that thought, my heavy eyelids slid shut, and I felt myself drifting off...

I awoke with a start.

The vines were gone, sunlight filling the cubbyhole. How long had I slept? Must have been a while. My back screamed in protest.

With a groan, I stretched as best I could within the confines of the cubby—only to still and dart my gaze in every direction. Someone had visited me. My canteen overflowed with water, as if I'd never taken a sip. A new dress lay folded at my feet, a handful of shiny gemstones resting atop the fabric. Best of all, there was a wooden bowl brimming with scrumptious red berries.

More gifts from Allura, I'd bet. Roth had her all wrong. Temperamental? No way. Try kind and thoughtful.

I downed the sweet berries in record time, moaning with satisfaction. I stuffed the gemstones into the bottom of my pack, my blistered shoulders weeping at the thought of added weight. No way I'd leave anything behind, though. In one of the bedtime stories Mom had told us, a princess had refused a gift, insulting the giver—a witch in disguise—earning a curse.

Pang. Mom and her stories. I wished I'd known they were based in fact. I would have listened better, would have asked more questions. Knowledge was as powerful as magic.

I palmed my compact and checked the glass. Unbroken, no cracks. Grief glinted in my eyes. Blood and mud caked my face. Berry juice had stained my lips scarlet red. Twigs and leaves tangled in my hair.

Taking a deep breath—pine and roses—I waved my hand over the glass. "Show me Hartly."

Waiting, waiting…again, nothing happened.

Dang it! I still needed to syphon. With no one nearby, I had a grand total of zero options. Except…

Deep roots. Bonum et malum. I might be linked to the forest—maybe even linked to Allura herself. Did she have power of her own? She must. How else would she aid the forest?

She knew I was a witch too, yet she seemed to like helping me. I doubted she would object to me syphoning from her. For all I knew, she'd be offended if I *didn't.*

I was decided, then. I would try to syphon from Allura.

Desperate and determined, I slid my free hand into dirt as soft as silk, closed my eyes and wiggled my fingers. The movement acted as a catalyst, my magical side reaching deeper and deeper.

A connection did not click; it strengthened. Oh, yes. Allura brimmed with power, a link already established between us. Noel and Ophelia were right. *Bonum et malum* had deep roots.

Suddenly I saw myself as a tree in her forest, planted the day Violet ate of the Tree of New Beginnings. And…and… No way. I thought I sensed… Mom?

Excitement shook me, but though I searched I found no evidence of her presence.

Bye-bye excitement. Hello disappointment.

Ignore. Move on. I syphoned like a boss, lava invading my veins, then spreading through the rest of me. My blood fizzed like champagne, muscles and bones energized.

When the process completed, I opened up my compact to peer at the glass. Foreverly grinned at me. White hair streaked with black had been braided in the shape of a crown, crystals rising from the strands. Bold makeup, a bloodred gown and a diamond choker with teardrop dangles turned her into a princess with edge.

"Mmm. Pure power," she purred with contentment.

No time to waste. "How is Hartly?"

"Missing you, but well."

"Nicolas hasn't hurt her?"

"He has not. Should we trust him? I'm unsure. Should we should trust Noel and Ophelia? Again, I'm unsure. Their intentions are hidden from me. Murky." She drummed her fingers, the metal claws clinking. "Right now, they are not our primary concern. There is something you need to see in Sevón."

"Show me." Had Roth and Truly already returned?

Ripples ran through the glass, erasing Foreverly. Princess Farrah appeared. She stood beside an ornate throne made of ice, and I smiled with affection. How I'd missed my old friend…a friend whose spine was rigid.

Something troubled her. I wanted to fix it, whatever it was, wanted to help her as she'd once helped me, distracting me from my troubles. And I kinda sorta considered her family now. She was Truly's girlfriend, after all, secret or not.

Farrah lifted her hand, palm up, and curled her fingers inward. Ice sprouted at the tips, an apple-size ball forming. My jaw dropped. What amazing magic!

Envy sparked, and there was no denying it. If I could create ice like that, I could return to Airaria, freeze Violet and win her realm.

And act the part of Evil Queen, doing awful things, betraying Mom?

Ugh. Way to ruin a good revenge fantasy. Lucky nonsorcerers. They could power a magical ability without syphoning and accidentally killing people.

I couldn't see Foreverly, but I heard her voice. "Those nonsorcerers have a self-charging battery, yes, and they do not need to take fuel from an outside source, but they cannot borrow or steal from others, so their loss. Plus, they are hypocrites. They often pay witches to transfer one person's power to another. That is how most royals acquire a magical ability in the first place. Of course, the ones they take from are willing to give."

An idea took shape. What if… No, surely not…but maybe? What if *Farrah* was Snow White, named for her magical ability?

Problem. Roth and Farrah would never be romantically involved.

Unless they were stepsiblings, with no blood tie?

No, they were definitely blood related. They had the same eyes.

I inhaled, needing as much oxygen as possible to jump these mental hurdles. In the earliest versions of "Little Snow White," Prince Charming never kissed her. He inadvertently removed the piece of "poisonous, poisonous" apple lodged in her throat.

So, their connection didn't actually require physical attraction, just love.

The idea deserved more thought. Later. Now I focused on the scene in the mirror. Behind Farrah was a magnificent wall of mirrors. At her sides, intricate wall murals that depicted icy mountains, fire-breathing dragons and a forest engulfed by flames. The only source of light came from a massive chandelier dripping with thousands of teardrop crystals.

Her father sat upon the throne, looking fatigued and defeated. A crowd of blonde females, anywhere from sixteen to fifty years old, formed a line in front of him. One by one, they stepped forward, held out their arms and curtsied.

Farrah waved each one away, growing more and more defeated, too. Was this some sort of tradition, like bring your blondes to the palace day? There was no sign of Roth or Truly. For that matter, no sign of Vikander, Saxon or Reese, either.

"Why do I need to see this?" I asked.

The scene diminished and Foreverly reappeared. "I have heard whispers that Noel had another vision concerning Roth's father, yet the details remain hidden from me. I only know that she spurred this proceeding, and it affects us in a major way."

Another mystery for my growing pile. Peachy. "So what do I do now? There has to be a way to keep the centaurs at bay. For good!"

"There is. Kill them."

How easily she offered such a brutal suggestion. "Do centaurs wield magic I can syphon?"

"Every creature in Enchantia has *power* you can syphon, though not every creature has an ability you can wield."

Good to know. But I still wouldn't kill in cold blood. "There has to be another—less evil—way to deal with my foes."

"If so, you need to find it fast," she intoned. "Remember Noel's warning. Diamonds are made with pressure and heat, trees are pruned to bear more fruit, and butterflies cannot fly without a fight. For you, the worst is yet to come."

13

In battle, stay calm, be smart.
Expect losses and a broken heart.

I left the safety of the cubbyhole. As I walked forward, the pink forest vanished, the blue one reappearing. How and why did that keep happening? *Had* I stepped through a series of doorways?

How soon could I step through another one? The centaurs caught my scent within minutes.

I sprinted over uneven ground, leaped over buttress roots, twisting here, turning there. Panting, sweating. Eventually, I lost my tail, but I didn't slow my pace, unease blending with urgency.

Rocks cut my feet as if my boots were mist. Thorns sliced my face and arms. Vines purposely tripped me. Trees and bushes often moved *into* my path. Ants that looked like flecks of lava crawled over my legs, burning holes in my pants. A bird crapped on my shoulder, and a cluster of grapes withered to dust before I'd managed to eat one.

I should have listened to Roth. This was Allura's doing, no doubt about it. I'd stolen power from her, and now she would make me pay.

"I'm sorry," I said between labored breaths. I trudged through a patch of land glazed with sticky tree sap. "I was desperate."

A tree limb smacked my backside, and I yelped.

"A spanking? Seriously?" As usual, I was torn about my reaction to everything. Part of me regretted what I'd done. Part of me…didn't. Fully charged, I could use the compact like GPS, a dot showing me which direction to travel to get to Sevón.

I reached out to Noel, seeking help, but once again she failed to respond.

Horned squirrels threw nuts at me. Spider-scorpions jumped from their webs to dangle in front of my face, attempting to scare the pee out of me.

"What do I need to do to make this right? I'll do anything."

Crickets stopped chirping. Birds stopped squawking, and locusts stopped rattling, silence encompassing the forest. Then…

Why, why, why?

Suddenly the rapid *thump-thump* of a stampede resounded. My nerve endings electrified. The centaurs were closing in fast. Too fast. The forest floor shook, the vibrations scurrying up my legs, tripping me.

I chugged along, racing for cover, wheezing every breath. When I tried to hide, bushes batted me away, leaving me out in the open, vulnerable. Message received. Apology rejected.

I would have to take a stand and fight. I had my magic and Mom's. I sucked in a breath. *That's right.* Mom had wielded illusion magic, and I'd stolen it. *Ignore the pang.* Why not try to use it? Once, she'd rendered herself invisible. Why couldn't I do the same?

I'd survive or die trying.

I gave a shimmy, letting the backpack slide off my shoulders. My muscles sang with relief. After dumping the bag's contents at my feet, I dropped to my knees and filled my pockets with Allura's gemstones. Then I returned everything else to the pack and refit the straps to my shoulders.

My heart a war drum in my chest, I patted the daggers sheathed at my waist. Still in place. Excellent. I positioned myself in front of a tree. *Hands are conduits.* I just needed to syphon. Who had better power than Allura?

Furious with the forest nymph, I decided, *Why not?* Still linked, I had only to point my fingers at the dirt to draw from her. Consequences be damned!

Power surged. I waved a hand over my body…

Expunged. Deleted. Erased, right before my eyes. Yes! Adrenaline pumped with new life as I freed two of the stones from confinement. Standing as still as a statue proved difficult, fight and flight going head to head, but I managed it.

The ground shook harder, leaves clapping. In the distance, limbs parted. A horde of centaurs galloped into the small clearing, carrying the aroma of hay, sweat and old pennies—blood. They'd killed something or someone. *Recently.*

I counted my opponents. Five…ten…fifteen. The moisture in my mouth dried. All males, all shirtless, all bulging with muscles and covered in scars.

They had waist-length hair plaited at their temples, the other strands free-falling over broad shoulders. Those wavy locks ranged in color, everything from the palest ivory to the darkest jet. Same with their skin tones. A good portion of the warriors were speckled, and not just with mud and blood.

They carted an arsenal. Spears, swords. Bows, daggers. The leader carried a scythe. At least, I assumed he was the leader, since he led the charge.

As they passed me, wind blustered, kicking up dirt. *Don't cough. Be silent.*

The second they galloped out of range, I would run in the opposite direction. *Hold. Hold.* Almost time…

The leader shouted, "Halt!" The others immediately obeyed. *No, no, no. Move on. There's nothing to see here.*

"I smell apple blossoms," he said, his deep voice crackling with impatience. "She's nearby."

I smelled like apple blossoms?

The horde turned, ready to backtrack. Okay, split-second decision time. Did I stay put and hope they couldn't pinpoint my exact location, or flee, leaving trackable footprints?

Here, now, I didn't want to be Snow White. I wanted to be the Evil Queen. I wanted my foes to bow before me, surrendering to my superior strength.

A goal for another day. Today, I'd have to run. Again.

Decision made, then.

Hoping to earn a head start, I tossed the stones as far as possible. The ensuing *clunk-clunk* drew their attention, and they bolted in that direction, only to stop and turn, facing me once again. The leader sniffed the air.

I reached out with a ghostly hand…a *mystical* hand…linking with a centaur. Why not syphon from my prey—weaken my prey?

My prey? I thought I was *theirs*.

As I drew power from him, I bolted. Limbs sliced me. With every step, my heart crashed against my ribs anew, as if trying to revive itself, and the gemstones clinked inside my pockets, announcing my location.

Keep going. Faster. I dashed up a hill, muscles burning. All of me struggled. I chucked one stone after the other, always in a different direction. My stomach bottomed out when the link with the centaur severed abruptly. Had he just—

Nope, not going there. Guilt was not my friend.

The illusion magic dissipated, a cold sensation flowing over me. I wouldn't panic. I wouldn't!

"There!" the leader shouted. I'd call him CL.

Pounding hooves, faster and faster. Sweat dripped into my eyes. Panting breaths singed my throat. My lungs constricted, and my limbs quaked with more force.

I rounded a tree trunk and threw another rock, directing my aim at the centaurs this time. Rinse, repeat. Round a tree, throw a rock, until only two stones remained. I hopped over a slithering root, threw—a meteorite, I realized at the last second, regret singeing me. I didn't want to part with Mom's keepsake.

The missile nailed a redheaded beast in the chest, his bellow of pain echoing through the forest. His legs gave out. He toppled and writhed, looking agonized.

Centaurs were sensitive to the meteorites?

Pumping my arms, I picked up speed. Passing a large birch, I chanced a glance over my shoulder. No! Two pursuers were almost upon me.

A vine shot out, snaring my ankles and yanking. Falling…

I never hit the ground. Fingers tangled in my hair and jerked me into the air. My scalp stung, the least of my worries. My captor flung me over his back, pinning me in place with a too-rough grip.

Cheers resounded, the others celebrating. The prize had been bagged and tagged.

I could have let fear choke me; already a barbed lump grew in my throat. But fear was just another face of evil, snuffing out hope.

I didn't think, just acted, pressing the remaining meteorite into my captor's flank.

He roared and reared up, tossing me to the ground. Impact proved jarring, nearly unbearable, but I didn't care. I rolled to my feet and darted left.

A wall of centaurs blocked me.

I darted right and drew up short. Blocked again. The creatures encircled me, radiating malice, and slowly inched forward.

"This isn't going to end well for you," I said, doing my best to sound confident. I held out the meteorite, all, *Behold your doom.*

CL stepped to the forefront, unfazed. He had black hair and fur, golden brown skin weathered by the sun, and eyes the color of whiskey. Handsome in a homicidal maniac kind of way.

He grinned, all satisfaction and glee. "Queen Violet says we are to kill you quick. We will obey...eventually. New toys are fun to break."

Though I was a mess inside and longed to shrink back, I pasted on a grin of my own. "You don't have to give me the hard sell. I know breaking you is going to be fun."

He scowled. Others snickered.

If he lunged at me, I would play dirty, going for the vulnerable groin. Or a flank. Perhaps an eye. Until then...

I held out my arms and spread my fingers, luxuriating in the newest rush of tingling heat, greedy for more. I had no idea which one I was drawing from, and I didn't care. *More. More!*

CL paled and edged back, muttering, "Sorceress." Maybe I'd linked with him. Terror darkened his eyes, and I luxuriated in that, too.

"Someone comes," one of his soldiers shouted.

Another foe? An ally?

Roth, Vikander, Saxon and Reese exploded into the clearing, as lethal as bullets, and I could have danced. I'd never been so happy to see someone I knew.

How had they found me?

Easy. Noel.

CL faced the incoming threat, forgetting all about little ole me. I struck, stabbing him in the human part of his gut. Not just stabbing—slashing. He cursed as blood and bile spewed out.

When he reared, intending to kick my face, I ducked, but not in time. Just before impact, Roth crashed into me, knocking me down and taking the blow between his shoulders. He grunted as we rolled in the dirt.

The moment we stilled, he surged to his feet, dragging me to mine. Our gazes met for a suspended moment.

"Stay back," he commanded. "A great oracle says you are to live, no matter the cost."

"But—"

He cut me off, charging into the fray. Man against beast.

My eyes went wide. If Roth or his men died because of me…

Some costs were too high!

Or not. I watched, dumbfounded, as the prince targeted CL with incomparable savagery. Every furious swipe of his sword suggested rage and vengeance versus protection. His men were no different.

The violence…a true bloodbath. The soundtrack. Grunts and groans, howls and curses. Saxon flared his wings, leaped into the air and used two short swords like scissors, cutting off a centaur's hoof. Vikander laughed as he skewered a centaur with a spear. A centaur collapsed a few feet away; Reese ripped open his throat.

So why did I want to smile? A chill swept through me.

Didn't matter. I would rather be of service—or part of me would. Argh! Torn again. The other part of me wanted to run and never look back.

Well, that part of me could suck it. I was fully charged and teeming with strength. I would help. Had I borrowed a magical ability, too?

"Look to the sky," Roth commanded as he moved in front of me.

Who was supposed to look to the sky? Me? Yeah, definitely me. He didn't want me to see his macabre handiwork. *Too late.* I could never unsee it—never wanted to.

As a centaur had thrust a spear in my direction, the prince had blocked, then kicked the beast in the chest, spun around and lopped off his head. Blood still arced from the severed artery.

Roth picked up the head, bowling-ball style, and lobbed it

at another centaur, who took the hit to the face, stumbled back and tripped over a fallen beast.

The epitome of fury, the prince advanced. His target had no idea Vikander was sneaking up behind him…swinging his sword… A second head plopped to the ground.

Do not vomit. Worse, do not enjoy *the sight.*

A spear slicked through Reese's side. Though he opened his mouth, no sound escaped. He banged a fist into his temple. To clear his head of pain? On his arms, his scales flared, the razor-sharp tips glistening with moisture. Only then did he dive into his opponent. Those scales sheared off a huge hunk of the centaur's torso.

I almost vomited, I also almost laughed. *What's wrong with me?* The two sides of me needed to merge or battle to the death; I couldn't take much more of this.

When a spine landed at my feet, minus a body, the soul-chill gained new ground. Finally, the nausea won. I hunched over and emptied my stomach. My knees buckled and I crashed to the ground.

Unfortunately, the commotion distracted Roth.

Distraction always came with a price.

As the prince turned to check on me, CL—the last remaining centaur—kicked his sternum and galloped away, soon disappearing from view.

Vikander and Saxon gave chase but didn't go far. The fairy darted to Roth's side, and the avian hastened to Reese's.

I wiped my mouth with the back of my hand and closed in on Roth, as well, a little embarrassed. I hadn't been of service at all. I'd been a hindrance, and he'd gotten hurt because of it. The force of the kick had sent him flying. He'd landed in a tangle of bushes and now lumbered to an upright position. He wheezed with pain, and concern nearly robbed me of sense.

Be okay, be okay, please be okay. "Roth?"

His wild gaze landed on me. Voice gruff, features pinched, he said, "You are well?"

"I am." If only I had healer magic. "How are *you*?"

"I'm fine." He rubbed his chest. "Or I *will* be fine. Just as soon as I collect your rescue tax. And your fool's tax. What were you thinking, entering the forest? I told you to remain behind."

14

One battle is done, but another looms.
Who walks away, who greets their doom?

"Queen Violet sent the centaurs to *murder* me. I was running for my life," I snapped. "But please. Tell me again how foolish I am for doing whatever proved necessary to survive."

He grumbled something unintelligible.

I left him in a huff, deciding to aid Reese. I patched the mer's injuries as best I could, considering our limited resources. When I finished, he took my hand in his and peered deep into my eyes. He said nothing, made no sound, and yet, in a perfect moment of understanding and peace, I *felt* his gratitude and adoration for Roth, a friend and honorary brother. I felt his deep respect for Vikander and Saxon. Mostly, I felt his desire to love and be loved.

How he shared, I didn't know, but I welcomed the insight. No matter how happy people seemed, they had hurts, too. Underneath our skin, we were all the same, fighting for a little slice of happiness in an unhappy world.

"Thank you," I whispered, and he nodded.

"Come," Roth said, closing the distance to help me stand. The battle had ended, yet he still exuded savage intensity. War must live in his bones. "We'll take you to our camp. We can protect you better there."

I could have given a token protest, but I wanted to see Truly too badly. "Thank you."

"Walk only where we walk. Touch nothing. If there's a risk to take, we will take it, and you will stand down. You will do what I say, when I say. Understood?"

"Hey, if you want to take risks while I stay safe, go for it. You'll hear no complaints from me. I'm happy to do my part— breathing—so you have a reason to go on."

Some of the intensity dulled at last.

During the twenty-minute trek, Roth kept pace beside me, the others lagging behind. With his long legs, he could have eaten up the distance no problem, leaving me in his dust.

I took advantage of our stolen moments together. "You said Noel told you where to find me. Does she speak inside your head?" Was he *bonum et malum*, too? Mom had mentioned *two* queens who'd partaken of New Beginnings.

He frowned before admitting, "Princess Truly is the one who speaks to Noel. But I never mentioned the oracle's name."

Oops. Guess I had no reason to hide my acquaintance with Noel. I was only surprised the oracle hadn't told everyone about my sorcerian ancestors.

She probably planned to blackmail me.

"Noel speaks to me, too."

First he projected astonishment, then curiosity.

"Did she tell you *why* my survival matters so much?" I asked. Maybe she'd given us different answers.

"Apparently, the fate of Enchantia rests in your dainty hands," he said, his tone dry.

Or not. "Clearly, you doubt Noel's claim. Has she been wrong often?"

Now he glowered. "Never."

"Yet you think she's wrong this one and only time?"

"I think she speaks in riddles, and I have yet to decipher this one."

Okay. Yeah. I knew the feeling. "Is that why you did the whole white knight routine?" Something he would regret as soon as he learned I was a sorceress. Unless I changed his mind. *We're not all bad, promise!*

"I'm a prince. I do what I want, when I want."

Ha! "You missed me. Admit it."

His glower returned a thousand times darker, and I grinned. He had a very evil queenish vibe right now.

Speaking of the fairy tale, what would come next? If Violet *were* the Evil Queen, and I were Snow White, then the centaurs would be the Huntsman, and I would soon meet and greet the Seven Dwarfs.

Excitement reenergized me, making me feel drunk and stone-cold sober at the same time.

But something inside me shouted, *You've got this all wrong.*

"Or," he said, "perhaps I hoped to receive another of your infamous tongue-lashings—without words."

As my cheeks heated, the tension he'd carried like a second skin began to fade.

"The girl who so boldly killed a troll blushes when we talk of kissing?" He laughed outright, and I noted a little of the rust had returned.

But oh, what a beautiful sound. I'd missed it, and I'd missed him.

His friends gaped at me as if I'd just walked on water.

"Tell me something about you," I said, switching tracks.

"Why?"

"Why not? It'll help us pass the time. And if we are going to end up kissing, I'd like to know you better first."

Intrigue lit his eyes. "Why don't you go first, then? Help *me* know *you* better—for our kiss."

Very well. "I like fresh tomatoes, but I hate sundried ones."

He gave me a look: *that all you got?*

Okay, okay. I popped my knuckles. "A year ago, I stood in line for twenty-two hours just to get my sister an autographed book."

"So you are stubborn and determined. Tenacious." He sounded impressed.

"Your turn," I prompted.

He thought for a moment. "Multiple maids have snuck into my bed and hidden, revealing themselves only when I crawled under the sheets."

I barked out a laugh. "Oh, my gosh. You're bragging!"

"Perhaps." His mouth curled up. "Or maybe I'm offering a suggestion?"

Heat bloomed in my cheeks, and he chuckled.

"Tell me something personal," I said, "that doesn't involve maidens."

Again, he did some thinking, "I have been referred to as the 'mince prince.'"

"Because you leave your opponents in little pieces?"

Clipped nod.

"That is..."

"Horrifying?" he asked, brow quirked.

"Hot."

He jolted, his intrigue back and brighter.

Vikander motioned for Roth, who nodded and motioned to Saxon.

As soon as the avian and his gorgeous wings reached us, Roth told me, "I'll be back in a moment. Stay with Saxon." After I agreed, he stalked to the fairy.

———

Keeping pace beside me, Saxon whispered, "As soon as the prince realized we were to rescue the flaxen-haired maiden with eyes like mirrors, he could not get to you fast enough."

My heart skipped a beat. "Why tell me?"

"I have noticed the way you gaze at him. We all have. But you are not the one for him, mortal. His cares about family, those of blood, and those he loves, and his kingdom. You do not qualify. If you pursue him, you will be hurt."

Ouch. I gave him my best man-eater smile. "Have you happened to notice the way *he* gazes at *me*? Maybe you think *I* will hurt *him*, yeah?"

"Exactly," he said with a nod, taking the air out of my tires.

"Look, I understand putting family first. I do it, too. But who do *you* think is the one for him?" The girl I'd seen in his bed?

"That isn't my story to tell," he said, then slowed his gait, falling several feet behind me.

Well. The guy had a highly effective way to end a conversation, that was for sure.

We reached their camp, a lovely site within a clearing, hidden by a wall of snapping flowers on one side and a towering cliff with a rainbow-colored waterfall on the other. Truly sat before a crackling fire, stirring the contents of a boiling pot. Behind her was some kind of telescope. A little farther, horses grazed in a makeshift stable.

She popped to her feet. "Everly?" She wore a dress more serviceable than fashionable, with a camouflage pattern in different shades of russet, amber and emerald. A bow strap crossed her chest, the weapon's tip rising over one shoulder. A quiver hung from the belt cinched around her waist.

My heart leaped, and I almost blurted the truth. *I'm your twin!* Last time, I'd decided to wait until I'd spoken with Violet. This time, I didn't want to risk Truly's distress or disbelief. If she booted me from the group before we'd had a chance to get to know each other, I'd never get over my regret.

Can't risk it. Until she trusted me—*liked* me—I had to stay quiet.

Still, I couldn't bring myself to treat her like a distant acquaintance. I dropped my pack, sprinted over and threw my arms around her. "I'm so happy to see you."

Though hesitant, she hugged me back. "I'm happy to see you, too. How was your meeting with Queen Violet?"

I winced as I drew back, and she patted my hand.

"That bad, huh?"

"Worse," I grumbled. "My mother—the woman who adopted me—grew up in Airaria." *Tread carefully.* I wouldn't lie, but I wouldn't be nudged from my current plan, either: win her over, then spill. "Mom loved Violet, and even encouraged me to seek her out. But within a minute of meeting me, the queen ordered her soldiers to attack. For no reason!" *Ignore the spike of hurt.*

She gave my hand another pat. "I'm sorry."

Reese passed us, then sat before the fire to do a more thorough patch-job on his wound.

"Prepare the camp," Roth called. "There's a sorcerer nearby." The disgust and disdain in his voice sent a shudder skidding down my spine.

"How do you know?" I asked. *Don't look guilty.*

He tossed a satchel in Vikander's direction. "I overheard the centaurs muttering about him." Expression softening, he said, "Do not worry. I will not let the sorcerer harm you."

"Thanks?"

As the fairy opened the satchel, revealing hundreds of metal shavings, I shifted from one foot to the other. *Don't. Freaking. Look. Guilty.* Having friends had never been so important.

Vikander held one of the shavings in his fist. The shaving grew, lengthening beyond his grip, then thickened. Soon, he held a spear with two pointy ends.

Awed, I said, "My mother used to read bedtime stories about fairies and their allergy to metal."

"Most fae are allergic to metal, yes. All but the House of Iron."
He winked. "If you think this skill is impressive, you should see
what I can do with the iron in my pa—"

Roth elbowed him in the stomach, the fairy's sentence ending in a gust of air.

I rolled my eyes. "How many have fallen for your roguish…
charm?"

"Countless." Vikander shrugged. "I'm an equal opportunity
charmer."

"You say charmer, we say annoyer." Saxon confiscated the first
spear and stalked to the camp's border. With his wings gliding
up and down, he hovered in the air while anchoring the weapon
to the ground, the shaft angled. A shaft he hid with foliage.

Reese watched his friends with a smile.

"So, fairies wield magic like witches?" I asked, keeping my
tone casual, acting as if I witnessed the instant making of a spear
every day.

"We do, just not in the way you mean." Vikander grabbed
another metal fragment and created a second spear. "We commune with an element. Earth, wind, fire, water. My family has
an affinity with earth, more specifically, iron. Hence they are
known as the House of Iron."

Fascinating. "Wait. I thought you were from the House of
Love." Which I now realized had been a joke.

A shadow passed through his eyes, there and gone. "I *was* part
of Iron, until I was disavowed."

"I'm sorry," I knew how bad it hurt to be rejected by family.

"*I* am sorry for the way my mother treated you," Truly
said. "She used to be kind and caring, if always fearful tragedy would strike me. Perhaps because my father blamed me for
every drought, broken trade agreement and kingdom dispute,
and often threatened to murder me. Over the years, Mother
grew more like him. The day he died, I swear she *became* him."

Did she not know Violet absorbed Stephan's seer magic? And

dang, how crappy was my twin's childhood? She'd been repeatedly blamed for disasters. I'd been showered with love.

Truly sighed. "She claims everything she does, she does to protect me and the kingdom."

Everything…like forcing her daughter to marry a guy she didn't want? I had to find a way to help.

Roth strode our way. Ignoring Truly, he picked up my backpack. "If you'd like to bathe, there's a pond on the other side of the waterfall. You'll be safe there. And private."

A ray of light lovingly stroked him, making his eyes sparkle. *Not for me, not for me.* "Washing off centaur blood sounds amazing."

"Come, then." He twined our fingers, his skin roughened by calluses, and steered me toward the waterfall. I relished the strength of his grip and the warm friction that sizzled between us.

"Take as long as you'd like. No one will bother you."

Cool mist caressed my face. "Will someone *drug* me?" I asked, remembering what he'd done at our first meeting.

Far from shamed, he unveiled a slow, wicked grin. "I didn't—don't—know you. I couldn't take a chance you would attack my men while they slept."

That, I understood. Still. "You seemed to know me the first time you glanced at me."

He stiffened. "I am a prince. I never explain myself."

"I am a prince," I mocked, and the corners of his mouth curled again. "Don't drug me, Roth. I mean it."

He offered no assurances, only said, "To protect my people, I will always do what needs doing. But in this case, I will consider your forgiveness the first payment for your mounting debt."

First payment? "I'll be happy to pay in full…*after* you've worked off your bad-decision tax."

A new laugh burst from him without a hint of rust. "Let me guess. I am to cater to your every desire?"

I fought a laugh of my own. "You are, yes. Just until your debt is fully satisfied."

He gently chucked me under the chin before handing me the pack. With an even gentler nudge, he urged me to walk through the water. The cold droplets rained over me, perfumed with water lilies.

I came out the other side and discovered a spacious grotto with an Olympic pool–size cenote, surrounded by a flat limestone ledge, everything illuminated by a swarm of lightning bugs.

Euphoric, I stripped down to a smile and wrist cuffs, then waded into the water. I sudsed up, scrubbed my hair and teeth, then washed my clothes. I left my hair down, letting the locks dry naturally, and returned the signet ring to my neck, then dressed in the outfit Allura had given me before I'd angered her.

The bloodred corset with boned inserts protected my vital organs. For added protection, I wore my black leathers underneath the skirt.

I picked up the compact, thinking to check on Hartly, maybe ask if there was a way to appease Allura. *Look. See.*

Yes...

"Everly?" Truly's voice echoed through the cavern. "Are you all right in there?"

"I am." I stuffed the compact in my pocket, gathered the rest of my things and slung the pack over my shoulder. "Everything okay out here?" I asked as I exited.

She greeted me with a nervous smile. "Noel—an oracle— just spoke to me. She says trolls are out, and their leader is determined to kill you."

"Me? But why?"

"You know the troll you killed? The one who attacked me?"

"Stumpy?"

Nod. "Apparently, he was the commander's brother. Warick— the commander—paid an oracle to tell him who delivered the final blow. He cared about nothing else. She told him your name and where you are located."

Great! Wonderful! "Would that oracle happen to be *Noel?*" Had she betrayed me?

No. Surely not. To truly destroy me, she had only to tell Truly and Roth what I was. Which put me on a clock. How much time did I have before she spilled?

"I don't know," Truly replied.

I tried to reach out mystically. *Noel? Don't tell anyone about me, okay, and I'll reward you handsomely.*

One minute, two. Silence. I ground my teeth.

Roth and Vikander worked, their pace frantic as they anchored a tarp overhead. Saxon remained in the air, fitting the material over the treetops. As soon as darkness moved in, Reese doused the firepit and peered into the telescope—or whatever the arm-length golden tube atop the tripod was.

The siren lifted his head and peered at me with an intensity I found unnerving. What had he seen?

Roth moved his gaze to the waterfall, noticing me at last. Or maybe not. He'd known just where to glance, as if he were acutely aware of my presence. He quickly faced me fully to give me a total body perusal.

Heat. Zaps of electricity teasing me, tempting me. Stronger than any drug.

Vikander noted his friend's distraction and grinned wide. He looked me over and whistled. *"That is how you dress to win a prince."*

A flush heated my cheeks, and I forced my attention back to Truly. "What's the tarp for?"

"May I?" At my nod, she appropriated my wet clothes. As she hung each sopping garment on a limb, she said, "Roth spent a fortune to have the tarp enchanted. Anyone who approaches it will temporarily forget their purpose and wander off."

If necessary, I could maybe possibly use illusion magic to hide us. To tell or not to tell?

No need to ponder. Not. A nonsorcerer's power never fluctuated. If these people didn't know what I could do, they wouldn't expect me to perform magic, and I wouldn't have to secretly syphon. If I needed to craft an illusion tonight, I would, and they'd never know.

As Truly led me to the firepit, I asked, "How long have you lived in Sevón?"

"A year."

A lot longer than I'd expected. "Why move there?" I barely stopped myself from mentioning Farrah and their relationship, a detail I wasn't supposed to know.

"When Father and Challen, the King of Sevón, agreed to an alliance, they sealed the deal by arranging the engagement of their children, the marriage set to take place on my eighteenth birthday. Challen insisted I live in his palace from then on. I think he knew I would not survive in Airaria."

Wait, wait, wait. Hold up. The two kings…their children… My world spun.

"You're engaged to *Roth*?" I screeched. I'd suspected the possibility and *discarded* it.

The entire group went quiet. Truly cringed, and Roth scowled—at me.

"Not happily," he snapped.

"Not even *close* to happily," she snapped back.

But not too long ago, I'd seen him in bed with a girl who wasn't his fiancée. Unless he was a cheater? Well, of course he was a cheater. He'd flirted with me while he had a freaking fiancée.

Now Ophelia's parting words made sense. *See you at the wedding.*

My guts contorted, the pain searing. One day, Truly—who liked Roth's sister—would become Mrs. Prince Charming. So the two disliked each other. So what? An engagement was an engagement, making the prince forever off-limits to me. And that was fine, whatever.

Actually, I'd already known he was off-limits, that he belonged with Snow White. So this shouldn't be a big deal. Besides, I'd only interacted with the guy a few times.

But, gah! This *was* a big freaking deal. He wasn't afraid of me. We'd joked about his benefits package. We'd laughed together, and I'd dreamed of more.

He should have told me he had a fiancée. Finding out this way...

Had Roth considered making me his side slice?

Humiliation blistered my cheeks, anger only adding fuel to the heat. In a roundabout way, this was Peter and Prom Queen all over again. I might as well be a spare tire; the crappy doughnut you used only when a good tire went flat. Handy to have around in case of an emergency, never good enough for daily use.

On top of everything else, envy poked at me. Did this mean Truly was, in fact, Snow White?

Snow White versus the Evil Queen...at war over a boy Truly didn't even like. A *beautiful* boy—the fairest of them all.

Was *Roth* Snow White?

Who was I, dang it? I just... I didn't want to be EQ. I didn't want to end up like Violet: a cold-blooded murderess, alone, afraid and despised. A true evil queen. Was she?

Argh! Mysteries sucked.

Ophelia suggested I work with the fairy tale rather than fight it. Sure thing, sign me up. Only one slight problem. I couldn't work with anything until I knew my role.

Truly nibbled on her bottom lip, reminding me of Mom and Hartly. Homesickness almost drowned me.

She whispered, "I've noticed the way Roth looks at you. The way you look at him. If you wish to win his affections, even his hand in marriage, I will help you."

Breathe. Just breathe. "Why would you help me?"

More nibbling. She looked left, then right, making sure no one had come closer. Still whispering, she said, "I'm in love with someone else."

"Who?" Would she trust me with the truth?

Twin pink circles painted her cheeks. Every inch a royal, she puffed up her chest, gearing for a fight. "Do you desire my help or not?"

Okay, so she wasn't ready to tell me the *whole* truth. Didn't matter. This was a great start. "I'm attracted to him," I admitted just as softly. "But I don't want to marry him. And I don't have the best history with boys, especially boys who are tied to another girl."

When disappointment darkened her features, I found myself adding, "Why don't you just break up with him?"

Her shoulders rolled in. "If I do, our kingdoms will war."

Well. A very good reason to remain engaged. If Violet had acknowledged our connection, I could have maybe possibly considered thinking about taking Truly's place. But she hadn't, so I couldn't. I wouldn't.

Also, if I *was* fated to be the Evil Queen, I *wasn't* destined for a happily-ever-after.

Fate, you cruel SOB. I hope someone ganks you.

In both versions written by the Brothers Grimm, the Evil Queen ended up in shackles...

And burned alive.

15

In life, there are risks you must take...
and desires you should not slake.

Night crept through the forest, bringing thick shadows and an eerie soundtrack. Muted screams, animalistic growls and whistling winds. I quaked. The temperature had dropped exponentially, my every exhalation misting in front of my face.

Light flickered from the firepit, spilling over us. Instead of retiring to the tents, we'd opted to huddle together for warmth, creating a beefcake sandwich.

From left to right: Reese, Vikander, Roth, me, Truly and Saxon. Strewn around us, weapons and unlit torches. Not too long ago, my...friends had eaten Truly's rabbit stew. I'd explained my vegan status. Ever the gentleman, Roth had gone foraging, providing me with a mouthwatering selection of berries and nuts...though I might not ever eat again. A tiny pixie had lived inside one of the walnut shells, and I'd almost eaten her.

Every two hours, someone walked the camp's perimeter and checked on our horses. Too keyed up to sleep, I'd volunteered to take a shift, or *every* shift, but I'd gotten flat-out refusals. I had yet to earn anyone's trust. Which was understandable. I didn't trust them, either. And I wouldn't. Not until they knew my secrets and liked me anyway.

Cold winds blustered, and full body shudders racked me.

I rolled to my side, facing Roth, seeking warmth. Only warmth.

He draped an arm over my waist and pulled me closer, his heady, Christmas-scented heat enveloping me. "Better?"

Mmm. "Much." The guy was a grade-A furnace, and much cozier than a blanket.

Red alert. He's engaged to your twin—for now. Do not *enjoy this.* Except Truly had all but begged me to take him off her hands. Because I was a giver, I wanted to make her happy.

He smoothed a strand of hair from my cheek and whispered, "I have a confession, sweetling."

I leaned closer. "Don't call me *sweetling* anymore." I liked it far too much.

"All right. I'll rephrase. I have a confession...my sweet."

I rolled my eyes.

"I dreamed of you before I met you," he said.

"You did?" Really? What had he seen? "A *magic* dream?" A *seer* dream?

Brighter firelight lovingly caressed his face. "I have no magical foresight, and I've never had a dream like this one, before or since."

"What did I do in it?"

"Are you sure you're ready for the answer?"

The way his lids sank to half-mast, I could venture a guess. We'd kissed, we'd touched. *More?* I cleared my throat and said, "Why would you dream of me, specifically?"

"The day Father announced my engagement, I visited Noel to

inquire about the union. She said I had asked the wrong questions, but I would find the right answers beneath the moonlight."

I recalled the way he'd pinched a lock of my hair and murmured, *Like moonlight*. The words had sounded like a prayer. Now I gulped.

Voice thickening, he added, "That is the night I had the dream of you. A very...*revealing* dream."

Oh, yes. We'd kissed and touched. I needed to refocus the conversation before I tried to make fantasy a reality. Topics to avoid: everything personal. I'd stick with business. "What kind of jobs are available in Enchantia for people like me? And don't say cook, seamstress or nanny. Go chauvinist on me, and I'll rip out your tongue."

"Is that what mortals call kissing—ripping out your tongue?"

I sputtered, and he laughed.

"I told you I would find a position for you on my staff," he said, "and I meant it. You'll be pleased to know my benefits package has been growing."

More sputtering, my cheeks all but roasting. Crafty, crafty prince. Only he possessed the skill to simultaneously make me blush, twitter with pleasure and shriek with frustration.

"You don't want me to sign on to your roster, Roth. I'll take you for every chest of gold you've got." A girl had to build her investment portfolio *somehow*.

He sifted strands of my hair through his fingers, mesmerized by his task. "Perhaps I think you're worth such an extravagant price. Perhaps I'll consider it a bargain. Or," he said, a teasing twinkle in his eyes, "perhaps not. You constantly insult and defy me."

"I've never insulted you! More than a couple of times," I grumbled. But I think he kind of *liked* being defied. "Is this my job interview, then?"

"You've already got the job. Consider this a...placement interview," he said. "Tell your prince what magical ability you wield."

My prince? This had turned into a fishing expedition, hadn't it? An opportunity to learn more about me, his dream girl. "What magical ability *you* wield? Tell me, and I'll consider thinking about the possibility of considering thinking about reciprocating."

He chuckled. "Singular creature. You and your secrets drive me mad."

"That just proves I'm *smart*. Secrets are armor. They protect you when enemies lurk around every corner."

"I am not your enemy."

You might be. "What about the sorcerer you mentioned?" I could fish, too. "What will you do when you find her?" Gah! "Or him. Or them!"

His disgust returned. "If they syphon, their hands are removed. That is the punishment for any theft."

React, and you'll give yourself away. But I couldn't stop the invasion of cold in my bones or the pangs in my chest. No hands, no magic.

Already I qualified for an amputation. If ever he learned the truth about me...

Well, screw him. If necessary, I'd cut and run. Yet I wanted to shout, *Why can't you like me for me? Be my friend!*

I rasped, "That's a little harsh, isn't it?"

"Trust me, I do not take such actions lightly. In the past, different sorcerers have become so powerful, they couldn't be stopped. Thousands of innocents died, just to fuel their ever-increasing abilities."

"What about an altilium...that I've overheard people talking about?" Truth. "Sorcerers syphon from the willing, no harm, no foul."

"The members are rarely willing. They are chosen for their abilities and held captive for the remainder of their lives. Even if they escape, they might not achieve freedom. They are mystically linked to the sorcerer, who constantly syphons their power, keeping them weak."

The two parts of me reacted differently. One understood the appeal of plugging into multiple batteries at once—power, there for the taking, always, ensuring I'd never be weak again; the other part of me understood Roth's disgust.

"How do they break the link?" I asked.

"If the sorcerer doesn't break it, distance or death is required."

Then and there, I made a vow to myself. If ever I created an altilium, the members would be willing, and paid.

"As a young boy, I spent months in an altilium," he continued, strained. "The day of my younger brother's funeral, a former overlord snatched me, my stepmother and my older brother and locked us in an underground bunker. Months later, we escaped… My mother and brother were killed in the process. I was the only survivor."

To lose so much, so quickly. "I'm sorry, Roth." For everything the prince had suffered…and everything we might suffer in the future thanks to his experiences. Former overlord—Nicolas or someone else? "I know the pain of watching a loved one die."

"I didn't tell you to gain your sympathy, sweetling. Only to warn you. Never trust a sorcerer."

Sweetling again. I let it slide, my mind in turmoil. What would happen if—when—Roth considered me a foe? An epic battle between Prince Charming and, say, the Evil Queen?

Clearly, he had no idea King Stephan had a sorcerer in his family tree. Otherwise, there'd be no engagement to Truly… who still hadn't exhibited a sorcerian trait.

For all our sakes, I needed to do as originally planned and prove good sorcerers existed. Could I? Maybe. Hopefully. Already he liked me and found worth in me. He'd *dreamed* of me.

But I'd get only one shot at this. I needed to think this through and figure out the best way to proceed. For now, I performed another subject change. "Is there a prophecy—fairy tale—about your future?"

He went stiff. "There is, but I do not speak of it, lest others try to mold themselves into a certain role."

Ahhh. Made sense. How many girls had pretended to be his Snow White?

So badly I wanted to admit my connection to the tale. We could discuss our thoughts, compare notes.

Reward—a partner and support system. Risk—inadvertently revealing my heritage.

I sighed and decided to change the subject yet again. Though I already knew the answer, I said, "Tell me why you're out here in this dangerous forest. You could be snuggled up safe and sound in your palace."

Raw pain darkened his eyes. "My father is gravely ill. I search for a way to save him."

"I'm sorry," I said, plucking at his shirt collar, wishing I could syphon his heartbreak.

"Tomorrow, I'm sending Princess Truly back to Sevón, where she'll be safe. She's a good tracker, but she's failed to find—" He pursed his lips. "Reese and Saxon will accompany her. You will go with them."

She'd failed to find what? The Apple of Life and Death? I wondered...the very apple used to harm Snow White?

Tomorrow, Ophelia would fetch Hartly. Going to Sevón meant seeing her sooner rather than later. But...

During our last interaction, I hadn't known I'd killed Mom. Now I knew it beyond a shadow of a doubt, and I wasn't ready to face my sister. The witch and oracle would guard her, and I would guard Roth.

"We should stay together, look out for each other," I said. Let the prophecy continue to unfold.

I could tell my words pleased him. Masterfully suave, he

moved closer to me before I realized he'd moved at all. "Perhaps you hate the thought of leaving me?"

"Perhaps you hope I'll refuse your offer so you have an excuse to keep your dream girl by your side?"

"Another body to protect. Another mouth to feed. Another burden to bear." Closer still. Even in the dark, I could see the wicked gleam in his eyes. "You think these things please me?"

I edged closer, too, a breath of air separating us. Never had I been so hyperaware of another person, of his breaths, and his touch, his scent. Our connection. *What are you doing? Draw back!*

I would…in a minute. Maybe two. "You won't even know I'm here."

"I have a feeling I will *always* know when you are near."

The grumbled admission should have elicited zero reaction inside me. *One day, he might want to cut off my hands. Never forget!* But it *did* elicit a reaction. Something beyond the heat and the tingles. Something lasting.

I asked, "How can you say such a thing? You don't even know me."

"I want to remedy that. I have *tried* to remedy that. Our first night together, you sidestepped my questions. *If* I allow you to stay, will you tell me more about yourself?"

"I'd rather pay a straggler tax."

His warm chuckle made me giddy. He reached out, watching as he circled his finger around and around my thumping pulse as if he'd never been so fascinated.

"Since you refuse to cook, sew or nanny for me," he said, "how will you pay me?"

"I could clean your tent." À la *Snow White and the Seven Dwarfs*. "Does the big bad prince know how to pick up after himself?"

"He does not," he replied, another grin stirring at the corners of his mouth.

Beautiful prince. "Fair warning. If I clean your tent, I will snoop through your stuff."

"I hope you do. I have nothing to hide."

Oh, the vast difference of our lives. I had *everything* to hide. "You won't let me stay out of the kindness of your heart?"

"My enemies say I have no heart."

"You definitely have a heart. It's fierce and protective." I'd seen him with his family. The gentle way he'd helped the king get to the table. The affectionate pat he'd given his sister. His willingness to defend Truly, someone he didn't even like, and his protection of me, a virtual stranger.

"You're right," he said, meeting my gaze. "You make it race."

"I do?" When a dark lock fell over his forehead, I didn't hesitate to smooth back the silken strands. Problem: each new touch made me crave another—crave *more*. But I didn't want to pull away, so, I didn't. I caressed the shadow beard on his jaw, almost moaning when the stubble tickled my hand. *More.* I pressed my palm against his chest and gasped. He hadn't exaggerated. His heart raced as fast as mine. "I do!"

He liked this. He liked *me*. I *had* to win Roth over and change his mind about the sorcerian. No ifs, ands or buts.

"Roth," I rasped.

"Everly," he rasped back, his voice devastating hypnotic. *More!*

The wind kicked up, a high-pitched whistle joining by the chorus of agonized wails. I tensed, my desires momentarily forgotten. "What is happening out there?"

"Focus on me, sweetling. Good, that's good." He shifted, tangling our legs together. With fingertips as hot as little flames, he stroked my arm up and down until I relaxed, then cupped my hip. "Tell me *something* personal. Do you have a significant other at home?"

"No...but you do." The reminder made me tense again.

213

Reminding me of flint, he said, "My father says I'm engaged. I do not agree."

"Why, though? Princess Truly is amazing. You can't do better." *What are you doing, playing matchmaker? Shut up!*

"I want more than she can give me."

Don't do it. Don't ask. "What do you want?" I croaked. Argh! I needed better impulse control.

A moment passed in silence. An endless moment, both too long and not long enough.

He placed his lips at my ear and breathed, "I want to look at a girl and know she's mine and mine alone. That I am hers. That we belong to each other, body and soul. I want the world to stop when we're together. I want to dream about her at night and wake for her every morning. I want to put her first, and know she does the same for me. I want…everything."

I will give you everything.

Oh, no, no, no. I would *not* go there.

"What about you, Everly?" His devastatingly hypnotic voice had returned, wreaking havoc on my self-control. "What do you want?"

More than anything I wanted… "Someone who isn't afraid of me. Who sees worth in me and accepts me just as I am. Someone who is proud of me, never ashamed." I knew I was revealing too much, my internal armor being stripped away, piece by piece, but I couldn't stop. "I want someone who would rather die than hurt me. But he *won't* die. He's too strong."

The prince's breathing quickened. My breathing quickened, until we were inhaling each other's air. Until the wants I hadn't listed overshadowed the others. I wanted him. I wanted to kiss him. I wanted his strong arms wrapped around me, his body flush against mine. I wanted—

To not set myself up for a fall. The tender things I felt for this boy were dangerous. *Want what you shouldn't, and you will pay a price.*

"Has someone feared you, sweetling? Hurt you?" he asked.

"Someone has—"

I yelped as a fist-size spider-scorpion skittered over the ground, just over Roth's head. For some reason, the abomination stopped to peer into my soul and hop up and down.

Grunts of pain joined the soundtrack, sounding just beyond the tent, and I wondered if my little visitor maybe kinda sorta hoped to...warn me about incoming trouble.

He—it—raced away before I could ask.

"Get up," the prince commanded everyone, the authority in his voice unmistakable. He reached for his sword. "Trolls are about to bypass our shields."

16

*The worst has happened, every path a disaster.
Behold! Destruction has become your master.*

As the boys freed the horses, letting the animals gallop away to safety, I slung my backpack over my shoulder and shoved the end of a torch into the fire, lighting the end. We'd find the horses after we'd dealt with our bloodthirsty intruders.

"Trolls fear fire," Truly reminded me, nocking three arrows at once. She dipped the tips in flames, and unleashed hell, setting one side of the tarp ablaze.

Fire...the instrument of the Evil Queen's demise. My knees knocked.

A volley of spears flew our way—the ones these boys had planted. Reese yanked Truly against his chest, acting as her shield. Roth did the same for me. Thankfully, no one got hit.

"Let's go," the prince commanded. He snaked an arm around my waist, keeping me upright as we hurried out of the clearing, into the darkest night. The others gave chase.

Saxon claimed the torch.

Roth readjusted, twining his fingers with mine. Saxon moved to Truly's side, using his wings to protect her from swatting tree limbs, ensuring she could run, aim and fire more arrows without pause. Reese and Vikander took up the rear.

The wind fought us, trolls in pursuit, too close for comfort. The cold singed my throat and lungs, but a surge of adrenaline masked the worst of my discomfort.

Between panting breaths, I told Roth, "You said trolls enjoy chasing prey. Shouldn't we stop and fight?"

"They can see in the dark." Madness and desperation tinged his tone—he longed to fight those who threatened his loved ones. "Until morning comes, they have a massive advantage."

As we ran, I searched for any sign of an invisible doorway, a way to hide, as I'd done with the centaurs. A shimmer, a glint. Something. Anything. Had Allura moved the doorways from my path in a fit of pique?

Vikander created and tossed metal spears. I glanced back, realizing he'd hit trees rather than trolls, who were roughly a hundred yards away, illuminated by Truly's trail of fire. The spears were as sharp as daggers from tip to tail. Whenever a troll slammed into one, he got sheared in half.

My twin released a new volley of fiery arrows. Then another and another. She never missed a target, her accuracy awe-inspiring. Even more shocking, her quiver never emptied, some kind of magic at play.

I could use a dose of magic myself, my muscles burning and shaking. *Can't slow. Can't—*

My boot slammed into a buttress root. Roth kept me upright, allowing me to regain my footing.

Whoosh. An ax soared between us, then embedded in a tree. Shock...fear...fury—they surged quickly, fiercely. How close we'd come to injury and possible death. How quickly life could change. If I didn't stop these trolls, one or all of us *would* die.

Truly loosed another round of arrows, heralding new grunts of pain. Flames crackled, charring foliage and tree bark, I hated what we were doing to Allura's territory. Would she blame us? Punish us?

A throng of trolls leaped from the trees, blocking our path. The hulking beasts possessed an aura of menace, their eyes neon red. Twining shadows and light fell over prominent foreheads, sharp teeth and jutting jaws. Some beasts had horns, most had tusks, but each and every one had dripping black claws. Weapons ranged from clubs to machetes.

We were surrounded. They'd *herded* us here, intending to pick us off. We were...defeated?

No, no. What had Hartly said to me? If there's breath, there's hope.

I wished I were stronger, but I wasn't. I could work only with what I had. Bottom line: I would *not* let these people die just to protect my secrets.

"Stay back!" I extended an arm, determined to syphon from a troll, and only a troll...yes! Connection. A tidal wave of power, allowing me to craft an illusion of a bigger torch and lunge.

With a collective hiss, the trolls jumped back.

The prince, fairy, avian and mer closed around Truly and me, their weapons raised and ready.

Heartbeat, heartbeat, heartbeat. A war cry pierced the night, trolls converging en masse. My guys swung their swords and spears. Metal clunked against metal, wood—and cut through flesh. Limbs piled around m, blood flowing in rivulets. Groans and groans created a horrid symphony. The scent of old pennies and emptied bowels permeated *everything*, and my stomach roiled.

I tried to link with more trolls—tried to *weaken* more trolls— but I hadn't practiced doing both at once, and failed.

Every few seconds, one of the guys ducked and Truly unleashed an array of arrows. No matter how many trolls those missiles felled, other fiends always swooped in.

Reese skinned his opponents with his scales. Saxon used the hooks in his wing-joints to rip out organs. Vikander forced any metal worn by his victims to lengthen and sharpen, growing *inside* the trolls.

My contribution? Watching. Maybe if I crafted a bigger, badder illusion, the army would retreat.

"Everly, look out!"

I turned at Saxon's shout, my heart in my throat. Too late. A troll had leaped from a tree, his gaze locked on me. Impact!

Except, it wasn't the troll who'd landed atop me. It was Reese. He'd gotten to me first. He stumbled backward, toppling to his butt. Blood gushed from two puncture wounds in his cheek—punctures meant for me; the muscle underneath looked like raw hamburger meat.

Rage-tinged horror engulfed me. Reese…hurt beyond repair…

Roth disemboweled the beast responsible for the mer's condition, words he'd once spoken rushing back. *Get fanged while you're with me, and I will kill you straightaway.*

No one in my group would be dying today. We would find a way to help the siren. No other outcome was acceptable.

Focus. The sooner the trolls were dispatched, the sooner we could save him.

Remaining crouched, I clasped Reese's ankle and dragged his heavy frame deeper into the circle. My body would shield his. I pressed my palm on the other side of him, flat on the ground, my fingers pointing toward the trolls. *Link.* I drew power, warmth and energy.

Trolls feared fire, so, I would give them fire.

Around us, an illusion of flames erupted, so real a white-hot breeze swept over us. Would my illusion actually burn someone's flesh?

I laughed, suddenly overcome with glee. *Burn, burn.* I wanted to hear the trolls scream. I wanted to dance in moonlight as their ashes twirled in the air.

Amid the flames, the army backtracked. One warrior proved slower than the others. My unwitting victim? I continued to draw. The flames spread, closing in on the horde, seeming to immerse the trees. Our foes continued to backtrack, fearful, and I *liked* it, reveled in it. Actually, *all* of me liked it; for once, I wasn't divided.

These monsters had hurt Reese and wanted to hurt everyone else. I would teach them the error of their ways. *Strike against me and mine…and suffer.*

Taking my illusion to the next level, I envisioned bomb blasts erupting, debris spraying. *Boom! Boom! Boom!* The ground shook.

Infected by panic, a troll shouted, "Retreat!"

The army ran as fast as their feet would carry them.

I held the illusion as long as possible, sweat dripping from different parts of me, my arms quivering. Still I syphoned from my troll. The distance didn't matter, I realized. I could do what other sorcerers could not and maintain the connection, my link too powerful to break.

Power on tap, yes, please, and thank you.

But if I drained him to death, I could keep any magical ability he wielded. Pros and cons, risks and rewards. *Resist!* What if I absorbed his evil on top of everything else, as Violet might have done with Stephan?

Another realization struck, sickening me: the day I'd entered Enchantla, I'd still had a link to Hartly. I'd *syphoned* from her. The distance hadn't mattered then, either. I could have killed her.

Tears scorched my eyes. Though I still maintained our connection, I ceased drawing from the troll. In an instant, weakness invaded my limbs. I slumped over, strong arms looping around my waist to save me from a face-plant.

The scent of cinnamon teased my nose. Roth! When had he knelt beside me?

He petted my hair, saying, "You wield illusion magic, then?"

"I do," I replied, my voice wispy from overexertion. Like I could really deny it. Did he suspect the rest?

"I know of another who had the same ability. Princess Aubrey Morrow of Airaria." Such a gentle tone.

He believed he'd solved the mystery of Everly, didn't he? That I was Aubrey's daughter and Truly's cousin. I did not correct him.

"I wish I could give you time to rest, sweetling, but we must move on." His expression hardened as he stood. "Reese must be...helped."

The siren lumbered to his knees, head bowed. The puncture wounds looked charred, blood and puss oozing from each. A scarlet rash covered half of his face.

Vikander and Saxon flanked his sides and stared straight ahead, strain knotting their shoulders.

Dread chilled every inch of me. What was happening?

Truly dropped to her knees beside me and peered up at Roth. "Please, don't do this. Just let him go. We can let him go."

Comprehension dawned, and I stared at Reese wide-eyed. This boy wanted only to love and be loved, and Roth planned to end him?

My chest clenched. "Roth," I croaked. "Don't. Give me a minute." I dug into my backpack, frantically searching for my compact. Argh! Where was it? "There has to be another way."

Roth moved in front of the kneeling warrior, a sword in hand. I searched faster, fighting the urge to vomit.

"Just give me a minute." Searching, searching. Had I dropped it?

Reese lifted his head. In his eyes frothed a mix of regret and resolve. "Do it," he told Roth, speaking up for the first time in our acquaintance.

———

I sucked in a breath. His voice reminded me of a lullaby, haunting and sweet. A strange calm settled over the group—over everyone but me.

"Yes," Truly said with a nod. "Do it."

I frowned. Why the sudden change? "There has to be another way," I repeated. If Reese died because he'd saved a sorceress, I would never assuage my guilt. There! Finally I withdrew the compact.

Reese caught my gaze and offered me a sad smile. "Let me die as I lived. By choice. With honor."

"No," I said, shaking my head. This could not be happening. "There must be an antidote. What about the Apple of Life and Death?"

"We're out of time." Regret and resolve frothed inside *Roth's* eyes. He bowed to Reese, saying, "I thank you for your service, my friend."

"My honor and my privilege," Reese said.

"Listen to me. There *must* be an antidote." But what if there wasn't? What if Reese turned into some kind of homicidal rage-beast and hurt Truly?

I divided once again, half of me ready to defend the siren until the end, half of me ready to do far worse to protect my twin.

Roth whispered, "We shall meet again." Then he swung the sword.

17

*Fight the good fight with everything you've got,
or even your smallest efforts will be for naught.*

Using a metal shaving and an enchanted cloth he'd saved from the fire, Vikander created a gurney. Roth and Saxon carried Reese through the forest. Sorry, the *pieces* of Reese.

I gave a humorless laugh. Guess Roth wouldn't be sending us back to the palace, after all.

One hour bled into another as we traveled. I remained in a state of shock, cold from head to toe and shivering uncontrollably. The others were in shock, too. No one said another word.

When we reached a suitable campsite, the guys set traps along the perimeter. I built a firepit, gathered twigs and used the box of matches to start a fire.

Settling before the flames, I mused about the day I'd first come to Enchantia, how I'd thought a land with such a charming name couldn't be so bad. What a fool I'd been.

I'd entered a bona fide nightmare…and I might be the evilest creature on the block, evidence continuing to stack up against me. The Evil Queen was a legit illusionist—check. She communed with mirrors—check. She hurt people and liked it, relishing her power—checkmate. I'd enjoyed torturing those trolls.

Evil wears many faces, and if you aren't careful, it will wear yours.

There were still flaws in my conclusion, of course. I hadn't suddenly started giving two craps about being the fairest of them all, and I had no husband or children…though "husband" might be symbolic of a romantic partner, and "children" might be… what? The fruit of our labors together?

Follow the train of logic. Let's say I was the Evil Queen, no ifs, ands or buts. How could I overcome my predicted end, avoiding shackles and flames, dying alone and unloved?

There had to be some kind of loophole. Most prophecies had one, right?

Prophecy: you can never speak the truth.

Loophole: you *can* tattoo the message on your body.

Prophecy: no warrior has the strength to defeat the villain.

Loophole: a scholar comes along and defeats the villain with her wits.

I palmed the compact I'd had so much trouble finding earlier. *Look, see. One peek, just one.*

Answers awaited me. I needed only to resume syphoning from the troll. What's more, I could inquire about Hartly.

Curiosity gnawed at me. I had to know.

Hating myself, avoiding my reflection—my eyes would be wells of grief and pain—I waved my hand over the glass. I whispered, "Show me what would have happened if Roth hadn't killed Reese."

Ripples, then Reese appeared. Dark hunger contorted his features. Shock hammered me as he launched himself at Roth. The two grappled, vicious to the extreme. Vikander and Saxon tried to help and got mauled. When Truly stepped in, she lost an eye. I linked with the siren and syphoned from him until he died…then *I* focused on the others with dark hunger.

Real life Truly eased beside me, her shoulder brushing mine. "How are you?"

Struggling to control my breathing, I closed the compact. *Focus.* I'd ask the mirror about Hartly after we'd retired for the night.

"I'm still shocked," I admitted. I understood Roth's reasons better, but I couldn't get past one fact: the (seemingly) easygoing prince who'd made me smile and ache for his kisses hadn't hesitated to lift his sword and remove Reese's head. He'd killed someone he loved.

"What happened?" I asked. "One minute you begged Roth to spare Reese, the next you agreed the siren had to die." No judgement, only genuine curiosity.

"With his voice, Reese could calm or incense legions. The better question is, why didn't he change *your* mind?"

Yeah. Why?

She added, "Trolls, centaurs and shifters are usually the only ones immune," and I knew. My connection to the troll had saved my mind. Oh, the irony.

"There really isn't a cure for troll venom?" I asked, voice wobbling.

"There really isn't." She plucked a blade of grass. "I just wish Roth hadn't been so cold, detached from emotion."

He'd been anything but cold. He'd been—was—agonized, which made his lack of hesitation a thousand times more astonishing. Why hadn't he placed the burden of responsibility on someone else? So that he alone would bear the guilt?

"What happens to the dead in Enchantia?" I asked. "Does the person's spirit move on, or cease to exist?"

"In Airaria, citizens believe the dead live in the sky, forever lighting our way. In Sevón, the dead are said to return to their roots—the forest—their power and magic made one with the trees. In Fleur, spirits are thought to be reborn. In Azul, spirits forever dance atop ocean waves."

Beautiful sentiments.

Morning arrived, light seeping through the overhead umbrella of leaves, a familiar cobalt glow encasing the trees. Squirrels hunted nuts and birds flittered about.

I marveled. We'd suffered a huge blow, but the world didn't care. Life rolled on, never missing a beat.

Maintaining heartbreaking silence, Vikander placed spears around the perimeter while Roth and Saxon built...

"What is that?" I asked Truly.

"A funeral pyre."

To say goodbye. *Pang.* "Your skill with a bow," I said, switching directions. "It's miraculous. And magical?"

She nodded. "When I first realized what I could do, I was disappointed. I'd wanted to control one of the four elements, like my mother."

"You shoot with one hundred percent accuracy, and your quiver never empties. You can play offense and defense, for yourself and others. That is amazing!" Enviable.

She flicked her hair over one shoulder, saying, "I can also throw blades, and when I use daggers, my magic always guides me, telling me where to cut to cause the most damage. I can mimic animal calls, and track anyone or thing."

"Amazing," I repeated, and she beamed. Everything she described...

Had I found the Huntsman?

Awe quickly morphed into dread. In the fairy tale, the Evil Queen and the Huntsman worked together—for a short time. EQ asked for the unthinkable, and the Huntsman betrayed her.

As soon as the boys finished the altar, Roth used flint and a dagger to ignite a torch, then motioned us over with a wave. We joined him, and Vikander and Saxon moved behind us.

Roth tossed the torch underneath the altar. Kindling quickly erupted with flames, the inferno growing, spreading. The soldiers assumed battle positions, watching as their friend burned. Pain turned their eyes into wounds.

By the time the flames died, night had fallen and only ash remained. But it was then, that moment, that the sense of gloom dissipated.

Roth rested a fist over his heart. "A life well lived is a life missed by others. You fought the good fight and ran a good race. We'll miss you always, Reese of Seaspray, but we will not mourn you."

The others mimicked his pose, fist over heart. "We will not mourn," they chanted in unison.

"We celebrate the time we had together," Roth said.

"We celebrate," they echoed.

"Death has lost its sting. The grave has lost its bite. May you forever abide in the peace of the hereafter." The prince knelt before the ash.

Again, the rest of us followed suit, and bowed our heads.

"Let your heart return to the earth." Roth planted his palm *inside* the ash.

We did the same, the warm mound shimmering with the same azure glow that pervaded the forest. A glow that grew brighter, brighter, before being absorbed into the dirt.

Let your heart return to earth. Had I felt the hearts of the dead—the source of the endless, limitless power—when I'd syphoned from Allura? The reason I thought I'd sensed Mom's presence?

Only when the glow died did the guys walk away. Their steps were lighter.

I remained in place, my thoughts riotous. I'd led a great life and had much to celebrate. Every time I'd laughed, I'd experienced a little miracle. And I'd laughed a lot. I'd had camaraderie, acceptance and comfort when times had been tough. I'd had a sister's unwavering support, and a mother who'd chosen to raise me, to love me; that meant something. But I needed to let go of the past and set my sights on the future.

I got it now, how I'd fought the prophecy and hadn't worked with it. You could not move forward if you were always looking back. Rather, you stalled out, rendered immobile, trapped in a ceaseless tug of war. The constant strain left you fatigued and vulnerable.

I will always love you, Mom, and miss you terribly, but I will mourn you no more. I will rejoice for the time we had and anticipate a reunion in the hereafter.

I drew in a deep breath...then let the brick wall around my heart come crashing down. I expected my body to crash, as well, but I remained on my feet, astonishingly steady.

"If you'll gather wood for a new fire," Truly said, breaking into my thoughts, "I'll set up a private bathing area. Vikander will make us a tub."

I stood. Roth and Vikander erected tents, while Saxon marched along the camp's perimeter, on guard. Back to business as usual.

"How will we fill the tub?" I saw no evidence of a pond or lake, or even a puddle.

"I have a bespelled canteen. It has been in my family for ages, and never runs dry."

What had *that* cost?

"As you gather the wood, try to garner Roth's attention," she said, waggling her brows. "Maybe bend over and wiggle around."

"I would rather teach Roth how to insert a tampon," I grumbled and strode away.

The prince watched me, a blank mask over his features.

Okay, maybe I would wiggle around a *tiny* bit. If I could help him forget his troubles, even for a moment, I would.

This was also a chance to advance my win-him-over plan, so he would never help Snow White shackle and burn me.

Whoa! Light bulb moment. In the fairy tale, Prince Charming worked with Snow White to murder the Evil Queen. Roth was tied to another girl *and* my death. How had I failed to connect the dots before?

I consider myself the Evil Queen now? For sure? No doubts?

No, I still had doubts. But I needed to proceed as if I didn't. Self-preservation said, *Attack first, die last.*

Another part of me shouted, *Leave while you can!*

No way. I wouldn't leave Truly behind. And I wouldn't give up on Roth. I was his dream girl—a reminder I would never tire of hearing. The way he looked at me...

If anyone could change the prince's mind about the sorcerian and overcome his contempt, it was me.

Goose bumps broke out over my arms as I gathered firewood. Firewood glazed with a strange pink powder. I frowned.

"Trying to poison me?" I asked Allura. "Go for it. You can choke on my bones, for all I care." She could have helped us today. To punish me, she'd let an innocent siren die.

I headed back to camp, stomping my feet with more force than necessary. A fist-size spider-scorpion dropped from a web, stopping me in my tracks. My heart lurched. The same fist-size spider-scorpion as before, the one who'd tried to warn me about the trolls? If so, he'd hitched a ride on something—or someone. I shuddered.

"Um...hi?" I said with a lame little wave.

Roth rushed past a tangle of limbs, murder in his eyes. "What is— Ah." He sheathed his sword. "I will slay this dragon with my boot."

"No!" Jumping into his path, I flattened my hands on his pecs. A puny action, considering his strength, but he halted anyway, his muscles flexing. "He's innocent."

"A spidorpion bites and stings, injecting his victims with two types of venom. One causes pain, one paralyzes. He will eat your eyes, a delicacy to their kind, and you will remain aware, unable to fight."

Another horror. Yawn. "There's been enough death for one day. Let's leave him to his business."

Did Roth just flinch?

"Spidorpions have a long history with those who wield magic, and a seething hatred for our kind. Witches use them for spells. Oracles use them to achieve an altered mental state. Sorcerers eat them to make their blood venomous—so they can paralyze and easily abduct their victims."

So this one *had* followed me. Not to help, but to hurt. "I get it. He hates me, and he'll attack at his earliest convenience." I shrugged. "So what?" He'd have to get in line.

The prince gave me an odd look but allowed me to walk— push—him backward. I glanced over my shoulder and expelled a relieved breath. The spidorpion had already disappeared in the foliage.

Saxon strode over to confiscate the twigs I'd gathered, his bracelets clinking together. I'd been meaning to ask him about those bracelets. What they meant, their purpose, that kind of thing. But he was gone a second later, marching off without speaking a word.

"Hold up," I called, about to give chase. "Some of the twigs are sprinkled with pink powder."

"That is fairy dust." Roth clasped my wrist, pulling my body against his, and motioned Saxon to continue on. "It'll help us relax."

Our chests bumped, and I tottered. I had to grip his shoulders for balance. He coiled an arm around my waist to hold me steady, and I gave a nervous little laugh.

"Smooth move, princeling. How many fair maidens have succumbed to your charms?"

His fingers flexed on me. "Do you think I'm evil now?"

See! I'd known he was agonized. I softened against him, saying, "I'm sorry it happened, and I'm sorry you were put in such a terrible position. You made a tough decision during a tough time. You did what you thought was right, your intentions pure. Your strength awes me."

He met my gaze. The vulnerability in his expression...the astonishment...was that a hint of adoration? Danged if I didn't soften even more. My opinion actually mattered to him.

I'd absolutely, positively made the right call by staying with him. I had this in the bag. Wait. Would he try to send me back to the palace without Reese? I asked, and Roth shook his head.

"You'll stay with me," he said.

Well, well. Soon, his one-star sorcerian review would get an upgrade, guaranteed. I'd make sure of it—for our well-being, *not* because my body shouted, *I will perish without his touch.*

Cupping his cheeks, I intoned, "*You* awe me, Roth."

The adoration intensified, so strong I felt it like a caress. I trembled and ached and maybe, just maybe, reflected an answering adoration right back at him.

Fool! Have you forgotten? He isn't yours. He'll never be yours.

Right. I'd have to continue winning him over without becoming emotionally attached. Or more attached.

My heart chuckled and tipped a hat at my mind. *Good luck with that.*

18

True love's kiss can break any curse...
or make your life ever so much worse.

O ne day bled into another as we searched for the Apple of
Life and Death. No one knew what we were looking for,
exactly. An apple tree? Some kind of artifact?

Roth said, "We'll know it when we see it."

Every day, he exuded more urgency, the pressure to return
to his sick father flourishing.

Again and again he told me he needed to save the king, that
Challen was a good man, beloved by his kingdom.

Beloved by his son, too. In a very un-Everly-like act, I'd
thrown my arms around Roth this morning, hugging him tight.
I knew the pain of losing a parent too soon. He'd already lost
his mother, and I didn't want him to lose another.

He'd hugged me back, his nose buried in my hair. We'd clung
to each other. I'd never wanted to let go.

"I know the apple is close," Truly said. "Every fiber of my being tells me I need only reach out to clasp it, but..."

Despite her ability to track anything, anytime, anywhere, we'd made no real progress. I both minded and didn't mind the delay. While I cherished the time I spent with my twin and Roth, who'd never made good on his plan to send us to the palace, I missed Hartly like crazy.

But I couldn't be swayed from my current path. Operation Like Me More was for my sister's benefit, too. Security for me was the same as security for her—if she was in Sevón.

Had Ophelia done as promised? What was Hartly doing right this second? Did she blame me for Mom's death?

I'd never been so desperate for information, but Noel continued to ignore me.

I couldn't ask Foreverly. I'd already severed my link with the troll as easily as I'd created it—with a simple mental command. I'd had to. The temptation to take more and more of his power, *all* of his power, had only magnified.

During our treks, Roth always claimed the lead and commanded me to stay close to his heels. He would hack foliage out of my way and use his body to shield mine from danger. Every evening he foraged for fruit and nuts while I washed off the day's grime. He never delegated the task to one of his men.

"I can find my own food," I'd told him.

"You can, yes. But I enjoy satisfying your needs," he'd replied, sending electric tingles down my spine.

Sometimes he combed his fingers through my hair, or massaged my nape, or rested his palm on my lower back. I remained in a constant state of anticipation, hoping he would do more.

Today, we slogged through a marshy field scattered with trees, the ground shaking intermittently. In fact, a new tremor hit, and we had to pause our procession. Leaves rattled with more force, limbs clapped together and birds took flight.

Wherever I happened to stand, the earthquakes worsened.

Allura's doing? I doubted I'd been forgiven, but she hadn't tormented me in days. Birds no longer crapped on me, limbs no longer swatted me and roots no longer tripped me.

"The tremors are coming faster," Roth said, his jaw compressed.

I clung to a brittle vine, my bones like tuning forks. "Truly? You all right?"

Like me, she clung to a vine. "I'm good."

At night, we shared a tent and talked until one of us drifted off. Getting to know her was as wonderful as I'd hoped, but it made me miss Hartly even more.

In one of our gab sessions, I'd told Truly more about her cousin, and she'd told me more about her—our—father, scaring me further. "There were rumors. Whispers that my grandmother had an affair with a sorcerian overlord, and my father was the result." Her face had scrunched with distaste. "Before King Challen accepted my hand in marriage on Roth's behalf, he had an oracle read me to ensure I had no need to syphon."

Would I receive a reading before I gained entrance into the palace? Would it matter if I did? Noel could have spilled my secret at any time but hadn't. Why spill it now?

Maybe I should just go ahead and confess? How would she take the news? Would she understand why I'd remained mute, and forgive me? Would Roth?

We'd been together awhile now, and I hadn't syphoned from any of my friends. Hadn't I proved myself?

When the newest quake ceased, we soldiered on. Sweltering temperatures had reduced my insides to a nice, bubbly stew, my skin the bread bowl. No flowers flourished in the area, no insects crawled about. Char and ash hung heavy in the breeze, ruining my lungs. I coughed and coughed and coughed.

Clearly, living things came here to die.

Roth shoved a limb out of my way. "Are *you* all right, sweetling?"

"I'm fine, thank you," I muttered. "What about you?"

"I'm with you. I'm good."

The things he said… There was no one sweeter than Roth Charmaine. And no bigger jerk. How was I supposed to remain emotionally detached?

About an hour later, I grumbled, "How big is the forest?" Translation: *How much farther do we have to go?*

"Endless."

Behind me, Truly groaned. "There are entrances hidden throughout. The entire woodland is comprised of different dimensions smashed together. Allura has been known to trap people in the worst ones, just for fun. Witches do it for the right price."

Well. Multiple dimensions explained how I'd escaped the centaurs. How I'd gone from a wonderland of exotic flowers and majestic wisteria to something like this, a hellscape littered with quicksand and the remains of gnarled trees.

"Give me a reason to push on," Vikander said from behind my twin. "Cast an illusion, Everly. Naked beauties all around, gender optional."

I rolled my eyes. The fairy and avian had requested an illusion countless times. I gave them the same answer as before. "Dance monkey dance. No. Sorry, not sorry."

"Your fire illusion was remarkable," Saxon said. "The finest I've ever seen."

"Thank you." While I liked the avian and would enjoy amusing him—he rarely relaxed and always stayed busy protecting his friends—I couldn't do it unless I syphoned. "My answer is still no."

If another emergency presented itself, I wasn't sure what I'd do. Take from Allura again?

My apple birthmark began to heat, startling me. I tripped and would have kissed dirt if Roth hadn't caught me.

—*Everly! Hello, hello. Testing one, two, three. Is this thing on?*—

Noel. I snapped, *What do you want?*

—*I have news. Hartly is alive and well!*

Relief rained over the boiling cauldron of my worry. But I said, *I reached out. You ignored me.*

—*I know, and I'm sorry. I'm only one girl. Granted, I'm an amazing girl. Some might even call me a fairy godfriend. But even I have limits. So many dominoes to line up, keeping you safe, staying ahead of our foes, planning the taming of the trolls, all to ensure Enchantia survives the wars to come.*—

So much to unpack. And she wasn't done!

—*Don't worry. I'll let you know when you need to tag in. Until then, let's chat about Roth. Are you still concerned he'll fall in love with Snow White and kill you off?*—

Well, I was now. Did Noel know something I didn't? *Are you trying to tell me something, Oracle?*

—*I feel your fear and it's driving me batty. You realize fairy tales are sometimes symbolic rather than literal, yes? I've mentioned that fact? Like, when you left the mortal world, your old life died, and you started fresh. A clean slate.*—

Are the iron shackles and fiery death symbolic?

—*Well, they aren't not symbolic.*—

What did *that* mean? Lost in thought, I plowed into a tree and ricocheted backward. Sharp pain in my forehead, blood dripping into my eyes.

Truly gasped. "Everly!"

Roth backtracked fast, sheathing his sword and clasping my face with his big, calloused hands. He studied the gash. "It's shallow. You'll heal without scarring."

Even with sweat-dampened hair and dirt-streaked cheeks, he remained the fairest of them all. The most beautiful being ever to live.

I'd wondered before but had dismissed the idea. Now I *really* wondered. *Could* Roth be Snow White, even though he was jaded and domineering? Could *I* be Prince Charming? I had charm, probably.

Frustration frayed my nerve endings. Would I never figure this out? Everyone I'd pegged as a player in the fairy tale had traits that fit multiple characters. Even me! And where did this journey fall in the prophecy?

"Let's get you patched up," he said, brushing his thumb over my bottom lip.

While Saxon played nurse, handing over supplies, Roth played doctor, cleaning and bandaging the wound. I let my mind wander.

As soon as possible, I needed to do an intense study of the fairy tale, especially the Enchantian version. A thousand times, I'd almost broken out the one by the Brothers Grimm, but I'd been too afraid the others would catch me and speculate about why.

I just... I suspected we'd entered one of the many time gaps in the tale. "Soon afterward." "Later." "One day." A point when a catalyst occurred, driving the characters from one action to another as they prepared to face the big bad.

Would we soon be fighting another foe? What would happen next?

"Better?" Roth asked me.

"Yes. Thank you." His concern for me was intoxicating,

His wishful gaze sought mine, and longing arced between us, stronger than ever before, nearly turning me inside out.

—*This is better than mortal TV!*— Noel's casual comment reminded me that my birthmark hadn't cooled; our mental connection remained active.

Beat it, Oracle. You keep Hartly safe and continue keeping my secrets, and I'll stop driving you batty with my worries. Deal?

—*Deal. Oh, and Everly? One last thing before I forget. This next part is going to sting.*—

What are you talking about? Sting how?

The birthmark cooled, silence greeting me. Danged oracle—and danged oracle yeah.

Another quake started up, the stoutest so far. I rocked back and forth, my brain slamming against my skull. A crack forked over the ground, separating me from Roth.

Anger burned the filter from my tongue, and I shouted, "Enough, Allura! Stop the nonsense."

The shaking ended, and every member of my group peered at me with confusion, maybe even fascination.

"What?" I stomped my foot. "She's being ridiculous."

Suddenly, I lost the foundation at my feet, the crack expanding, land crumbling. I screamed as I plummeted into a dark pit. Roth lunged for me—

Yes! He caught my hand in his, his vise grip strong enough to crack bone.

I dangled there, frantic. Roth hung over the outer edge of the pit, the tendons in his neck strained.

"Don't let go," I beseeched. I kicked my legs, searching for a toehold. "Please, Roth."

"Never," he vowed.

The ground gave a stronger shake, and I whimpered.

"Saxon?" Roth demanded.

The avian stood behind him, features dark with concern, wings flapping. He gripped the prince's ankles, ensuring he wouldn't slide away. "The pit is too narrow. I cannot fly inside it."

"Wildander," he demanded next.

"Working on it," the fairy said. As Truly handed him metal shavings, he created and planted spears on both sides of Roth, giving the prince hand and foot rests.

"I'll pull you up as soon as I'm stabilized," Roth told me. "Any minute."

With Prince Roth Charmaine on the case, I had no need to panic. "Thank you. I—" Something hard and strong clamped around my ankle and yanked. "Roth," I shouted, kicking my legs once again.

"Everly!"

Yank, yank. I fell deeper, and Roth fell with me, refusing to let go.

"Losing my grip," Saxon snarled, attempting to lift us both.

I couldn't let Roth and Saxon hit bottom with me. Doing my best to sound calm and assured, I said, "Release me, Roth. Now."

"Never," he repeated with just as much conviction.

I pried my fingers from his, one by one.

"Everly, don't. Don't!" He tightened his hold...

"I'm glad I met you, Roth. I love you, Truly. Vikander, Saxon, you aren't so bad."

"Everly!"

My hand slid free, and I tumbled down. Impact! Pain! The rocky ground pulverized my legs, and the backpack I'd insisted on carrying myself nearly broke my spine. Stars flashed over my vision, and my stomach heaved.

When I was able, I dug inside the pack and withdrew a dagger and a flashlight. Then I clambered to my feet.

What monster would I be forced to face this time? Some type of mole shifter?

The flashlight illuminated a narrow carven with crystal walls, and open passages into other caverns. Water dripped, the sweet scent of roses somehow overshadowing the muskiness of earth.

"Everly!" Never had Roth sounded so rattled. "Stay where you are. I'm coming for you."

"I'm okay," I called. Oh, crap! A boy stood a few feet away, and I nearly jumped out of my skin. He loomed inside one of the passageways. "Stay where you are!"

He was over six feet tall, leanly muscled and as beautiful as he was frightening. He had a mass of curly blond hair, blue eyes and tanned skin, his features too perfect to be real. In black leather, with a sword rising over his broad shoulders, he looked like a fallen warrior angel.

He inclined his head in greeting. "I apologize for causing the quakes," he said, his voice deep and melodious. "I had orders to speak to you, *without* slaying your companions. Since the prince would attack me on sight, I had to get you alone."

Allura hadn't been responsible for the quakes? *My bad*, I thought, patting a cavern wall. "You caused the quakes, just to speak to me without Roth's interference? Why? Who are you?"

"I am Tyler, and I am at your service. After years away, our overlord has returned. He says I am to guard you with my life."

Our overlord. Tyler was sorcerian—and he knew *I* was sorcerian, too. "What makes you think I'm like you?"

He frowned. "You are the niece of Nicolas Soren, yes?"

Niece, not stepdaughter? How could... Unless...

I replayed Truly's confession. A former sorcerian overlord was rumored to have had an affair with our grandmother. Nicolas was that overlord's son. Nicolas, who'd admitted he might be the new overlord.

Nicolas, brother to Stephan and Edwin...my *legit* uncle?

"How were you able to speak with Nicolas?" I asked, heart misfiring. "He's still in the mortal world." Right?

"He is not. He found a way home, and he's searching for your sister." Moving too swiftly to track with the naked eye, Tyler clasped my forearm. Where we touched, I blistered.

Wincing, I wrenched away. The faint outline of a palm print remained.

"What did you do to me?" I demanded.

"I gave you a way to contact me. If ever I'm needed, just fit your palm over my print," he said, "and I will find you."

He'd *marked* me? I ground my teeth.

"Everly!" Roth's voice. Louder now. Closer.

The sorcerian narrowed his eyes and rested his hand on the hilt of his sword.

"Go," I whispered, waving Tyler away. "I decline your offer of protection. I've gotten good at protecting myself." *Better that way.* I would never betray myself. What's more, I didn't want Tyler and Roth fighting. Someone would die.

"We *will* see each other again. Soon," he said.

A prediction or a threat?

He held my gaze as he stepped back…soon vanishing in the shadows. Perfect timing. Using tree vines as rope, Roth was lowered directly in front of me.

Cuts and bruises marred his face, and blood splattered every inch of his exposed skin, yet he'd never been more beautiful.

He looked me over. "Any injuries?"

This boy… Despite the danger, he hadn't hesitated to come to my rescue. Because he liked me. Because he didn't know who or what I was—yet.

Foreboding flared to life once again. I'd told Noel I wouldn't distract her with my worries. What good had worry done me anyway?

I needed to win Roth over faster. I needed to admit the truth and face the fallout, whatever it was. Because being with him felt…inevitable, with fate playing matchmaker.

19

Your dreams have come true.
Why are you so blue?

Once we cleared the overly hot, pit-filled wasteland, we crossed through another invisible doorway. Dimension. Whatever! We entered a land of blue. Blue trees, blue flowers, blue mushrooms plucked straight from Alice's Wonderland.

"Anything?" Roth asked Truly.

"Always! The apple is close," she said, frustration pulsing from her. "I don't understand why I can feel it, but not see it."

Vikander motioned to me with a tilt of his chin. "Perhaps the apple isn't an apple at all."

Roth and Saxon stared at me and nodded.

They thought *I* was the apple? I frowned. Was I? I supposed I could be. I was *bonum et malum*, after all. But then, so was Truly.

Maybe, "the" apple referred to two apples. One life, one death. One saved. One killed.

I gulped, then shook my head. "Sorry, guys, but you've got the wrong girl. I'm not a healer or a killer." Not purposely. Although, I *could* syphon from multiple healers, steal their magic, and save King Challen. Life and death from one little apple baby.

Trepidation twisted my stomach. But again, I wouldn't be killing anyone. Not healers. Not Snow White. By the sheer force of my will—and each of my decisions—I would never be the apple.

"We've lost the trolls." Saxon landed in front of us, tucking his wings into his back.

The brutes had caught our trail again this morning, their commander's determination to slay me unwavering.

"And the centaurs?" Roth asked.

Yeah. Violet's horde continued to chase me. So far, we'd managed to evade it, too.

"No sign of them," Saxon replied.

A family of pixies glided over, elegant and graceful, pulsing with iridescent lights as they performed tricks and flips around the avian and the fairy, as if showing off.

Vikander shooed them away. "Thieves and mischief-makers, the lot of them."

"We'll stop here and set up camp," Roth called.

Here—a small clearing surrounded by towering fruit trees. No apples, dang it. Would we ever find the (real) Apple of Life and Death?

Roth grabbed the satchel he always kept close and stalked off. Just before he disappeared in the forest, he tossed me a heated glance over his shoulder.

Every sensation he'd ever roused in me flared anew, leaving me breathless. How could one person affect another so strongly with a simple look?

Vikander grabbed the bag of iron shavings and began nailing spears around the perimeter, as usual. Saxon erected tents, then fed and watered the horses. We'd found them several days ago, unharmed. Truly prepared food.

I was tasked with gathering firewood and digging a firepit. With my backpack in place, I headed down the same path Roth had taken. The desire to see him, to *be* with him, tempted me beyond measure.

Detecting splashing sounds, I quickened my step. I had to push past a hedge of flowers and dodge a swarm of bees, but I found a lovely pond, the water clear as crystal.

Roth discerned me as he swam. After smoothing wet hair from his brow, he walked forward. The closer he came, the more I saw of his incredible body. Those broad shoulders. The rippling muscles in his chest. The pierced nipples and elaborate tree tattoo, with swirling limbs forming varying patterns. A shiny red apple dangled.

A tree with an apple. Coincidence? "Maybe *you're* the Apple of Life and Death," I said. He kept walking, about to reveal his lower half... I spun around, my cheeks burning as if I'd returned to char-o-land. He was naked, wasn't he?

Magnificent male. The epitome of perfection.

Don't stare at him. But I really, *really* wanted to...

A few feet away, a pixie was busy gathering his clothing. Intending to steal the garments?

"Get lost," I said, waving my hands. Wait. What was I doing? Helping Roth cover up all that muscly goodness? For shame!

The pixie giggled as she flew away without his clothes. Dum mer

"Did you miss me?" Roth asked, material rustling as he dressed.

"I'm, uh, on the hunt for firewood." *But yes. I did.* I spied several stray limbs not too far away, layered with pink fairy dust. Sweet! When burned, fairy dust smelled like caramel.

"I'll gather firewood while you bathe," he said. "I promise not to peek...more than a few dozen times."

Laughing, I spun back around. He hadn't donned a shirt, only pants. The waist dipped low, revealing a dark goodie trail. *Eyes up!* Right. Cheeks flaming all over again, I looked over the rest of him. From shoulders to ankles, he was littered with gashes and bruises. Each one served as a reminder: he'd put his life in danger to save mine.

As he prowled toward me, my heart thudded. He stopped only a breath away—still too far. With two fingers under my chin, he gently nudged my gaze to his. Water droplets clung to his lashes. His irises burned white-hot with zero frost.

I breathed deeply. His cinnamon and nutmeg scent had a piney layer, crisp and clean, and well within the Christmas wheelhouse. My new favorite smell.

"But," he added, "you'll owe me a wood-gathering tax."

I snorted. "What is today's currency?"

"More of whatever I'm seeing in your expression."

"Admiration? Or drool?"

A husky laugh teased my ears. "I want both," he said. He stepped back to pull on one boot, then the other, but draped his shirt over his arm. "You know what else I want from you, sweetling?"

A kiss? *Please, be a kiss.* "Tell me."

"Information," he said, and my good humor drained. "You are smart and brave, but secretive. You rarely reveal personal details about your life. You are a contradiction. You keep a mirror close, but you do not care what anyone thinks of your appearance. You are protective of Truly, and genuinely like her, but you sometimes watch her warily as if you expect her to hurt you. Vikander amuses you, but you prefer Saxon because he is also protective of Truly. As much as I have watched you, you have watched me, just as warily as Truly. You carry a book about an Evil Queen and a girl named Snow White, which makes me wonder if you are part of my prophecy."

My eyes widened. And he thought *I* was smart? My perceptive prince had me pegged to a T. I wore my wariness like a second skin.

I should have realized he'd seen my book the morning he'd dug through my bag. *Breathe, just breathe.*

"Am I right?" he asked softly.

"I don't want to talk about this." Not yet. I wasn't ready.

He sighed and traced a fingertip along my jaw. "One day, Everly, I hope you'll trust me. Until then…"

Everly, not sweetling. Until then…what? We couldn't be friends?

Tell him something personal. One little tidbit. Trust begat trust, and I needed his trust.

"There *is* a prophecy." I peered down at my wringing fingers. "One I think we have in common."

"And who do you think I am?"

I licked my lips and admitted, "I think you are Prince Charming. And not just because of your title and last name. When you smile, you charm the uncharmable."

He blinked, surprised. "Perhaps my advisors never made such a connection because they've never seen my smile?"

"Who do they think you are?"

"The Huntsman."

Was that who he most identified with? "I think Truly is the Huntsman. Her magic fits. Though I admit I change my mind about who is who all the time."

"You are not alone. I once considered Truly the Huntsman, as well, but I now see her as one of the seven protectors of Snow White…who I believe is my sister."

Seven Protectors. Yes. A perfect description.

And dang, but I liked this, liked bouncing ideas off each other and comparing notes. If Farrah was Snow White, maybe *Truly* was Prince Charming.

"Who do you think *you* are?" Roth asked.

Never mind. I didn't like this. "Maybe I'm the boar the Huntsman kills," I grumbled.

"You *are* a tasty piece of meat…"

I snorted, and he added, "Perhaps I've been wrong about myself and Farrah. Perhaps I am Prince Charming, as you believe, and you are Snow White. This hair…the color of moonbeams and frost." He pinched a flaxen wave between his fingers. "Your passion for life fits. You tease princes. You protect princesses and poisonous spidorpions with the same fervor."

Me? Passionate?

He snagged me around the waist and pulled me closer. I leaned against him, resting my ear against his chest. The swift beat of his heart soothed me. Sunlight had warmed his skin, the decadent heat seeping past my clothing.

"Any ideas about the Evil Queen?" Maybe I'd been worried for nothing. Maybe I simply hadn't met the real one. Or maybe I was right about Violet.

Petting my hair, he said, "Soon after my mother died, my father married Farrah's mother. In fact, the day she gave birth to Farrah is the day the prophecy was spoken. As desperate as my stepmother was to preserve her youth and beauty, I always believed her to be the Evil Queen."

I kissed his chest directly over his heart, and said, "She was cruel to you?"

"At times. But I loved her. She was the only mother I knew."

"I'm sorry."

Still petting. "In the prophecies, death isn't always physical, you know."

"I know. But…"

"But still you worry," he said.

"I have a sister. Hartly. She communicates with animals. What if *she* is Snow White? What if you fall in love with her at first sight?" As I spoke, I realized the fear had been inside me all along; it had just been hidden by my worry about my heritage.

"You should fall in love with her, and you could! She's wonderful, and she's here. Ophelia brought her to Enchantia."

"I could, but I won't." He sounded certain.

"How do you know?"

"I just know," he said. "How can I want one, when I crave another?"

He'd just…he'd admitted he craved me. Who did that? And when could I get him to do it again? "Wh–what if *Hartly* is the boar?"

"Then I'll pay Ophelia for a protection spell. I'll pay Noel for insight and answers."

"Really?"

"Really." He rubbed the tip of his nose against mine. "I had planned to summon the witch and oracle anyway, to pay for *your* protection spell, and insight about your future."

Reeling, I leaned back to thump my chest. "Your, as in *mine*?"

"You and no other." His eyelids turned heavy, his voice thickening. "I want you safe, Everly. Always."

My heart swelled with lo— like for him. So much like. "I don't know what to say, Roth."

He cupped one side of my face, holding my gaze, and swiped his thumb over the rise of my cheek. Then he leaned down and pressed his forehead against mine as if I'd become some sort of lifeline. "Say you're glad you met me when you aren't afraid you'll die."

"Are you kidding? I am! The gladdest."

The corners of his mouth quirked. "I'm glad I met you, too. Now, go for a swim and cool off. I'll take care of the fire, tax free. But only this once."

"Thank you, Roth."

"For you? Anything. Always."

Here it was, an opportunity to reveal my secret. *Do it. Tell him.* He would be upset at first, but he would soon realize I was still me; I was still his sweetling.

The way he looked at me...the way he teased me and comforted me... He *couldn't* hate me. Everything would be okay.

So why did the foreboding come back stronger, as if my heart knew something my mind didn't? As if my present and my future were about to collide...

20

*If a warning sounds deep in your soul,
pay it heed or pay the toll.*

Roth strode off, a tower of strength and beauty. Everything I'd ever wanted. I stood there, my emotions running the gamut. I was falling for him, my mission to remain detached forgotten.

But I wouldn't let myself worry. Not because I'd promised Noel I'd do better, but because I knew Roth would catch me.

Only seconds later, a grinning Truly came bounding past the wall of foliage. "The prince told me to relax with you, that he would start the fire and prepare dinner."

Could he be any sweeter?

"What have you done to him?" she asked with a laugh.

"What do you mean?" I stripped down to a bra and panties as well as the necklace and signet ring. No way I would risk a theft-by-pixie. But I'd have to be careful. *Can't let her see the starburst pattern*. If she noticed, she would have questions I wasn't ready to answer.

"You've changed him. Once, he had stone around his heart. Somehow, you chiseled it away." She stripped down to a loose tank top and pair of pantaloons, the outfit reminding me of something I'd once seen in a history book. Half prim, half proper, all old maid.

"You've seen me, right?" I fluffed my hair.

Another laugh burst from her.

I waded into the cool water and dove under the surface, every speck of dirt dissolving from my skin. Truly dove in next.

When she came up for air, I said, "Truly, you know I consider you one of my dearest friends, right? I don't just like you, I love you."

"Um…" She nibbled on her bottom lip as she swam a circle around me. "I consider you a dear friend, too, and I have no desire to hurt your feelings. I'm just not interested in you romantically, Everly. I'm sorry! I'm in love with someone else."

I fought a smile. "I'm not interested in you romantically, either." *By the way, I'm your sister. Surprise!* "So, who is it you love romantically?"

A pause. More nibbling. "Roth's sister," she whispered. "Princess Farrah Charmaine. I miss her so much. She's the most amazing person I've ever met. Kind, compassionate. Generous. Witty. Fierce."

The fact that she'd trusted me with the knowledge—I wanted to bang my chest like a gorilla. Such sweet progress! The fact that she rambled on about the girl—adorable. "Thank you for telling me."

"Please don't mention this to Roth. He doesn't know. Actually, no one but Saxon knows. Our parents would not approve, for a royal must do her duty and produce an heir," she said, reciting what she'd probably heard her entire life.

Though I already knew the answer, I said, "Does Farrah feel the same way about you?"

"She does. But she loves her brother, too, and she would rather die than hurt him."

"Roth has mentioned her a time or two, and I could tell he adores her and wants her to be happy. If being with you makes her happy…"

"Yes, but he still cannot break our engagement without starting a war between our kingdoms." Dejection settled over her, her shoulders rolling in. "A selfish part of me wants him to do it anyway."

"If he is Prince Charming, but you are not Snow White, he won't marry you and there won't be a war." Right? This fairy tale had a happy ending for everyone but the Evil Queen.

Her jaw dropped. "You know about the prophecy?"

"I do. I've discussed it with Roth because…it's my prophecy, too. I don't know what part I play, exactly, but I'm here to find out."

"So many things make sense now," she breathed. "Namely, why I've felt connected to you from the start."

Because we are sisters. Twins.

Tell her.

And ruin this ease we had? No! Not yet. But soon.

The longer I waited, the more betrayed she would feel. I got that. And no matter what, Truly would still like me. Just as Roth would. I was certain of it now. Mostly certain. I just needed to find the perfect time and place…possibly when we reached his palace.

She floated on her back. "I think I'm the Huntsman, or one of the Seven Protectors."

Well, well. Someone else who identified with more than one character. If only I knew what it meant. And it *had* to mean something.

Before she could ask which part *I* played, I told her, "I have an idea. While we're on this quest for the apple, let's forget about prophecies and wars. You're just a normal girl, engaged to a normal boy, and I'm the magnificent femme fatale determined to steal him away from you. I'm going to step up my game."

She snickered. "I meant what I said. I've never seen the cold-as-ice prince so fascinated by another person."

This wasn't the first time she'd referred to him as ice-cold. And yeah, I'd had the same impression once or twice, especially when his eyes frosted over. But honestly? He was mostly fury and passion, with a fervent zest for life.

"What kind of girls does he usually prefer?" I asked.

"A variety. Only one of his relationships ever lasted—that I know of—but he ended things the day his father announced our engagement."

Okay. I maybe might have possibly experienced a slight, teeny-tiny, hardly worth mentioning, unexpected prick of jealousy. "Who was she?" *And how soon can I drain her?*

Whoa! Where had *that* thought come from?

"She's one of his sister's ladies-in-waiting," Truly said.

"Tall, short? Curvy, thin? Mortal or mythical?" *Stop!*

"Short. Curvy. Mortal. Her name is Annica, and she's all that is kind and graceful." A teasing light glowed in my twin's eyes. "This news upsets you?"

"Yes! Right now, I want to drop-kick Annica into the pit I escaped." I bet she was the girl I'd seen in his bed. His usual type.

"But," Truly added, "she never made him laugh."

"*Of course* she didn't." I preened, smoothing a lock of wet hair from my brow. "Where others fail, I prevail."

Another snicker.

We splashed around, and after a while, my fingertips resembled prunes. We got out and dried off, and Truly dressed in a clean, well-made and serviceable gown.

"Where do you guys get your clean clothes?" I asked. I'd

asked before, but no one answered me. "I've never seen anyone do laundry. Or carry a bag of supplies, for that matter."

"I'm not supposed to say, since others would kill to possess it. But it's you, so... Roth has an enchanted satchel," she admitted with a grin. "It was a gift from his father. You've seen it. The one with the metal shavings. It has the power to produce any tangible item we request, as long as it fits within the cloth."

Amazing!

As she left to join the guys, I thought I spied a shimmery entity hiding in the shadows. Curious but leery, I made my way over to investigate...and found a cluster of berries and a gorgeous dress made from moss and flower petals.

More gifts from Allura? Had I been forgiven? "Thank you," I called.

Wanting to look my best—only because I had more charming to do, definitely not for any other reason—I brushed my hair and pinched my cheeks for color. Using the berries, I stained my lips a stunning bloodred. After donning the new dress, I spun in a circle and laughed. The best part? I smelled magnificent, like a summer garden.

When I checked my appearance in a compact, I longed to see Foreverly. Alas. There was no sign of her.

"I need a permanent power source," I muttered to a tree. Just in case something went wrong. "Will you share with me, Allura? Pretty please."

One minute, two. No response.

Sighing, I returned to camp. Everyone sat before the fire, a waft of dark smoke carrying the fragrance of caramel and cotton candy. Roth perceived me first, then the others. Conversations ceased. I'd never been shy, but here, now, I battled an intense surge of nervousness as if I'd just bared a part of my soul.

Roth looked me over slowly. *Achingly* slow. He stood, closed the distance and lifted my knuckles to his mouth. One kiss, only one, and I felt singed to the bone.

"You are a goddess," he said. "The living embodiment of the moon. Both ice and fire."

His praise went straight to my head, as potent as the wine he'd once given me. "You are..." *Everything.*

In a white tunic that molded to the rows of strength in his chest, black leather pants and combat boots with blades attached to the toes, he looked every inch the warrior prince.

Firelight adored him, the flickering flames paying homage to his arresting features. Light and shadow embraced him, one after the other, like warring lovers fighting for his attention. *My turn. No, mine.* I yearned to brush my fingers through his windswept hair.

And how had I ever considered his eyes frosted? Those sham-rocks *smoldered.*

Sorry, Annica, but this girl will not share. I hadn't fought for Peter, but I would fight for Roth.

"You cannot think of a single word to describe me?" he asked, almost pouting.

I chuckled at his very human reaction. In our time together, I'd seen many different sides of Roth. Confident. Amused and amusing. Angry. Hurt. Remorseful. Arrogant. Protective. But never vulnerable—until now.

And it was then, at that moment, that I knew beyond any doubt. I *had* gotten the fairy tale wrong. Even if I was the Evil Queen, my demise by fire would not be literal. This amazing boy would help me torch the past and start my new beginning.

"I can't think of one," I finally said, and he frowned. "I can think of hundreds. *Glorious* being at the top of the list."

My reward: a slow, sinful grin and heavy-lidded eyes. "That is compliment enough. For now."

"Find a cave," Vikander called.

Saxon guffawed. Giggling, Truly slapped the fairy's chest.

Roth mumbled something about making the fairy eat his own teeth, then escorted me to the firepit. I eased beside Truly, accepting a wood plank topped with a veritable feast of vegetables and fruits. When the prince attempted to sit at my other side, Vikander hurriedly scooted over, blocking him.

I smothered a laugh. Truly tried to do the same but failed. Vikander and Saxon offered wide, toothy grins, daring the prince to comment.

Expression inscrutable, Roth settled *behind* me. Resist the urge to lean against him? Impossible. Between my shoulder blades, I felt the erratic pounding of his heartbeat, a mimic of mine.

"I appreciate the feast," I said. "My compliments to the chef."

"The fruits fell from trees as I walked past, as if in offering." Roth's warm breath fanned my crown. "I stumbled upon the vegetables. A garden unguarded by man or beast."

I toasted the trees with a jug of wine. "To Allura, then."

As we passed around the jug, I missed the convenience of ceramic mugs. Considering who I might be, though, I supposed I should prefer to drink from the skulls of my enemies.

"You always smell incredible," Roth whispered, his voice like gravel. He traced his nose up the column of my nape, inhaling deeply. "Like apples dipped in honey. I *love* honey-dipped apples." The dark, primal look he gave me…

I couldn't mask my shiver. Seriously, was this boy even real? Or had I somehow conjured him from a dream?

Even when he became absorbed in a conversation with Saxon, some part of him remained attuned to me. As he played with my hair, I closed my eyes and savored the sensations. Peter had never acted as if touching me was a privilege. He'd never openly admired me, or held me just to keep me close.

How had I missed the warning signs?

Feeling a gaze upon me, I cracked open my eyelids. Vikander watched me, with his head tilted to the side, his eyes swirling…holding me captive…swirling, mesmerizing… Dizzy, I rubbed my temples.

"Think I drank too much wine," I muttered.

Voice soft, Vikander asked, "Are you here to harm Prince Charmaine or Princess Truly?"

"No, of course not." The words left me of their own accord, just as soft as his. We were in our own little world. "I love Truly. I like Roth." Did I love him, too?

Oh, crap. Did I?

No. Not yet, I rushed to assure myself. In that regard, fear had aided me, preventing another Humpy Dumpty fall.

"What of King Challen, Roth's father?" Vikander asked. "Or his sister, Princess Farrah? Do you plan to harm them?"

"No," I said, the word slightly slurred. *Still so dizzy.* "I want to save his father and love his sister. Angel." I frowned. "Something's wrong. My head…"

"Enough," I thought I heard Roth snap from a great distance.

"Nothing's wrong." Vikander released my gaze and stared into the fire. "Everything's right."

The dizziness fled, the world coming back into focus. Saxon was engaged in a conversation with Truly. Roth glared daggers at the fairy.

A sickening suspicion got tangled up in my mind. Somehow, Vikander had forced the truth out of me. I would have answered anything he'd asked.

Anger seared me like a hot poker. "How did you do that?"

He hiked one shoulder. "I asked questions, and you answered."

"He mesmerized you. A fairy trick," Roth explained, the words as sharp as a blade. "He magically coerced you to respond to his queries honestly."

Vikander pursed his lips, all *come on, bro.*

"I told you not to do it," Roth said to him. "You disobeyed, I punished."

I bristled. "Unless you want to uncage my rage, Viks, don't do this again."

"Why?" Voice like silk, the fairy asked, "Do you have something to hide, Everly?"

Yes! "*Everyone* has something to hide. Including you, I'm sure."

He narrowed his eyes, black lashes glittering as if dipped in stardust. He opened his mouth to say more, but Roth cut him off.

"You will *not* mesmerize her again. She is off-limits to you, always, in every way."

I didn't mean to, but I smirked. *Take that, mesmerizer!*

"Know this, and know this well." Vikander raised his chin and directed his next words at me. "I will do *anything* to protect Roth. Cross any line, risk any consequence. Long ago, I pledged my life to the betterment of his, and I refuse, absolutely refuse, to break a sacred oath."

"I understand the need to protect a loved one." I admit, I would have done something similar if someone had come sniffing around Hartly or Truly. "But we've been together awhile now. Why not interrogate me earlier?"

"You had no influence on the prince back then."

And I did now?

Roth offered no argument or rebuke, so maybe I *did*.

"Strip away my free will again," I said with gritted teeth, "and I *will* retaliate."

"What will you do?" Vikander took a page from my playbook and rolled his eyes. "Illusion me to death?"

His mockery chafed. I could do things. Tons of things. He had no idea. If I so desired, I could syphon his power right now. I *should* syphon his power.

My fingers twitched, temptation beckoning. *Reach out. Take. Make him eat his insults.*

But that was what he hoped for, wasn't it? To goad me into performing. The more he knew about my abilities, the better he could protect the prince, if ever I attacked. In the end, I said, "Pray you never find out."

Truly leaned around Vikander to meet my gaze. "You're probably wondering about the best way to harm a fairy. Unfortunately, there isn't one. They regenerate too swiftly. Well, from everything except the touch of a necromantic sorcerer."

"You wish to harm me?" Vikander flattened a hand over his heart. "Mission accomplished, princess. Words hurt."

She rolled her eyes, too.

I flipped through my mental files, the ones containing info I'd gleaned from Mom's long-ago bedtime stories. "Necromantic is...communicating with the dead?"

"That is one of the definitions, yes," Roth said. "Another is when the sorcerian have syphoned too much power from others, turning their blood black with antimagic."

"Antimagic?" I asked. I'd never before heard the term.

"When magic has become toxic, a single brush of the sorcerer's skin against yours is as painful as it is lethal."

Great! Another worry to cart around. Not only could I syphon others to death, I could take too much and kill innocents with a touch. Go me.

Seeking comfort, I shifted and sank deeper into Roth. How quickly I'd come to rely on him. The one thing I shouldn't do. What if I lost him? What if I lost them *all*?

I gazed around at our group, wondering for the millionth time what part Vikander and Saxon played in the fairy tale.

I'd told Truly to forget the prophecy while we pursued the apple, but my survival depended on my choices. Even if Roth hadn't been fated to bind me in iron and set me on fire, he *was* destined to fall in love with Snow White. One look at the girl's dead body and his feelings for me would wither. Even his dream girl couldn't compete with true love.

Perhaps Vikander and Saxon were two of the Seven Protectors. A fairy godfriend and his magic wand?

Godfriend—a word Noel had used. *On the right track, I know it.*

So badly I wanted to summon Foreverly and learn her thoughts. Too much time had passed since we'd spoken.

"I've seen you in this state often," Roth said, his warm breath fanning the shell of my ear. "You stare off in the distance, your worry palpable. Not knowing what is bothering you...it makes me feel like I have a thorn stuck in my brain. I can think of nothing else. The desire to slay your dragons and present their heads at your feet becomes all-consuming."

How did I tell him the girl who refused to lie had been living one since the moment we'd met?

"Tell me *something* about yourself," he intoned. "Anything."

"You know everything that matters."

"Do I?"

"Yes!" Being a sorceress *shouldn't* matter.

When I offered no other reply, he huffed with frustration.

"Ah, is the big, bad prince pouting?" I asked, hoping to tease him from his dark mood.

"The big, bad prince is brooding. There's a difference."

"Ooh la la. Do tell."

"Pouting—childish. Brooding—practically a mating ritual. Admit it, you can barely keep your hands off me."

I laughed, but quickly sobered. *Look. See.* The impulse bombarded me.

Look. See. Do not delay.

I unearthed my compact and held it close to my chest. Had something happened? I needed to know. I needed to know *now*.

Without a power source, I couldn't summon Foreverly.

Think, think. But my mind refused to cooperate, different thoughts set on shuffle. Hartly was in trouble. The time gap had ended, and the fairy tale prepared to reveal another scene.

21

Secrets are there, yours for the taking.
Please be careful, the beast is awaking.

I lay atop a pallet of furs, the compact still in my hand. A few feet away, Truly slept on a pallet of her own. Her deep, even breaths harmonized with the forest choir: chirping crickets, buzzing locusts, croaking frogs, singing birds and howling wolves.

Instinct continued to scream at me, keeping me awake. *The worst has happened. Look. See. Do not delay!*

Noel? I mentally shouted. *I need another reassurance. Tell me Hartly is okay. Tell me Truly isn't in danger. Tell me Roth is on the right path.*

Not knowing why I felt such foreboding, I could easily consider Hartly both well and hurt. I could imagine danger both headed for Truly and not headed for Truly. I could believe Roth was both my friend and my enemy.

Silence.

Noel! If you continue to ignore me, we're done.

I waited.

Waiting…

Inside me, urgency and frustration were a ticking time bomb.

If you won't tell me, I'll be forced to syphon from one of my companions.

Still waiting… *Tick, tick, tick.*

I ringed my fingertip around the compact. Should I at least *try* to summon Foreverly without syphoning from someone else?

Little hinges creaked as I opened the lid—oh, sweet goodness. Tired eyes stared up at me, glassy with panic. My cheeks were pale, my pale hair tangled from tossing and turning.

"Tell me why I'm feeling such a dark premonition," I whispered.

Tick, tick—

Boom! The bomb exploded, decimating my resistance. *No more waiting.* To find answers, I needed a power source. I wouldn't syphon from Truly, even though we had a wonderful bond in place already. *(Note to self: Were bonds the same as links?)* I wouldn't syphon from Allura, either. Lesson learned. Three potentials remained: Roth, Vikander and Saxon.

They had supply; I had demand.

What magical ability did the prince wield? Once, he'd touched me and my pain had faded. Would he notice if I borrowed a mere drop of his power, especially if I took it while he slept? He'd probably recover by morning. And really, he'd said he wanted to help me. Had he meant it?

Risk: after spending time in an altilium, he would hate the sensation of linking and syphoning.

Could I really hurt him in such a way?

No. I couldn't. And I wouldn't. The experience would be different with me. We liked each other. I just… I didn't want to link with Vikander or Saxon. I wanted Roth. Only Roth.

Reward: saving Hartly, if necessary. And if my win-him-over plan failed, I could weaken him and strengthen myself. *Attack first, die last.*

I curled my hands into fists. Why was I even debating this? The prince *owed* me power. A consolation gift for breaking my heart in the future.

And he *would* break my heart.

With Peter, I'd never been emotionally invested. Looking back, I saw the truth so clearly. With Roth, I'd tried to remain detached…on occasion, whenever I'd remembered. But here I was, obviously attached. He intrigued, amused and delighted me. The slightest graze of his fingertips made me burn. His protectiveness thrilled me, and his sense of humor left me giddy.

But the secret sorceress would never win the beloved prince. I'd been fooling myself. Because if I admitted my secrets and asked to borrow some of his power and he refused, I would resent him. I would blame him for whatever travesty occurred.

I couldn't come out and ask him, either. He might rally his defenses, stopping me before I started.

If I was going to do this—successfully—I couldn't warn him ahead of time. I had to violate his trust.

Unease clambered inside me. *Oh, looky. Everly is torn in two again.* Part of me wanted to end this now. The other part of me wanted to do anything, hurt anyone, to save my sisters.

Did they need saving? Until I spoke with Foreverly, I wouldn't know.

I had to know.

Very well. Decision made. I would do it. I would syphon from Roth.

I *must* be the Evil Queen.

How could I take from Roth, when I couldn't see him? Always before, I'd had a direct sight line to my battery. Or in Mom and Hartly's case, that unshakable bond. What if I accidentally took from Truly?

I imagined the layout of the camp. The prince slept in the tent next to mine. Saxon slept in the one next to Roth's, and Vikander patrolled the camp's perimeter. Maybe if I angled my hand in the prince's direction?

I rolled to my side—and my whole body jerked. The spidorpion was perched at the edge of my pallet.

When my heart decided to restart, I whispered, "What do you want?" Why continue to follow me? I frowned as I studied him. There was something different…his poor tail! The stinger had been removed. "What happened?"

The little monster skittered over—and bit my wrist. Pain spread through the rest of me, an avalanche of fire and ice. I wanted to scream, *needed* to scream, but I couldn't use my muscles. I melted. I froze. My vision hazed, and my head spun, around and around and around.

Breathe, just breathe.

Trying. Trying so hard.

An eternity passed, or maybe just a few minutes. Any second I would die…

But the pain, heat and cold began to ebb at last. Suddenly, I could breathe again. Gradually, I refocused.

The little POS watched me with his beady eyes.

"I saved you from death by boot, and you punish me for it?" No wonder I'd always hated arachnids. Jerks! At least I knew I would recover from a bite. "Thanks *tons*."

Truly stirred behind me, and I stilled, my heart galloping.

You imprisoning me, yes.

Once again, my whole body jerked. The words had drifted through my mind, clear as a bell. Just as Noel's had. Which meant I'd heard his thoughts…the way Hartly heard animal thoughts? Crappity, crap, crap! Was I syphoning from my sister?

I checked my internal power gauge but felt no influx of power.

Still whispering, I demanded, "How are you talking to me?"

—*I do trade. I no sting, but I speak to you.*— He hopped up and down on the pillow. —*We friends now, me and you. Yes, yes?*—

He'd traded his stinger for a way to communicate with me? *Me?* Who would demand his stinger as payment for— Never mind. A mercenary witch. Maybe even Ophelia. But why?

"I'm not worthy of such a sacrifice," I told him. "Go and get your stinger back."

—*We not friends?*—

Were his eyes…watering? Great! Now *I* wanted to cry. "Fine," I said. "We're friends. But my advice hasn't changed. Go get your stinger."

Hop, hop, hop.

His excitement was contagious. "What's your name?"

—*No name.*—

That wouldn't do. "How about I call you Phobia?"

—*Everly and Phobia friends.*—

"Everly and Phobia friends," I echoed. "But friends don't hurt each other, okay?" *Take a lesson, Morrow.* I cringed. "You don't use me as a snack pack, and I won't stomp on your guts."

—*No snack pack, no guts.*— He scampered off, disappearing under the tent, his steps jaunty.

Bite, bam, thank you, ma'am. Whatever. I had more pressing matters to attend to.

Heart a war drum, I reached out and flattened my palm on the ground, just like I'd done amid combat with the trolls. I angled my fingers in the direction of Roth's tent and gasped. In an instant, my fingertips heated, power pouring through me. I didn't have to establish a link first? We had one already?

I drew from him. Mmm. More! Had I ever experienced anything so sweet?

What was *he* experiencing?

Guilt scorched me. I turned my attention to the compact. As usual, ripples heralded Foreverly's appearance and excitement followed it. I'd missed her!

Her makeup was bolder than usual. Currently, she had the smokiest smoky eyes that had ever smoked. Even better, she had *Scarlet Letter*–red lips. A ruby choker adorned her neck, and a scarlet halter top barely covered her chest.

My girl had style.

She'd changed her hair, most of the strands jet-black. Only the locks framing her face remained silvery-white.

"You know why I summoned you," I whispered.

"Look," she said, waving her hand. As she faded, Nicolas took her place. "See."

Fresh tears welled. Despite everything, I missed my stepfather's stoic presence. Not that he was stoic right now. He scowled at Ophelia, rancor smoldering in his eyes.

The witch stood inside my living room, Hartly at her side. Wearing a dress she'd made from one of Mom's old comforters, Hartly clutched Thor close to her chest.

My tears spilled over, the sight of her as much a torment as a soothing balm.

Nicolas spat, "I won't let you take her from me, witch. We go together, or not at all."

"I owed, I offered. She accepted." Ophelia spread her arms in a gesture of innocence. "*She* understands the troll commander cannot be allowed to murder Everly. For the good of Enchantia, he must travel a different path."

Terror clogged my throat. Hartly and the troll commander... a couple? No wonder Foreverly didn't trust the witch and oracle. From the beginning, the deceitful pair had planned to offer my sister to a savage killer.

"Don't do this, Harts," I whispered. Could Nicolas talk Hartly out of it?

Why hadn't Ophelia gone back for Hartly sooner? Unless... Was I seeing into the past?

Surely not. Why feel foreboding over something that had already happened?

He debuted his *oh, really* expression. To Ophelia, he said, "Explain why the troll commander won't kill *Hartly*, or use her as bait to draw Everly out of hiding."

I wasn't hiding!

"Trolls have but one *maritus*," the witch replied, "someone they do not harm for any reason. We believe Hartly is the commander's, that she alone can—" Ophelia frowned, shook her head. Glowered. "You're syphoning from me. Disgusting leech. How are you doing it? I have blocks."

Confirmation! Some people had an ability to erect blocks.

Nicolas grinned, unrepentant, maybe even a little cruel. "I *always* find a way."

Ophelia stepped toward him. "I will rip out your heart!"

He stood his ground. "Rip away. I'm sure it will tickle. But there is nothing you can do to convince me to let you abscond with my stepdaughter. I vowed to protect her, and I will."

Go Nicolas!

"I do not need to convince you of anything," the witch said with a grin. "I need only take her."

"Hartly," he snapped.

"I'm sorry, Nicolas." My sister gave him a sad smile. "I hate to leave you behind, but just because I hate it, doesn't mean it's wrong. If I fail to return to Enchantia tonight, trolls will attack Everly, and she will die. If *I* must die to save her, so be it."

"Hartly," he snapped again, his tolerance eradicated. "Everly is stronger than you think. She can emerge from any battle victorious. Let her. Why risk yourself for the girl who killed your mother?"

I sucked in a breath, a dagger of pain nearly flaying me alive.

Hartly jutted her chin. "I do not blame Everly for what happened. Had you or Mom warned us… Well, it doesn't matter now. What's done is done." A fat teardrop slid down her cheek. "Goodbye, Nicolas. I love you, and I hope to see you soon."

Reeling…

My wonderful, amazing sister still loved me, her support unwavering.

Smug, the witch clasped Hartly's shoulder, then waved her free hand. A second later, darkness dominated the glass. Then Hartly, Thor and Ophelia reappeared, surrounded by trees and a familiar azure glow, hundreds of animals vying for my sister's attention.

She laughed and spun. "I'm here. I'm really here!"

My foreboding skyrocketed. Yes, she was here. Without protection and as ignorant as I was.

"Are you ready to meet your troll?" Ophelia asked.

She nibbled on her bottom lip. "You swear Thor won't be hurt?"

"I do. I swear it."

"Then yes." Hartly shuddered but squared her shoulders. "I'm ready to meet the troll commander and save my sister."

22

Hurting others comes with a great cost.
Piece after piece of your heart, until you are lost.

Had I seen into the past? Or the present? Either way...
On a mission to find Hartly, I jolted upright. What
if she *wasn't* the commander's *maritus*? Another word for "soul
mate," I'd bet. What if he hurt her?

I yanked on my pants and boots, terror and rage battling inside
me. Terror centered around Hartly's well-being. Rage wanted
to punish Ophelia for her betrayal.

My birthmark began to burn, signaling an incoming call from
Noel.

—*I know you don't understand why.*—

I spit curses at her before snapping, *You're right. I don't understand why you would put an innocent girl in danger.*

—*For the salvation of the land, sacrifices must be made. I told you,
war comes. Good against evil. I've seen what happens if evil wins. So
I need you to trust me, your mediocre friend.*—

I don't care about coming wars. I care about my family. And you just put my family in danger. Pause. Deep breath. When did Hartly arrive?

—*When else? The very day Noel had always planned.*—

Blood roared inside my ears, my head going light. *Days.* My sister had been with the trolls for days, while I'd vacationed with Truly and Roth. *Why am I just now sensing trouble?*

—*Because things aren't going as planned?*—

My temper sharpened. *We're done. Don't contact me again.*

—*Why are you so upset? I've seen Hartly's future. As long as she remains in the troll dimension, she doesn't just survive. She thrives.*—

You're still talking?

—*Oh, Everly. Is this really the hill you want to die upon? Fair warning. Every decision has a consequence, and you're not gonna like this one.*—

My birthmark cooled.

Screw her! I grabbed my cloak and did a quick pat-down. Necklace, wrist cuffs and daggers. Check, check, check.

Truly slept on, undisturbed.

Still linked to Roth, I waved my hand over the compact and whispered, "Show me the best path to reach Hartly."

New ripples, then an aerial view of the camp appeared, a path highlighted, again like GPS on a smartphone. We were so close! Only a five-minute run apart.

Urgency invaded my bones. I waved a hand a second time, cloaking myself with invisibility, then raced out of the tent. Moonlight painted the land in black gold. The temperature had dropped significantly, a storm brewing. Frost drizzled the trees.

Charged by adrenaline and Roth's power, I quickened my pace, passing Vikander, sprinting around trees and rocks, jumping over vines. No shouts of alarm sounded; relief gave my feet wings.

Another fifty steps, and I would reach Hartly…

Faster… I huffed and puffed. My nose burned. My lungs, too.

Red eyes watched me from the trees. Buttress roots even slithered out of my way. Almost there…

Someone tall, dark and leanly muscled stepped into my path. Unable to slow my momentum, I slammed into him and ricocheted backward. When I landed on my butt, I lost my invisibility. I jumped right back up, swinging my fists.

He moved out of the line of fire and into a beam of moonlight, revealing familiar features. Dark blond hair, golden skin and amber eyes.

"Nicolas?" I said and gasped. He wore a black tunic and leather pants, not the button-down and slacks I'd seen him in only minutes before.

"None other."

I threw myself into his arms, shocked but happy. And guilty! Why had I ever doubted him? "How are you here? I saw the witch take Hartly and leave you behind." Yes, he'd syphoned from her, but he'd lost the connection as soon as she'd returned to Enchantia. He couldn't syphon from a distance the way I could. Or could he?

"I already had a way home. I would not have traveled to the mortal world without one," he said. "I chose not to use it until the witch came for Hartly."

"Where is she? Do you know?" According to the map, she should be five feet away.

"I have been searching for days. Tracked her here, then lost her trail."

Fear devoured my calm in one tasty bite. "The mirror says she's here."

"Here but not here. The trolls must have taken her to another dimension. With the witch's help."

Hate the witch! Will kill Ophelia for this.

As long as she's in the troll dimension, she won't just survive. She'll thrive.

"We need to find the doorway." Or shift the curtain.

"Not a doorway. All access points are sealed with magic. We need a portal and a key."

Like, a literal key? "Are you still linked to Ophelia? Can you syphon from her, and use her magic to create what we need?"

"I have saved the power I took from her, but it's a minute amount. Not nearly enough." He ran a hand over his face. "I must set up another altilium."

"You can create a portal and key if you have an altilium?"

"If I choose the right members, yes."

"I'll...help." For Hartly? Anything.

He projected surprise. "I've been gone so long, I don't yet know who can do what."

"What type of magic do you need the members to wield?"

Rather than answer, he said, "In the mortal world, I offered shelter to Enchantian refugees, as long as they spilled information about royals and witches. *That* is what I was doing when Aubrey... When she died." His voice cracked, and he pulled his gaze from me as if he couldn't bear to face me. "The information has proven faulty, however. In the past few months, many royals have passed away."

"If it's the last thing I do, I will find and save Hartly." Had Noel told the truth about her safety? If I had to syphon from her and Ophelia, I would.

"You should go, *niece*," he said. "I will stay. I will find her."

Niece. "Are you really my uncle by blood?" More staunchly tied to me than Aubrey, my aunt by marriage.

"I am, though not even Aubrey knew it. Not until the end." A flash of grief in his eyes, quickly gone. "Years ago, an oracle found you and sold the information to your father. Stephan had always regretted his inability to kill the babies conceived after the consumption of his apples. He'd tried with all but Truly, of course, yet fate always stepped in, ensuring someone showed up and saved the children every time. He asked me to journey to the mortal world—to behead you."

Why, why, why did the reminder still hurt?

"I fell in love with Aubrey instead," he continued, "and decided to stay in the mortal world, lest the king send someone else to kill you. And he did, time and time again. Your mother never knew, because I took care of it. I should have forced her to return to Enchantia before…"

Before I killed her.

And he despised me for it. I saw it in his eyes, heard it in his voice, and I couldn't blame him.

"You need to stay away from Hartly," he said, "or she will suffer the same fate."

I wrapped my arms around my middle and just…shattered. Was he right? If I harmed Hartly, I wouldn't recover. Ever.

The frantic *thump-thump* of footsteps disrupted the quiet. Panic seized me, but there was no time to act. Roth and Saxon exploded past the trees, their swords drawn.

The prince noticed me, then Nicolas, worry and relief transmuting into rage and loathing. He halted in front of me, using his body as a shield.

Saxon flew over the sorcerer and landed behind him.

Tyler revealed his presence, zooming from the inky darkness to flank the avian, pressing the tip of a sword into Saxon's neck.

"Don't!" I shouted. "No one has to get hurt today."

"You." Accusation turned the word into a dark curse as Roth glared at Nicolas. "The overlord's son. I have waited years to face you. Now here you are, daring to abduct someone under my protection—daring to syphon my power."

I struggled to breathe, *in, out, in, out*, every exhalation accompanied by a wheeze. Had *Nicolas* helped imprison Roth and his family?

"I dare many things, oh mighty Prince of Sevón," my stepdad said, his voice pure silk. "Tonight, abduction and syphoning are not among them."

Shame and guilt twined. Letting Nicolas take the fall for my crime would be so easy. And because of their past interactions, Roth would believe my stepdad culpable, no matter what he claimed. *The temptation…*

I had a choice. I could continue keeping my origins a secret—and remain fearful of Roth's reaction, like a coward—or I could admit the truth, as I'd needed to do for days.

Besides, why did the opinion of someone who might come to despise me matter?

Please, don't despise me.

"He didn't steal from you, Roth," I said, shaking in my boots. "I did. I—I am a sorceress. I am Nicolas's niece and stepdaughter."

Comprehension seemed to dawn in waves. First, he radiated shock. Then he stiffened. Then he tightened his grip on the sword hilt. His muscles knotted, and rage electrified the air.

"Roth," I croaked. "Please don't—"

"I'll deal with you in a moment." He glared at Nicolas. "I'm going to enjoy killing you."

"Perhaps," my stepdad said, "but you are too weak to succeed."

Too weak, thanks to me. *Strangling…*

"I'd link and make you weaker, but it seems I've been link-blocked." Nicolas winked at me and said, "Good girl. Now be a better girl and deal with your new pet. Keep him out of my way, and I'll rescue your sister."

Only one sorcerian link at a time? *So much to learn.*

My stepdad walked toward. He was about to knock into Saxon—

Nope. He ghosted *through* the avian and sidled up to Tyler, rattling me. "I will do whatever proves necessary to help Hartly," he said. "Will you?"

The two sorcerers vanished in a blink, leaving me to wonder if they wielded illusion magic, too, or if they could teleport. How many magical abilities did they wield?

Why leave me, really? Because I was well trained in self-defensive and able to care for myself, or because they did, in fact, need me to keep Roth busy?

Either way, I was on my own.

Roth wasted no time, spinning to face me, his eyes as frosty as his mountains. Guess it was time to deal with me.

"You stole power from me, weakening me minutes before I faced a hated foe," he snapped.

"I did." I squeezed my eyelids closed. Able to breathe again, I inhaled deeply, exhaled heavily. What to do? A lie might help tonight's situation, but it would taint every other encounter we ever had. "I'm worried about my sister. I didn't know Nicolas had come—"

"I *told* you I would help Hartly," he interjected. "You could have asked me for power."

"Like you would have said yes. You kill sorcerian, Roth, you don't aid them." I moved closer, hoping to touch him. Needing to. "What I did was wrong. I knew it, but I did it anyway. A mistake I regret with every fiber of my being. I'm sorry I hurt you, but I'm not sorry I learned about my sister."

He sprang out of range, avoiding contact. "You regret it with every fiber of your *sorcerian* being." Was that disgust in his eyes, in his voice? Or despair? "You hid your origins from me."

"Think of everything you've said about the sorcerian. Can you blame me?"

"You *used* me," he snarled. "From the beginning, I was a means to an end."

"No." I shook my head. "Never."

"You are a sorceress. Related to the son of the man who abducted and tortured my family, who laughed as we suffered and ignored us when we begged for help. Like him, like them all, you steal from others with no thought for the well-being of your victims."

His words hit me like fists. *Punch, punch, punch.* I recoiled, just kind of crumpling into myself, instinct ensuring I protected my vital organs.

I thought I'd shattered before. Wrong. "I've been with you for weeks," I croaked. "I syphoned from you once. Once!"

"You are evil. You are—" His eyes widened, and I knew. He'd just pegged me as the Evil Queen.

"I didn't pick my lineage out of a catalog." I hadn't signed up for Evil Queen tryouts. "Fate chose for me. Why am I being punished?"

"Fate didn't choose to syphon from me tonight. *You* did."

That was fair. A dagger to the gut, but fair. My throat clogged. I blinked back tears and choked back sobs. With my actions, I'd killed Roth's affection for me, adding fuel to the fires of his hate…almost as if I'd fed him a poisonous apple.

He would never forgive me, and I couldn't blame him, either.

Glaring at me, he said, "Bind her." His frigid voice froze my soul.

Wait. Did he say *bind* me?

Saxon moved closer without a word.

I leaped into motion, running fast…faster. But the avian dove on me, knocking me to the ground. Just before we landed, he drew my arms behind my back. Though I fought, twisting, punching, kicking, he secured my wrists together, using my own cuffs against me, wrapping the garrote wires around the leather.

Landing jarred me and jumbled my thoughts. I was too fraz-zled to react as Saxon confiscated my daggers and compact.

Roth observed the entire exchange, silent, his body like stone. His every breath was ragged, his hands fisting and unfisting.

"Please don't do this," I whispered.

Unfazed, he said, "The time for conversation is over."

Rejection. Anguish. Shock. They packed a punch as power-ful as his words. "Why don't you bind me yourself? Unless the big bad princeling is too afraid to handle his dream girl?"

A muscle jumped beneath his eye, making me think he felt as I did. Rejected, anguished and shocked.

Guilt punched me harder than anything else. I'd hurt him deeply, inexorably.

If I could manage an illusion, I could escape, giving Roth time to calm while I searched for Hartly.

Knowing action would unleash magic, I tried wiggling my fingers, but nothing happened. I tried yanking my wrists apart, but the wire sliced into my skin, the pain excruciating. I hissed and stilled. Okay. So. I needed full mobility to use my magic.

"Just let me speak to Princess Truly," I said, "then I'll be on my way. You'll never have to see me again." The moment the words left my tongue, I wanted to snatch them back.

I didn't want to cut him from my life. We could fix this.

"Your word means nothing to me. Less than nothing." He motioned to Saxon.

The avian pulled me to my feet. I wrenched from him and lurched toward Roth.

"Ophelia delivered Hartly to an army of trolls," I rushed out. "Let me save her. I know I don't deserve your trust, but I'm begging you to give it to me anyway."

Tension strung his body as tight as a bow. "With my voice, I can compel, forcing others to do anything I desire, even against their will. For years, I have refused to use my ability. Then you came along. When your head hurt, I told you to feel better, and you obeyed."

Fear iced my heart. "Please, Roth. Don't—"

Staring at me with brutal intensity, he said, "You will return to camp, Everly. You will not syphon from Vikander, Saxon or Truly. You will not hurt them, period. You will not escape. Go. Go now."

His voice...deep, husky and mesmerizing, far more potent than Vikander's. Though I did everything in my power to remain in place, compulsion annihilated my free will. I placed one foot in front of the other, marching forward, heading back to camp, unable to stop myself.

Dress for the job you're going to want...the King of Compulsion's obsession.

Noel's words. Roth, the King of Compulsion.

If I was his obsession, I could get through to him. I *had* to get through to him. "I'm sorry for what I did to you," I shouted. "Don't punish Hartly for my mistake. She's in danger. If something happens to her, I will blame you as much as Ophelia and Noel. We will become enemies."

"How have you not realized the truth?" he called, merciless. "We are *already* enemies."

23

Time is of the essence and quickly running out.
Fight, fight, fight and ditch the overgrown lout.

Though I stumbled on my return to camp, I did not fall. Though tears filled my eyes, I did not cry. Though my world crashed and burned around me, I did not crumble again. I had breath, so I had hope. I had fury and hate. I would escape, and I would find Hartly. Somehow.

I just needed to syphon from Roth. And I could. The link remained. What's more, he hadn't compelled me to stop, not with him. Unless he *wanted* me to keep doing it so that Nicolas and Tyler couldn't syphon from him? Or maybe he'd omitted the command on purpose, to test me?

I'm ready for my F, Professor Roth.

Not yet, not yet. First, I needed my hands free. Then I would use his magic against him. In the clearing, when he'd ordered me to go back to camp, I'd had no immunity to it, even though his power swam in my veins. Therefore, he would have no immunity against my compulsion...

Silly prince. He'd underestimated me to his peril. I almost smiled.

Truly entered my line of sight. Suddenly, I wanted to cry. Clad in a nightgown and cloak, with a bow slung over her back and a quiver dangling from her side, she paced in front of our tent. Vikander stood behind her in battle position, ready to attack any foe who dared approach.

I stepped on a twig, drawing her attention. She whimpered with relief. "Thank the stars! You are safe." Noticing my bonds, she frowned. "Why is she tied up? Free her immediately, Saxon."

He'd followed overhead and now landed at my side. "She is a sorceress. The one who syphoned from Roth. We caught her scheming with Nicolas Soren, son of the former overlord."

"No." Truly shook her head, dark hair dancing. "You're mistaken."

"He's not." I lifted my chin, as Hartly had done. "I'm a sorceress, and Nicolas is both my uncle and my stepfather." *Surprise! He's your uncle, too.*

She recoiled, hissing, "Monster!"

And I'd thought our parents' rejection had hurt. This one cut deeper. Stephan and Violet hadn't known anything about me, while Truly knew more than most.

"I feared you were going to be locked inside an altilium." Disgust all but dripped from her. "But you're one of *them*. You do the locking."

Ignore the pain. "I'm not just one of them. I'm the best of them." Why had I let myself be ashamed of my origins? I could do things most people couldn't. "I wish I'd taken *more* from Roth."

She clutched her stomach as if hoping to ward off a sudden ache. Vikander regarded me with curiosity, and Saxon blanked his expression, revealing nothing.

I didn't need these people! I didn't.

I just needed Harts.

"If my sister is hurt…" I contorted this way and that, pulling the garrote wire taut. Again, the pain was excruciating, threatening to fell me. Worth it! I slid my bound hands under my butt, then worked my legs behind my arms, one at a time, without toppling. "Heads will roll."

"Place her things in Roth's tent," Saxon told Vikander, handing off my precious possessions, "then help me check the perimeter for other sorcerian."

"Am I to restrain her further?" Vikander asked.

"No need. Roth has compelled her." Saxon turned to Truly. "If she asks for aid, shoot her."

How easily they spoke of harming me.

How easily you harmed Roth.

I gulped. The guys marched off. *Now or never.* I swallowed my guilt and fury, choosing to muster on. "Listen, and listen well. You and me? We are sisters. Twins. King Stephan is my father, and Queen Violet is my birth mother. Nicolas is your uncle."

"No." She stumbled back. "You're lying."

Full steam ahead. "Our father ordered our deaths. Violet and Aubrey tried to escape with us, but they were caught. Aubrey got away and took me to the mortal world, along with her daughter, Hartly. We remained there until Ophelia came with news of Stephan's death."

"That cannot be. I…I am not a sorceress."

"Our magical abilities are different, just like our hair and eye color. You are more like Violet, and I'm more like King Stephan. You might not need to syphon, as I do, but you do have a connection to the sorcerian. The rumors about our grandmother's affair with the overlord are true."

Paler by the second, she shook her head. "You have no proof of this."

Despite my bonds, I was able to reach up and yank my necklace, breaking the chain. I tossed both pieces of jewelry at her.

Again, she stumbled back. The necklace and ring thumped against the toe of her boot.

Another shake of her head. "This proves nothing. Rings can be stolen. Where is Aubrey? I've seen her portrait. I'll recognize her. Or not."

"I told you. She's dead." Miserable, I admitted, "I didn't know what I was, or what I could do...didn't know I'd stolen from her every time I'd used my magic. I—I killed her."

Shake, shake, shake. "I would be a fool to trust you. You'll say anything to gain an ally." She started to turn away.

I rushed out, "You've felt our connection from the beginning. It has nothing to do with the fairy tale, and everything to do with us."

Pause. A tear trickled down her cheek, nearly breaking me all over again.

I might not need her, but I wanted her. I still loved her.

"Why would my mother keep you a secret?" she asked softly. "Why would Ophelia and Noel?"

"Violet believes I will steal her crown. Ophelia and Noel are schemers. Everything they do serves an endgame I'm not privy to. I only know they delivered Hartly to an army of trolls." And turned me into a powder keg ready to blow. *Calm. Steady.* "Hartly is my sister by heart and cousin by blood. *Our* cousin. And you're right. I'll do anything to save her—but what I will or will not do doesn't change the truth."

I stepped forward, hoping to clasp her hand. She stepped back. *Ignore the flare of pain.*

"If ever Roth learns of our connection," I told her, "my fate will become yours."

Behind me, leaves and limbs clapped together. Heart in my throat, I spun. Roth stalked into camp, his scowl darkening the closer he came to me. "Attempting to work your wiles on another victim, sorceress?"

"Like it's hard?" I offered a smile with bite. "I had you panting for me in record time."

He ran his tongue over his teeth, the picture of exasperation. "You act as if I'm the one who did something wrong. I'm not. You are the liar. You are the thief."

"You're right," I said, all sugary sweetness. "I should have confessed my secrets, even though your hatred for the entire race was crystal clear and I feared you'd cut off my hands. What a fool I was. When the next prince comes along, I'll tell all. Do you think he'll tell me if he's engaged to another woman like you...oops, never mind."

He jerked his narrowed gaze to Truly. "Return to your tent, Princess. The sorceress will spend the night with me, and I will ensure she does not hurt anyone else."

All innocence, I said, "The good prince wants to have a pants party with the bad sorceress? Is it my birthday, or yours?"

Looking like the world's worries had settled on his shoulders, he scuffed a hand over his face. What, he'd expected me to take every insult he dished? "Are you *proud* of the trouble you've caused, sorceress?"

"Who wouldn't be? If only I'd caused *more*." As he sputtered, indignant, I raised my chin even higher. "I've made mistakes. Some intentional, some accidental. If you want to yell at me for syphoning from you, go for it. I deserve it. I betrayed your trust in more ways than one. But I won't accept blame for every mistake every sorcerer has ever made."

He gave me a gentle shove toward the tent. I stumbled inside. Before coming in behind me, he called, "Whatever you overhear, no one enters."

As the tent flap fell into place, I caught a final glimpse of Truly and her disgusted expression.

Watch Everly pretend her heart isn't crushed. Loathed by my parents and *my twin sister.*

Fate—2. Everly—0.

"You will go to the bed and sit," Roth said, his voice like smoke, filling me up. "You will stay there until I give you permission to rise."

Another compulsion. My feet walked me to the furs of their own volition. *Hate this! Hate him! Hate myself.*

"Admit it," I said as I clumsily sat. "Compulsion is the only way you can score a girlfriend."

The muscle started jumping in his jaw again. He sat at a desk made by Vikander. Tomorrow the fairy would use his magic to return that desk and chair to metal shavings.

Roth poured himself a drink of...whiskey? Down the hatch.

"You said you despise your magic and never use it," I said, as if he needed the reminder. "How wonderful that you decided to make an exception for me."

He poured, downed and stared at the daggers in the center of the desk. My daggers.

I'd never been inside his tent and now studied every detail. A small hole in the roof vented smoke from a central firepit. Only four pieces of furniture—the desk, the chair, a metal trunk and the pallet of furs created by the enchanted satchel.

Once he'd teased me about his need for a maid. A total exaggeration. He kept everything neat and tidy. Just the way he wanted his life.

"I didn't imprison you, Roth. I didn't kill your mother and brother, either."

"Nicolas's father kept us locked in a dungeon for months," he snapped. "At first, he used me to keep my mother and brother docile. When he realized what I could do, my age mattered little. He syphoned from me, too. I *felt* it, every time. The loss of strength. The flood of weakness. Then *you* syphoned from me, treating me as he did. As if my only value came from my magic."

Strangling again. "I apologized, and I meant it. I'm sorry I hurt you. If you need to spill my blood to forgive me, so be it. Spill my blood. Then we can part ways."

Dark, silken locks tumbled over his forehead. He thrust a hand through the strands, a gesture of pure frustration, yet he had a boyish aura. A lie! He wasn't a boy—he was a royal warrior.

"If I let you go," he said, "you'll steal from others. *Harm* others."

"I might *borrow* from others, but I never purposely harm. I just… I do what's necessary to protect myself and my family."

He poured another glass of whiskey, downed it. "I think I've found what I've been searching for. So. Tomorrow we will begin our journey to Sevón."

He'd found the apple? "I don't understand."

"How many times was Truly certain we had neared the Apple of Life and Death? Yet we never stumbled upon it. Now I know you have the ability to syphon from healers, killing them while bringing life to another. Life and death. You can deny it all you want, but I know you are the apple, Everly."

"Maybe I am," I whispered, shocking him.

He did a double take, as if I'd sprouted horns.

"But you… You are a hypocrite, Roth. You'll make use of my abilities as long as they help you. You'll take any measure to save your family, no matter how despicable, but woe to anyone who does the same for theirs."

Done with him, done with this day, I reclined on the pallet. Phobia! My heart leaped. He perched on the pillow.

—*I bite prince. You run.*—

Darling spidorpion! He'd just shown me more kindness and support than my own twin. *You don't want to help me.* I projected the words at him, the same way I'd done with Noel, hoping he would hear. *I use magic, which means I'm your worst enemy. Plus, I can't run from here. Compulsion won't let me.*

—*We not enemies. We friends. I help friend.*—

He did hear me. He also knew everything about me and liked me anyway. *Thank you, sweet Phobia, but I must decline. If you help me, the prince could hurt you. I'd rather you stay alive and well.*

—I help.—

Maybe you can, without going near the prince. Can you break the wire binding my wrists? Dare I hope?

While Roth downed another shot, hopefully too distracted to notice, Phobia crawled over my arm to gnaw on the wire.

One minute passed, two. The wire finally snapped, and a mewling sound escaped me. The little baby had done it!

Thank you!

"Hey. What are you doing?" Had Roth slurred his words?

What to do with my newfound freedom?

Pretending my wrists were still bound, I gave him the finger. "My mother told me evil can wear many faces. FYI, tonight it wears yours."

He poured and downed another shot and grumbled, "What does FYI mean?"

"It stands for *focus, you idiot.* Hint—you're the idiot. One day, the day you smarten up, you'll regret your treatment of me."

He poured, downed. Dare I see this drinking as a vulnerability—for me? If he passed out before I'd gotten him to undo his compulsion...

"Stop drinking and start enjoying the moment," I said. "You have me at your mercy, princeling. So, show me mercy."

Poured. "Do you think I have mercy to spare for a sorceress?" Downed.

"I'm the one bound and under threat. What do you have to drink about?"

He glared at me. "Sorcerers are parasites. Leeches."

His insults were like barbs, lodging deep in my heart, leaking poison.

"Sorcerers are also as human as you, with feelings, hopes and dreams." Using the lewdest, crudest tone I could manage, I said, "Or are you trying to hint that you'd like me to suck on you?" Considering how many innuendos I'd had lobbed at me, I had a ready store on tap.

He choked on the next shot.

I eased upright to offer him my most maniacal grin. This time, he didn't laugh.

If I did what I was about to do, he would hate me more. And always.

Could he hate me more?

"Roth?" Using the link between us, I syphoned a stream of his power, taking as much as I could, as fast as I could. In seconds, compulsion tingled on my tongue.

He paled and tottered on the chair.

Guilt flared. I'd just hit him with the same weakness, reminding him of a past he'd rather forget.

Before he could stop me, I said, "You will give me permission to rise from this pallet and say nothing else."

He had opened his mouth, but no sound emerged. He leaned back, disappointment settling over his features. If my heart hadn't been a pile of rubble, I would have shattered again. This *had* been a test, and I'd just failed.

Don't care. Voice breaking at the edges, I added, "You will not speak again until I give you permission. You will not attack me or hurt me or follow me when I walk out of this tent. And I *will* walk out of this tent."

Scowl returning, deeper and darker, he stalked across the tent, closing in...

24

*The deeper you wade into trouble,
the quicker your life becomes rubble.*

I halfway expected the prince to laugh in my face. Instead, he obeyed my every command, fury shimmering in his eyes.

"You may rise," he said with gritted teeth.

Laughing, I stood and patted his cheek. "Good boy. Now sit on the pallet."

Though his muscles bulged, signalling he fought my compulsion, he sat. He watched, seething, as I gathered my things and sheathed my daggers at my side.

"I'm curious," I said. "I know you wanted to test me, but you're also smart enough not to let a sorceress get the upper hand. Why didn't you compel me to stop syphoning from you?"

Silence.

How—oh. "You will answer me," I said, "then return to your silence."

A vein popped out in the center of his forehead. Again, he fought compulsion. Again, he failed.

"I knew you couldn't syphon from me, despite the link between us, as long as your hands were bound. I hate that link... but I like it, too. I feel you here." Glaring at me, he gave his chest a hard pound. "Didn't want it to end."

I didn't... I couldn't... He liked me despite everything?

Or he had. Until I'd acted like the Evil Queen.

"I feel sorry for you," I told him, wanting him to hurt as I hurt. Sue me. "I could help you in a thousand different ways. I could *harm* you in a thousand different ways, too. Guess which way I'm leaning."

He made a choking sound.

Pretending to check my reflection, I opened the compact. With a twirl of my fingers, I summoned Foreverly.

She appeared with a sad grin. "I know you desire answers about Hartly, but Ophelia has hidden her. However, the witch cannot block the whispers of the forest's inhabitants, and they say Hartly is unharmed."

Unharmed—for now—but probably terrified. Whatever fate befell my sister would befall Ophelia, Noel and all the trolls, as well.

I'd never been so excited to hurt another person.

Rather than thank my inner self aloud, I winked and shut the compact, then turned to Roth, who examined me with a furrowed brow.

"What?" I asked with a shrug. "I'm beautiful. I like beautiful things." I performed a slow spin. "Though the view from behind is just as spectacular, is it not?"

His expression said, *The next time I get my hands on you...*

As I approached him, I couldn't help but draw a parallel between Violet's life and my own. She couldn't blame fate for her predicament. Her own choices had led her down that dark,

dark road, reducing her to a cautionary tale. Those choices had shaped her...just as my choices would shape me.

Could I have been better, if I'd chosen better?

I patted his cheek. His thick shadow of stubble tickled my skin, just the way I lov—liked. *Ignore the arc of pleasure.* Pleasure was temporary. Revenge would last a lifetime.

"I could drain you to death and keep your magical ability forever," I reminded him. "There's nothing you could do to stop me. I *should* drain you. Otherwise you'll use the ability against me."

A vein bulged in his forehead as he continuously balled and unballed his hands. The muscle started twitching under his eye. All of his fury tells at once. Good. I'd made an impact.

"But," I said, "I'm a better person than you are. Clearly. I have mercy." I *wasn't* evil, and I would prove it. "I will allow you to live. After I find Hartly, I'll even go to your kingdom and save your father. On *my* terms. *If* I can. I'll syphon from healers, if they'll let me." I wouldn't kill them.

I made no mention of my plans for Ophelia and Noel. I hadn't yet worked through the details.

"Think of the irony," I said. "You despise the sorcerian, yet it is a sorceress who will save your father."

Tendons in Roth's neck pulled taut, his pulse hammering.

I sighed with faux regret. "Well, I must be off. Things to do, other people to save."

His eyes promised, *I will find you.*

My grin replied, *You can try.*

I moved to the tent's exit and paused. Should I make a pit stop in Truly's tent and speak with her one last time?

Despite our differences, I loved her. And, whether she accepted it or not, she needed me. One day others *would* find out about her connection to the sorcerian.

So, yes. I would make a pit stop. First, I had to get past Vi-

kander and Saxon. They stood outside the prince's tent, waiting
for his next set of orders.

My ears twitched, their whispered voices drifting on the
breeze...

"—certainly picked the right female," Saxon was saying. "She
makes him laugh. He never laughs. The problem is, amusement
is addictive. I fear he'll find a reason to forgive her."

"Let me put your mind at ease," Vikander replied. "He won't
forgive her because she makes him laugh. He'll do it because
he wants to *bed* her. I know romantic entanglements outside of
marriages, rituals and ceremonies are forbidden to avian, but I
thought I'd taught you the signs of amour."

Bed *me*? The parasite? The *leech*? I wished!

Fool! I had one way out of here—illusion magic. The guys
knew I could become invisible, and they might be on the lookout for footprints and the like. I'd have to go a different route.

Still linked to Roth, I pictured what I wanted and waved my
hand. Between blinks, his image was superimposed over mine.
Wow! My hands appeared so much bigger, so much darker, with
a light dusting of hair.

I glanced at Roth over my shoulder and grinned. "Admit it."
Sweet! I even had Roth's deep tenor. "You're more attracted to
me right now."

The vein in his forehead throbbed. The muscle under his eye
jumped faster. His hands *remained* balled.

"Tsk, tsk," I whispered, just in case the others listened in.
"Careful or you'll have a stroke."

I turned away before Roth could castigate me with his gaze.
Showtime. *I am the freaking Prince of freaking Sevón. Confidence
matters.* Chin lifted, scowl and broody arrogance in place. *Let's
do this.*

Hoping no one could hear the thunder of my heartbeat, I
stomped out of the tent. The fairy and avian shot to attention,
each one speaking over the other.

Vikander: "What did you learn?"

Saxon: "What is the plan?"

I held up a hand in a bid for silence. As soon as they complied, I said, "Go to your tents. Now."

Though they appeared confused, they didn't protest. They simply obeyed.

I've got this. I marched into Truly's tent, where she paced back and forth, once again wringing her hands.

The moment she spotted me—I mean Roth—she skidded to a stop. "D-did you kill her?"

Would you care if he did? "No one is killing anyone tonight." Very softly, I added, "I'm not the prince. I'm Everly, and I'm leaving this camp. Any interest in coming with me?"

"Roth," she said, and it was clear she hadn't listened. She stepped toward me, paused, then took another step. Tears had reddened her eyes and streaked her cheeks. "I know my opinion has little sway with you, but I need you to hear me. You should not kill her. Death is permanent. You can't change your mind after it's done."

Not exactly a declaration of love, but a good start. Taking a gamble, I waved a hand over myself, magically erasing the illusion.

She gasped and stumbled back. "Everly?"

"The one and only. Like I said before, our cousin needs rescuing. Once she's safe, I'll heal Roth's father. If I can. You can come with me." *Please, come with me* "We can do this together."

"I... No," she shook her head, bi-colored hair swishing over her shoulders. "I won't go."

Another rejection, as expected. *No big deal. Move on.* "Very well. I guess this is goodbye, then. If something happens to me, know that I love you, and I wish you the happiest of happily-ever-afters."

As Truly trembled more forcibly, I turned away before my willpower deserted me. Different noises erupted outside the tent.

Voices...hushed, rushed conversations...footsteps. Dang it! Vikander and Saxon had already figured out the truth.

No matter. To catch me, they'd have to find me. I waved a hand, conjuring invisibility, old faithful. If they found my footprints, they found my footprints. The risk could lead to a great reward. Freedom!

I bolted from the tent without delay and darted into the forest...and slowed.

I tried to quicken my pace but continued to slow. *Come on, come on!*

Finally, I stopped altogether. Though I fought, sweat beading on my brow, I couldn't move. My feet planted like cinder blocks. I lost my hold on the illusion, and I was too panicked to get it back. Dang, dang, dang.

Silly Everly. Roth's compulsion remained in play. I *couldn't* escape.

Heavy footfalls escalated in volume, until they reminded me of thunder. I even heard the rasps of my pursuer's breath...the swish of leaves... Birds took flight, and insects quieted. Who would I face? The fairy or the avian? Did it matter? The end result remained the same: *back to Roth I go.*

I bit my tongue, tasting blood. I'd failed Hartly, and I'd failed myself. All I could do now? Brace for impact.

25

Kiss me once, kiss me twice.
I will be your favorite vice.

A hard weight slammed into me, knocking me down. My pursuer hadn't realized I'd stopped, obviously, or he might not have sacked me like a quarterback.

I was flipped midair, allowing my captor to absorb the worst of the impact and cushion my fall. He didn't hesitate to roll me to my back, however, pinning me with his weight.

Roth!

From chest to toes, he stretched atop me. We glared at each other, our breaths ragged. Azure mist rolled through the forest, underscoring the rugged masculinity of his features. I saw fury…and desire?

"How is this possible?" I demanded.

He snarled but didn't speak. Because he *couldn't* speak. I had to give him permission first.

"Tell me," I demanded. "Speak."

The explanation came roaring from his tongue. "The bane of any compulsion? Other people. They are never bound by the same constrictions. Vikander sensed something was off and snuck into my tent. I couldn't move from the pallet on my own, so he carried me out. I couldn't follow you on my own; so Saxon flew me overhead."

Ugh. I'd made some beginner's mistakes. My commands should have been more specific. Noted. I would do better this time.

I prepared to issue another round of commands, but the POS beat me to the punch, growling, "You will *not* compel me again. You will not compel my men or Princess Truly. You will not syphon from me, my family or my friends. Or Noel or Ophelia. Or the citizens of Sevón."

The newest compulsion brutally murdered the words on my tongue. "If I can't syphon," I grated, "I can't protect myself."

I waited, hoping he would retract his final demand...

He went a step further—in the other direction. "To ensure you will not syphon from anyone I did not name, you will wear a torque," he said. "No longer will you be a danger to others."

Ignore the panic, forge ahead. I wouldn't give this smug prince the satisfaction of asking what a torque was, or how it worked. *Hate him!*

Using my silkiest tone, I said, "Look at you, loving your magic. If you lost the ability to compel, would you try to power-up in other ways, like, say, hurting innocent people? No. Not the mighty Roth. What if you had to hurt others to save your father or Farrah? Would you do it then?"

His lashes nearly fused. "Still unrepentant. Still proud of your actions."

Proud? No. "Should I apologize for doing everything possible to escape my jailer? Should I be drawn and quartered for attempting to save myself? No, that isn't terrible enough. The punishment should fit the crimes. I should be forced to listen to you prattle on about how evil I am. Yeah. That's the winner. That'll learn me *real* good."

Why didn't I just keep my mouth shut? Why did I continue to needle him?

Did I *want* him to snap?

Yes! Then the longing for him would fade.

"You represent everything I despise," he hissed.

The insult might have hurt more if I hadn't felt the evidence of his desire pressed against my belly. "Do I, then?" I all but purred. "Are you sure?" I'd seen this boy in battle. He'd been steady as a rock. Afterward, he'd killed his friend without hesitation. Now? With me? He *trembled*. I had power over him. Him! The strongest person I'd ever met. Delicious, irresistible power, no magic required.

The knowledge softened and emboldened me. I added, "For the sake of accuracy, let's ask the monster in your pants."

Growling noises rumbled in his chest. He looked ravenous, and dang if it didn't awaken an answering hunger in me.

"By the way," I said, "your face didn't get the memo. The way you're looking at me...as if I'm everything you've ever craved..." Dang it! That look started to mess with my head and make me wish for things I shouldn't want. Like forgiveness and a second chance. "You don't hate me, princeling. You hate that I'm still dressed."

"I will not crave a girl like you. I refuse." His muscles seemed to plump with aggression. "You are too bold, unpredictable and brash."

In other words, nothing like Annica, the lady-in-waiting he'd dated. Another insult blunted by his physical reaction to me. Blown pupils. High color. He clamored for every breath.

"Are you insulting me," I quipped, "or helping me draft a résumé?" Prince Roth Charmaine could refuse to crave me for a freaking eternity, but he already freaking craved me.

Expression tormented, he said, "I am fighting for my life."

I hadn't experienced pangs of regret since I'd let go of my grief. Now? *Pang, pang, pang.* They wouldn't stop. "You prefer wilting flowers?" I wanted to stroke my fingers through his hair, wanted to sweep my tongue into his mouth and slowly rip off his clothes. *Fool!* "Do you *dream* of wilting flowers?"

He ignored the questions, instead expanding the list of my perceived faults. "You are selfish. Greedy."

"I think you mean *protective* and *determined*."

"Devious. Untrustworthy."

"To my enemies, yes. I'm all of those things and more."

"Shameless," he spat.

"Don't forget unrepentant." As I spoke, his attention remained fixed on my lips. Lips I wetted languidly, dragging a ragged groan from him. "Poor Roth. How *hard* it must be to admire the very thing you claim to hate."

Who am I? When had I learned to tease and taunt like this?

Voice rough, he said, "You are wrong for me in every way."

My heart missed a beat, my lungs constricted, my skin pulled taut over my bones and rational thought fled. "I'm sure you're right...but you crave me anyway. Maybe you crave me *because* of those things."

He peered at my lips, so I wetted them. "Lord help me," he murmured, "I do crave you anyway."

The admission shocked me. "Does my Prince Charming want to be bad? We should star in a reality show. Fairy tale princes gone wild."

"Bad. Yes. Let this be bad." With a groan of surrender, he pressed our lips together and thrust his tongue into my mouth.

The smooth taste of whiskey seduced my senses. I wanted more, needed it, my resistance gone. Who was I kidding? My resistance had fled long ago. Control? I had none. The past and future ceased to exist. I became hyperaware of Roth, clinging to him. Clinging to this one perfect moment, losing myself... never wanting to be found again.

I was desperate for more, for all, for *everything*. No, no. I wanted freedom. I dang sure wouldn't offer this boy something he hadn't earned and didn't deserve. Any second now, I would wrench away, laugh cruelly and call him a fool for falling for my act.

Any second...

After everything he'd done, how could I want him? I didn't know. But...

I did. I wanted him. Frantic, fevered, I poured myself into the kiss. Forget wrenching away. I'd already jumped off the bridge, so to speak. A crash was inevitable. Why not enjoy the fall?

When he remembered what I was—and he would—he would shove me aside. He desired my body, yes, but he didn't like the rest of me. Understandable. I was a chink in his emotional armor. Because *of course* the big bad sorceress used magic to trick him into playing a rousing game of tonsil hockey.

He lifted his head to stare at me, as if starved for another glimpse of my face. His eyelids hooded. In the golden glow of moonlight, arousal stamped the planes and hollows of his face.

No, don't stop. Not now. Wasn't done, need more.

Between panting breaths, he said, "You taste like apples. As sweet as you smell. You *are* the Apple of Life and Death, Everly."

No. Absolutely not.

But maybe?

Worry later. Savor now. Already I could hear a new countdown clock in my head. *Tick, tock. Tick, tock.*

"Stop talking," I said, sounding drunk. His heady scent fogged my head. "Start kissing."

"What are you doing to me?" he demanded.

See? Already he sought some way to blame me for his desire. "I'm using magic to rouse your passions. Obviously."

He groaned again, a sound of pure agony. "Don't stop."

I jolted, astounded by his willingness. He jolted, too.

He pressed his forehead against mine and inhaled my air. "You should walk away," he said. "You should return to camp before we do something we'll forever regret."

"I think we'll regret this regardless." With one hand, I sank my nails into his back, his thin tunic offering little resistance. With my other hand, I yanked his head closer to mine. "But let's make sure."

He claimed my lips once again, licking into my mouth, sucking on my tongue. Our breaths turned ragged.

He cupped my backside, using his hips to wedge my legs farther apart, then rocked against me. I gasped, pleasure storming through me. More kissing, tongues seeking.

I tugged on his hair and rubbed the softest part of me against the hardest part of him. My blood morphed into kerosene, and he lit a match. I *burned* for him. Any lingering reservations wafted away in a puff of smoke.

But…this wasn't enough. Not for either of us. He angled my head and took my mouth deeper, devouring me as if he couldn't get enough. As if I was the last meal before his execution. As if he'd finally found the treasure he'd sought his entire life. As if the world began and ended with me.

As if I meant something.

But the kiss was a lie. I meant nothing to this boy. Less than nothing. Why had I insisted we keep going?

To Roth, I would forever be a parasite.

I should pull away, as originally planned. Why wait for him to do it? I should walk, no, run, as fast as my feet would carry me. *I* would be the one to reject *him*.

He slanted a kiss against the corner of my mouth, peppered sweet little nips along my jaw and ran the lobe of my ear between his teeth. I moaned and writhed—so good!—and prepared to stop him…

He trailed his fingertips down the column of my throat... across my collarbone...lower...

Shivers. Goose bumps. "More," I begged. Except, I became aware of swishing leaves, two pairs of footsteps.

I stiffened and managed to rasp, "Incoming."

Ever the warrior, Roth set me on my feet and unsheathed a dagger. Sweat sheened his brow, and a flush painted his cheeks. He labored for every breath. So did I.

When he stepped in front of me, becoming my shield, I felt like a little girl at Christmas. Hopeful. Maybe we could work through our differences after all.

Roth wiped his mouth with the back of his hand, expunging any trace of our kiss, and my hope withered. Another rejection, worse than the last. I nearly wept with mortification and resentment.

How could I kiss someone who despised me? Did I have no self-respect?

A stupid tear fell unchecked, but I hastily wiped it away. This didn't matter. *He* didn't matter.

Vikander guided Truly past the trees, a sword in his hand. Anger crackled in his eyes, and blood and dirt smeared his torso. Truly wore just as much blood and dirt. She also had bruises on her wrists.

"What happened?" Roth demanded. "Where's Saxon?"

I rushed around the prince to examine my twin. "Are you all right?" The bow arched over her shoulder. The quiver and never-empty canteen of water hung at her side.

"I—I am fine." Her chin trembled. "But Saxon..."

"The centaurs found us," Vikander explained. "Everything happened so fast. They appeared out of nowhere." He threw a glance over his shoulder, checking to make sure he hadn't been tracked. "They caught the princess, but Saxon snatched her back. In the process, he was injured and knocked out. The bastards fled with him. They plan to offer him in trade, I'm sure. Saxon for Everly."

"They *dare* harm my people?" The patent stillness of a predator came over Roth. He'd selected the night's prey, and it wasn't me. I'd been granted a reprieve. "Escort Everly and Truly to the palace. Lock Everly in the tower. She isn't to leave, but she isn't to be hurt, either. Make sure she's given food and water. I'll deal with her as soon as I've found Saxon."

Ignore the hurt.

Despite the odds stacked against me, I gave pleading one last shot. "Let me go, Roth. Hartly isn't sorcerian. She's an innocent, and she needs me. After I find her, I'll present myself to your father, you have my word."

His gaze met mine, and I knew. I *knew.* He wouldn't be showing me an ounce of mercy. Not now, not ever. "I said I'd help your sister, and I will. After I retrieve Saxon, I will find her." Thrums of compulsion brewed in his voice as he added, "You will go to my palace. Along the way, you will not attempt to escape. Upon my return, you will heal my father."

The commands slammed into me, *boom, boom, boom,* breaking down my remaining defenses. I'd failed to escape. Now I couldn't even try. Like a fool, I'd kissed my enemy, revealing my most secret vulnerabilities and desires. I deserved this fate, I really did.

"Why must I wait until your return?" If I needed to heal the king to meet the conditions of Roth's compulsion, I wanted to do it sooner rather than later. *Then* I could launch an escape. Maybe. Probably. "What if he dies?"

"I want to watch over—him," he said. Why the hesitation? "Noel assured he will survive until my return."

Oh, yes. I remembered. Tone dry as Airaria's sand, I said, "Believing her is smart. Oracles *never* mislead or misdirect."

He pursed his lips. But he also voiced an amendment. "If my

father is going to die, you will heal him before my return." Done with me now, he refocused on Vikander. "Do you have it?"

Clipped nod, even as the fairy remained on the lookout for centaurs.

"Do it," Roth said, pitiless.

My skin crawled. "Do what?"

Vikander faced me, then reached out as if to choke me. Too late, I realized he held a sliver of metal in each hand. Before I could dart away, the metal grew and thickened, curving into a band, one end meeting the other. *Click.* The edges fused together, a cold, heavy weight settling over my neck.

The torque, I realized with a frisson of fear. No matter how hard I tried, I couldn't rip it off.

Just like that. My link to Roth fizzled, the heat in my fingers cooling. No magic, no power. I'd been hobbled, rendered helpless.

Shock…

Rage…

But I revealed nothing to Roth. I would not give him the satisfaction.

"I've changed my mind," I told him. "I don't think you're Prince Charming or the Huntsman. I think you are the Evil Queen."

Did he just recoil?

I lifted my chin. "Only minutes ago, we spoke of regrets. News flash. You'll be bearing the brunt of them. I could have been a powerful ally for you and your family. Instead, I'll be your worst enemy."

The muscle jumped in his jaw, faster than before. He gave me a last sweeping glance, projecting fury, longing and yes, even regret, before nodding at Vikander. "Go."

26

They say pride goes before every fall.
I say take someone with you—take them all.

For three stress-filled days, we traveled from sunup to sundown, sometimes riding, sometimes walking, occasionally stopping to eat and rest our horses. I remained in a constant state of agitation, tension burning through my bones like acid, fraying my nerve endings.

I wasn't the only one struggling for calm. Allura was ticked off again. Trees vibrated and leaves quivered. Limbs slapped us while roots tripped us.

Countless times, I'd wanted to shout for help, but Roth's compulsion kept me silent. I'd wanted to syphon…anyone, but the torque kept me powerless.

Never had strength mattered more. The stronger I was, the less I could be hurt.

Face it, if I'd had more magic, more power, I could have prevented this from happening. I could have protected myself.

If I had more magic and power, I could protect myself and my loved ones *forever.*

My only source of hope was Phobia. Twice I'd observed him in the trees, following me, ready and willing to bite my companions if ever I gave the command.

My main source of upset was Roth. Had the centaurs captured him?

I don't care, I don't care, I don't care.

I'd made zero headway with Truly, yet my stupid heart would not excise her. Okay, okay. I'd made *some* headway with her. On more than one occasion, I'd caught her studying me, pensive. But it didn't matter. I wasn't so pathetic I would settle for scraps—yet.

Most of all, I wondered about Hartly. Despite the stay-out-of-my-head order, Noel had popped in with daily reports.

—*Nothing has changed. All is well.*—

—*Daddy Dearest is searching...but I'm not sure he's searching for Hartly. Speaking of, your sister-cousin is thriving in her new home.*—

—*What has four thumbs and a massive crush? The troll commander and Hartly!*—

Noel's assurances meant nothing to me. While she couldn't lie, she *could* misdirect, as I'd reminded Roth. Hartly and a troll? No.

Yes, she saw the best in people. Yes, she believed hurt people often hurt others, that they needed love to heal. But trolls were dangerous and irredeemable, their bites toxic.

You judge all trolls for the actions of a few? Sorcerers are dangerous, too, yet you expect a free pass from Roth.

My guilt proved as frigid as the wind, ensuring I never warmed up. I exhaled, mist wafting in front of my face. Vikander and Truly seemed impervious to the cold, while I shivered nonstop, my teeth chattering.

"Are we there yet?" I asked for the thousandth time. Annoying the fairy amused me. If I wasn't complaining, I was singing, just for the pleasure of watching him cringe.

"Almost," he muttered.

I should have rejoiced.

Why wasn't I rejoicing?

When our horses trotted past a mighty pine, a beam of sunlight found me, the sky no longer obscured by a canopy of leaves. *Too bright!* My eyes burned and watered. I blinked rapidly, trying to take stock of my new surroundings.

I tamped down a cry of protest, my insides raw, as if I'd been scrubbed with sandpaper. We had exited the forest, I realized. This. This was why I hadn't rejoiced. *Not ready to say goodbye.*

I'd never really met Allura, who'd often reminded me of a recalcitrant child, but I had to respect her. She'd judged me for my actions, not my origins.

To be fair, Roth had judged me for my actions, too. I'd hurt him, and he'd retaliated. But he'd been predisposed to hate me.

Stop thinking about him. I'd been knocked down, but I would rise. Fate *expected* me to rise.

Red birds soared across a blue sky filled with pink clouds. Such vibrant colors! Like a painting come to life. Mountains consumed the horizon, trees scattered here and there. Was that... it was! Beneath multiple layers of ice was a yellow brick road. Well, a gold brick road.

We're off to see a wizard. The heartless tinman (me), the cowardly lion (Vikander) and the brainless scarecrow (Truly).

Eventually we reached a charming village smaller than the one I'd seen in the mirror, nestled in a river-rich valley. No avian or palace in sight. People draped in furs meandered along the streets. Some led animals, some led carts. Dark smoke rose from a blazing firepit, where a minotaur blacksmith hammered a sword—I wondered if he and the centaur got into turf wars. Next door to a tavern, a rotund baker sold fresh bread. The scent of yeast made my mouth water.

"You're failing at your job, you know," I told Vikander. We rode the same horse, with me perched in front.

"How so?"

"Both ordered you to keep his new pet fed and watered. For good reason! When hungry, my breed bites. So, do us both a favor and fetch my next meal."

The fairy chuckled. "I'll take my chances."

My torque drew curious stares. Vikander got smiles and catcalls, while Truly received envious glowers from fair maidens who probably hoped to win the bachelor prince's rotted heart.

After another day of nonstop travel, we reached a second village, the one I'd seen in my vision. Miners hauled wheelbarrows piled high with shimmering stones. Avian flew above, and vendors hawked their wares below, selling everything from jewelry to meat on a stick.

We passed Noel and Ophelia's shop—Magics, Foretellings and More—and I balled my fists so tightly, my nails cut into my palms. I wanted to leap off the horse and attack. Alas. No sign of the devious twosome.

A commotion erupted behind us. People shouted warnings, pandemonium sweeping through the village. Racing footsteps pounded against the ice. Different items fell from the tables. Truly paled, and Vikander cursed. I turned and swiveled my head, looking for the source of the panic.

A large shadow fell over us, blocking out the sun, and my curiosity gave way to dread.

"Look out!" Truly shouted.

Something dagger-sharp pierced each of my shoulders, and yanked me into the air. I hissed at the sudden onslaught of pain. Craning my neck, I saw that my attacker had the head and wings of an eagle, with the body, tail and back legs of a lion. *Griffin*.

What had Mom told me about them? What, what?

At the last second, Vikander latched on to my ankle, trying to hold me down with his weight. The griffin merely dug his talons deeper, lifting *the fairy*, too, nearly wrenching my shoulder out of its socket. Muscles pulled and tore. I gagged, nauseous. *So dizzy.* As the pain escalated, unbearable, I screamed. Any second, my arm would rip off.

Breathe, just breathe. Black dots wove through my line of sight as I used my free leg to kick Vikander in the face. "Let go!"

He tightened his grip. "Can't! He'll eat you."

"Let him!" *Kick, kick.* Finally! The fairy lost his grip and dropped, allowing the griffin to soar away with me. The worst of my pain eased, the dizziness and nausea fading, but I remained a prisoner, the creature's talons embedded deep. "You're not going to like the taste of me. I'm bitter and tough. I bet the fairy is tender and juicy, seasoned to perfection."

He squawked as he whisked me beyond the village, past an overcrowded valley where soldiers trained with swords and spears, and over an unoccupied hill. At last, he retracted his talons. I screamed and flailed as I tumbled through the air, but nothing slowed my momentum.

This was it, then? The end?

I crash-landed, impact emptying my lungs. Bones cracked. Jagged icicles knifed from the ground, cutting me as I rolled; I left a trail of blood in my wake. Even when I stopped, the world spun on and on and on.

Focus! Fueled by white-hot rage and soul-curdling fear, I spat out a mouthful of blood and came up swinging. But the creature flew away, leaving me in the presence of a hated foe.

Noel, the redheaded, purple-eyed she-devil, stepped from the shadows. Finally! I bowed up, ready to pounce. As before, she wore golden armor and wrinkled clothing. A style I now understood. She spent most of her present in the future.

"Please accept this gift." She lobbed a shard of glass at me. "Ophelia enchanted it for your use as a token of our goodwill. You can view anyone, anywhere, even Hartly, but only in present time. The best part? You don't need access to your power or magic to use it! Just remember, when you see, others sense."

Truth? Lie? Either way, I clutched the shard to my chest. *My precious.* "This will not save you from my wrath. Nothing will. You endangered Hartly."

Her purple eyes flashed with fury of her own. "To save her. To save you. To save us all. Not that I'm a savior. Not that you are a savior, either. Far from it. If left unchecked, your evil will infect us all. But, if everyone makes the right choices, hint hint, everything will turn out grand.

"No one makes the right choice every minute of every day," I snarled at her. I advanced a step, only to collapse when my ankle buckled. Searing pain shot up my leg, and stars winked through my vision. I swallowed a scream.

"True," she said. "But you see only in part. One day, you'll see clearly. You'll love this land and its people, and thank me for keeping wars at bay."

"Maybe, but that day isn't today." I lumbered to a stand. Though I wobbled, I took another step in her direction.

"Hartly remains unharmed," she said. "You know I speak true."

"I know you misdirect. I know you must be stopped, and I'm the perfect girl for the job. Right now my evil doesn't feel very checked."

Or I would have been, if the griffin hadn't broken through a wall of clouds, swooped down to capture the oracle and flown away. I screeched with frustration.

As soon as I quieted, I heard the *clomp-clomp* of galloping horse hooves. Vikander had given chase. Because of Roth's compulsion, I couldn't mount an escape…but I *could* prepare for my imprisonment.

Moving at the speed of light, I tore a strip of cloth from the hem of my skirt, anchored the enchanted glass to the inside of my thigh, and sprawled across the dirt as if I was knocked unconscious. I would bide my time, hide my rage and think. Hopefully I would find a compulsion loophole. If not, I would meet the conditions of Roth's commands, *then* escape.

You will go to my palace. Along the way, you will not attempt to escape. Upon my return, you will heal my father.

I'd have to convince the king he couldn't afford to wait for his son. Other people could "force" me to disobey the prince, after all.

With King Challen healed, the compulsion to stay put would be nullified. In theory.

There was only one way to find out...

Let's say it worked. Let's say I healed the king and nullified the compulsion before Roth's return. Two problems still remained. The torque, and an inability to syphon from a Charmaine or any of Roth's people. That particular order hadn't come with an expiration date. So, I wouldn't be able to commune with a mirror, cast an illusion or weaken my foes. Someone would give chase.

Wait. I could cross the torque off my list of problems. If I couldn't syphon while wearing it, someone would have to remove it. But even without it, I couldn't syphon from Roth's healers. They were citizens of his kingdom and off-limits. Unless one of the prince's commands superseded another? Like, I couldn't syphon from the citizens...unless I did it to heal the king.

Again, there was only one way to find out.

Evil, Roth? You haven't seen anything yet.

We reached the palace at last, and the sheer magnificence blew my ever-loving mind. The mirror had not done it justice. Backlit by a mountain of ice, the sprawling three-story structure looked like it had been plucked from a dream. Between the second and third levels was a massive stone walkway where guards marched back and forth. Both the left and right sides had a copper-roofed turret.

"There will be serious consequences if you try to harm Roth's family or any of his people," Vikander said.

"Look at my glorious neck accessory. What harm can I possibly do?" *Underestimate me. Please.*

My tasks were set. (1) Convince the king to let me heal him. Or try. (2) Escape the palace without the torque. (3) Return to the forest to find Hartly. (5) Get stronger.

I'd once hated the way people feared me. Now, I craved that fear. I wanted people to know: screw with me and mine and carnage will follow.

Brimming with anticipation, I studied the landscape, my escape route. Hills carpeted with flowers of ice created a breathtaking pathway straight to the palace. A pathway that ran alongside a rushing river littered with bobbing icebergs. Steam curled from a moat filled with molten gold.

A stunning marble waterfall—or goldfall—occupied the center of the driveway.

Vikander stopped the horse and dismounted, then helped me to my feet. The wounds in my shoulders throbbed, and prickles of pain erupted over every inch of my lower half. Still, I pasted on a smile. Reveal weakness? Never again!

Multiple guards rushed over to aid Truly, all male, and all wearing the same blue jacket, tan pants and knee-high brown boots.

"What do the stars signify?" I asked Vikander. Some men had stars sewn into their sleeves, others did not.

"The numbers of battles waged on behalf of the kingdom. The color denotes number. Bronze means one. Silver means ten. Gold means twenty. Guess who has more stars than anyone else?"

"You?"

"I'll give you a hint. He began his military training at the age of three and has already led his army through two wars. Successfully!"

"So?" I'd known Roth was strong. And brave. And resilient. *Not that I admired him anymore.*

"So. He has killed enemies and watched friends die. He has loved and lost. Has hurt, and has been hurt by others. But he has always persevered. You will not break him, Everly, but you could win him, if you fought for him half as much as you fight for your sister." Vikander led me up the steps, where another contingent of uniformed guards stood sentry. Truly stayed close and quiet, and I tried not to drown in my guilt.

"When will someone fight for *me*?" I muttered. When would I be the prize?

A pair of guards pushed open the lofty double doors, allowing us to enter without a hitch.

More guards waited inside, lining the walls, each man holding a golden staff. Some of the soldiers leered at me, some scowled. No one projected any hint of concern.

Ah, we were back to business as usual. How nice for me.

I marveled at the luxury surrounding me. Elaborate chandeliers. Intricate murals. Paintings framed in gold. Diamond-studded *everything* and gold-veined floors.

Greetings to Truly and Vikander rang out. "May you find gold."

Then, whispers began to rise from the ranks. Either Roth had somehow sent word of my upcoming visit, or Noel had spread a little gossip. I heard:

"Evil sorceress." "White hair." "Is she the one?" "Does she have the mark?" "Is our kingdom saved…or doomed?"

What mark?

So everyone reviled me. So what? Their opinions meant nothing. I just…

I hadn't fit in at home. I hadn't fit in with Violet, and I wouldn't fit in here. When would I ever find my place?

"You." Vikander pointed to one of the soldiers. "Escort Princess Truly to her chamber."

I shared a final look with my twin. *Trust and help me, or share my fate. The choice is yours.*

She went with option two, blanching and glancing away. As she vanished around a corner, I heard her say, "Forget my chamber. Take me to Princess Farrah."

Familiar pangs of rejection cut through my chest. Very well.

Her life, her loss. I'd lived seventeen years without her; I could live the rest without her, too. And I would. I wouldn't even miss her. Really.

An older man with dark brown skin, wild blue hair and a short stature hurried over, a stone tablet in hand. He wore a velvet robe. "Vikander. Nice to have you back."

One of the Seven Protectors?

"Roycefus," Vikander said with a nod. "Where's the king?"

"In the library." Roycefus looked me over. "Is this the Apple of Life and Death?"

"I prefer Everly. Or call me Glorious One. Roth does." I offered my hand for a shake.

He arched a blue brow in question, then lifted my hand to his mouth and kissed my knuckles, surprising me. I detected no malice, only welcome. "I am pleased to meet you. I am King Challen's chief advisor." His dark gaze swung to Vikander. "Shall I inform the king of your arrival?"

"Yes. I'll head to the library as soon as I've secured the prisoner."

"Her room is ready," Roycefus said. "I selected the best suite in the east wing."

"No." Vikander shook his head. "She'll stay in the tower."

Despite the advisor's protests, Vikander ushered me down a maze of hallways and up a different flights of stairs.

At the top of a turret, we came to a circular hallway, with no added adornments anywhere. The stone walls were crumbling, the floor dingy, several doorways loomed.

Each door possessed a small barred window. Through all but two of those bars, prisoners watched us, projecting fear, loathing and hope. No one uttered a word.

My stomach sank, and my blood flash froze.

A new guard stepped forward and bowed his head. "We welcome you, Vikander. We have prepared the biggest room for the prince's...guest, as his messenger requested."

So, Roycefus had ignored the prince's order? I liked him even more.

"Ooh la la," I said, hiding my dismay behind a smirk. "I get the biggest room in the dungeon—sorry, *tower*. How lucky am I?"

The fairy trailed the guard, dragging me along. We stopped at the last door on the right. Keys rattled. The lock unlatched. Hinges squeaked and dust swirled. Suddenly, nothing separated me from my captivity.

"What's the number for room service?" I asked. "And I'd like to lodge an official complaint with management. If this is prepared, I'd hate to see unprepared."

Vikander nudged me inside while remaining in the hall. *Squeak. Thud. Rattle.*

My heart made similar noises. "I won't forget this," I told him.

"I'm certain you won't." He peered at me through the bars, saying, "I won't apologize to a sorceress."

"That speaks of *your* flawed character, not mine."

He shrugged, unconcerned. "You will stay here until Roth's return. As ordered."

I heard him issue orders to the guards. "No one goes inside. No one talks to her. No one *looks* at her. If there are any problems, you will summon me, and only me. Understood? I will oversee her care."

A chorus echoed. "Yes, my lord."

I tuned them out and scouted my accommodations. A narrow cot with a ratty blanket. Scratched up walls splattered with flecks of dried blood. A dirty stone floor. An unlit fireplace with heaps of ash. Lastly, a bucket. The toilet?

Inhale, exhale.

Look on the bright side. Time alone means I can spy and plan.

I stumbled deeper into the room and sat in the farthest corner from the door, with my nose facing the wall. Wasting no time, I withdrew my sliver of enchanted glass.

27

A lock is a lie, an illusion of capture.
The real jailer is desire, oh, the rapture.

"Show me Hartly," I whispered, my chest tight.

My sister's image appeared in an instant, love for her swelling my heart. She was alive and well, as promised, but confirmation was my undoing. Hot tears streamed down my cheeks.

She huddled in the corner of a tent, petting Thor. Mud caked her hair and smeared her dress. The same dress she'd worn in the last vision. Thankfully, she wasn't chained or bound.

A female troll I'd call Trollina (because why not?) meandered about, tidying up and chattering. "I like you, I really do. You are so nice. That is why I'm going to be honest with you, even though lies would make you feel better. I don't know if anyone has ever had the courage to tell you but…you are hideous. Probably the ugliest girl I've ever seen." She winced. "I am sorry! I know the truth stings. But you don't even have tusks! Maybe if we cover your face, he'll forget about your ugly exterior and fall in love with your beautiful interior?"

Hartly? Hideous? *You've got to be kidding me!*

"Thank you for the tip," Hartly said and rolled her eyes.

Trollina continued, sounding genuinely upset on my sister's behalf. "I believe we can be best friends. I don't care how ugly you are!" All eagerness and innocence, she nodded. "Yes. We're going to be best friends. I'll fight anyone who makes you feel bad about your grotesque face."

A big hand tipped with claws shoved the tent flap out of the way. In stalked a large troll with horns, features carved from granite, and bulging muscles covered in tattoos and piercings. Fury crackled in his eyes as he stepped closer to Hartly.

I tensed. To my sister's credit, she didn't cower or cry. In fact, she remained calm and met his stare.

"I'm so glad you're back," she said, blowing my mind.

Trollina bowed. "Please be kind to her, brother. She can't help her ugliness."

"Enough." Gaze locked on Hartly, he dismissed the other girl with a tilt of his chin.

As soon as they were alone, Hartly rushed out, "Did you harm my sister?"

"I did not." He unsheathed and dropped weapon after weapon, leaving a pile on the floor. "Centaurs attacked her camp. She and the other female escaped, but their avian friend sustained injures during his capture. The prince gave chase, but he was injured, as well."

Roth was injured? *I don't care, I don't care.*

Hartly paled. "Where are Everly and Truly now?"

"You may rest easy. They are in the Empire of Sevón, where the centaurs cannot reach them."

"Can you?" Hartly asked, setting Thor aside. "Will you?"

"I can, but I will not. I'm too busy taming my war prize. You are here to please me, so please me. Bathe. Finally! Your stench offends my nose."

"Well, your face offends my eyes, so we're even," she said, then sniffed. "I'm sorry. That was mean. And false! I'm lashing out because I'm worried about my sister. Until you forgive her for killing your brother, I'm on strike. I won't bathe. I won't eat. I won't sleep."

"I could *make* you do those things," he announced.

Two griffins swooped through the hole in the roof, took a post at Hartly's side and squawked, daring the troll to approach.

"Go ahead," Hartly said with a sugary sweet tone. "Try. Dare you."

Go, sis, go!

Excitement blended with eagerness, pulsing from the troll. He *wanted* to cut through the griffin. Then he stiffened and turned, searching the tent. "Who dares to watch us?"

Gah! He'd sensed me? Oh, right. Noel had warned me of the possibility. *You see, they sense.* I stroked the glass, saying, "Show me Roth."

The prince appeared, blood dripping from gashes in his forehead, shoulder and side. Despite his obvious pain, he wielded two short swords against three centaurs, moving with savage elegance and expertly sidestepping blows.

Tension stole through me, turning my muscles to stone. A group of centaurs surrounded him. One horseman used a spear to distract, while another reared up and kicked him in the sternum. He flew up and back, flipping midair and crashing into a tree.

My breath caught in my throat. Why didn't he use his magic and command the centaurs to turn on themselves? I knew he hated the ability, but come on! If you had a skill, use it. Otherwise, you'd end up torque'd and locked in a cell.

Maybe he *couldn't* use his compulsion? What were the parameters of his ability? Or maybe the centaurs were protected in some way?

I needed to know! The more I knew about Roth's weaknesses, the better I could defeat him. And I *would* defeat him. Me. Not these centaurs. *Come on, Roth! Win this.*

With a roar, he threw himself back into the fray. His speed wowed me, and his skill left me reeling. Though the odds were stacked against him, he landed more blows than he received.

Where was Saxon? I scanned the surrounding trees. A blue feather balanced atop a pink leaf, the end soaked with blood. My chin trembled, a single thought knocking me for a loop: Schrödinger's avian.

"Give us the fugitive," a centaur said, "and we will give you the avian."

"I don't want you to give me the avian," Roth countered, sinking his sword into the speaker's torso and twisting the blade. "I'm going to *take* him from you."

As blood and guts spilled, the sound of footsteps reached my ears. Someone approached my cell! I tossed my cloak on the cot and hastened to hide the sliver of enchanted glass, just in case someone gave me a pat-down. Where, where? There! Behind a loose stone in the wall. Then I stood. Just in time.

"Open the door."

That voice! Princess Farrah Charmaine. A whisper of hope drifted through me. What if Truly had changed her mind about me and convinced the princess to set me free?

"I'm sorry, Your Majesty," the guard began, "but Vikander ordered us not to let—"

"I am your princess, and you are subject to my rule—and my punishment," she interjected with a slight tremor, clearly un-used to taking charge. "If you force me to issue the same com-mand twice, *I* will force you to live the remainder of your days in a cell of your own."

I gave her a mental standing O.

The soldier mumbled something to someone else—I thought

I heard Vikander's name—before obeying the princess. Keys clanged together, hinges squeaked and the door opened.

Tremors rocked me. Farrah entered, my angel in the flesh. I released an embarrassing whimper. For months, I'd considered this girl a friend. I'd watched her help others time and time again. If she turned her back on me...

She was resplendent in a pale pink gown and a thousand pounds of jewelry. The sparkle... *No! Focus.* Two other girls followed on her heels. Truly, who kept her gaze downcast, and Ophelia, who stared at me with unwavering satisfaction.

My warm fuzzies turned to rage, and my hands fisted.

Truly had yet to wash off her travel grime, and Ophelia wore more armor than usual. Expecting a fight?

Farrah stopped a few feet away from me and, to her credit, she appeared unafraid. "I am Princess Farrah of Sevón, the only daughter of King Challen, and sister to Prince Roth." Pride layered the words. She was even more beautiful in person, with flawless skin the color of porcelain, bright green eyes a shade darker than Roth's, bloodred lips, and hair so black it appeared blue, braided into a towering crown.

Remember the mission—heal the king, escape. "I'm Everly, captive of Prince Roth, potential healer of King Challen. Unless I'm too late? How badly has he deteriorated?"

Fear flashed over her expression, reigniting my guilt. The modern-day nightingale had done nothing to earn my wrath, I just... I needed her cooperation,

I'd make it up to her later.

"My father is deteriorating at an alarming rate." Head tilted to the side, eyes like wounds, she said, "But according to Roth, we are not to host the healing ceremony until his return."

"Ceremony?" No one had mentioned a ceremony. I could syphon and use whatever magic I gained, no more, no less.

Farrah advanced on me, the epitome of grace. She trusted me not to attack?

"I do not know what the ceremony is supposed to entail," she said, "and I'm sorry. Our witch and oracle have been vague."

I flicked Ophelia a quick glance. "What a shocker."

Taking my hands in hers, Farrah said, "I'm also sorry for the horrors being done to you. You are a sorceress, yes, but I will never cheer the suffering of another."

"Free me, then." I could have begged, but pride kept me silent.

"Noel says you are needed here, in this cell," Ophelia said.

Oh, she did, did she? My narrowed gaze slid to the witch, the oracle's best friend. Not a single glimmer of remorse.

"Everly." Farrah squeezed my hands, an offer of comfort. "If I do it, if I go against Noel's advice, will you submit to Ophelia? She will bespell you, ensuring you never again need to syphon power from another."

They could do that? Permanently hobble me, no torque required?

Panic turned my every inhalation into a dagger, slicing my throat, my lungs. I shifted my gaze to Truly. She was waxen, agitated and close to tears, but she said nothing in my defense.

Walls seemed to close in around me, and breathing became more difficult. I returned my attention to Farrah, to our joined hands. The edge of her glove had rolled back, revealing an apple-shaped birthmark identical to mine.

My jaw went slack. Like me, she was *bonum et malum*. The most powerful of her kind. No doubt her mother was the second queen, the one who'd worked with Mom and Violet to steal those apples.

A witch and oracle had helped, too. Ophelia and Noel's mothers? Of course, I thought next. Our roots run deep.

Grinding my teeth, I said, "I like you, Farrah. I always have. But your offer is not a kindness. It is a cruelty. A lifetime of weakness. I refuse."

"But—"

"Please, see yourselves out." I wrenched free and eased upon the cot with as much dignity as I could muster.

Farrah remained in place, wringing her hands. "Everly," she said, and I got the impression she was attempting to align her thoughts. "I was born to privilege, riches and power. Things most others will never experience. All my life, I have tried to share my blessings with the less fortunate. The thought of hurting someone, anyone, makes me sick. But I *must* protect myself from you. I *will* protect myself."

"Let me go with my magic intact, and you'll have nothing to fear from me, ever. I—" Realization hit, and hit hard. She'd pegged me as the Evil Queen and herself as Snow White.

Bile burned the back of my throat, eroding my calm. The truth was so clear. Princess Farrah. Farrah. Fair-rah. Fairest. The fairest of them all. Beloved by Prince Charming because of familial connection, not a romantic one. Wielder of ice magic, creator of snow. White snow. Snow White.

Farrah Charmaine *was* Snow White.

Truly was the Huntsman, who saved Snow White and tricked the Evil Queen.

"That's right," Farrah said, sounding both sad and weary. "I am Snow White, Princess of Ice, and you are the Queen of Evil."

Just then, breathing wasn't difficult; it was impossible. Before this, Roth had believed any death on my part would equate to a new beginning. I had agreed with him, hoping against hope. Until now.

"I've known about the prophecy all my life," Farrah continued. "I worried I might become the Queen of Evil, so I worked hard to prove I'm good. I don't want to war with you, Everly. In war, innocents get hurt. But I meant what I said. I will protect myself, even if I must accept a truth I've denied for years—defeating you is my destiny."

28

Storms might rage in your past,
but the tempest cannot last.

As my world spun off its axis, Farrah and Ophelia exited the cell. Truly lingered behind.

"I consulted Noel," she said softly, fiercely. "She said I do *not* have a sister. But—" My twin pressed her lips together, while giving her next words careful consideration.

Ignore the hurt. I was so danged tired of ignoring hurts. "You don't have a sister but...what?"

"But I could if I wanted one," she snapped. "She probably meant I could have one if I pressured Queen Violet to have another child."

Ignore. The. Hurt. But oh, wow, the pain threatened to rip me asunder. "You're right. You do *not* have a sister. Not anymore, anyway. I'm disowning you."

She opened and closed her mouth, then left without speaking

another word. What? I'd expected her to fight for a relationship with me? A vile sorceress and unwitting murderess, too weak to defend herself. The devil to Farrah's angel.

Truly left, and my frustration bubbled over. I threw back my head and screamed until my voice broke. Panting, I tossed my only blanket across the cell. Then I tossed the cot, too, the wooden legs splintering.

My eyes blurred as I beat my fists against the rocky wall, uncaring when I left smears of blood behind. Painful stings flared and faded. I didn't want to be the Evil Queen. I just didn't. Like Farrah, I wanted to be a better person and I wanted to keep myself and my loved ones safe. So, what made her good, and me bad?

What was the difference between us?

In the ensuing week, I talked myself into summoning Tyler. He'd given me the mark for a reason. Why not use it? But. Though I tried…and tried and tried…placing my hand on the faint print he'd left behind, nothing ever happened. Either he'd lied to me, or I needed magic to activate the mark. Stupid torque!

Vikander brought me three meals a day. Twice, he created a metal tub from a metal shaving and filled it with water from the enchanted canteen. *Cold* water. He then sent a maid to scrub my back and style my hair.

I would have welcomed the help, but he'd sent Annica, Roth's former girlfriend. The smoky-eyed beauty with curves for miles I'd once seen in a vision.

When she'd laughed and told me, "Princess Truly spoke of you to Princess Farrah, and mentioned Prince Roth's abhorrence to you." I hadn't punched her—proof I wasn't the Evil Queen. Such restraint!

Also, I *still* wasn't jealous of Farrah's beauty. Her strength was another story. *Gimme!*

Footsteps sounded. Who would visit me this time? Vikander? Truly and Farrah?

A familiar symphony played. Rattling keys, squeaking hinges. As the cell door swung open, I shoved the sliver of enchanted glass inside my pillow and sat up on my brand-new cot.

In walked Roycefus, the king's top advisor. He wore another velvet-soft robe and carried the same stone tablet.

Clad in a serviceable brown dress made from lava ants and poison ivy—surely—I didn't feel like a lady, so I didn't bother acting like one. "What do you want?"

He scanned the cell, features pinched with disapproval. "King Challen would like to meet you, but he's in no condition to climb the tower steps. Therefore, I will escort *you* to *him*."

"Is he getting weaker?" He must be. Before this, he'd expressed zero interest in me. Or... "Has Roth returned?" Anticipation sang in my blood, a melody both hypnotic and grating. I'd checked the glass mere hours ago, but I'd seen nothing. Why? Was he...? No! He lived. I would believe nothing less. "Am I supposed to perform the healing ceremony?" Whatever it was. No one seemed to have a clue.

"The prince has not returned, and no preparations have been made for the ceremony. But King Challen *has* weakened." Very well. I would use this meeting to advance my plan.

Trying to disguise my eagerness, I eased to my feet. "Well? Let's get this over with."

He led me out the door, and I wondered—again—if he was one of the seven.

A guard stepped forward to offer his assistance, but Roycefus waved him away. "According to Princess Truly, she cannot mount an escape. Brute force is unnecessary."

"How...kind of the princess to share my plight with others," I muttered. Meanwhile, my mind shouted, *Betrayer!*

As the advisor led me around corners, down hallways and different flights of stairs, the furnishings became more elaborate.

Even the air changed, warming and sweetening. Quiet voices created a cacophony of sound, and I picked up a smattering of words. "Sorceress." "Prisoner." "Healer."

Finally, we reached the room I'd seen in my vision—the one with the wall of windows overlooking the mountain. A crystal chandelier hung from a circular cutout of stained glass. Cream-colored stucco walls boasted swirling designs. An ivory grand piano occupied one corner, a small table another. A marble hearth crackled with flames.

The king reclined upon a plush couch, wearing a plain white tunic with an ankle-length hem. A nightshirt? He'd lost weight. His already-thin hair had thinned some more, and his weathered cheeks had sunk in.

Keen intelligence glowed in his emerald eyes—eyes so like Roth's. *Pang.* While his body had deteriorated, his mind remained sharp.

Armed guards watched me from posts throughout the room, ready to pounce as Roycefus led me to the chair directly across from the king.

Challen waved his advisor away, saying, "I will speak with the girl alone."

Clipped nod. Roycefus gave my hand a comforting pat before stalking to the door. None of the guards followed, so I guessed they didn't count as observers.

"I am honored to make your acquaintance," Challen said.

"Then you must have forgotten I'm an evil sorceress."

"Are you evil, then?"

Leaning back, I kicked up my feet, resting my heels on a coffee table made of emeralds. "I'm not *not* evil."

He thought for a minute, then sighed. "Ever since my son sent a missive attempting to end his engagement to Princess Truly, I've been eager to meet you."

What! Roth had asked to break his engagement, despite the potential for war? "You should do it. If they get hitched, they'll make each other miserable." *Helping Roth carve out a better future while you suffer? Fool!*

"They might be miserable," he said, "but they will live, and that is what matters. That is why I fight to survive. Why I will do *anything* to survive. Other kingdoms would raze us to the ground, just to gain control of our mountains and the precious stones we mine. My battle magic stops them from even trying."

I perked up. "Battle magic?"

Nod. "I am able to predict an enemy's every move and create the perfect counterstrikes."

I took his words for what they were: a warning. "So what does your battle magic tell you to do about me in general?"

He heaved a weary sigh. "To free you."

Seriously? Hope bloomed, only to die a quick death when he added, "But I will not. As my body weakened, my magic has weakened, as well. No longer can I trust its leadings. Instead, I rely on my oracle. She claims you will save me."

Oh, really? "What did she say, exactly?"

He closed his eyes and recited, "With hair as pale as moonbeams, eyes like mirrors framed in gold, and an apple forever within reach, she will burn with fury and save the mighty King of Sevón."

I remembered the second vision I'd had of this man, as different blondes introduced themselves and revealed their palms and wrists. He'd been hunting for me even then, searching for the girl with an apple forever within reach.

"So sure I have an apple within reach?" I asked, stroking my fingers over my wrist cuff.

"Prove you do not. Remove the cuffs."

I narrowed my eyes. "I will willingly, happily save you. Today. If you vow to free me afterward, and if you remove the torque. I cannot syphon from healers while I'm wearing it."

"I'm sorry, Everly, but I cannot let you go. Not today. Not

ever." Sadness emanated from him. "You play a part in Farrah's fairy tale."

Her fairy tale? As if the rest of us merely served as fodder to advance her plot. Hardly! "You are sentencing me to life in prison for crimes I have yet to commit." The fury he'd mentioned? Yeah, it already blazed in my heart.

"I do realize this, but I will not be swayed. The well-being of my children, and my kingdom, comes first."

The envy I had for Farrah doubled. Tripled. She had something I'd always wanted but had never received—a father's unconditional love. "You think you can change fate?" I asked.

"I think I must try."

"Then stop courting my wrath. Right now, I can forgive my mistreatment. I want to help you, and I want to move on. But the longer you lock me away, the more I dream of retaliating."

Just as stubborn as his son, he said, "That is a risk I'm willing to take."

Swallow your frustration. Remain calm. Denial today didn't have to mean denial tomorrow. I could change his mind. I *had* to change his mind.

Or maybe I had to *goad* him into performing the ceremony sooner rather than later? "Then I've just moved Farrah's pain and torment to the top of my To Do list. Roth has spot number two. Too bad you won't live long enough to protect them. Wanna bet on when you'll die?"

If he were anyone else, if the situation were any different, I would have been mortified by my conduct. But the Charmaines had stripped me of everything but my wits—and my temper.

With determination and desperation calling the shots, I looked him over and smirked. "My guess? You'll die in a matter of days. You've been getting steadily worse, I'd guess, growing a little weaker every day?" I leaned forward and smiled cruelly. "In the fairy tale, Snow White's father dies soon after the Queen of Evil enters their lives."

He went ghost-pale. "Guards. Escort the prisoner to her room."

Two soldiers stomped over to haul me to my feet. I was shoved none too gently into the hall.

"Careful, boys." I batted my lashes at one, then the other. "My online review is already hovering in the one-star range."

Just as the door closed behind us, I heard the king command, "Fetch Noel. Quickly! I must consult my oracle."

I grinned and practically floated back to my cell.

29

With this ring, I thee wed.
With this dagger, your blood runs red.

Only an hour later, Annica marched into my cell with a basket of goodies: a white gown, sparkly slippers and an array of toiletries.

I bathed in Vikander's tub, happy to be clean again, then sat before the unlit hearth. No one trusted me with a fire. Annica brushed my hair a bit too roughly, then styled the locks into elaborate braids around my head.

I dressed after secretly tying the enchanted glass to my thigh. The white silk gown molded to my curves. The slippers were a perfect fit, as well.

"Why so fancy?" I asked, pulling at the torque. The metal remained in place.

"I do not know," she muttered. "I do what the king commands."

"And you'd rather be anywhere else, helping anyone but the sorceress."

"Yes! Especially the girl foretold to harm our beloved royals."

More hate. Yawn. I searched the basket, hoping to find a mirror. "I hear you used to date—sorry, *court* Roth."

She ripped the basket from my grip, snapping, "We ended our relationship when the king announced his engagement."

So, a year ago. Unless she was lying. Instinct told me she wasn't, that she would be bragging if she'd nailed him since then. Which meant I'd seen the past. Which meant my magic was amazing!

"Did the *honorable* prince promise you a happily-ever-after and then renege?" I asked with an exaggerated pout.

She sniff-sniffed. "He didn't need to promise me anything. His eyes spoke for him."

So she'd woven a pipe dream. "What are *my* eyes telling you?"

She studied me and laughed. Laughed! "You want him, and you actually believe he'll want you back. You, a sorceress."

"That *never* gets old," I muttered.

"Hear me well, sorceress. I grew up in this palace, and I love the Charmaines. There is no finer family in all the lands. If you hurt them in any way…"

Such vehemence. Then and there I knew beyond a doubt I'd found one of Farrah's Seven Protectors.

In order to craft a better defense and offense, I needed to identify all seven. I hadn't wanted a war, but the Charmaines had given me one.

I had more questions for Annica, but Vikander entered the chamber, looking dapper in a white jacket with gold trim and black slacks. His dark skin glittered more than usual

With a tilt of his chin, he dismissed the lady-in-waiting. As soon as she scurried out, he pinned me with a glare. "The ceremony isn't supposed to take place until Roth's return. Whatever you said to move up the timetable, you're going to regret it."

I wanted to whoop with excitement. And cry. "Why?"

"Noel explained the healing ceremony to us."

Uh-oh. "And?"

"Congratulations. You're getting married."

I fought. I fought so hard, but Roth's compulsion forced me to walk to the ballroom, where the marriage ceremony would be held. One step, two. Three. I couldn't stop.

Marry Challen...

Even the idea sent me into a tailspin of panic because (1) I was only seventeen and had no desire to tie my life to another person in holy matrimony; (2) I had no desire to marry the old king, specifically; (3) If I did marry the king, fate would win this round.

I would officially qualify as the Queen of Evil. No symbolism required.

"Don't make me do this," I pleaded. Hating him, hating myself.

"I must. I am bound by duty." Merciless, Vikander ushered me deeper into a ballroom.

Heavy breaths sawed in and out of my mouth. Light flickered from golden sconces, highlighting intricate wall murals. Brighter light spilled from a massive chandelier, glistening crystals illuminating a large crowd of onlookers—a sea of unfamiliar faces, sparkling jewels, lace gowns and velvet suits. Every gaze rested upon me. Some people watched with pity, others with envy or intrigue.

If not for the torque, I could have drained everyone and blown this joint for good.

I would do anything for power right now.

In attendance, countless fairies with glittering skin in various shades of white, black and brown as well as winged avian, with skin in various shades of purple, blue, red and green. There were a handful of minotaurs, centaurs and creatures I hadn't come across before. Like the woman with tiny snakes attached to her scalp (gorgon), the man surrounded by a strange red glow (phoenix) and the teenage girl with a beaked nose, feathers instead of hair, and tiny, delicate wings (harpy). Some attendees wore wrist cuffs, some didn't.

Oh, look. There was Roycefus, standing with the other advisors. He seethed with disapproval, so I crossed his name off the Seven Protectors list.

Problem was, he didn't protest. No one did.

Close to hyperventilating, I searched that sea of unfamiliar faces. Surely there was one person with honor or integrity, who would stand up and defend me. Someone? Anyone?

Someone fair—

I laughed without an ounce of humor. Fair. Finally, I understood what EQ had meant in "Little Snow White," when she'd requested the "fairest of them all."

The fairy tale was unfolding right before my eyes.

If Snow White was the fairest, as the fairy tale promised, she would offer me aid.

Afraid to hope, I scanned the crowd once again. There. Farrah and Truly pushed their way to the front, both wearing pale pink gowns and enough jewels to sink a ship. How sweet. They'd dressed for the occasion—Everly's downfall.

Did they protest? No.

Why, why, why had I rushed this ceremony? Why hadn't I waited for Roth? "How would you feel if someone stripped you of your free will and forced you to marry someone you didn't love?"

Truly opened and closed her mouth before averting her gaze.

Behold, the Huntsman's betrayal.

Tears welled in Farrah's eyes, but she spoke not a word.

All hope burned to ash, and burrowed deep into my heart. Every beat gave me life and poisoned me anew.

"Your brother will be furious." Or mildly perturbed. Though he despised me, he would never force me to marry his father.

Despite his faults, he *was* fair. "He commanded us to wait for his return."

Silence.

Had he even heard of these nuptials? Would he rush to the rescue any second? I needed to stall, just in case. Threats wouldn't work. I needed to run, hide.

Preparing to bolt in three...two...one!

Nooo! Compulsion forced me to take another step, another and another, until I stood beside King Challen, the groom, who leaned against a cane, sweat dotting his brow.

Until Roth released me from the compulsion, I had no choice but to follow through with this indecent proposal.

Any second now...

No harried footsteps. No shouted command to stop.

Don't cry. Never reveal a weakness an enemy can exploit. Hysteria loomed. "How will a wedding ceremony heal you, King Challen?"

"I don't know. I'm told it will."

"Don't believe everything you're told! Take what I said, for instance. I was wrong to taunt you. You're not going to die today or tomorrow." He *might* die today or tomorrow. His breaths now rattled. "Please, don't do this." Begging again? When would I learn? Begging revealed weakness as surely as tears and would get me nothing but censure and disappointment.

Anguish darkened the king's eyes. I thought I'd reached him. Then he tottered, nearly falling over. "I'm sorry, Everly. We do this today. I vow."

Murmurs rose from the crowd, the sea of people parting. Ophelia and Noel strode down the newly created path. The witch wore a skimpier-than-usual leather ensemble, and the oracle wore a kind of frilly pink bathrobe. Her feet remained bare.

"Everly! So good of you to come to your wedding." Noel smiled and waved. "All is well, I hope."

I'll see you at the wedding.

Never in a million years would I have guessed Ophelia had referenced *my* wedding. "Get me out of here, and I'll pay anything." I would even forgive her for her crimes. "Help me!"

She scratched her head and looked up at the taller Ophelia. "I thought that's what I was doing."

"It is." The witch eyed me expectantly. "Some people don't know when to be grateful."

Hate these two! I wished I'd never promised safe passage if ever I ruled a kingdom. Because if this wedding persisted, I would be ruling *this* kingdom. "Contact Roth." My gaze darted between them. "Tell him what's about to happen."

"Are you kidding?" Noel spread her arms, all *does no one ever listen to me anymore?* "He might put a stop to it."

I withered. Alone, outnumbered and outmagicked. A true damsel in distress.

"Isn't this exciting?" Remaining out of my strike zone, Noel climbed onto the royal dais. "A wedding and a funeral, both in one day. A beginning and an end."

Funeral? Whose? Mine? Had to be. No one else was panicking, as if they knew a secret I did not.

"Vikander." Swaying, inhalations more labored, Challen said, "Begin."

A scowling Vikander moved beside the oracle and the witch. I glared bloody daggers at him.

Though stiff, he launched into a speech about husband and wife loving, honoring and protecting each other. After a while, I lost track of his words. Blood rushed through my head, my ears ringing.

Vikander wore a mirrored pin on his jacket. I stared at my reflection, willing Foreverly to appear and tell me what to do.

I stared at the exit, willing Roth to rush through it. Or even Nicolas.

If the torque came off, I could try to summon Tyler again.

"Everly." Challen wheezed. "Say the words."

Any. Second.

My heart hammered against my ribs as if trying to hang a picture there. One of a husband, his wife and her two stepchildren.

"I. Do," Challen said. "Say it."

I gave a violent shake of my head. *Come on! Someone, anyone, object to this.*

Roth didn't burst into the room.

Tyler didn't appear.

My twin remained quiet.

Wanting to vomit, I met Vikander's gaze. The glitter in his skin swirled like mist. His emotions affected his appearance?

"Do you take King Challen Charmaine to be your lawfully wedded husband?" he asked, his voice tight. "Yes or no?"

I opened my mouth to say *I don't*. No way. Not now, not ever. I would fight this marriage with every ounce of my being. The words that rolled from my tongue? "Yes. I do."

Nooo! The compulsion had overtaken me. Now, the words reverberated in my mind, *destroying* me. A white-hot tear streamed down my cheek.

Vikander wilted, saying, "You may now crown and kiss your bride."

Someone handed Challen a crown made of crystals. The king placed the symbol of my new status atop my head and planted a quick peck on my cheek. I stood there, stunned.

"All hail the King and Queen of Sevón," the fairy muttered.

The crowd erupted into wild cheers. It was done. I had married the king—I had married Roth and Everly's father. In one fell swoop, I'd become a queen and a stepmother, and developed a deep hatred for my stepchildren, who'd helped make this day happen.

The prophecy had unfolded, just as predicted.

Welcome to my new reality.

I had officially become the Evil Queen.

30

Leave him in the dust,
and his heart will rust.

My entire world crashed and burned. I felt like a fish caught in a net, struggling to no avail. Dazed and horrified, I offered no protests as Noel and Ophelia led me from the room, King Challen following at a much slower pace behind us.

King Challen. My husband.

I whimpered. Just before we exited, I looked over my shoulder and zeroed in on Truly. She sobbed quietly, her arms wrapped around her middle.

Boo-hoo. Poor Truly. At any point, she could have protested. Instead, she'd remained silent, and I'd been served to the king on fine china that definitely hadn't been on my registry.

Noel had nailed it. Truly and I *weren't* sisters.

"Give her to me." Vikander closed in, saying, "I will return her to the tower, where Roth wishes her to stay."

"No, no, no, little fae. There's another ceremony to complete," Noel replied. "Sorry, but your invitation is nonexistent."

"*Another* ceremony?" I squeaked.

"Because of Challen's condition, we must make the healing as easy as possible, which means he needed a familial bond with you," she explained.

"Let me annul the marriage to Challen and marry Roth, then." I'd rather hitch my wagon to my enemy—and crush—than his father.

"The closer the bond, the better the result," Noel said. "Now, the time has come to offer true love's kiss."

Gross! "I will *not* be kissing the king." Or doing anything else to or with him. "In the actual fairy tale, there are *zero* mentions of true love's kiss. Especially in regards to the Evil Queen."

"Just as death does not always represent death, a kiss does not always represent a kiss."

"What does it represent in this case?" What were they trying to make me do?

She smiled, her eyes going blank. "Around and around and around they go, where they stop, nobody knows."

Nonsense—what did it mean? Was she in the midst of a vision? "What do you see? Tell me!"

"I see what could be, what would be, what should be, what will be, what can't be, what won't be…"

She was still muttering when we entered the throne room, smaller in size but devoid of people and guards.

Challen entered at last. I was married to an elderly man. I had two stepchildren who despised me, the fairy tale grinding on. At the moment, I had no power or hope. Did I even *want* to heal Challen? No. The desire to cause pain *seethed* inside me. And I could… I didn't need to wait for magic.

I threw a punch at Noel, but she expected the action and jumped out of the way. Rather than pausing to formulate a plan of attack, I used my momentum to my advantage, spinning and kicking, nailing Ophelia in the stomach.

Air gushed from her lungs as she hunched over. I experienced the barest hint of satisfaction. *More!* I threw another punch. Prepared this time, she blocked. Before she could deliver a punch of her own, Noel stepped between us.

"Shall I explain what happens next?" She looked at me, brow arched. "Witches cannot steal power the way sorcerers do. But a coven *can* work together to collect and extract power from one body, then transfer it to another. That is how many royals acquired their magic."

More fuel for my fury. "The sorcerian are universally hated for stealing power. Now you're going to steal mine, but that's okay because the king is dying? *Hypocrites!*"

"No, no. You've got it all wrong." Noel patted the top of my head, all *there, there.* "*We* are not going to do anything. The coven will do the honors. Plus, you won't have to live as an empty husk without magic. I promise! When the ceremony ends, only one royal will live. The other will be dead, if I wasn't clear."

Empty husk? Bile burned my throat. I was to be killed—*sacrificed?* Dead at seventeen, the fairy tale unfulfilled? Surely not. "In the prophecy, the *king* dies after he marries the Evil Queen," I reminded Challen. "Why are you willing to risk yourself?"

"Desperate," he rasped. "Dead anyway. Must try."

"Of course you must," I screeched. "For your children and the kingdom, right? Well, I call foul! You're doing this because you're a selfish bastard."

He blanched, but said nothing more.

"Ah. The coven has arrived." Noel grinned and clapped. Clapped. Thrilled to ruin my life.

Great, sweeping tremors moved through me.

A door opened. One after the other, seven women in hooded black robes glided into the room. Not a single footfall resounded.

Panic and hysteria surged within me, threatening to slay what remained of my sanity. *Seven* witches. As in, Seven Protectors? Had I gotten things all wrong?

The members of the coven formed a half circle around me.

"Let's get the queen ready for the ball." Noel placed a hand on each side of my torque. *Click.* The metal split in two, the pieces clanging on the floor. So quick and easy, making a mockery of my efforts. "Torques made by fairies can be removed only by another fairy. Remember that."

Finally, an act of kindness. A mistake on the oracle's part, and one I would happily exploit. I cracked the bones in my neck, rolled my shoulders, flexed and unflexed my fingers, preparing to strike. Syphon first, attack second.

—*I will help you survive this, but you must swear not to kill the Charmaine siblings.*— Though she had turned away from me, Noel spoke inside my head.

I paused, considering her words. *I would be a fool to trust you again.*

—*If you do not trust me, you* will *die today, and Roth will die later.*—

That sounds like a you *problem. If I die, I won't care what happens to Roth.* I needed to stop chatting and focus, so I could syphon. So why was I hesitating?

—*I have never lied to you. I cannot. Think back, remember my words.*—

Today she'd said one royal would live and the other would die...but she hadn't specified that I would be the one to kick it.

My eyes widened. Would *Challen* die?

—*This is the only way to get everything you've ever wanted, Everly. That is my gold star guarantee.*—

Everything I'd ever wanted versus dying. Maybe she was telling the truth, maybe she wasn't.

Did I really want to blow this opportunity?

Did I have a choice? If I couldn't circumvent Roth's compul-

sion, I couldn't escape. This way, at least, I might—might!—
have a way to protect myself.

I told her, *I agree to your terms.* Desperate times, desperate
measures. *But I have two caveats. One, I won't attack a Charmaine
sibling unless I need to defend myself. And two, all bets are off when
Roth returns.*

*—Very well. You have a deal. Now, here is my aid. Do not use your
magic, Everly. Let this ceremony take place.—*

Sickness curdled my stomach. *That's it?*

"Return the torque to her neck." Challen coughed, blood
spraying from his mouth. "Without it, she can syphon from us."

"The collar keeps power trapped inside her, and you want to
draw her power *out*, correct?" Noel said. "Besides, a plain, ordinary sorceress cannot syphon from witches who are guarded
against such things. And Roth compelled her not to syphon
from you or your people."

What felt like a thousand invisible hands swept me off my
feet, forcing me to lie flat on my back midair. I had no foundation, and I pitched this way and that. My sickness worsened.
Though I kicked and clawed at air, nearly tearing my shoulders
from their sockets, I remained in place.

The fires of fury went head-to-head with an ice storm of fear.
Too late to change my mind and launch an escape. "Let me go!"

*—You can thank us later. We prefer gift baskets filled with the hearts
of our enemies.—*

"This is where we bid you adieu, Your Majesty." Noel spoke
out loud this time. To me, she said, "The king offered us a mea-
sly chest of gold to perform this ceremony, so of course we declined. So he hired witches from another kingdom."

Something about her tone…and the gleam in her eyes… She
was trying to tell me something, but my mind was a jumbled
mess, and I couldn't figure it out.

She blew me a kiss, and then she and Ophelia left. *Abandoned?*
I won't cry.

As the double doors closed with an ominous *click*, Noel whispered to me, —*Here's to New Beginnings, Everly.*

They *had* abandoned me, unwilling to witness my demise. *Foolish Everly!* I'd had an opportunity to strike, but I'd wavered, allowing an oracle I despised to fill me with doubt.

Panic screwed with my focus. What was I supposed to do now? The witches were guarded against syphoning, and Challen didn't have enough power to flicker a light bulb, much less help me fight off an entire coven.

"B-begin," he said, his voice nothing but fumes.

The witches glided closer, forming a complete circle around me. One unsheathed a dagger, metal glinting in the light. Better to stab me to death?

I screamed and flailed for freedom, then grunted and groaned from exertion, my gaze returning to the doors. *Come on, come on.*

Roth.

Hartly.

Nicolas and Tyler.

Truly.

Vikander.

Even Noel and Ophelia.

Anyone!

The witches chanted words I couldn't decipher, their voices melodic but emotionless. Air heated, electric pulses flashing like lightning strikes. Every point of contact felt like a needle prick against my skin.

One after the other, the women sliced their palms and flung blood over my body. Soon, my wedding dress had more crimson than white. Tears brimmed, obscuring my vision. *On my own.*

This was it, then. The end. I wished I'd had a chance to say goodbye to Hartly and Nicolas. Wished I'd never come to Enchantia.

Giving up so easily?

Yes! What other option did I have? I wasn't a plain, ordinary sorceress but a—

I sucked in a breath. *That's right.* Everly Morrow was no plain, ordinary sorceress. I was the Evil Queen. I was rooted in the Enchantian Forest, and more powerful than most.

I *was* the Apple of Life and Death.

The witches began to dance around me. Around and around and around.

I stilled, Noel's gibberish helping me focus at last.

Realization: I didn't need to annihilate any mystical shields. To link with me and draw out my magic, these women had to drop their guard all on their own. I had only to wait...

The only obstacle? Roth's compulsion.

But wait! He'd compelled me to leave his people alone. The witches were not from his kingdom.

More of Noel's nonsense made sense. In her own way, she *had* helped me.

One royal *would* die today, but it wouldn't be me.

As for the witches...they weren't characters in the fairy tale but instruments of Challen's demise. His battle magic had warned him to let me go, but he'd refused to listen. Today, he paid the price.

I closed my eyes, inhaled, exhaled, centering my mind. Once Mom had likened magical power to a string. As the witches used their combined power to clasp *my* string, pulling, pulling me, weakness washed through me.

Now!

I clasped my string, too, pulling...pulling, regaining my power. At the end of my string, I found *theirs.* They'd hitched their wagons to mine. Pulling. Harder. Faster.

The tips of my fingers heated, strength flooding me. Seven witches, seven times the power. I wanted to laugh with glee. Pulling, pulling. The coven chanted at a lower volume, their dance slowing. Hoods fell back, revealing eyes aglow with fear and confusion. The blade clattered to the floor.

My merciful side said, *Show mercy.*

My vengeful side replied, *These witches agreed to kill me for a chest of gold. They can spare more power!*

Pulling. The heat intensified, my cells ablaze, using my organs as firewood. Sweat beaded on my skin. Did blisters erupt? Any second, I would melt, yet I never ceased pulling those threads.

What magical abilities would I obtain?

"What's happening?" Challen asked, sounding weaker.

Power nearly split me apart at the seams. Just a little more… one last tug…

A witch collapsed, then another. *Thud, thud.* Soon, the rest followed. Unconscious or dead?

Did I care?

Next, *I* dropped with a hard *thud.* My plaits came tumbling down, curls falling over my face. As I smoothed the locks away, lines of fire raced from the tips of my fingers to my shoulders. I gritted my teeth and lifted my arms to the light. My jaw nearly unhinged. Black veins had surfaced, branching here, there, everywhere.

When sorcerers have syphoned so much power from others, it seeps into their blood, turning their veins black. Touching them skin-to-skin is as painful as it is lethal.

The witches were dead. I'd killed the entire coven and stolen too much power.

Suddenly I wanted to laugh. Too much power? *Tsk, tsk.* Such a terrible problem to have.

"Everly," Challen said, barely audible now.

I snapped my gaze to his. "Are you asking for my help? I remember asking for yours—to no avail." I stood, a little giddy, and a lot drunk on power. So glorious!

Only two slight problems remained.

1. Challen wasn't healed.

(A) To heal him, I would have to give him my power.

(B) No witches had survived, so no one could perform the ceremony.

2. Roth hadn't returned, so I couldn't leave the palace.

If Challen touched me... I wouldn't have a marriage problem.

"You've killed me," he rasped.

Oh, no, he didn't. "I will not carry blame. I warned you about this. Had you shown me an ounce of compassion, I would have moved mountains to save you." The pitch of my voice escalated with each new word. "You just had to go and use force, turning a potential savior into a definite enemy. So, no. I didn't kill you. You killed *yourself.*"

He wavered, his cane shaking. In his expression, defeat battled remorse. "Do it, then. Syphon from me. Kill me and acquire my battle magic. But please, I beg you, use it to save the kingdom and my children, not to harm them."

"You heard Noel. I *can't* take it. Your son ensured I couldn't syphon from a member of his family."

Defeat marred Challen's features. He hobbled toward me, every step an illustration of agony. I stumbled back, bumping into the throne, then falling into the seat with a *humph.* It wasn't made of ice, as I'd once assumed, but glass.

A wild thought pricked my mind: *there is no throne more perfect for me.*

Focus! I gripped the arms. "If you touch my skin, you *will* die. Instead, hang on as long as you can." *Give Roth a chance to say goodbye.*

"Told you." Still he kept coming, until he stood mere inches away. He dropped the cane and gripped the throne, finding balance. "I'm dead either way."

To prevent any accidental contact, I settled my hands on my lap.

"What I did to you was wrong," he said. "What I planned to do, even more so. But I ask you to forgive me, to spare my children, and treat them as your own. They are your family now. I ask you to be better to them than I was to you. Please! I ask you to be better to them than *they* are to you."

I owed him no favors. I owed his precious children even less. But I wasn't a monster—I hoped. I couldn't let him die without offering some kind of assurance. "I promised Noel your children would be safe as long as they refrained from attacking me." If they *did* strike at me...

Who was I kidding? They *would*.

Must take precautions. "What is your battle magic saying now?"

Already pale cheeks became ashen. His inhalations turned shallow, coming more swiftly. "Evil...is a choice. Do not...make my...mistakes." He reached for me, saying, "Battle magic says... I must die...so they can...live. This time...I listen."

I lurched back as far as possible, avoiding his fingers. "Don't!"

He simply followed me, closing in, finally brushing my cheek. Skin-to-skin. One touch, only one. A second later, his knees gave out and he crumpled, cracking his head on the floor. Blood pooled around him as he expelled his last breath.

31

Red wedding, stony heart...
no longer will we be apart...

I gripped the arms of the throne, blood leaving my frigid fingers in a frigid rush. Heart racing, I scanned my surroundings, noticing smallish mirrors hanging on every wall, strategically placed to give the sovereign a 360-degree view of the room. The blood-soaked wedding gown chilled me to the bone, and I shivered. The king's body lay at my feet like some macabre offering. Somehow, I'd entered a nightmare from which I couldn't awaken, one I would forever dub Schrödinger's king.

I had both healed and not healed Challen. I had both killed and not killed him.

Loophole: he wasn't sick if he was dead.

Roth and Farrah would be devastated by his loss. The *entire kingdom* would be devastated. The evil sorceress would be blamed, and rightfully so. While I hadn't purposely killed the king, I *had* purposely killed those witches—and I'd loved it. But

I might be a monster, but I didn't regret my actions, or what had followed. Or maybe I did? I wasn't sure what I felt anymore.

The only thing I could do now? Fight to ensure no one else ever held my fate in their hands. I didn't even want *Fate* to hold my fate. I wanted to run from this place, run and never look back.

I had to try.

I stood on wobbly legs and approached the wall of mirrors behind the throne, blanching when I had an up-close view of my reflection. Tangled flaxen locks just as blood splattered as my dress. Black lines ran through every inch of exposed skin as well as my eyes. I could be a poster girl for *eerie*.

I wasn't linked to anyone, so I wasn't syphoning. But I had all the excess power stored up, desperate to be used. "Take me to the forest," I muttered, reaching out. When my fingers encountered a solid block, I cursed. What I didn't do? Give up—

Not for a solid hour.

With a screech, I pounded my fist into the glass. Despite the king's death, Roth's compulsion remained in effect. Until the prince returned, I couldn't flee the palace.

Stuck here. Timing unknown. Legs unsteady, I plodded back to the throne and drew my knees to my chest, feeling utterly alone.

I wanted to hate Roth for everything that had happened. And maybe a small part of me did. The other part of me missed his ridiculous taxes, and how safe I'd felt in his arms.

Torn in two yet again. My chin trembled, tears stinging my eyes. What was I doing, missing my *stepson*?

Forget him. Focus! What to do? What, what? Pride wouldn't let me cower or hide. These people had schemed to make me their queen; now they should have to deal with the consequences. I couldn't lash out at Noel and Ophelia. Thanks to our hasty bargain, they had safe passage in my kingdom from now until forever. And, according to prophecy—

The prophecy! Razors slashed at my chest, my lungs deflating. We'd reached a tipping point in the fairy tale. The time the Evil Queen tried to kill Snow White.

I wouldn't renege on my promise to Noel, so I wouldn't be harming Farrah. But I *would* offer Fate a big screw-you and banish the girl.

Evil is knowing what is right but doing what is wrong anyway.

Evil is a choice. Do not make my mistakes.

Mom would have been proud of me. Maybe. Probably. Challen would thank me. Would Foreverly agree with me?

My tremors degenerated as I peered at the mirror closest to me. I waved my hand to unleash a stream of power and summon my staunchest (and only) ally. Instead, I somehow caused a pile of dirt to appear in the middle of the room. I frowned, then waved my hand again. Another pile of dirt appeared. Why did—

Ahhh. I'd killed the witches and stolen their abilities. One—or all?—must have created dirt the way Farrah created ice.

Their bodies still littered the dais, the sight of them scalding my eyes. I croaked, "Mirror."

Foreverly materialized, her friendly face making my heart swell. She wore a spectacular gown made of ivy and bloodred roses. Living snakes coiled around her forearms, and spidorpions hung from her ears.

"My, how things have changed," she said. "From prisoner to queen, an army at our beck and call."

Yes, but just as quickly as I'd gained the title, I'd lost it. "How is Hartly?" Hours had passed since I'd last checked in.

Foreverly tilted her head, listening to whispers I couldn't hear. "The troll commander had hoped to tame her, then use her to draw you out, but she continues to defy and intrigue him. He spends his time fighting his attraction to—quote unquote—*the hideous mortal.*"

I stiffened. If only I'd had such success with Roth. "If the commander *bites* her—"

"He knows he'll lose her."

"Show her to me."

Ripples. A spacious tent. Hartly faced away from me, feeding treats to birds, rabbits, deer and foxes. *Darling sister. Miss you so much.* No sign of the troll commander.

A fluffy bunny nipped her finger, and she laughed. A genuine sound of amusement, layered with zero concerns. My relief doubled. "Show me Roth."

Foreverly resurfaced, saying, "He is beyond our sphere. Ophelia hides him."

I would summon her for a chat, then. Later, after I'd dealt with my Farrah problem. "Are you ready to face our foes?"

"Ready, willing and able. All your life, you have hated how others fear you. Now you *need* that fear. Use it."

Yes! "Guards!" I readjusted my crystal crown. "Guards, get in here." *Head up. Shoulders back. Spine fused with steel. Legs down. Ankles crossed. Casual but authoritative.* I twirled one quaking finger, an illusion of cold disdain settling over my features, masking my ashen cheeks and wild eyes.

Just in time. The double doors were thrown open, two soldiers plowing inside the chamber.

The moment the carnage registered, they ground to a halt.

Though I wanted to fold into myself and explain what had happened, I announced, "I am your sovereign, crowned this very day. Kneel before me or suffer."

Radiating disbelief and dismay, they looked from the bodies to me. Me to the bodies. Back and forth, again and again. Ultimately, they sank to their knees.

Get this over with. "You will find the princesses Farrah and Truly, the maid Annica and the fairy Vikander. You will bind their arms behind their backs and bring them here."

"The likelihood these soldiers will obey? Abysmal," Foreverly said. "They revere the royal family, especially the princesses. Unless forced, they will never willingly endanger the Charmaines."

I doubted the men could hear her; their expressions never changed.

I would have to use force. Groaning inside, I said, "If you fail me, others will suffer." Others—like myself. "I can imprison your families. You can listen to their screams of pain." Not a lie. We *could* do those things. But we wouldn't.

The men paled.

Foreverly told me their names, as well as the names of their loved ones, and I repeated the information. They shook with fright.

"Shall I go on?" As tightly as I squeezed the throne, I expected my knuckles to split my skin at any moment. I comforted myself with the knowledge that I would make up for every terrible act I committed as soon as I'd secured my safety.

"No need. We understand the consequences of disobedience," one guard assured me. "We will complete our mission."

"You will complete your mission...what?" I demanded, playing my part. Cold, callous.

"Y-your Majesty," the other stuttered.

"That's right. I am Queen Everly, your majesty. I will be a benevolent ruler, you'll see. I offer competitive overtime rates and incomparable medical insurance." Though they looked confused by my words, I shooed them off. "Go. Fetch. And spread the word. Anyone who doesn't wish to serve the new queen may leave my kingdom or die." Again, not a lie. At some point, everyone died.

A guard motioned to the sea of dead bodies, saying, "Would you like us to..."

Cold. Callous. "Leave them." For now. Let Farrah think the worst of me, like everyone else. "A girl should enjoy her handiwork, yes? Now, go!"

They raced off, and I sagged against the throne. Would they

ditch the palace, gather their families and run? Maybe they would return with the entire army and attack me.

I should prepare. Weapons, I needed weapons, just in case my magic faltered. I swept my gaze over the king and whimpered, guilt rising. *Focus.* Two daggers hung from his belt.

Feeling gutted, I leaned down and drew a blade from its sheath. Then, I waited. When the guards came back, I shot to my feet, my heart a cannonball against my ribs. An army *had* tagged along, and each man thrummed with aggression.

I raised the dagger—

The prisoners! Astonishment and satisfaction unfurled. Farrah, Truly, Vikander and Annica were clustered together, their hands bound behind their backs. They glared at me as if I'd just had them imprisoned...oh, wait.

The fact that I'd given an order and the guards had obeyed... well, that was big. Huge! My reward for having power, and oh, the headiness. For a moment, I forgot the tragic events I'd endured to get here. Only a moment.

Roycefus pushed his way to the front of the group, the disappointment in his gaze giving me a major case of the pangs. "Your Majesty," he began. "I must council you against—"

"I like you, Roy, I really do. But if you do not hold your tongue, you will join the ones you seek to protect." *Can't trust him. Can't trust anyone.*

He quieted. Good. I'd meant what I'd said. I did like him, and I didn't want to kick him out.

When the group stopped just below the dais, I disregarded the ragged, gnawing pain in my chest and told the guards, "Help the prisoners kneel before their new queen."

Though the foursome fought, they couldn't defeat the masses and crashed to their knees. My satisfaction deepened. Truly and Farrah were disheveled, hair tangled, lips swollen, gowns wrinkled. No doubt my summons had interrupted snuggle time.

Annica bowed her head and sobbed.

Vikander was shirtless, his pants unfastened, his lips as red and puffy as the princesses'. Snuggle time had been interrupted for him, as well. Far from cowed or upset, he looked somewhat proud—of me. Which I didn't understand! He'd borne no love for the king?

Doesn't matter. I had four prisoners—Snow White, the Huntsman, and two of the seven. I needed to smoke the other protectors out before they had a chance to ambush me.

One problem at a time.

I peered at Farrah and suddenly understood why the Seven Dwarves had sung their song. "Hi…ho."

Farrah pleaded with her eyes. "I know you are angry with us, Everly, but—"

"Anger doesn't begin to describe it," I interjected.

"You must—" She looked down, noting her father's body for the first time. His blood had begun to congeal, turning black. A scream ripped from her. She attempted to scramble to her feet and launch forward. Per my order, the guard held her in place.

Guilt pulverized me, and regret slashed me. *Mask in place? Reveal nothing.*

"How could you do this?" Truly demanded.

I rallied quickly. "Me? How could *you*? To save his life, the king had to end mine. I was to be a sacrifice. But you knew that, did you not? Perhaps you even wanted me dead?"

"No!" she shouted, but I didn't believe her. *Fight the pain.*

When Farrah choked on her sobs, my twin nuzzled her cheek, offering comfort. All the while, she glared at me.

Hate me? Get in line.

Knowing my life depended on my next actions, I stood slowly, regally, and announced, "Because of your actions, I was crowned Queen of Sevón. You caused this. Part of me wants to kill you for it. However, my dear, departed husband of five seconds used his dying breath to beg for mercy—for his children. I have decided to honor his wishes." I made no mention of my vow to Noel.

Everyone scrutinized me as if I were a viper poised to strike. I couldn't fault them. A viper by any other name…

"Truly," I said, "you will move into my old room." The Huntsman would not be aiding Snow White, and Snow White would not be turning on the Huntsman, if ever she learned of Truly's connection to the sorcerian. Added bonus: if Snow White feared for her girlfriend's life, she would not attack the palace.

A gaggle of protests sounded, each at a different volume.

I spoke over them. "Farrah, Vikander and Annica, you are hereby banished from my kingdom."

More protests.

"If I were as evil as you," I said, "I would cut off your hands before sending you off, hobbling you the way you hobbled me." The temptation… "If you dare return for any reason, I will slay you without a moment's hesitation."

32

Just when you get bored,
in comes the horde.

Roycefus summoned a witch who had the power to teleport big groups—not Ophelia, thank goodness. To get her to help, I had to pay with a vow. As long as she didn't turn on me, I would not syphon from her.

Overflowing with power, I remained seated on my throne and peered into the mirror, observing as the witch deposited Farrah, Vikander and Annica in the Enchantian Forest. I also watched a set of guards escort Truly to her room in the tower.

By the time my enemies were settled in their new homes, the black lines had disappeared from my skin. I could no longer use magic without syphoning.

Rather than link with someone else, I focused on the remaining guards and stood. "I want a patrol sent to the Enchantian Forest to search for Prince Roth and Saxon. They are hidden by magic. Find and help them. I expect daily reports of your progress. You are not, I repeat, *not* to bring them back or kill any forcerian in the process." Nicolas and Tyler were still hunting for Hartly, and I wanted nothing to interfere with that.

They nodded and dashed off.

"You," I said to Roycefus. "Escort me to Prince Roth's private bedchamber." I wanted privacy and a bath. What better place?

"Of course. This way." He led me from the throne room, saying, "We should discuss your schedule. As queen, you have many duties."

Was he serious? "Don't act as if you're glad I'm in charge." Part of me still expected him—everyone—to side with Farrah. I remained on alert, lest anyone decided to attack.

"What do feelings matter? Challen made you queen. Long ago, I vowed to serve the royals, whoever they happened to be." He chatted about upcoming meetings, barely pausing to breathe.

When he spouted off rules of comportment for queens but not kings, I held up my hand to stop him.

"I will do what I want, when I want," I said. "In my queen-dom, girls have the same rights and privileges as boys."

As soon as we reached the bedroom, I shut the door in his face, ending the conversation and barricading myself inside. After everything that had happened, I needed a moment alone to breathe and to be, or I would snap.

The room's splendor staggered me. A square dais had four massive pillars made of marble, one in each corner. A chandelier hung from the ceiling, directly over the bed. Roth's scent wafted from the sheets. A padded bench rested against the bed's footboard, the legs carved to resemble dragons. Beside the solid gold nightstands were potted plants. The hearth crackled with flames; the servants must have expected Roth's return. No artwork decorated the walls to reveal the prince's aesthetic preferences. Why?

A cold breeze whisked through an open bay of windows leading to a balcony that overlooked the surrounding mountains. A wet bar contained various bottles of whiskey. How many times had he entertained Annica?

My hands fisted. Atop the desk were stacks of paper and a metronome.

I picked up one of the books. *Annals of Enchantia, Volume 111*. As I thumbed through the pages, I found a copy of "Snow White and the Evil Queen." Roth had highlighted it, as well as a copy of "Snow White and Rose Red," and added a hand-written note. *Are the two tales linked?*

SWARR featured two sisters raised by a loving mother. One day, the siblings freed a ferocious bear from a trap. Later, they freed an evil dwarf from the same trap. Despite their good deed, the dwarf tried to kill them, and would have succeeded if the bear hadn't returned to kill the dwarf. When Rose Red kissed the bear in thanks, he turned into a handsome prince, his curse lifted. The two married soon after. Snow White married his brother.

There were definite parallels between the story and my life. The couples: me and Roth, Truly and Farrah. Like the bear, Roth considered his magic a curse. Like the evil dwarf, Farrah lashed out at me after I was kind to her.

Roth had studied other fairy tales, even the ones that had nothing to do with his own. He'd written notes about the ones he believed had been activated in each of the four kingdoms. "Beauty and the Beast." "The Little Mermaid." "Cinderella." "Sleeping Beauty." "Rumpelstiltskin." "Hansel and Gretel." "The Frog Prince." And "The Swan Princess."

Though intrigued by the others, I returned my focus to "Snow White and the Evil Queen." As I'd been told, both *mother* and *stepmother* were used interchangeably to describe the Evil Queen, and the Seven Dwarfs were touted as the Seven Protectors. No mention of true love's kiss. There *was* a fairy godfriend slash witch who popped up any time Snow White required aid.

Snow White. Not the Evil Queen.

Also, in the Enchantian tale, the Seven Protectors had names. Sparkles, Wingly, Hickey, Verity, Petal, Crusty and Viper.

Sparkles—Vikander. Wingly—Saxon. Hickey—Annica.

Could Truly be Verity? Did she do double duty in the tale?

What I wouldn't give for concrete answers!

After setting the metronome into motion—*click, click, click*— I strode into the private bathroom. Just as elaborate as the bedroom, with a gold toilet, clawfoot tub and sink.

At one end of the tub, a small vase hovered midair. Nothing anchored it in place. Not the wall, not a hidden wire. When I brushed my hand over it, hot water poured out, filling the tub.

I laughed, amazed. Magic plumbing. Being queen was fun!

QUEEN OF SEVÓN
DAY 2

I woke with the rise of the sun, enveloped by Roth's delectable scent, surprisingly refreshed and ready to conquer the new day.

As I stretched, I realized a stalk of ivy had grown over the far wall. A soft blue glow enveloped the leaves.

"Spying on me, Allura?" I asked. Why would she bother?

I sighed. I had spying of my own to do. Had anyone planned my assassination?

I rolled to my side and freed my sliver of enchanted glass from confinement. "Show me the servants and guards currently in the palace."

Rooms appeared, one after the other. Silence permeated the air, but no one actively plotted my murder. Maybe these people would grow to like and trust me one day. If given the chance, I could be a good queen. No, a great one.

I checked on Hartly—doing well. Roth—still blocked by Ophelia.

Farrah—living in a small cabin in the Enchantian Forest.

"We cannot leave Truly with that...that monster," she told

the others. She sat at a table, her eyes swollen and red. "We *must* save her."

I had to admire her courage.

"You're wrong. Everly will never harm Truly." Vikander—aka Sparkles—sat at the table, as well. He leaned back and crossed his arms. "We must stick to the plan and find Roth and Saxon."

Envy twisted Farrah's features.

Snow White is jealous of the Evil Queen? What a delightful twist.

"Your confidence is misplaced," she said. "I can't... We need... *I* need Truly." A sob broke free. Then another and another, until she was snot-crying into fistfuls of her hair.

Annica—aka Hickey—sat at her right and reached over to pat her hand, offering comfort, but Farrah was beyond consoling.

"My mother's things are in the palace," she said between sniffles. "Everly will destroy everything, just to spite me."

Wrong. I knew the pain of losing a mother and, no matter how much I disliked the girl, I would never add to hers.

"That's enough, Princess." Vikander's harsh tone lacked mercy. "I provide shelter, food and protection for you. In return, I ask only that you cease crying, clean up the cabin, wash my clothes and cook my meals. In other words, you will make my life easier, not more difficult."

Ooh la la. How very Seven Dwarfs of him.

"Show me Nicolas," I said.

The scene morphed. My stepdad camped out in the forest. He perched before a firepit, sharpening a sword alongside Tyler, preparing to "question another troll." The one chained to the ground a few feet away, I assumed.

"Show me Violet," I said, tensing.

Morph. The queen had sealed herself inside a greenhouse, alone, to pull weeds and prune a large tree that was surrounded by thorns as long as my legs. The branches were jet-black, heavy with bright red apples.

The Tree of New Beginnings?

———

"Ridding the world of evil is good," she muttered. "*I am good.*"

She saw herself as a hero? A humorless laugh escaped me. May I never be so deceived.

I'd had enough. I ended the vision with an angry swipe of my hand.

Only seconds later, a knock sounded at my door.

I pulled myself into an upright position as Roycefus entered. A gaggle of maids spilled in from behind him, everyone loaded down with armfuls of fabric.

"You're awake. Excellent," he said with a nod of approval. "I will wait in the hall. Join me when you finish, and I will escort you to a meet and greet with your generals. Afterward, you will speak with Cook about your meal preferences. Anything special you'd like for lunch? Oh! I have rescheduled all other meetings. They take place tomorrow."

So much to do! I groaned. "Breakfast first. For lunch, I'd like a vegetable pot pie." The last meal I'd shared with Mom. "Today I'd like to go over the laws of the land."

"What you want, you shall have." He clapped his hands and exited the room.

The signal to help me, I supposed. The maids leaped into action, tugging me out of bed, brushing my hair and trying to brush my teeth. *That* I did myself. Despite my protests, they stripped me, sponged me off and dressed me.

Another maid strolled into the room, a bowl of oatmeal—porridge—in hand.

I took a tentative taste. Mmm. Not bad. I thought I detected ginger, saffron and cardamom. "Thank you, Roycefus," I called, knowing he was responsible.

He struck me as a straight shooter, who rolled with the flow. But I wouldn't—couldn't—trust him. I had to keep my guard up, and expect an ambush at every turn.

"So, what do you guys normally eat here?" I asked the maids.

Someone said: "Mostly trenchers, King Challen's preference. On special occasions, he requested a meat pie."

Another added: "There's a flour mill behind the castle. Breads are Cook's specialty."

Mom had mentioned trenchers. Bread bowls filled with meat, an array of vegetables and even fruit.

When I finished my meal, the maids turned their efforts to the cleaning of my room.

I stepped into the hall and said, "You mentioned other meetings."

"Yes." He led me through the palace. "While Sevón's leadership has changed, the need for trade agreements has not. You must be introduced to dignitaries from other kingdoms. Do you have any experience with negotiations?"

"I do." Thanks to my summer classes. "I'll make you proud."

He heaved a relieved breath. "You also mentioned learning our laws."

"My mother told me about the Enchantian version of divorce. Namely, the beheading of a wife who doesn't conceive during the first year of marriage."

"A barbaric law," he said.

"I want it changed. How do I go about it?" Did I need to present any amendments to any groups?

"You tell me what you want the law to be, and I have papers printed to distribute to your citizens."

"Excellent. From now on, a husband may be beheaded if he fails to please his wife."

Roycefus's eyes widened.

I smiled sweetly and continued our conversation. "Will the generals balk at my leadership?" I asked.

Took a moment for him to dig his way past his shock. "The generals are not happy you killed their king. But because you syphoned his battle magic, they will forever obey."

Gah! Everyone believed I'd syphoned Challen's magic—the one thing I hadn't done!

"Tell me about the prisoners in the tower," I said, switching gears. "Are they sorcerian?"

"They are not. They are mortals who owed King Challen money, or insulted him in some way. Violent offenders and those with special abilities are kept in the dungeon below."

I pressed my tongue to the roof of my mouth. "Let the ones in the tower go with my compliments. Everyone but Princess Truly." Would Roth protest upon his return?

I kind of...hoped so. I missed arguing with him.

"Yes, Your Majesty." Roycefus used a magic pen to make a note in his stone tablet.

Being queen came with perks and responsibilities, but I was up for the challenge. So why did my nausea return and redouble as we entered the throne room?

To my surprise, the meet and greet passed without a hitch. In fact, as servants filled everyone's goblets with sweet wine, the vibe was almost jovial.

Afterward, Roycefus oversaw the release of the prisoners, and I met with Cook. She was quite old, with frizzy silver hair, stooped shoulders, and pale gray skin. Corpse walking. I thanked her for the porridge and did my best to put her at ease, but she refused to look at me.

She only perked up when I requested two slices of the vegetable potpie. One for me, one for Truly.

I carried both to the room in the tower. I sat at the edge of the bed and held out a plate and an extra fork, but she humphed and turned away.

"I won't break bread with the destroyer of Sevón," she said.

Whatever. "Your loss." I'd put her in my old cell, and had it filled with every luxury but freedom. "As a nickname, Destroyer of Sevón gets my gold star of approval. How about DOS for short?" I tasted the pie… Sweeter than I preferred, but not bad.

"How easily you mock me," she snapped. "My twin would not treat me this way."

"But I'm not your twin, remember?"

"You *believe* you are, despite disowning me."

"Which is why I'm protecting you."

She snorted. "Imprisoning me is protecting me?"

"Yes! What do you think will happen if—when—Farrah learns of our connection?"

Paling, she said, "Going with Farrah or staying with you should be my choice. *Mine.*"

My stomach gurgled, seeming to wring out bile. A sharp pain seared my side.

"Are you all right?" Truly asked, mildly concerned.

Though heat rushed from my face, sweat beaded on my brow. Black dots consumed my line of sight. I labored to my feet. *Dizzy.* Another gurgle, another pain. I whimpered.

The urge to vomit overpowered me, and I dove for Truly's bucket-toilet. Goodbye, potpie.

The potpie! The unexpected sweetness. Had Cook…poisoned me?

I stumbled to the door, saying, "If you want to go, fine. Go. I won't stop you."

Truly followed me into the hall, and I thought—hoped—she would accompany me to Roth's chamber, that she would care for me until I recovered. But she ran away as if her feet were on fire, choosing Farrah. Again.

The loss shredded me. When would I learn?

Crap! I wasn't going to make it. Halfway to my destination, I stopped, hunched over and vomited.

"Sorry," I muttered to the maid standing nearby.

Roycefus came up behind me and told the girl, "Clean the mess."

"Yes, sir," she responded.

Throat raw, I said, "I think Cook poisoned me. I want her locked in Truly's cell until I'm well enough to speak with her."

"Of course," he said. "In the meantime, I will search the kingdom for healers."

"What happened to the old ones?"

"It is my displeasure to inform you they have abandoned us."

Not us. Me. I blinked away my tears as I locked myself in Roth's room. *This is for the best.* I couldn't defend myself. I couldn't risk another betrayal.

I had to get better on my own.

QUEEN OF SEVÓN
DAY 6

I wasn't getting better on my own.

After I'd run out of potpie to barf, I'd puked up stomach lining, a lung and a few thousand pints of blood. When my latest round of heaving had subsided, I'd crawled into bed and burrowed under the covers.

I'd been there ever since.

A foul taste coated my tongue, my throat dry as the desert. I needed water, but I didn't have the energy to fetch any. Fever ravaged my mind and body.

Noel had attempted to mind-speak with me a few times, but I'd faded in and out of consciousness and couldn't recall what she'd said.

At some point, I remembered Tyler's lifeline and lifted my hand over his faded print. Maybe he would come, maybe he wouldn't.

Allura's ivy continued to grow over the walls.

Now, I rolled to my side and caught sight of Phobia. The little darling had followed me all the way to the palace.

—*Friend hurt?*—

Yes, Phobia. Friend hurt.

I thought I saw Tyler, standing beside my bed, his arm banded around a guy I'd never met. A hallucination?

"Syphon from the healer, Everly. Now."

No, not a hallucination. With a mewl of pain, I stretched out my fingers. *Link.* In an instant, streams of heat and power flowed through me, calming my stomach and soothing my throat. The fever cooled, intelligent thought flickering to life.

Tyler had actually come, had actually helped me. But how had he gotten in?

I severed the mystical connection to the healer and blinked. The unfamiliar male had collapsed in the sorcerer's arms.

"You will strengthen now," Tyler said, hefting the healer over his shoulder. "Color has returned to your cheeks."

"Did I kill him?" *Please say no, please say no.*

"He lives, though that is more than he deserves, considering he left you in such deplorable condition. As for Cook...she does *not* live. Nicolas drained her."

Nicolas was here, too? Where? Did I care that he'd killed the woman who'd tried to kill me?

I kind of...didn't.

Liking your title of Evil Queen a little too much, eh?

Tyler regarded me curiously. "You need to punish your people for their crimes or they'll strike again."

I pushed a tangle of hair from my damp brow. "What, no lessons about choosing good over evil, forgiveness over hate?"

"Do you want to live?" he asked, one brow arched.

"More than anything!"

"Then no. No lessons." He turned away, only to pause. "Be leery, Everly."

"Be leery of what? Who?"

"Everyone."

Was he trying to tell me something? Maybe. His gaze darted away from mine as if he couldn't bring himself to face me. Then he resumed his journey to the door, saying, "We haven't found your sister, but we *have* found your prince. Ophelia locked him and the avian inside a dimension of their own. I left a key in your bathroom. You may use it to scry him."

"Scry?"

"Your magic. When you have visions, you scry."

Still so much to learn. "Thank you."

He glanced over his shoulder, grinning a scary grin. "Don't thank me. One day, I'll demand repayment."

QUEEN OF SEVÓN
DAY 7

I soaked in the tub, steam rising from the water. Again and again, my gaze returned to Tyler's gift. A full-length mirror, propped against the counter; the frame had a keyhole up top, dead center, and a hook on the side, where a golden key dangled.

What would happen if I inserted the key in the hole? Would I scry and see Roth? Or would I create some sort of doorway our enemies could use to enter the palace and attack? I'd only just regained my strength. Could I risk a battle with unknown foes?

I wanted to trust Tyler—Ty. And I *should* trust him, right? He was a sorcerer, considered evil by most, and I barely knew him... yet he'd helped me more than anyone else. I just... I couldn't figure out why he and Nicolas wanted me to contact a prince who would behead them both at the first opportunity.

I was missing a piece of this puzzle. But what?

After drying and styling my hair, I dressed in an azure gown that molded to curves. In deference to Aubrey, I refused to wear the royal jewels...though I was more tempted every day. Why deny myself life's simple pleasures?

A stalk of ivy reached out to pet my arm. The foliage now covered the bathroom walls as thickly as the bedroom. Would the entire palace soon become a secret garden?

"Why won't you reveal yourself to me, Allura?" I waited. No

response. "Why do you watch me?" Was I a novelty? An exotic animal at the zoo?

Knock, knock. I walked into the bedroom as Roycefus entered.

He wore a purple robe, as usual, and carried a stack of parchment rather than a stone tablet. "You'll be pleased to know I have hired a new cook and rescheduled your meetings for today. If you miss another one, you risk offending other kingdoms."

Ugh. "Very well. I'll attend." I hesitated to join him. "Hey, Roy. You know Farrah is part of a fairy tale, right? She is Snow White, and she has seven protectors."

"And you think I am one of those protectors, determined to end you before you can harm her?"

"Are you?" Petal, Crusty and Viper were up for grabs.

He wagged the pen at me. "While I abhor violence, I understand the need for war. I will not betray you, Everly. On the other hand, I will not harm the princess, either."

My admiration for him skyrocketed. "I apologize if I offended you. That wasn't my intension. You are a good man, Roy. One of the best." I closed the distance, even more at ease with him. "Please, lead the way."

He patted my hand, letting me know all was forgiven, then headed for the throne room. "Are you wearing your listening ears today? Because I have information you need."

"Hit me."

He shrank back, with his hand pressed over his heart. "You heard me say I abhor violence, yes? I will not hit you, even if you demand it."

I fought a smile. "I meant, tell me what you want me to know."

"Oh. All right. Yes." Some of his tension drained. "Fleur wants gold and precious gems from us, things they use to build grander homes and more dangerous weapons. In return, they offer honey and herbs only they can harvest. Azul wants our lumber and our gold. We were on the verge of war, until their emperor died in his sleep. The new ruler made peace with your late husband while your stepson was away."

My late husband. My stepson. I shuddered. A full-body quake.

"Azul controls most bodies of water, and they offer coral and seafood in trade." He held up one of the papers, revealing a map of Enchantia. "Airaria will request safe passage through Sevón to more easily reach Fleur. They offer meteorites and sand. We use the meteorites for weapons, and the sand for mortar."

"As soon as Queen Violet learns I'm in charge, she'll balk. She despises me more than most." And I didn't care. I didn't!

"Personal feelings have no bearings on kingdom business," he chided.

I couldn't argue, because he wasn't wrong.

"More than anything," he said, "Sevón needs access to Azul. Like every kingdom, Azul has new leadership, but we have yet to reach an accord. Also, it wouldn't hurt if we convinced more witches, oracles and fae to move here. I tried to set a meeting with the sovereign of each faction, but they refuse to come near a sorceress. Please, you must not syphon from anyone today. Doing so will violate trade law and leave us destitute."

We reached the throne room, and I paused to offer him a jaunty salute. "I'll be good. I'll even win us that water route. Oh! I need you to send someone to buy every full-length mirror in every village around us. I want a life-size looking glass in every room of the palace." My escape hatches, in case something went wrong.

He looked confused, but he made a note. "It will be done."

Guards stood at attention as we entered. I strode forward, my head high, and eased atop my throne of glass. Roy looked nervous as he stood at my side and motioned for the first representative. I would enjoy matching wits with others and winning concessions for my people. Proving my worth. And one day, one day soon, this Evil Queen would be touted as the One Who Gets Stuff Done.

★ ★ ★

Exhausted mentally, emotionally and physically, I made my way to Roth's bedroom. For hours, I'd employed the four tricks I'd learned in business class. Never let them think you are in a hurry. Always be willing to walk away. Never give without taking. Never be afraid to fall silent.

No matter how many insults were hurled my way—sorceress! murderess!—I'd maintained my calm. Well, I'd maintained my calm until someone insulted Roycefus. Then I'd buried the offender in dirt, forcing his people to dig him out.

I'd allowed no one to intimidate me. I'd smiled constantly as if I hadn't a care, and made sure to exaggerate my Oklahoma twang while asking for more than we'd needed and offering less than they'd wanted.

As promised, I'd won a better water route. After the last meeting, Roycefus had rushed off, jubilant, eager to share the news with the palace staff.

Now I tossed and turned in bed, despite my state of exhaustion. After one hour…two…I gave up and moved to the desk, where I worked a mechanical puzzle I'd found in Roth's closet. A true brain stumper. I don't know how long I played, moving pieces around, before a familiar voice interrupted.

"Puzzles? Boring!"

I jerked up my gaze, and found Noel sitting at the end of the bed, her ankles crossed as she swung her legs.

"Play with *us*," she said. "We're ever so much more fun."

Ophelia leaned against a pillar, watching me, her expression dark, brooding.

I didn't bother asking how they'd gotten inside.

Safe passage. Can't strike. Had they touched the mirror and key Ty had given me? I maneuvered to peer into the bathroom, relieved to find nothing had been disturbed.

"I like what you've done with the place," Noel said, motioning to the ivy. "It's very…alluring." She laughed at her own joke.

"What do you want?" I asked, not even trying to mask my irritation.

"So many things." She sighed. "Did you know our mothers once served yours? They helped Violet, Aubrey and Malinda—Farrah's mother—steal apples from the Tree of New Beginnings."

"I suspected," I admitted.

"After Reba gave birth, she spoke your prophecy. King Stephan killed her," Ophelia said, voice tight.

"Reba?" I asked softly.

"Noel's mother. My mother is—was—Teegan," she replied just as softly. "Stephan killed her, too. He would have killed us, as well, if Reba and Teegan hadn't planned for every eventuality. A witch stepped in to protect us with her magic and kept us hidden in another dimension for years."

That, I hadn't known. "One of my parents helped yours, the other hurt yours. Is that why you sometimes help me, sometimes hurt me? Tit for tat?"

Ophelia blinked with surprise. "We have never hurt you."

"To see the rainbow, you must first survive the storm." Noel drew a heart over my comforter. "I think Ty is my rainbow." She fanned her cheeks. "Never thought I'd go for a sorcerer, but he is changing my mind. And he's such a surprise! I can't predict his actions."

I yawned, nearly cracking my jaw. "*Ty* is the reason you risked my wrath to come here?"

"Your wrath?" Ophelia chuckled. "Aren't you adorable! You're nothing but a tame house cat."

I would show her a tame—

No, no. Let her continue to underestimate me. One day, she would learn better. But not today. Today, I smiled, all sugar without spice.

"We came to warn you," Noel said, then frowned. "Right?" When Ophelia nodded, she breathed a sigh of relief. "Save Roth and forfeit your crown. Leave him be and keep it. The choice is yours."

"I arranged imprisonment for him," Ophelia told me. "Sealed him inside a private dimension. You're welcome. The moment you use the key, the seal will break. He'll find a way out."

"I need a minute to mentally catch up. You trapped him for *me*?" I thumped my chest. "But why?" Would he snatch the crown from me? Try to kill me?

The witch hiked a shoulder. "When my favorite oracle tells me to give you time away from a prince, time to toughen you up so that you'll make a better, wiser queen, I give you time away from a prince."

"My reign as queen doesn't affect you," I said.

"I told you. Our fate is tied to yours." Noel smiled, though she looked sad, not amused. "I also mentioned you will become a diamond. And do you recall how we create a diamond?"

"Heat and pressure," I grumbled.

She grinned, proud of me. "When all is said and done, you are going to sparkle, Everly Morrow."

QUEEN OF SEVÓN
DAY I DON'T KNOW, AND I DON'T CARE

After my visit with Noel and Ophelia, I had posters made and passed out in surrounding villages, advertising for members of an altilium. Three forest nymphs applied for the job—Daphne, Skye and Belladonna. Sent by Allura, they'd said, with instructions to help me however I needed.

Her support floored and confused me.

I'd syphoned enough power to summon Foreverly and, with her help, hired a contingent of personal guards.

I now had a direct power source, anytime, anywhere, and I loved it.

Yesterday, I'd thrown a party, inviting the citizens Roycefus referred to as "courtlings." The "upper class" and their associates.

A huge crowd had come. Among them, fawners and snubbers. The worst of the worst. Most of the guests had stood in place, silent and miserable.

I knew the feeling. I rarely slept, my mind too wrapped up in Roth. Where was he trapped, exactly? Was he hurt? In pain? Did he blame me for his current predicament?

Did I want to keep my crown while he suffered? No.

Before I could talk myself out of it, I stomped into my private bathroom, swiped up the key—so cold—and shoved the metal into the mirror's keyhole.

Roth appeared in the glass, as beautiful as ever. No, more so. My heart rate doubled, tripled, a fever spreading over my skin. His inky hair was wind-blown, his green eyes bright. He was shirtless, and I was parched. I drank him in. The muscles. The tattoos. The pierced nipples. My kryptonite. His dark skin glistened with sweat as he swung two short swords at nothing, practicing his technique.

Saxon stood a few feet away, wincing when he flared and contracted his wings. Flared. Contracted. Scabs littered the hard, outer rim.

For weeks, I'd been lugging around ten thousand pounds of tension. Suddenly, every bit of it evaporated, relief nearly knocking me to my butt. Both males were alive and well.

"What's the first thing you're going to do when we break free?" the avian asked Roth.

Tone dry, he replied, "What I want to do isn't the same as what I'll get to do."

A smile lit Saxon's face. "What you want to do—or who?"

I studied the other dimension—so weird! The sky was green, with trees hanging upside down, raining leaves over the fluffy white clouds Roth and Saxon stood upon. A star streaked under their boots.

Roth went still. His gaze skidded over me, then returned in a hurry. Awareness singed the air.

"Everly?" he rasped.

He could see me?

"I knew it!" Saxon said. "About time you admitted it."

The prince stepped toward me, and I gasped. He *could* see me. Then he started running, Saxon on his heels.

Unless I did something, they would use the mirror as a doorway, just as I'd feared, and enter the bathroom.

Going to blame you for Challen's death.

I trembled as I ripped the key from the hole. Roth vanished, the glass hardening, the doorway closing.

A reprieve. It wouldn't last long. I'd broken the seal on the other dimension. Roth would escape, and soon. He would return to the palace, and we would have a showdown.

I stumbled to the bed, my heart racing faster.

For the first time in forever, I slept deeply.

33

It's time, it's time, the toll is due.
Pay up, pay up, and say adieu.

I awoke with a dagger pressed against my throat. Ice-cold steel, a warm drop of blood sliding to my collarbone. Keeping my eyes closed and remaining (seemingly) relaxed proved difficult, but I did it. *Think!*

"Put the torque on her, Vikander," Farrah commanded quietly. "What are you waiting for?"

Well, well. Snow White had returned to challenge the Evil Queen. Not exactly sticking to script, were we? SW had just borrowed a play from EQ.

How had the group gotten past my new guard? Or had my new guard worked *with* them? I'd heard grumblings among the soldiers for days as they'd speculated whether or not I'd actually acquired the battle magic.

"Sorry. Must have left my iron shavings in my *other* pants," Vikander replied, as breezy as could be. He was *helping* me?

Think! I had to act before the two—

"She's awake." Farrah pushed the blade deeper into my neck. Voice soft but fierce, she said, "I'm not going to murder you, Everly. Not yet. Sit up nice and slow."

Giving up the charade, I opened my eyes and met her gaze— she projected pure emerald ice. Colder than the ice dagger she held. Her long, dark hair was tangled, her face dirt-streaked, and her eyes red-rimmed.

"What happened to never cheering the suffering of others?" I asked. Mind abuzz with shock, distress and the anticipation of battle, I sat up slowly, as ordered.

"You happened. Fate tried to warn me, but I didn't listen. Now? My ears are open." Farrah backed up, one step, two, but kept the ice dagger pointed in my direction.

Linked to my nymphs, I syphoned just enough to craft an illusion. In it, I remained seated on the bed. Next, I crafted a second illusion, this one of invisibility. The real, invisible me rolled to the other side of the bed, undetected.

I paused to make sure no one could see past the illusion. Annica blocked the exit, glaring at FE—Fake Everly. Truly stood at the foot of the bed, an arrow aimed at FE, tears glistening on her cheeks.

Betrayer! So she was crying. So what? Vikander sat at the desk, thumbing through the trade agreements I'd left there. Did my success shock him? I'd benefited the kingdom in ways Challen had not.

Focus. The mirrors beckoned me. Best route to reach one?

"We can't allow you to roam free," Truly said, and hiccuped. "Please, cooperate. We don't want to hurt you."

They were planning to lock me away again before they killed me?

"I do," Farrah whispered, her voice ragged. "I want to hurt you. I want you to feel my pain."

Well, well. Snow White wasn't as sweet as predicted, just as I wasn't as evil.

"Why aren't you afraid?" she demanded, glaring at my illusion. "React!"

Oops. The magical version of me expressed zero emotion. I twirled my finger, and FE smiled. Gah! Twirl. Frown.

"My torment is amusing to you? I ignored the prophecy," Farrah said, sniffling "I had a chance to defeat you, right from the start, but I let you live. I hoped against hope, believing there was something good in you. But there isn't, and there never will be. Now, I will teach you to fear me." Her expression hardened more with every word.

With a gut-wrenching cry, she lunged at FE, pushing the ice dagger into my throat.

Took a moment for my brain to compute what had happened. A murder attempt. An actual murder attempt. By Snow freaking White. I reeled.

Truly shouted, "No!" She dropped her bow and ripped the dagger from Farrah's grip. Then she paused and frowned. "There's no blood. No wound."

Heart caught up in a wild dance, I dove over the mattress, crashing into Farrah. We hit the floor and rolled, and I exchanged invisibility for an image of Farrah. As we grappled, no one would tell us apart.

We punched, kicked and blocked, and it was clear she'd had training. As many blows as I landed, I received. Adrenaline dulled my aches and pains: a split lip, a black eye, cracked ribs and a bruised midsection. She didn't emerge unscathed. A gash bisected her forehead. One of her eyes swelled shut and blood poured from her nose.

"Who is who?" Truly cried.

I edged Farrah toward the closest full-length mirror, where Foreverly watched us. The moment we were close enough, I shoved Farrah into it—through it. Then I followed her through, my heart guiding us to…the throne room. We slammed into the floor, hard, and stars flashed through my vision.

The guards posted along the wall jerked to attention.

"Stay back," I commanded, jumping to my feet.

Farrah spun, taking in our new surroundings. Comprehension dawned; I'd given away my secret. She knew I had seer magic.

Good! I wanted her to know. I wanted her to fear me, and back down. I would make peace with her…and have a better chance of making peace with Roth.

Soon, he would return. The thought made me ache with wanting. We could give fate an FU. No more imprisonments, banishments or murder attempts. No more looming death by fire.

No more prophecy.

Farrah and I circled each other. Blood dripped from her nose and mouth, and fury festered in her eyes.

I dropped the illusion, saying, "I don't want to fight you, Farrah. Your family hurt me. I hurt your family in turn. Let's end the toxic cycle."

"You killed my father. I will *never* forgive you." She waved in my direction, unleashing a torrent of magic.

Led by instinct, I waved in her direction, too, unleashing my own magic. Between us, a spray of ice collided with a stream of dirt. Problem: I burned through power fast.

How much longer could I continue syphoning from the nymphs? How weak were they now?

"I hate you," Farrah spat. "I want you consumed by pain, as I have been."

"We don't always get what we want, now, do we?" I quipped.

Truly, Vikander and Annica must have followed the commotion; they sprinted into the throne room. Other guards trailed them, quickly forming a circle around us.

Dang it! I hurried to project another illusion of Farrah.

"Please don't hurt her, Farrah," Truly cried. She looked between us, frantic. "She's... Everly is my sister. My twin."

Shock! She believed me?

"I suspected the truth, but I didn't... I couldn't... Believing meant losing you," Truly said, wiping away a tear. "But if you kill her in cold blood, I'll lose you anyway. Look what happened to my mother after she killed my father."

A high-pitched, ragged sound seeped from Farrah, a mix of rage and pain. "Y-you are a sorceress?" She gave a violent shake of her head. "No. You can't be. You just can't."

"I'm sorry." Truly wiped away more tears. "I've never needed to syphon, but I *am* related to Everly. When she told me of our connection, my heart shouted, 'Yes!' I tried to convince myself otherwise, and I suffered for it. We all did."

Farrah's expression fell, her eyes windows to an endless pit of anguish. Her world had just crumbled around her.

I experienced a pang of sympathy. Been there. But I wouldn't let my emotions alter my current path, so I had to keep up my charade. I had to mimic her reactions and echo her words.

"Y-you lied to me," she said to Truly. "You *used* me."

Mimic. Echo.

"No!" Truly gave a violent shake of her head while glancing between us. "I never used you."

"You spied on me and reported back to her. I know it," Farrah bellowed.

"Did you laugh about my torment?" I asked.

"I would never do something so despicable." Truly sniffled, and her agony almost felled me. "How can you think such a thing?"

"Because I don't even know you!" Farrah shouted. "You are not the girl I thought you were. You protect a sorceress, the girl who murdered my father. I *hate* you. Guards! Seize her! Seize Princess Truly."

Threaten my twin and suffer. "No one moves."

The guards halted, unsure what to do or who to obey.

Burning with rage, I zeroed in on Farrah. A section of her bodice had ripped.

In the fairy tale, EQ choked SW with a bodice...

Thanks for the tip. I sprang at her. We slammed together, smacked into the ground and rolled. I let her whale on me, not even trying to shield myself, too busy hunting for the dangling material...there!

I worked my way behind her, wrapping the cloth around her neck. One hard tug, and I cut off her airway.

She clawed at the makeshift noose, but I held on tight. Reaching back, she batted me. Wham. Wham. Anytime she made contact, a patch of my skin iced over.

"Do not do this, Everly," Truly begged, and I realized the illusion had faded. "Please."

"Once, I spoke those same words to you," I snapped. "Refresh my memory. Didn't you do it anyway?"

She flinched, but also nocked and aimed an arrow—at my face. "I won't let you kill her, and I won't let her kill you. Just... move away from each other. Please!"

"She threatened you," I reminded her. "She hates you now." Just as I'd warned.

Saxon charged into the room, his massive wings tucked into his side as he pushed through the crowd. He assessed the situation, fury darkening his expression.

In reflex, I tightened the material around Farrah's neck. Strangling noises left her as she wiggled against me.

I casually said, "Welcome home. Where's Roth?"

"I flew, he rode," the avian replied. "He will arrive before the sun sets, and expects his sister to be healthy and whole. Let her go, Everly. Now."

Oh, yes. Saxon was absolutely, positively Wingly, one of SW's Seven Protectors.

I'd wondered if Truly did double duty as the Huntsman and

a protector. Considering her relationship with Farrah had just tanked

Getting ahead of myself. They could make up.

So, I'd leave Truly on the list. Three protectors remained. Maybe Roth did double duty, as well. Prince Charming and Crusty. Or Viper. Nah. Crusty all the way.

Voice terse, Saxon said, "Do you want Roth to lose his sister the same day he finds out he lost his father?"

Oh, crap. I loosened my grip. "I could kill you without a qualm, Farrah," I rasped in her ear. "And I will, if you dare to threaten someone I love again."

I could change the present, and the future. One decision at a time. One action at a time.

I released Farrah and shoved her away from me. Gasping for breath, she collapsed and curled into the fetal position. With all eyes on her, I dashed toward the nearest full-length mirror. Closing in...

"No!" Saxon shouted.

Faster... almost there...

The avian rammed into my back. I fell and landed face-first. Pain. Darkness. I tumbled into an endless pit, one final thought wafting through my mind. *The worst is yet to come.*

I awoke with a jolt, chilly, damp air engulfing me. Memories surfaced. The return of Snow White and four of her protectors. Truly's acceptance of our blood connection. My defeat.

Now I stood upright, shivering. I frowned. My toes were burning hot and freezing cold at the same time because—my eyes widened. A big block of ice covered my feet. Water dripped from it, a shallow pool forming around me.

Confused, I looked around. Sunlight filtered through the lone window, highlighting a wealth of twirling dust motes...and a familiar room. I withered. I was back in the tower.

I still wore my nightgown, but something cold and heavy

rested against my neck. Suspicious, I reached up and groaned. Yep. The torque. Once again, the ability to syphon and use magic had been taken from me. I was powerless, defenseless. Weak.

I set my hand over Ty's faint mark. Though he hadn't felt my summons the last time I'd worn the metal collar, I prayed he would feel this one.

"Truly," I shouted, fighting for freedom. Was she nearby, in a cell of her own?

I heard sniffles behind me and craned my head around.

Farrah wiped the tears from her cheeks with a shaky hand. "Your twin is locked in her bedchamber. She's alive."

My heart acted like a bomb, exploding with every beat. Fate's chosen Snow White stood next to a guard...who held a barbed whip.

It was then, in that moment, that another puzzle piece clicked. The Evil Queen's obsession with beauty had nothing to do with appearance, and everything to do with strength.

To me, nothing was more beautiful than strength. It was the most beautiful attribute anyone could have. I mean, look who I'd crushed on. Roth Charmaine, the strongest boy in all the land.

Strength was even more beautiful now because I had none, and Farrah had it all. So, yes. The Evil Queen *did* envy Snow White for her beauty. Greatly.

"Truly is your girlfriend," I snapped. "I know you don't hate her as you claimed. You love her. So help her, don't hurt her."

"Do not blame me for her circumstances. I am not the one who kept secrets." Hurt mixed with anger, dripping from her words. "As soon as Roth arrives, he will decide her fate. And yours."

Would he spare us? "Why not kill me as you threatened?"

"Oh, I'm tempted. But Noel says your end could spur Roth's. Since I'm unwilling to risk his life, I must settle for making you regret everything you've done to us, and ensure you never do it again."

My death could impact Roth, just like my life supposedly impacted Noel and Ophelia? How? Why? "Perhaps you are the Evil Queen, eh?" The girl I'd once considered an angel now clung to hatred and grief, and enjoyed hurting another living being. The same was true of me. Maybe we should start a club.

Why did fate consider Farrah a heroine worthy of love and me a villain worthy of pain? Better PR?

The guard lifted his arm to uncoil the whip, then lashed out. *Crack.* I tried to hold back the scream Farrah so desperately wanted to hear, but I failed. Searing agony consumed every inch of me.

The next three blows came in quick succession, and I squeezed my eyes shut, doing my best to focus on something, anything else. A future with Truly and Hartly. And Violet? Would she change her mind about me if I proved I didn't want her crown?

I wanted my own. And I wanted…Roth. But he would never again want me back.

Crack.

I craned my head again and met Farrah's eyes. Was that…dismay darkening her expression? Had she just flinched? "I never hurt you like this," I said, wheezing. "Just banished you."

"What you did to me hurt worse than a beating!" she cried.

Crack, crack.

My whimpers and gasps were as unstoppable as the pain. After the tenth blow, I lost count. Only pride stopped me from begging for mercy I knew I'd never receive. I longed to pass out, prayed for the sweet bliss of darkness, but I remained conscious, hyperaware of the guard's every move.

Don't break down. Don't give Farrah the satisfaction.

I thought of Roth, and his immeasurable strength. Would he cheer Farrah for her deeds?

Crack.

The pain was excruciating, and growing more intense between every lash, the anticipation of the next blow almost as bad as the blow itself. Soon, breathing became an agony, too. I couldn't... I needed...

Crack.

Argh! I twisted to avoid the next lash. A mistake. The whip's tail struck the back of my thigh. My nightgown offered no protection, the material shredding, floating to the floor like confetti. I felt as if I'd been dipped in gasoline and set on fire. My vision blurred. My knees buckled, and I fell, the block of ice tipping, leaving me trapped on all fours.

Crack.

The whip snaked over my shoulder, slicing into my collarbone. Black dots peppered my vision. Bile rushed up my throat and spewed out of my mouth.

Like my nightgown, my pride got shredded. I began to beg. "Please don't...please...no...stop." There went the last thread of my dignity.

As suspected, I received no mercy. The blows continued to rain, until two sets of footsteps registered.

"Y-you deserve this," Farrah said. "Maybe, if you experience the consequences of hurting others, maybe if you hurt yourself, you won't m-murder some other girl's father."

Two sets of footsteps registered.

"Enough!" Vikander shouted. "Roth never wanted her hurt."

"Roth doesn't know what she's done," Farrah choked out, and I thought she might be crying again. "She killed the king, stole our palace and ruined my Truly."

"She did two out of three of those things. But she also left things in better shape than she found them," Vikander said.

"Princess," Saxon said, so soft, so gentle. "I'm not asking you to stop. I'm *telling* you to, as your friend and sworn protector. If you persist, the girl will die and Roth will hate you. *You* will hate yourself."

"You are wrong," she whispered, broken. "I already hate myself. But I cannot allow this girl's crimes to go unpunished."

Lost in a haze of pain, I was vaguely aware of rustling clothing, more footsteps, the slam of a door and the clink of a lock… of the agonizing passage of time, light slowly conceding victory to darkness…of Vikander and Saxon returning to clean up my vomit and blood, then chip away what remained of the ice, finally freeing my feet.

Saxon carried me to the bed I'd given Truly and laid me on my stomach. Despite his gentleness, I received a new lesson in agony.

Raw inside and out, I choked on a sob. I'd known cruelty like Farrah's existed, but I'd never expected to be a victim of it again…and again. Had I been stronger, the whipping wouldn't have happened. The *marriage* wouldn't have happened.

I had to get stronger.

Then, I could escape. I could forget.

No! Forgetting would be foolish. I needed to remember, always. The memory would stop me from making any more mistakes. Like wanting the wrong person, or showing mercy to an enemy.

I should have killed Farrah when I'd had the chance.

The door swung open, and Saxon and Vikander stilled. A dark figure stalked inside the room with all the confidence and authority of a warrior king who'd never known defeat. Roth!

Too broken to move, I took in as many details as possible. He seemed taller and more thickly muscled, his windblown hair longer. His torn white tunic and black leather pants were streaked with mud and blood, as if he'd run here. A gash marred his brow, and a bruise painted his cheek, as if he'd fought, too. His chest rose and fell with rapid succession, and a fine sheen of sweat damped his face.

Once, his glittering green irises had excited me. Now? They stirred hate—I hated my desires, I hated his presence and his absence, and most of all I hated his scent; it transported me back to the Enchantian Forest, to a time when we'd lain before a fire, stolen heated touches and whispered secrets in the darkness.

Fool! I'd made nice with my foes one too many times. The result? Rejection and pain. Well, no more. Never again!

At least the final caveat of Roth's compulsion had been met.

As he stepped toward me, I tensed. The action, though slight, caused pain to rack my body. My stomach gave a violent heave. "Stay away." The words were barely audible, my throat still raw from my screams. Shame stabbed me.

To my surprise, Roth screeched to a halt. Before he veiled his expression, I thought I spied horror and rage so hot he could torch the world and laugh while it burned. "Everly," he said with a moan.

"Are you happy now? The evil sorceress, the parasite—your dreaded stepmother—got what she deserved, eh? Tell me. Is this the royal girlfriend experience?"

"I didn't want *this*. Didn't know what was required of you."

Some part of me longed to hurt him as deeply as I'd been hurt. "I would have moved mountains to save your father. Because I liked you, and wanted you to like me back. But you were never going to like me. You are judgmental and prejudice, and you don't deserve my friendship. Just…go away and never come back."

34

Tell the truth or tell a lie.
Are you ready to say goodbye?

Roth did leave, and I hated him even more for it. But he returned an hour or so later, surprising me. But then, he must enjoy seeing a sorceress reduced to such a pitiful state.

"You may enter," he said at my side.

Confused, I snapped, "Your *mom* may enter."

His brow wrinkled, but he waved at something—someone—beyond my sightline.

Shuffling footsteps… A gaggle of servants swarmed into the cell, carrying goodies or cleaning supplies. Guards entered, too, with a more comfortable mattress unsullied with my blood, a privacy screen for the bathroom bucket, clean blankets and new clothes.

Roth hesitantly asked, "You see my mother's ghost?"

You've got to be kidding me. "No ghosts," I replied, too tired to explain the intricacies of mom jokes.

He slid an arm under my breasts and thighs, then carefully lifted me. As servants exchanged the mattresses, Roth held me against his chest. I fought the urge to curl into him.

The guards finished quickly and exited, taking the old mattress with them. Just as carefully as he'd lifted me, Roth deposited me atop the new, softer bed.

A handful of servants remained, scrubbing the chamber from top to bottom.

A glint of light drew my attention to the floor. My sliver of enchanted glass! It must have fallen from the sheath on my thigh when Roth carried me over.

One of the servants bent down to pick it up. I panicked and threw myself over the side of the bed. Fire erupted over my back anew, and I cried out.

"Stop that," Roth said, and he almost sounded concerned. "You could have opened your wounds."

I swatted away his hands and crawled to the shard—*ignore the pain, breathe*—snatching up my only means of spying on my enemies.

Once again, the prince lifted me as gently as possible. He returned me to the mattress, new lances of pain shooting through me.

"Let's see what you risked everything to acquire." He lifted my hand and pried my fingers away from the glass.

Though I tried, I couldn't stop him. If he took it away... "That's mine! Give it to me!"

He narrowed his eyes. "Are you planning to end your life with this?"

Farrah must not have told him about my ability to scry—yet. "And deny you...the pleasure of...torturing me?" I did the whole bat my lashes at him routine. Maybe he would react better than Challen's guards. "Everyone deserves to...look at something pretty. I just happen to prefer…that something to be me. Don't worry…want to live long enough…to watch your kingdom fall."

Shut up! The best time to antagonize your jailer? Never.

React? Oh, yes. A muscle jumped in his jaw—one of his biggest tells. I'd angered him.

Even still, he released my hand *without* confiscating the sliver of glass. "You carried a mirror through the forest and constantly reached for it."

Be quiet. Offer no response. "You and I have…something in common, then." The next words spilled from my tongue unbidden. "We both like…to look at me."

"Or you fit a certain character's profile," he said softly.

"Aw, look at the handsome prince. Putting pieces of the puzzle together. Well, maybe I do fit a specific profile…but only because…she is…misunderstood."

He studied me for a long while, the wheels in his head obviously spinning.

When I had my breathing under better control, I said, "If you let me go, today, now, I will forgive you for what's happened. I made the same offer to your father, but he declined. Will you be as foolish?"

His expression hardened. "You are too dangerous to roam free, Everly."

"Only to those who wrong me, Roth."

"Citizens are demanding your head. You are the most wanted woman in the north."

"So?"

"Violet has offered a reward for your heart. You are not safe outside these walls."

"Is the big, bad prince worried about his captive?"

"He…is. If I let you go, someone will attack you. Here, at least, you are safe."

"Yes, suuuper safe. Just ask my back. Or your former cook.

She poisoned me on my second day as queen. If not for a sorcerer's aid, I would have died."

He pursed his lips before turning away and barking, "Leave us."

"But, my lord—" a servant began.

"I wasn't asking," he snarled.

What, he didn't want witnesses when he tortured me? "Hate you," I croaked.

The servants exited, leaving behind a bowl of water, unused rags and jars of…stuff. I guess I was supposed to clean and bandage my wounds by myself. Good! I would do a sucky job, considering my limited range of motion, but at least I wouldn't have to endure—

Roth eased beside me, and a scream of frustration blended with a sob of relief.

"What are you doing?" I asked.

"What needs to be done. If I do not patch you up, infection will set in." He cut away what remained of my soiled nightgown, and draped my lower half with a soft blanket.

"Why bother? I'm a parasite, remember? A leech you compelled not to syphon from your people. The very people who wished me the most harm. To use my magic, I had to syphon from noncitizens. They are volunteers, and if you dare hurt them…"

I couldn't see his face or read his expression, but I felt his body stiffen. "They are free to leave the palace," he said. "You have my word. I also release you from compulsion."

Of course he did. "Only because I *can't* syphon now."

"The torque saves you from the need. That isn't a bad thing."

"You're right. It's awful. Terrible. I'm vulnerable to attack."

As he washed away dirt, sweat and debris from my back, I did my best to breathe through the pain and almost hyperventilated. "You must heal," he said. "We are in the middle of an argument, and you need to heal and finish it. Don't be a quitter."

Quit, yes. "Stop, please stop," I beseeched.

"I'm sorry, sweetling, but I must. The worst is almost over." He smeared some kind of numbing cream over my back, and I experienced my first moment of relief.

Once, he'd had the magic touch. Today? Not so much.

Clutching the sliver of enchanted glass to my chest, I pleaded, "Send someone else to bandage me. Your touch sickens me."

"You are despised kingdom-wide. I'm the best you're going to get. I don't trust anyone else to tend to you properly."

"I don't trust you."

"I'm not going to hurt you, Everly." Anger layered his voice. "Tell me what happened."

"And relive the worst moments of my life? Hard pass."

Still, he pushed. To distract me—or himself? "Rumors suggest you murdered my father seconds after your wedding."

Should I tell him about the second, secret ceremony? Why waste my breath? He would never believe me. In the end, I just said, "Rumors are *always* true."

He stiffened further.

"What are you going to do with me?" I asked.

"I don't know." His ministrations remained gentle as he applied other salves. "I'm furious with you. Furious with my sister and father, too. Furious with Noel and Ophelia. Mostly furious with myself. And shocked. And in mourning."

With my cheek pressed into a pillow, I studied him more intently. Lines of tension branched from his eyes. Eyes that were haunted, and haunting, and filled with despair. The lines bracketed his mouth, as well—a beautiful mouth that had kissed me one moment and condemned me the next.

He said, "I don't know if you are evil or innocent. Or both. I'm afraid to find out. I hate what you did to my father, and I hate what was done to you. I hate the pain you are suffering."

His word elicited a familiar pang, but I said, "I don't care."

"This morning, I escaped an upside-down dimension with Saxon. We intended to hunt for your sister at long last, but Noel and Ophelia sent word of my father's marriage and death. Saxon flew to the palace, and I rode the horse to ground. Then I ran."

Pang, pang. "Don't care."

"Before coming to your room in the tower," he said, "I sent my most skilled trackers to find Hartly."

PANG. "Get out. Please! Before I rip open my wounds and try to kick you out."

He must have sensed my seriousness because he finally left, closing and locking the door with an ominous clink.

I traced my fingertip along the edge of the enchanted glass, my entire body shaking, new tasks taking shape in my head.

Escape with Truly. Remove the torque. Set up a new altilium. Strengthen myself, and weaken everyone else. Return to the forest. Maybe Hartly and her troll would let me crash at their place.

My final task: *destroy the Charmaines.*

Until I'd dealt with them, I would never be safe.

Over the next week, I slept whenever possible and hurt constantly, fury my constant companion.

Roth visited three times a day to change my bandages and bring me a meal worthy of a queen. I never had to worry about poison, since he acted as my taste tester.

One morning, he even gifted me with a full-length mirror, *despite* knowing I could scry when I wasn't torque'd. Either Farrah had blabbed, or he'd connected all the dots on his own.

I wanted to ask why he'd given me such a gift, but I didn't. I could guess the answer: (A) I was weak, and couldn't use magic; and (B) he hoped to ease his conscience for my mistreatment.

Whatever. There were two silver-lined clouds in my crapstorm of misery. I used my abundance of free time to spy on Nicolas and Ty, Hartly, and each of my enemies, and I had friends!

To my surprise and delight, Phobia had shown up with another spidorpion I'd named Webster. Currently the two spidor-

pions were positioned at the head of the bed, observing me as
I tried to sit up.

—*Rest. Friend heal.*—

"I will," I told him. "But first I need to pee."

Roth had entrusted the ultra-smug Annica to help me with
my personal needs. Because, according to her, "He trusts me.
He *loves* me."

Having his former girlfriend slide a bedpan between my legs
and clean me up afterward... I *seethed* with humiliation. I would
do this on my own or die trying.

"Why don't you guys do something helpful," I grumbled.
"To escape, I need to get out of the torque. To get out of the
torque, I need a fairy."

They scampered away, disappearing beyond the wall.

I shouted, "No! Come back. Please, come back. I'm sorry. I
shouldn't have snapped at you."

But they didn't come back. Rather than break down and sob,
I gathered what remained of my determination and continued
my battle to leave the bed. Blistering pain shot down my spine,
but I finally, miraculously, achieved an upright position. Three
cheers for me!

Dizziness swamped me as I threw my legs over the side of the
bed. Movement of any kind was sheer torture, pulling on both
scabbed and raw tissues, but I slowly added weight to my feet,
until a ray of sunlight and warmth streamed over me. Success!

Remaining hunched over, I hobbled across the cell, used my
bucket and hobbled back to the bed. Yes! I'd done it!

Though my body demanded rest, I sat, then stood. Sat, stood.
Lay down, sat up, stood. The more I practiced, the easier the actions became. Finally, I could stand without praying for death.

As a reward, I lay on my stomach and freed the sliver of enchanted glass from the stuffing of my pillow. "Show me Hartly."

Yesterday, I'd checked on my nymphs. During my battle with
Farrah, I'd nearly drained them, and I had yet to forgive myself.

My sister's image appeared, a beam of happiness lighting up my soul. She'd finally taken a bath. Dressed in a pretty pink gown, she sat atop a tree stump, holding court for a pack of wolves. Thor perched on her lap, king of all he surveyed.

"Make the animals go away," the troll commander demanded, pacing before the group.

"Sure thing, Warick," she said, petting a wolf behind the ears. "Just as soon as you vow never to harm my sister."

"My men are holding off your friends as gently as possible because I decreed it so. An act of mercy on my part," Warick said. "One word from me, and a massacre will occur. Make. The. Animals. Go. Away."

"Make. The. Vow," she snapped. "Until then, the animals will continue to protect me."

"*I* am your protection. I told you I would never hurt you."

"You are my captor. There's a difference."

Pride suffused me. *Gisno Hisnartlisny!*

"I am your future husband. Me," Warick said, beating on his chest. "You are my war prize. You bow to my dictates, not the other way around."

"Yes, but why was I given to you?"

He ran his tongue over his teeth. "To spare your sister. Which I have done. Which I will continue to do."

"And?" Hartly insisted.

"And, I have done everything you've required of me. I have stopping using my venom and walked away from potential kills. Things I did to make you happy."

"And?" she repeated.

"And nothing," he said through gritted teeth.

A long moment passed, various emotions flashing over her features as she weighed her options. When her eyes widened and her jaw dropped, I knew she'd stumbled upon a revelation.

She shooed the wolves away, stood and crossed the distance.

Warick watched her with an aura of wariness. "Why did

you send the wolves away, when I did not give you what you wanted?"

"I like you, Warick, despite everything, and I've decided to give you my trust, without getting a promise from you. I see your heart, even when you try to hide it from me. You are a good man. Hopefully you see my heart, and what Everly means to me."

He inhaled sharply, exhaled heavily. "Your heart is too soft."

"So guard it well," she said.

He opened his mouth. Closed it. Then he closed his eyes and inhaled with more force. Facing her, he snarled, "I will command my armies to protect your Everly, when the time comes. I vow it."

"Really?"

His nod was clipped, even angry.

Hartly unveiled a slow smile before throwing her arms around him. After a slight hesitation, he returned the hug, all of his angst vanishing. Then he just appeared shell-shocked.

I sympathized. Hartly had made a kind gesture, and he'd reciprocated. If only my captors could be won over so easily!

Warick stiffened and frowned. Palming a dagger, he spun in a circle, scanning the area. "Who is there? Show yourself."

I cut off a groan. With the enchanted glass, people always sensed me. I ended the connection, lest I be found out.

"Show me Truly," I said.

A chamber appeared, the focus on a large bed with a gossamer canopy flowing over four posters. The walls were vibrant pink and patterned with roses, with golden crown molding up top, and matching wainscoting below. A plush rug boasted a colorful tree of life, the branches pointing to a rose quartz fireplace, a gold desk and a vanity made from diamonds.

Truly crouched on the floor, with her back pressed against the bed, and another beam of happiness lit my soul. Whatever our differences, I would never forget the way she'd defended me.

Now she was using a table knife to remove a foot-long sliver of wood from the bed frame. Then she carved an arrowhead at one end. Ohhh. Was she planning to fight her way out?

When she finished, she rushed to the desk, then used a quill and jar of ink to scribble a note on a small scroll. *Airarian princesses are prisoners in Sevón. Send help.*

After wrapping the scroll around the arrow, she sealed the paper closed with hot wax and Aubrey's signet ring. I whooped with surprise. Truly had saved it!

She grabbed her bow and moved to the balcony, where she aimed and fired, her magic ensuring the arrow reached her intended target, whatever the target happened to be.

"Show me Roth," I said, bracing. The sight of him always screwed with my mind. And my heart.

Truly faded as the prince materialized. No, sorry, the *king* materialized. His coronation had taken place yesterday morning, with thousands of subjects flocking to the palace to bear witness.

Excitement had been palpable. What I would have given to tailgate!

Mortals and creatures of myth had come, most I'd recognized, some I hadn't. I noticed the lack of trolls, however. And the lack of sorcerian—at least, none that I could tell.

When the ceremony had ended, the crowd had cheered with wild abandon. Everyone loved Roth and rejoiced over the evil sorceress's defeat. Heck, even I lov— liked him. Despite everything that had happened between us, I craved his time and attention. Why, why, why?

In the glass, Roth strode out of a mine. I watched, dumbstruck, as he ripped off a blood-soaked shirt.

Mouthwatering prince. Soot covered his cheeks. Gashes and blood littered his chest. Even injured, he pulsed with strength and vitality.

A group of men huddled nearby, their wounds being doctored by the avian who flew in with medical bags.

"I found the last one," Roth croaked, "but he didn't make it. I'm sorry."

The others bowed their heads, grieved. There must have been a cave collapse.

My head bowed. I should have done more for the miners when I was in charge.

Different people tried to speak with Roth, but he motored on. One man offered a coat, but he declined, seemingly unaffected by the cold. His hair was a mess, damp with sweat. Thicker-than-usual stubble adorned his jaw.

No doubt he'd rushed to the mines straight from training. He wore black leather pants and combat boots with blades attached to the toes. A spiked ring adorned each finger. The cuffs around his wrists were spiked, as well. Sheathed at his waist, daggers with brass knuckle handles.

When he reached the village, different citizens approached him. Some flirted, some played coy. Roth greeted each newcomer with less and less patience, his expression becoming harsher, his voice becoming gruffer. That gruffness intimidated his legions of admirers, both male and female, sending them fleeing.

Farrah waited at the border of the village. She fell into step beside him, a fancy yellow gown swishing around her ankles.

I nearly choked on my deepest, darkest fury.

Twirling a dagger-sharp icicle between her fingers, she said, "We need to talk, Roth."

"Not now, Farrah."

"Please, Roth," she beseeched. Breath misted in front of her face. "Roycefus told me you've missed meetings. Important ones. Every day your mood grows fouler. I fear your new duties are destroying your happiness."

The responsibility of running a kingdom *was* a heavy burden to bear, but Roth had the necessary skills and stamina. In that regard, we were alike. Ruling his people would satisfy him as nothing else ever had, putting his need to protect others to good use. He needed only a good foundation of support—something I hadn't had.

"I know the answer to your problems. You require a wife, Roth." She twirled the icicle faster and faster. "Someone to help you navigate these trying times. Queen Violet promises war, and our people blame you. They think you are dishonorable for ending your engagement with Princess Truly. Of course, they don't know she is the sister of a sorceress. If we host a ball, we can invite available princesses from other kingdoms. You can wed the one of your choice. The right one will double our armed forces *and* give our people a new queen to adore. They'll forget about Truly, and Father's murderous bride."

They entered the palace. In the foyer, Roycefus inserted himself between the royals to tell Roth about some rescheduled meetings. Farrah's ladies-in-waiting trailed behind, Annica among them.

With the heel of his palm resting on the bridge of his nose, Roth rubbed his temples, his fingers on one side and his thumb on the other. "I need an hour," he told his advisor, then switched directions.

Visibly upset, Farrah said, "No, you need to finish our conversation. Please, Roth."

He ground his teeth, but offered a stiff nod. "Come."

The princess and her ladies dogged him. But a glare from Roth caused the ladies to stop. Only the royal siblings entered the throne room. The king eased onto his throne and appeared to bite his tongue as Farrah prattled on.

"I'm in no mood for a ball or a wife," he finally snapped. "I'm not certain other kingdoms are even interested in forming new alliances. They are dealing with prophecies of their own. Chaos reigns."

I released a relieved breath.

Farrah wrapped her arms around her middl, as if to protect her vital organs.

Roth tensed, guilt flashing over his expression. "I didn't mean to shout at you. My apologies."

What a sap! So why did I admire his kindness?

"Do you desire Father's murderer?" she asked, the icicle shattering in her grip. "Saxon told me you couldn't keep your gaze off her during your travels. Now you visit her every day."

I practically foamed at the mouth with curiosity, desperate to hear his response.

Annica did, as well—neither Farrah nor Roth realized she stood behind the door, listening to their conversation, anger tightening her features.

Roth pressed his lips into a thin line. "Everly is...a problem, but she's *my* problem."

Ugh. If he had feelings for me, he'd just denied them. As Peter had done. Could no one want me and admit it to others?

"You know what?" he said, a calculating gleam in his eyes. "We *should* throw a ball—for you. You may have your pick of royals. *Your* marriage will double our armed forces and appease our people."

As she floundered for a response, I snickered. *Sucks when the tables are turned, doesn't it?*

She closed the distance, crouched next to the throne, and clasped his hand. "This isn't about me. Let me plan the ball, brother. We'll start small. Princess Ashleigh of Flour has acquired four dragon eggs, which makes me think her fairy tale is 'The Little Cinder Girl.' She would be a powerful ally. Or what about Azul? Reese's sister—a siren duchess—can compel, like you. Already you have something in common. Were you to marry her, all of our water problems would be solved."

The muscle jumped beneath his eye, faster than ever before. "Very well. Plan your ball, invite the Azulians. But I will not be choosing a bride."

A cool tide of relief washed through me.

Farrah beamed. "Thank you, brother. You won't be disappointed. Now, if you would be so kind as to grant one last boon... I would like to visit Everly. Before you say no—don't say no! I hurt inside, hurt so much, and I *need* her to hurt, as well. Then I can heal."

"You will stay away from her," he barked, startling her. And me! How could he be so terrible and so wonderful at the same time?

Tears pooled in Farrah's eyes. "But, but...why? Have you forgotten what she is? What she's done? What she'll do?"

Hate her!

"I've forgotten nothing, but I do not want her harmed." His tone sharpened. "I love you, Farrah, but you are not to whip her again. You are not to strike her, or put a bruise on her, or scratch her. Do you understand?"

"She's evil! Her family killed ours. Have you forgotten what happened to our mother and brother inside the overlord's altilium? Everly herself slayed our father and an entire coven of witches. She tried to strangle me. Prophecy says she'll attempt it twice more. Stop protecting her."

Yes, Roth. Stop. Help me hate you, too.

Suddenly, his spine jerked ramrod straight, his gaze darting around the room. Like everyone else, he'd sensed me. He settled his hand on the hilt of a dagger, and I ended the connection.

My reflection stared back at me, my disappointment clear. Briefly, I considered spying on Queen Violet, but discarded the idea. She only ever ranted about how I'd ruined her life, and I'd had enough rejection for a hundred lifetimes. Maybe tomorrow.

Sighing, I returned the glass to my pillow and eased up. A slight scuffing noise drew my gaze to the floor. Phobia and Webster had returned.

"Thank you for coming back." With a laugh, I maneuvered to my knees. "I missed you so much, and I'm so—" I frowned.

A web trailed behind them, a bejeweled comb caught within the gossamer strands.

"Thank you?" Why would they gift me with such an item?

The answer slammed into me, and I laughed harder. In the fairy tale, the Evil Queen defeated Snow White with a corset—check—then a poisoned comb. I could do the same.

"Why, you smart little devils, you." I pumped my fist toward the ceiling. "What I need next is a fairy's hand. The fairy body may or may not be included. You guys think you can provide one?"

They hopped up and down, eager to please.

Well, then. I'd found my way out. I only needed time.

35

Beware false hope and its lures.
Seek the truth and its cures.

By the third week of confinement, my back had mostly
healed, and my limbs had full mobility. I could sit, stand
and pace like a boss, with only a few aches and pains. Not that I
had much room. My cell was spacious, yes, but the rocky walls
had begun to close in.

I'd reached out to Noel many times, hoping to trick her into revealing any flaws in my escape plan, but I'd received no response.

Roth had cut his number of visits. He came once every evening, and sent Annica in his stead once every morning—the
girl he trusted to deal with my "lady stuff." How did he not
see her awfulness?

A few days ago, I'd told Roth, "Real smart move, having
your ex tend to me. That isn't uncomfortable *at all*."

"I know her. She does as ordered."

"How boring for you."

He'd narrowed his eyes and added, "I can trust her not to harm you."

"Can you?" Annica might not be Hickey, I decided. She might be Viper.

She brought me food and other necessities, and even tidied up my cell, but she did so while muttering insults and death threats. Twice, she'd hit me with a broom, and I'd had to stop my precious spidorpions from attacking her.

Not yet, my darlings. But soon.

When we made our escape, Phobia and Webster could do whatever they wanted to her, with my blessing. They'd become my best friends, saving graces and passport to fun. They kept me sane in an insane world, saving me from the tempting allure of depression and self-pity. They deserved the best, always!

The sweethearts had even introduced me to a whole slew of other new friends. The "dregs" of the palace. I was the most popular girl at Tower High. *Hair fluff.* And yeah, okay, since I'd released the other prisoners, I was the *only* girl at Tower High, but whatever. I'd developed a special connection with Cuddles the boa constrictor, Boomer the feral cat and Crouton the bird. Although, I had nothing but love for my rats and lava ants. And my squirrels, racoons and dogs.

I'd noticed a correlation: the mangier the animal, the more it liked me. Which I didn't understand. I didn't wield Hartly's magic, so how and why did I draw the critters in the first place? Because of the earth magic I'd taken from the witches? My connection to the Tree of New Beginnings? My tentative friendship with Allura? Like calling to like?

Now, as I lay in bed with Cuddles curled atop my belly, breathing in the pervasive scent of fur and the subtle hint of Christmas Roth always left behind, I watched Dust Mote TV, the only channel I could access. Because of the frigid temperature, the lava ants had burrowed inside the mattress. They heated the fabric, creating my own personal electric blanket.

When the time came, I held out my arm and said, "Bite me, darling Phobia." Like all spidorpions, my baby created two different types of venom. The one that flowed through his little fangs caused instant pain and paralysis. The one that flowed through his stingerless tail caused death in high doses.

—*Again?*— He made a twittering sound. His version of a moan.

"Again," I confirmed. "And give me more venom this time." If I couldn't get my hands on poison, I had to *become* poison. And I could. I remembered what Roth had said. That some sorcerers ate spidorpions to acquire venomous blood, that spidorpion venom wasn't normal; it possessed a thrum of magic, and with the torque, I stored any magic I received.

I would strengthen, even while wearing my stupid metal collar. I would become living poison. A weapon.

Helpless? Me? Never again. But I wouldn't harm my babies to get this done. I would rather harm *myself*.

At first, I'd instructed Phobia to bite me at breakfast, lunch and dinner. We were now up to eight times a day. Since we'd started, I'd burned up with fever, basically boiling inside. Worth it! As I stored more and more of the venom's magic, my blood became more and more deadly—to others.

Phobia remained reluctant, but he denied me nothing. He crawled up my arm and bit. I felt the sting, but not the inundation of heat and pain. I frowned.

"Again," I said. "You, too, Webster."

Bite. Bite. Just as before, I felt the sting, but no heat or pain. I laughed. We could finally move on to stage two of my plan. Human testing.

"Gang, we are one step closer to freedom," I announced with a grin.

Both spidorpions gave me a look—*Who are you?*

"What?" I asked, and yeah, I sounded maniacal and creepy. "A frightening laugh is mandatory for a villain. Now that I've nailed mine, I should update my résumé." Nah. I'd rather play *Where's Roth.*

I moved Cuddles to the mattress, kissed his adorable face, then stood at the edge of the bed to peer out the barred window. Thanks to Annica and her broom of doom, my bruised ribs protested.

Icy wind blustered, summoning goose bumps to the surface of my skin. So high up, I could see mile after mile of snowcapped mountains and, in the far distance, the barest hint of the Enchantian Forest. Avian warriors glided through clouds, riding bright beams of sunlight. In a nearby pasture, sheep with translucent wings and cows with braided red fur grazed. People of every size, shape and color worked alongside a variety of creatures. Mining had been temporarily suspended. Now, the worker bees carried bags of grain or wheeled manure out of barns. Stable hands walked horses and unicorns, children played, and armed guards staffed a parapet atop a border wall, surveilling the kingdom. The centaur blacksmith worked on a pair of horseshoes today, the sound of his banging hammer music to my ears.

Through the enchanted glass, I'd heard whispers of discontent from both palace guards and everyday average citizens, just as Farrah had claimed. The bulk of Roth's subjects feared what would happen if Queen Violet made good on her promise of war.

A small copper-colored snake slithered under my door, snagging my attention.

—*He comes, he comes.*— Phobia's voice shouted inside my head.

He? As in Roth? "I'm not excited, *you're* excited. Go, go," I whispered, making shooing motions. My friends scattered, hiding in an assortment of places.

I performed a mental inventory of my two most treasured items. Enchanted glass—inside the pillow. Comb—under my mattress. Excellent!

The broom was in position, and the spidorpion bites were—oops, not yet hidden by the sleeves of my shirt. I hurriedly rolled down the material.

My heart performed a tap dance as I settled at the edge of the mattress, doing my best to appear nonthreatening and innocent. One way or another, I would be testing my venomous blood today.

Only a few hours ago, I'd pricked my finger and smeared the blood over the broom's handle. The next person to clean the cell...

I grinned. Oh, how I loved the irony and justice of it all. The broom was used as a weapon against me. Now, I would use the broom as a weapon against my foe.

So you enjoy repeating Violet and Farrah's mistakes?

What? Who? Me?

A familiar melody started up, distracting me. The rattle of keys. Creaking hinges. Footsteps. In strolled King Roth and his mouthwatering cinnamon scent.

Shock. The excitement I'd denied. Relief. Happiness. The fury I could never shake. Each emotion delivered a one-two punch to my solar plexus, sending me on a wild carousel ride and stealing my breath. Was he more muscular than yesterday? He was definitely more beautiful. He exuded raw strength.

Here was a boy...a man whose enemies should do everything possible to avoid him in a dark alley. Or a well-lit garden. And here I was, missing his hugs.

As I jumped up, a twinge of pain made me cringe.

"Sorceress," he said with an incline of his chin. An *endearment* I despised. "You are hurt. What happened?"

Argh! He always noticed everything about everything. "Don't act as if you care."

"I would give anything *not* to care," he groused.

Oh, that burned! "Boo-hoo. Poor you. You have the hots for

a spectacular sorceress." I rubbed my fists under my eyes, mim-icking tears. "The travesty!"

He tilted his head and raked his frosty gaze over me, as cold as Truly once claimed. So why did I heat up? And how did I become more acutely aware of my clothing—a thin knee-length tunic and a pair of panties?

"You'll have to forgive my state of undress, kingling." The huskiness of my voice startled me. Even more stunning, the pulse in my neck fluttered so forcefully, I thought it might be attempting Morse code: *kiss me, touch me.* "Had I known you'd *honor* me with your company, I would have worn…less."

His pupils flared, scraping away the frost.

I'd once thought to encourage his goodwill so he wouldn't strike at me, as fate seemed to want. In spite of everything that had happened between us, I could see the plan still had merit. I just had to remain detached this time.

Not a problem. I'd learned my lesson well. Fall for Roth and suffer.

Heart dancing wildly, every beat shouting *distance, distance, distance,* I raked my gaze over *him.* As usual, he wore a well-fitted white tunic and black leather pants, no speck of dirt or wrinkle in sight.

"No training today? Or did you play hooky to come here and punish me?" I could think of no other reason for his earlier than normal visit.

"Why would I punish you?" he asked. "Is there a crime you'd like to confess?"

"There is, yes. Yours. You didn't snap up your dream girl while you had the chance. Look at all this goodness." I waved a hand over my body. "Now it's too late. I've met someone new. A sorcerer. The fallen angel to your devil in disguise."

He flicked his tongue over an incisor. "Give me a name."

Such vehemence. "Do you remember the blond hottie with

Nicolas? His name isn't your business. Want to know what I like most about him? He's never called me a parasite."

Rage exploded in Roth's eyes, discharging bombs of tension throughout the rest of him. Muscles knotted. Hands balled. Vibrated limbs. "You've had contact with him? When? How?"

Jealous, my king? Or just worried I'd found a way out? "I have my ways," I all but purred.

He bared his teeth and took a step closer, only to pause. "I didn't come here to argue with you. I want to move you to a more comfortable room and—"

"No! I'm staying in my cell. It's mine." Mostly, my friends could come and go here without being stepped on.

"Very well," he said, then we lapsed into silence. A group of men arrived, bringing a small table, two chairs and a good-size box with elaborate carvings.

The servants never glanced in my direction. They came in, deposited their burdens, and left, shutting the door behind them.

Roth waved to the table, saying, "Sit. Please." He'd gotten control of his temper. "I'd like us to get to know each other better."

I *longed* to get to know him better. But I studied my nails and said, "You assume I want to get to know you better."

The diabolical jerk called my bluff. "If you'd rather be alone, I'll leave."

"No," I rushed to say, then inwardly cursed my gullibility. I tried to recover. "I'm bored, and you could be a…tolerable distraction, I suppose."

He looked smug. Too smug.

I added, "I'm impressed. You went to a lot of trouble for our first date. If only I'd known you ascribed to the 'Beauty and the Beast' method of romance. You can make the girl love you…if you lock her up long enough."

His smugness vanished, and I preened, all innocence, a smile growing.

Wasn't long before he smiled, as well. "Your barbs are sharp, but the wounds are worth the reward." He traced a fingertip along the corners of my mouth.

Too flirty! I cleared my throat. "Yes. Well. Stop being nice to me." *Smooth as butter, EQ.*

"Let's see if I can—" He went still. "Careful, Everly. There's a spidorpion on your bed."

"A spidorpion? Oh, no. That's...terrifying?" I turned, blocking Roth's path, and mouthed, *Go.* At top volume, I shouted, "Get out of here, you filthy abomination."

I think my sweetie rolled his eyes, but he also scrammed, so no harm, no foul.

"There," I said, pretending to sag with relief. "The horrid creature is gone." I turned back to the king. "Now, then. You were saying something about being desperate to get to know your dear, dear stepmother."

He blanched. "Do not refer to yourself in such a way."

"Why? Thanks to you and your magic, I'm a bride and an insta-mom."

Several beats of brusque silence.

In the end, he moved on, saying, "We're going to play a game."

"A game to get to know each other?" Um, why not just ask each other questions straight up? "What game?"

"Inquisition."

"Never heard of it." With a false air of lassitude, I eased into a chair.

He sat as well and opened that elaborate box. Inside, a type of chessboard and toy soldiers. "Magic ensures we are honest with each other."

Color me intrigued. If I could use this game to my advantage...

"Each player has an army," he said. "I will ask a question or request information and you will respond. If you respond truthfully, you can advance a soldier. If you refuse to respond, *I* can advance a soldier. If you lie, one of your soldiers will die."

In other words, truth was a weapon against your enemy, and lies were a weapon against yourself. "How will you know if I'm telling the truth?"

The corners of his mouth twitched. Dang it, how could I find him charming, even now? "Go ahead. Try it and find out."

Surely he wouldn't know. He must think the threat of defeat would trick me into being honest. Not that trickery was necessary—which proved he *didn't* know me.

"If you move a soldier to a certain block, you can gain a special power, or send us into a rapid-fire-question round," he continued. "The more complicated the question, the more detailed the answer, the more choices our soldiers have in terms of advancement."

"Give me an example of a special power."

"Making a soldier a turncoat who kills his comrades."

Neat! "I assume the winner receives bragging rights, nothing more?" Though the true prize would be the information we garnered.

"Yes. Exactly."

The wooden soldiers were shockingly lifelike, some mortal, some mythical.

"I'll start us off easy," Roth said. "Tell me your full name, title and age."

"Hey! You're not getting a three for one special."

He shrugged, sheepish. "You can't fault a guy for trying."

"Yes, I can. But I won't." I decided to lie, as he'd suggested, just to test the waters. "I'm Everly Hartly Morrow, current Queen of Sevón, future Queen of Airaria, and twin to Truly."

My eyes widened as my soldiers began to *move*, coming alive. Though they remained inside the confines of their individual squares, they ducked, leaned or contorted as one of Roth's soldiers knelt down, anchored the end of his rifle to his shoulder, and fired off a shot.

Boom!

I yelped. Smoke wafted from the gun's barrel as one of my players fell face first onto the board.

Shocked, I zoomed my gaze back to Roth, whose irises sparkled with a hint of merriment.

"Told you," he said, smug once again.

"My name is Everly *Solene* Morrow," I said, basically vomiting words. I waited, hopeful, but the soldier never revived. I put a trembling hand over my mouth. "He's dead. Because of me."

"I'm sure his family will be well compensated."

"Family?" The heat in my cheeks drained, leaving me chilled. I whimpered.

Roth gave me a confused look.

Vision blurring, I picked up the fallen soldier. I expected blood, some sign of life or death. Instead, I found a little piece of wood, nothing more, nothing less.

"Everly. Sweetling. I apologize for teasing you." Soft, gentle tone. "The soldier isn't dead or alive. The pieces were made with enchanted wood and bespelled by a witch centuries ago. I promise you, the soldier felt no pain and has no family. He will revive for the next game."

"But…how can that be? Enchanted or not, bespelled or not, wood cannot craft an—an illusion on its own."

"Magic survives even when the one who used it dies. Much like our hands, or a unicorn's horn, an enchanted and bespelled object is a conduit. The witch's magic flows through it, activated by our verbal cues—like spells. We see the end result," he replied, sliding one of his pieces to a new square.

Argh! I hadn't meant to ask a game question, wasting a turn. And had he mentioned a unicorn's horn?

He leaned back in his chair, anguish settling over his features. "Tell me about the day my father died."

I didn't want to tell him, but I wanted him to know the truth. He *deserved* to know. How would he react?

"Thanks to your compulsion," I began, "I couldn't say no

when Challen commanded me to marry him. Immediately after we spoke our vows, he escorted me to the throne room. Seven witches joined us. They suspended me midair and danced around, chanting and flinging their blood on me. I would be the last to bleed, a living sacrifice, my life force transferred to the king. But I drained the witches before they could drain me."

He sat still and stoic, emotionless, and it added fuel to the flames of my never-ending fury.

Burning with it, I added, "The very thing you hate—my ancestry—was the very thing that saved my life. I went necromantic, black lines appearing in my skin. The king advanced on me. I warned him what would happen if we touched, but he reached out anyway. He died seconds later."

Guilt and sorrow flashed in his eyes. He shifted in his chair, saying, "I'm sorry I placed you in such an awful situation."

Once I'd snidely told him, *I apologized, and I meant it. I am sorry I hurt you. If you need to spill my blood to forgive me, so be it. Spill my blood. Then we can part ways.*

I hadn't understood then, but I did now. Sometimes apologies weren't enough.

"I'm sure you are," I snipped. "Just not enough to fix your father's mistakes."

"I told you. Keeping you here ensures your safety."

"Lie!" I'd never played chess or commanded an army, so I wasn't sure what my best move would be. I decided to edge my men to one side, while keeping them grouped together. But when I tried to slide a soldier with a sword to the right, it wouldn't budge. Huh. I tried to him in the other direction—success!

My turn to ask a question. Something *intentional*. I needed to throw Roth for a loop without wasting another opportunity to learn more about him.

Different questions vied for the privilege of being spoken.

I met his gaze and said, "Do you plan to free me one day, or kill me?"

36

Whether wrong or right,
you must have might.

Seconds ticked by in silence, Roth's eyes becoming endless wells of grief. The very emotion I'd spied in my reflection after Mom died. Though I'd made peace with what happened, regrets still haunted me, ghosts determined to stalk me wherever I ventured.

Would ghosts of the past forever haunt the king?

He'd come here to learn something specific. But what? Surely he'd known I would ask about his intentions; surely he'd already drafted a response. Unless I'd made him rethink his strategy?

He blanked his features and said, "I have no desire to kill you, Everly."

"But?"

"But I will do whatever proves necessary to protect my family and my kingdom. Always."

A warning Saxon had once given me…a lifetime ago. My silly heart reacted as if hearing the news for the first time, aching in revolt.

Unacceptable! I would not start caring about this boy again. "You mean *my* kingdom."

Features—remained blank. Hands—white-knuckling the arms of his chair. He was not unaffected by our topic of conversation. "Queens by marriage do not rule a kingdom. Descendants do."

When he reached out to move one of his soldiers, I latched on to his wrist, stopping him. "Your reply is unclear, and clarity matters," I said. "You will protect your kingdom. Got it. Does that mean my actions will spur your own, or that you'll kill me no matter what I do?"

He peered at me, laser-focused, until I squirmed in my seat. "Since my return, I've met with seven different oracles. They had the same warning. As soon as you are free, you and Farrah will war, but only one of you will walk away."

Me! Me! I would be the one. "Let me go right now, and I will put you and your family in my rear view. We'll end the cycle of hate. Or make the predictions a self-fulfilling prophecy and keep me here. When Farrah strikes at me again, and she will, I *will* retaliate."

He shook his head. "You will stay here, where I can guard you, where you have no need to syphon and hurt others."

"I won't hurt anyone! Not again."

"You cannot guarantee such a thing." He sighed. "I'm not sure what I'll do with you, sorceress, but you may rest easy about one fact. I will tell you my decision as soon as I make it, giving you time to prepare."

I released his wrist and instantly missed his body heat. *Stupid!*

He slid a player closer to mine. Meaning, he'd told the truth. Meaning, he remained honorable, at least in this regard; I could work with honorable.

"Did you leave a boyfriend in the mortal world?" he asked.

Uh, why did he care now? He hadn't wondered when he'd held me in the firelight, or kissed the breath from my lungs. Maybe he hoped to use the guy against me?

Watching him closely, I said, "I left a *former* boyfriend, Peter. I embarrassed him, so we broke up. Apparently, all the men in my life suffer from such an affliction." I moved a soldier. "Noel said your father would live if you found the Apple of Life and Death. Well, you found me, and he's dead. So what gives? And why trust her?"

"I asked her about this. She reminded me that she told me the *King of Sevón* would live, not King Challen. You killed one king, and saved the other—me. Half death, half life."

Well, well. A loophole. *Should have known.* But when had I saved Roth? The battle with the trolls?

"How did this Peter win you?" he asked, backtracking.

Ugh. Still harping on this? I needed to redirect him, and fast, before his line of questioning made me want bad, bad things. Like more kisses.

Putting an annoying amount of smirk in my tone, I said, "Why do you care? Are you thinking about lowering yourself to audition for the role of my significant other?"

"Answer the question, sorceress." His snippy tone would have delighted me under any other circumstances. "Actually, no. I'd rather know why was he embarrassed of you. I doubt he knew you were a sorceress."

My cheeks heated. I'd never felt so exposed. Wanting to shore up my defenses, I allowed my vengeful side to respond. "I'll answer two questions for the price of one. Because I'm generous like that. Firstly, he won me by writing sweet notes and making up excuses to come see me. He didn't imprison me, prevent me from searching for my missing sister or negate my magic with a metal collar. Secondly, he was embarrassed because I'm so different from *normal* people." I used air quotes. "I can stare at a mirror for hours, so of course I'm vain. I don't always smile, so of course I'm grumpy and cold. I don't always care what others think of me, so of course I'm a snob."

Roth rubbed two fingers along the dark stubble on his jaw, giving nothing away.

Resentful, I moved a player. "You once admitted you hate your magic. Tell me *why* you hate it."

He braced, admitting, "My youngest brother, Dominik, used to follow me everywhere. One day, I was injured during training. I wanted to rest, wanted peace and quiet, but Dom stayed close, talking nonstop. Looking back, I realize he was concerned about me, and hoped to make me feel better. But I was in pain and irritated, and I snapped. I told him to not speak another word, to go away and never come back. Seemingly innocuous commands. I had no idea that my ability manifested, that I'd compelled him. He did go away, and he didn't come back. We found his body weeks later. He'd left and the elements killed him."

Roth relayed the information with zero emotional inflection, yet I would swear I tasted his torment.

"I'm so sorry." Though he hadn't asked, I admitted, "I know the agony of accidentally harming someone you love. I drained my mother. If not for me, she would still be alive. While I've let go of my grief, my heart remains scarred."

"Scarred. Yes," he rasped, advancing a soldier. "Those scars are a constant reminder of the worst mistake I ever made."

I nodded. "I keep hoping better things await me in the future. Alas."

Guilt flushed his cheeks. "What is your natural magical ability? The one you were born with."

Once again, I had conflicting desires. I didn't want to tell him, but I didn't want to lose the game, either. "Mirrors. I acquired the ability to scry when my mother died." I let my soldier chase his. "Did you know our sisters were in love?"

"Yes."

When he said no more, I protested. "You shouldn't get to advance a soldier for a one-word answer."

"Then ask another question."

I racked my brain and came up with "If you weren't royalty, what would you be?"

"A soldier of war," he offered without hesitation. "Combat is what I know, what I'm good at." He advanced the same soldier as before, then motioned to my midsection. "How did you get hurt? More specifically, what happened to damage your ribs?"

Curious about his response, I answered, "You can thank Annica, the one you trust above all others. She likes to hit me with the broom."

He went still, tenser than before. "I'll take care of it."

His tone… I'd never heard such menace. I almost felt bad for Annica. Almost. "Maybe I'm lying." I hadn't moved my soldier yet, so he had no idea whether I could or not. "Maybe I hurt myself, hoping to gain your sympathy."

"I *wish* you would accept my sympathy. Instead, you only ever give me a tongue-lashing. Especially when I do something nice."

Did I really? And did he maybe kinda sorta…like it?

"You have my word," he added, that menacing tone back. "Annica will not harm you again."

Ohhh. What was he planning to do? "I won't say thank you." My tremors restarted as I made another move on the board. "Do you ever think about our kiss?"

During a prolonged beat of silence, I thought he would pass, refusing to answer. Then he said, "Constantly."

My trembling grew worse.

"Do *you* think about our kiss?" he asked, and I would swear he held his breath. "Do you think of me at all?"

I could not be so foolish, or so brave. So, I danced around the issue, saying, "I think about you…occasionally." I thought about him occasionally, and frequently, and yes, constantly.

The light in his eyes dimmed. I'd hurt him.

Good!

But now I wanted to sob.

We moved our soldiers, and I noticed he had access to a wider range of squares. I needed to up my game!

"What is the real reason you wanted to play Inquisition with me?" I asked. "What is it you want to know?"

Gaze unwavering, he said, "I need to make a decision about you, one way or the other. Your presence here…torments me. I thought the game would help." He tapped a square, and his soldier moved there, closer to mine. "Did you enjoy being queen?"

We were just going to blaze right by the comment about being tormented by my presence? Okay, then. "Yes and no. I like being in charge. I can't deny it. I like power and value strength. Yet, even when I used my power and strength to make life better for my subjects, I received criticism and death threats."

He listened and stiffened.

I followed his lead and tapped a square. My soldier moved closer to *his,* all on his own. "You know Truly is my sister and related to a sorcerer," I said. "Are you going to harm her?"

"No. I had her locked in her chamber as insurance, not punishment. You won't leave without her. You won't hurt my sister while I hold yours. And Queen Violet won't attack the kingdom while her daughter is here."

He made another move on the board, and relief overwhelmed me. He'd meant what he'd said. "I'm surprised you didn't lock her in the tower with me."

"And let the two of you plan an escape together? No."

Smart. "Tell me about your childhood."

"You already know the highlights. I'm the second son of Challen, King of Sevón. Far too young, I began my military training. I've lost a mother, a stepmother and two brothers. I'm nineteen years old and responsible for millions of lives."

The more I got to know Roth, the older he seemed. Nineteen? Try thirty. Experience could do that to a person, I supposed. I felt ancient. Like, forty!

He slid a soldier away from mine, saying, "Tell me about *your* childhood."

What to admit, and what to hide? "As an infant, I was sent to the mortal world because my father wanted to kill me. My aunt raised me. I've been loved, and I've been hated. After Mom died, I found out my entire life was a lie. I learned about Violet and Truly, and I was so excited to meet them. When I came upon Truly first, I decided not to tell her who I was. I believed Violet and I would tell her together." I tried to sound flippant. I just sounded bitter. "The same day you escorted me to the palace, she ordered her guards to kill me." *Don't care, don't care.*

He grew more and more stiff.

I moved my most menacing soldier into the fray, and said, "Do you wish you'd never met me?"

Silence. One minute passed, two, every second more soul-crushing than the last.

"It's not a head scratcher, Roth. Answer the question."

He drummed his fingers against the table. "Things would be easier if we'd never met. That much I know."

Ouch.

"But no," he said, and sighed. "I cannot regret meeting you." Not giving me a chance to respond—not that I knew *how* to respond—he asked, "I know you are an illusionist and a scrier. What other magical abilities do you possess?"

Translation: How many people have you drained to death, Everly?

Too many. "Pass," I said. Let him wonder what else I could do. Perhaps he'd grow to fear me like so many others. Then he'd think twice about treating me badly. The fact that the desire to sob intensified? So what?

He quirked a brow and moved one of his soldiers, intrigue reigniting the light in his eyes.

My turn. "What do you know about Queen Violet's transformation from beloved mother to homicidal maniac?"

Shrug. "She was your father's fourth wife. The other three did not conceive an heir within the first year of marriage, and the king oversaw their executions. Anytime I visited Airaria, or the royal family visited Sevón, Violet remained quiet and subdued, reminding me of a volcano about to blow. Tension thrummed from her, and she snapped her responses to people."

"That law is barbaric."

"Agreed. Violet has since abolished the practice in Airaria, just as I have abolished it here."

"No," I said with a shake of my head. "*I* abolished it here."

A grin teased the corners of his mouth. "Yes, I heard about your amendment. Wives are allowed to kill their husbands at any time, if they are not pleased."

"What can I say? Payback sucks."

The grin flashed, mega-watt, but it didn't linger. "I had to abolish your law, too. But I digress," he said. "The biggest of Violet's changes came after she murdered your father. Perhaps because she'd taken the first step down a very dark road."

"Every journey begins in such a way. Our choices steer our course." Hint, hint. *You're headed down a very dark road yourself, princeling.*

Could the same be said of me?

"What were your hobbies in the mortal world?" Roth moved a soldier…who then gunned down one of mine.

I nearly swept the pieces to the floor in a fit of pique. I. Hated. Losing. "I took classes. I learned how to dance, swim and fence. I read novels and trained in self-defense. Once a week, Mom made us sit before a hearth and knit. As long as I was with my family, I was happy." I would give anything for one more hour with my loved ones—heck, one more minute.

He belted out a laugh. "I can't picture you with knitting needles…for anything other than stabbing an opponent."

"I'm quite good." I fluffed my hair. "I've knitted a cap that looked like a brain, socks decorated with pole dancers, and a cover for a guy's...you know." Mom had always dreaded the unveiling of my handiwork.

He belted out another laugh, but quickly sobered. No matter. Power went straight to my head. Even locked up, torque'd and bearing the title of "former stepmother," I affected this boy.

I moved a center player toward my others, to act as a guard, and launched into my next question. "What are *your* hobbies?"

"I have no time for hobbies. I take meetings, negotiate deals, prevent other kingdoms from allying, train, and oversee disputes between citizens. I used to enjoy puzzles."

"Why not now? Those puzzles helped calm me after a long day at the royal office."

His eyelids hooded, delicious tension wafting from him. "I knew you'd stayed in my bedroom. Your scent permeates every inch."

Shivers rocked me in my seat. "You're welcome."

He noticed, and I didn't have to wonder how he felt about it. Those hooded eyes all but smoked with heat. "Just so you know, you impressed me. You completed one I'd struggled with."

I gave my hair another fluff.

"To answer your question," he said, "I stopped working puzzles when I discovered the fun I could have with girls."

I snorted. "Of course you did."

"You impressed me in other ways, too. Roycelus read me transcripts of your meetings. You negotiated masterfully."

The compliment stunned me. "Thank you."

He grinned as he made his next move. Crap! He'd boxed in several of my soldiers.

Despite Roth's success, he sobered. Grim, he said, "Tell me, sorceress. Do you enjoy ending lives?"

"No," I said, the denial bursting from me. "Are you kidding?

418

I've been torn in two, one half grief, one half sorrow." *Revealing too much. Must hide my vulnerabilities.*

My soldier fired off a shot, killing one of his.

"Do you blame me for your father's death?" I asked.

Silence, thick and oppressive. Then, "I do, and I don't."

"That isn't an answer."

"Yet, it's the only one I have to offer," he said.

Turned out, his answer was good enough to move a soldier into the square just vacated by the dead soldier, but not good enough to fire off a retaliatory shot. "If I freed you today, what would you do?"

Was he considering freeing me? Hope burned bright, the lone star in a vast expanse of darkness. Such silly hope. "I would return to the forest. I like it there. I would search for Hartly and succeed where others have failed."

For some reason, my admission angered him; he stroked his jaw a little too forcefully. Could he not abide the thought of losing me? Had I moved into his head without even trying, now living there rent free?

"Your mother tried to kill you," he said. "Why not remove her from her position and rule Airaria?"

"Because I'm dumb and still hope for reconciliation? Because I love Truly? Because the citizens would treat me as poorly as yours did? Take your pick." But...my greedy side kind of wanted to do it anyway. First, I needed to consider the risks and rewards. "By your logic, I should take Sevón from you and Farrah."

Just like that, the anger got mowed down by guilt.

Between us, we carried a full set of luggage, every piece filled to the brim.

I moved a player toward an empty square, closer to his line of defense. He stared at my fingers as if fascinated, and something wicked came over me.

Voice a sultry caress, I said, "Do you want to touch me, Roth?"

His Adam's apple bobbed as he swallowed. "Pass."

He'd already admitted he thought about our kiss. Why not cop to a desire for more?

I advanced my soldier directly in front of his. The little guy fired off a killing shot, and I experienced a flicker of triumph. *Must win* more.

Roth took the newest loss in stride, calmly stroking two fingers over his chin. "Do you think of yourself as evil, Everly?"

A loaded question, if ever I'd heard one. "Here's what I think. My mother—the woman who raised me—told me evil is knowing what is right, but doing what is wrong anyway. Forget about me for a moment. You and Farrah act as if there are good times to do terrible things...but only to save yourselves. Whether wittingly or unwittingly, you cloak your actions in a guileless veneer, claiming you're saving innocents while destroying other innocents along the way. But anything for the greater good, right?"

"Everly—"

"No! The sorceress isn't done talking." Game forgotten, I snapped, "Until I was forced into an untenable situation, my only crime was stealing power I knew you would recoup. But *I* am the evil one? Because I have a sorcerer in my bloodline? Because I disagree with your methods and motives? So be it. If you are heroes, I'd much rather be the villain. Which means, yes. Yes, I think of myself as evil. It is a badge I will forever wear with pride." Evil queen? Full steam ahead. "But I can't help but wonder how you and Farrah will react when the tables are turned, and a certain sorceress does terrible things to *you* in order to save herself or someone she loves."

His spiky black lashes nearly fused. His jaw displayed a cruel slant, and the tendons running along the sides of his neck pulled taut. His shoulders squared, a blockade between me and the rest of the world.

I knew I'd reached him.

Finally, he said, "Farrah grew up without a mother because of me. Because I wasn't strong enough to stop the sorcerer. She is flawed, yes, but the same is true of us all. We have done terrible things, yes, but so have you. Deep down, I know we will all do much, much worse to protect the ones we love—which means the prophecy will come true. You will hurt the princess…for a time. Then she will destroy you. *I* will destroy you. I won't want to, I'll hate myself, but in the end, good will triumph over evil."

How easily he spoke of my destruction. I'd reached him all right, but I'd failed to win him over.

Feigning confidence, even as despair stabbed at me, I said, "Tsk, tsk. If you won't trust your heart more than prophecy, you are the one who fulfills it, Roth, not me."

37

What's done is done.
Fight until you've won.

Time passed at a crawl and at lightning speed. Weeks. Months. My birthday came and went. I only knew because Roth told me, and he only knew because Truly told him. He'd tried to throw me a little party, bringing me cake and a present, but I'd declined both. Until I reunited with Hartly and Truly, I had nothing to celebrate.

Okay, that wasn't true. I did have something to celebrate. He continued to visit me every day at sunset. Not once did he hurt or insult me. We never finished our game, too afraid to ask any more questions, but he always brought gifts. Those, I accepted. A gorgeous claw-foot tub with an enchanted spout to replace the metal basin Vikander had made for me. A new and lovely privacy screen. A wardrobe filled with finely made garments. Elaborate metal face masks preferred by the avian, a part of their culture. Thin, lightweight armor. Jewelry. Soft blankets. Potted plants. Mirrors of every size and shape.

I would say, "This doesn't make my imprisonment any better, princeling."

And he would reply, "But it doesn't hurt, either, sorceress."

"Just let me go," I would then demand.

"I cannot. You killed seven witches."

"In self-defense." But deep down I knew I could have weakened them and achieved the same result.

"One day, you will commit crimes against my sister."

"Your sister has *already* committed crimes against me."

He never had a response for that one, only an involuntary response: a ticking muscle underneath his eye.

Yesterday, he'd switched things up, giving me a basket of yarn and knitting needles.

"Do not even think about stabbing me with those needles," he'd said, his eyes vibrant with merriment.

But merriment had quickly turned to heat. Nowadays we couldn't look at each other without electrifying the air around us.

I couldn't even think about those unfulfilled desires without melting. Once or twice I could have attacked him and mounted an escape, successful or not, but I hadn't wanted to injure him.

This is you, remaining detached?

Think of something else before you electrify yourself.

Right. The gifts. I'd think about the gifts. My favorite was a box of books filled with different volumes labeled *Annals of Enchantia.* Just like the one I'd found in his bedroom! I got to learn about Enchantia's history—witches hoping to hide from persecution inadvertently shifted the curtain between dimensions for the first time. I got to study Allura and the forest, royal families, and every magical species in the land.

Second favorite: the puzzles.

A few days ago, he'd stomped into my cell, all but vibrating with strain. I'd convinced him to work one of the more elaborate puzzles with me, and the strain had melted from him, amazing me.

This boy... He liked me. And whether he admitted it or not, he needed me. Every time he visited, he would laugh at my sass, and I would tease him about his stodginess. He'd begun lingering, staying later and later.

Last night, we'd lain in bed—an Enchantian scandal in the making, I was sure—and talked for hours.

Careful. Electricity sparking...

I didn't care. I loved the memory so much, I wanted to relive it every day for the rest of my life. He'd questioned me about my negotiation techniques, hanging on my every word, and then we'd discussed our prophecy.

When did "my" prophecy become "our" prophecy?

We'd fallen asleep face-to-face, one of his strong arms draped over me, and I'd loved it. When I'd awoken, however, he'd been gone, and I'd been crushed.

Was the ecstasy I found in his arms worth the despair I faced with his desertion?

It must be, because I hoped he returned tonight and every night after. The joy I felt in his presence...

Worth it. Worth anything. Even though it frightened me. I think it frightened him, as well.

Detach! Detach!

I wasn't sure I could.

To my consternation, I could no longer spy on him, either. He'd visited Noel and Ophelia to buy a spell to "block whomever is using magic to watch me."

"Are you sure you want to block her?" Noel had asked. "I'm giving you a bargain, yes. You must only vow to give Ophelia and me safe passage in your kingdom forever and always. Still. Are you sure?"

"*Her?*" he'd demanded.

She hadn't confirmed or denied my identity. Instead, she'd

replied, "Keep things as is, and you can put on a real show for her. Strip slow and bathe, maybe. That'll teach her a lesson she'll never forget." She'd wiggled her brows. "Or would you prefer she didn't know you shout her name whenever you get personal with yourself?"

His lips had pulled back from his teeth in a show of irritation. "What you're hinting at is impossible. Everly cannot access her magic. Therefore, she cannot be the one who is watching me."

Noel had shrugged, saying no more.

Now I had to get my thrills—I meant, my *information*—spying on everyone else.

Hartly and Warick were sickeningly flirty. Her love had tamed the beast of beasts, and the bulk of trolls marveled that their commander had fallen for such a "hideous" girl. Thor was revered by all.

Truly continued to prepare for escape. I'd observed her as she'd created and shot new arrows and notes, communicating with someone in the Enchantian Forest. But who? Someone who carried the message to Violet? Allura, maybe?

I'd begun to wonder if Allura was part of the fairy tale. Snow White ran through a forest, after all. The Huntsman slayed a boar there. The Seven Protectors supposedly lived there.

Nicolas and Ty continued to search for Hartly. At least, I assumed they did. They never left the Enchantian Forest. They definitely didn't know how happy and content she was.

Farrah had been planning the ball in Roth's honor, determined to help the king pick a bride to ease his "burden-filled life." Never mind the fact that the kingdom ran like a well-oiled machine.

Roth cared for his people, often risking his life to better theirs. In return, servants and soldiers alike eagerly did his bidding. But beneath their reverence, I sensed frothing fear. No one could soothe his temper or predict how he would react to a situation.

Case in point: no one expected him to exile Annica, the

broom-goblin, but he did it. I hadn't had the pleasure of witnessing the event, I'd only heard about it secondhand, when two servants—I'd dubbed them Thelma and Louise—had come to clean my cell in Annica's place.

The first day T and L had shown up, I'd gotten to check off one item on my To Do list. Thelma had touched the broom handle and dropped as if I'd kicked her feet out from under her. She'd writhed for several seconds, agonized. Both Thelma and Louise had blamed the spidorpion they'd seen earlier, and I'd let them. A mistake. When Louise next saw Phobia, she'd tried to stomp on him.

I'd jumped up and drop-kicked her for real. When she'd climbed to her feet, ready to backhand me, Thelma had caught her wrist and said, "Remember what happened to Annica? She struck the prisoner, and King Roth banished her *forever*."

Inside, I'd erupted with surprise. Outside, I'd schooled my expression to project only smug superiority. I'd told the servants, "Spread the word. If you see an insect or critter of any kind, anywhere in the palace, you do them no harm. Understand? They are under my protection. I always find ways to retaliate against my foes. Ask Annica. Oh, wait. You can't."

Now I stood on my bed, peering out my window, a cool breeze wafting into my cell. Stalks of ivy had grown over every wall, the leaves soft as they petted me.

Last night, when Roth and I had our sleepover, he'd pinched a leaf between his fingers and said, "Allura watches over you. Why?"

I'd told him I didn't know, and I didn't. But I suspected…

In the *Annals of Enchantia*, Allura was touted as a "rare triad." A nymph, a witch and an oracle. The Tree of New Beginnings supposedly belonged to her, not Violet, not Stephan. If true, I belonged to her, too.

A shout drew my attention to the icy courtyard below my

tower, where Roth and his army trained. They used to practice farther away.

I'd asked Roth why they'd moved, and he'd grumbled, "I
want to keep you within my sights."

I believed him. He wanted me within his sights...because he
wanted to show off. Proof: he continued to glance up to assure
himself I remained at the window.

Any other day, I might have cheered and shouted inappropriate comments until he laughed. Things like, *Pin him down
and kiss him hard—I would!* But not today. Maybe not ever again.

Tomorrow, the royal ball kicked off. Servants and guards had
been rushing around for hours, frenzied as they finished last-
minute preparations.

As jubilant as Farrah had been, I'd begun to suspect Roth had
finally agreed to pick a bride.

If he got married...

I pressed my tongue to the roof of my mouth to silence a
scream.

Roth and Farrah were out there enjoying their lives while
ruining mine. One day, they would regret it. One day soon. I
planned to mount an escape as soon as the ball began.

Something pulled my gaze beyond the mountains...to the
edge of the Enchantian Forest. I sucked in a breath. Was that...
could it be...Nicolas, Ty, Hartly and Warick?

Shaking from top to bottom, I dropped and grabbed the enchanted glass. "Show me Hartly." Nothing. "Show me Nicolas and Ty." Again, nothing. Argh! Why go on the fritz now?
"Show me Farrah."

At last! The princess perched atop Roth's throne. All around,
servants scrubbed the walls and floor. "You are no longer welcome here," she announced.

Ooh la la. What was this? A firing? I loved when I caught an
inciting incident.

Noel and Ophelia stepped from the shadows.

The witch offered the princess a dark, sardonic smile.

The oracle offered a sunny one. "You've never needed us more. But all right. What the doomed princess wants, the doomed princess gets!"

Farrah cringed but didn't reverse her decision. "You poison Roth's mind every time you tell him Everly both is and isn't the Evil Queen. He needs to stop visiting her, stop playing house."

Whoa. Hold up. Noel couldn't lie. So, what made me the Evil Queen, and what made me *not* the Evil Queen?

Too tired to deal with further emotional upheaval, I stuffed the enchanted glass in my pillow and waited for Roth to finish his training. He would visit. We would talk and laugh, and he would hold me.

Waiting… Still waiting…

Footsteps resounded. I couldn't contain my excitement, I whispered, "Go, go." My critters scampered to their hiding places.

A freshly bathed Roth strode into the cell, another gift in hand. A shoe-size wooden box. I lifted the lid to find…a bloody heart?

He read my confusion and said, "The centaur who escaped us in the forest came back for you. I…handled him."

I hugged the box, my new favorite gift, but also I gave him my usual spiel. "This doesn't make my imprisonment any better, princeling."

"But it doesn't hurt, either, sorceress."

"Just let me go."

"Say those words again in two days, and we'll talk." He sat beside me at the edge of the bed.

What! Did that mean he planned to let me go? I climbed atop his lap, determined not to react to his words. Two days from now wasn't today, and only today mattered. "Did you miss me?"

"Yes," he said, not even trying to deny it. He wrapped his arms around me, holding me close.

"I shouldn't find comfort with you," I muttered.

"I know." He sounded remorseful.

I breathed him in, the scent of pine strongest, reminding me of our time in the forest.

Combing his fingers through my hair, he said, "What if I took you on an excursion?"

My heart skipped a beat. "Where?"

"The village. We can shop."

A day with Roth. A normal day—or date. "I'm in! When do you want to go?"

"The day after tomorrow."

Again, such a specific time. Why? Oh, yes. The ball. Envy and anger sparked.

Reflexes too swift to track, he set the box on the floor, twisted and tossed me onto my back. Looming over me, pinning me with his weight, he grinned with wicked delight...and began tickling me.

"Stop! I'm going to pee my pants!" I told him between giggles.

He settled beside me and draped his arm over my middle, his warm breath fanning my face. Goodbye, amusement.

I wouldn't be here in two days. Tomorrow, I would escape. Nothing would stop me. Never again would I spend a night in the agonizing rapture of Roth's embrace.

"There's so much I long to tell you," he said. "So much I long to do with you, for you."

"Like...kiss me?" We hadn't kissed since our time in the forest.

"Yes," he said, a hiss.

Passion-fever heated every inch of me. "What are you waiting for?"

"While you are trapped in here, I do not deserve to kiss you."

I rested my head in the hollow of his neck, suddenly, exquisitely, deliriously happy. I'd won him over. I knew it!

We fell asleep like that. I awoke certain he would cancel the ball and set me free. But once again, he was gone. No note. Servants still rushed around preparing for the ball

Don't care what Roth does or doesn't do. This is for the best. I would be leaving today. I needed to get used to being without him.

Where was my detachment now?

With a screech, I tossed my pillow against the wall, only to remember my enchanted glass was still inside it. I scrambled over. *Please be intact.* Yes!

Sunlight streamed through the window, urgency, excitement and nervousness consuming me...and maybe a little dread, too. I had a ball to attend, a king to usurp and no fairy godmother to make me presentable.

No, not true. I was my own fairy godmother, and there was none better.

"Today is the day," I announced. My friends had come out of hiding. "Today we escape."

First up—preparation. As I bathed, brushed my teeth and styled my hair in an elaborate half plait, my spidorpions performed the most important task of the day. Would they succeed?

Twitters of excitement provided the perfect background music as I dressed in a scandalous silver gown threaded with gold. One of Roth's gifts. *To match your eyes, sweetling.*

I anchored a shard of glass to my thigh, donned a sapphire choker above the torque, and an array of bracelets on each wrist—my makeshift cuffs—then studied my reflection. Missing something...

Phobia and Webster entered the room through a crack in the wall, dragging a length of web behind them. Anticipation swarmed me. Had they done it?

Yes! In the web was a bloody, severed thumb.

I laughed, overjoyed. Cinderella had rodent helpers. I had spidorpions.

During my spying, I'd watched different fairies who lived in the palace. One male had patted the backsides of female servants, no matter how many times they'd protested.

"I'm so proud of you, my loves!" I bent down to pick up the thumb. "Did you cut off the fairy's other fingers and scatter them about, so no one would realize the thumb was missing?"

—*We did!*—

I pressed the appendage against the torque...*please, please, please.* The metal separated, the pieces falling to the floor, and all the magic I'd stored up surged through me.

Relief nearly buckled my knees. I collected Phobia and Webster, one in each palm, and lifted the little darlings to my ears. They used their stingers to hang from my lobes, the perfect earrings.

Days ago, Vikander had visited. He hadn't come inside, he'd just tossed a tiny, lightweight metal stinger through the bars in the door.

A prosthetic for your pet, he'd said. *Allura asked, I granted.*

I hadn't known the fairy and the nymph were...friends?

I'd stood before the ivy and told the forest nymph, *I want to give you something in return. I have nothing to offer but my thanks and appreciation, and I offer both liberally.*

—*We leave tower now?*—

Phobia's voice drifted through my head. "Soon," I said. "After stage two."

If I took off, Roth and Farrah would come after me, because they saw me as a weakling, someone easily subdued. I had to prove I was a foe with whom one did not screw.

I had to attend the ball.

I put the pieces of the torque on the bed and rolled my head back and forth. I had to be careful. Because of the spidorpion venom and its mystical pulse of power, I could use magic, yes, but it was untried. And how long before I burned through it?

I'd be better served syphoning. But the moment I syphoned,

word would spread, everyone suspecting the sorceress had gotten free.

I could syphon from Allura. And maybe she wanted me to? That pulsing, flashing blue glow seemed to say, *Syphon. Syphon. Syphon.*

Such power...no one here would know...

If I was wrong and I ticked her off, she might try to keep me out of the forest.

Can't risk it. I broke my sliver of enchanted glass in half and handed one of the pieces to an adorable rat I'd named Bitsy. "You know what to do."

Off she raced, other rats chasing after her.

I settled Cuddles around my neck, then clutched the remaining sliver of enchanted glass to my chest and paced. Five...ten... fifteen minutes passed. My army watched from various locations within the cell, their excitement unmistakable.

Lord Nut Sack—Nutty—perched on the bed, eating pecans and acorns, leaving a mound of debris behind. "You're lucky I'm blowing this joint," I said, wagging my finger at him.

He held an acorn in both of his tiny hands and rocked his hips, all bow-chicka-wow-wow.

Phobia translated. —*You want some of his nuts?*—

I rolled my eyes. My amusement didn't last long, overshadowed by impatience. "Why hasn't Bitsy returned?" And dang it, the ivy continued to call to me. *Syphon. Syphon. Syphon.*

No! I'd wait for my plumming to pay off and syphon from Farrah once I had her locked in this tower.

Finally, the rat darted from the hole in the wall and squeaked.

Again, Phobia translated. —*She do good. Just what you wanted.*—

Excellent. Bitsy and her crew had scared Farrah's ladies-in-waiting. Then, during the commotion, they'd slipped the second sliver of enchanted glass in the princess's pocket, ensuring I could have a private meeting with her, without leaving my cell.

"All right. Places everyone. It's showtime." I trembled with excitement and nervousness. The moment of truth had arrived.

My critters raced to their assigned stations.

"Here goes." *Deep breath in, out.* I lifted my piece of enchanted glass.

"Show Farrah to me, and me to Farrah. Let us see, let us hear…" Could I bait the princess into visiting my cell before the ball, *without* causing her to alert Roth? My entire plan revolved around her reaction to our conversation.

Of course, I'd worked up a plan B, C, D and E, just in case I failed.

Don't fail.

The nervousness won, sweat dotting the back of my neck. I *had* to bait her. I had to trick Farrah the way the Evil Queen tricked Snow White. And I could. I now knew the chinks in her armor.

Her image appeared. Her dark hair had been twisted into an elaborate crown of braids, her cheeks rosy. Her lips were apple red, her dress as white as snow. How innocent she appeared. Like the angel I'd first believe her to be. How deceptive.

She stood in the center of a crowd of servants, issuing instructions. Waiting for her to walk away proved difficult, but I managed. Then, it happened.

The moment she was alone in a hallway, I pasted on my game face and said, "Hello, Princess. It's Stepmother dearest calling. How about we have ourselves a mother/daughter chat, hmm?"

Gasping, she spun. Her gaze darted this way and that as she searched for me.

"There's a shard of glass in your pocket," I said.

She withdrew it, changing my view. Our gazes locked.

The roses drained from her cheeks. "How are you doing this? You still wear the torque."

I smiled slowly, tauntingly. "Do I?" I stroked Cuddles. "Do you like my dress? Your brother gave it to me. Just between us,

I think he secretly hopes I'll throw my heart in the ring and vie for his hand in marriage."

"No. No! You're in the tower. Trapped."

"Maybe I'm standing right behind you."

I knew chills had raced up her back when she whirled.

I laughed. "Made you look. With my illusion magic, I can become *anyone*. Just ask your brother. Or not. For all you know, I'll don his face as soon as we end our conversation. I could be anyone, anywhere…"

"But—"

"If you didn't want to deal with an irate sorceress, you shouldn't have locked anyone away." I gave a mocking wave with my middle finger before dropping the glass and doing something I'd been dreading…

I stomped on my precious shard, ensuring Farrah couldn't spy on me.

Would she come to the tower to make sure I was here? Hopefully, I'd instilled so much doubt, she wouldn't trust anyone she came across, even Roth. She would need to see me in the tower first. If not…

I would deal. If the prince showed up in her stead, I would do to him what I planned to do to Farrah. Nothing would sway me from this path.

Tremors beleaguered me anew as I picked up the comb my spidorpions had stolen for me. Earlier I'd soaked its teeth in my blood. The poison would subdue my next visitor, whoever it happened to be, just long enough for the final stage. Three…

Come on, come on. "Where are you, Princess?"

Finally! Hurried footsteps. Panting breaths.

Relief showered me, drying my perspiration. "Get ready," I whispered.

Metal clinked and hinges squeaked. Among my army, exhilaration skyrocketed. They'd waited for this moment, too.

Farrah stalked inside the cell, accompanied by a cloud of floral perfume. Two guards dogged her heels. More bodies than I'd hoped, but nothing I couldn't handle. The door closed, sealing us all inside.

"You lied! I knew it!" Scowling, she raised her hand to blast me with a stream of ice. But she'd underestimated me and overestimated herself.

The mistake would cost her dearly.

I had already stretched out my hand. Now, I began to syphon, drawing as much power from her as I could. At the same time, Boomer, my feral cat, leaped onto her back, scratching her, while one of the snakes dropped from the ceiling to wrap around her wrists and press her hands together, "disarming" her. As she opened her mouth to scream for help, *I* struck, slamming the comb deep into her neck.

The poisoned prongs embedded in muscle. She jerked and collapsed, momentarily paralyzed. I dropped with her, shoving a rag into her mouth and securing it with a strip of fabric.

Phobia and Webster dove from my ears. One landed on each guard. A quick jab, jab of their stingers, and out popped their eyeballs. Oops.

Swords dropped. The *guards* dropped. A boa constrictor wrapped around each man's mouth, squeezing to silence their screams. Other snakes bound their hands and wrists.

I continued to draw from Farrah. Using her power, her magic, I bound each of my foes with shackles of ice, freeing my army.

So close to freedom myself!

Farrah bucked, banging her head against the floor as if knocking on a door for help.

"Uh-uh-uh." I tied her long braid around the leg of my bed, forcing her to still or go bald. Drawing, drawing…

I wanted more; I wanted *all*. Never again would Farrah have the means to harm me. Released from Roth's compulsion, I would let nothing and no one stop me from draining this girl to death.

No! Resist temptation. If I killed her in cold blood, I would be a murderess. Officially. An evil act by an evil girl. More like Violet than I wanted to be.

There was still goodness inside me, and I would prove it.

"Keep the princess and guards quiet," I told my army. "If the worst happens and our prisoners are discovered, run. We'll meet in the Enchantian Forest."

Farrah's eyes spat contempt at me.

"We don't have to be enemies just because fate decrees it." I returned Phobia and Webster to my ears. "Let's think this through. Prophecy says I try to kill you three times. First with the corset—done. Next with a comb—done. Finally with the apple. After that, you and Roth are supposed to kill *me*. In a very unheroic way, I might add. Except, multiple sources claim death could represent a new beginning. I want a new beginning. So, why don't we jump to our happily-ever-after? You leave me alone, and I'll leave you alone. Or ignore everything I've said and come after me. I'll steal your magic, your title and your family. I'll leave you destitute."

Fury joined the contempt.

"Let's be honest. You are dim-witted—even the Brothers Grimm knew it—and need time to consider my offer." I reached into the wardrobe and selected an ivory half mask with wing-tips on both sides, a fan of peacock feathers rising over the brow like a crown.

Giddier by the second, I approached my full-length mirrors. I'd lined them up side-by-side, one pressed against the other. "Mirror," I said, taking a little more power from Farrah. Just a bit, yet it pitched through me, hot and bubbly.

Foreverly appeared in the glass. Today she wore bold makeup and an even bolder black gown, the deepest V showing off her cleavage. Spiked metal bands circled her neck, more deterrent than decoration—protection against a torque, no doubt.

"All hail the mighty Queen of Schemes and Poisons." She

smiled, proud, and curtsied. "You'll be happy to know Princess Truly escaped the palace."

Really? "When?"

"Only a few minutes ago. No one knows she's missing—yet. She's currently in the forest, meeting with Hartly, Warick, Nicolas and Ty."

I *had* seen Hartly and the troll! But how had Truly gotten to the forest so quickly? "I will join them...later."

"First, you must attend the ball," Foreverly confirmed.

"Yes." And not just to prove my strength. Vengeance beckoned...

Roth had ruined months of my life, so I would ruin his party.

"You cannot let him form a marriage alliance with Azul," she said. "He will become too strong."

"Stop a marriage. Check." For me to strengthen, my foes had to weaken. "Can I bring others through the mirror?"

"Of course. I don't want to brag, but I am pretty incredible."

And modest. "Any advice for me, oh incredible one?"

"Yes," Foreverly said and grinned. "Show no mercy."

38

What's theirs is yours.
Prepare for wars.

The throne room appeared in the glass next to Foreverly. The space brimmed with people and creatures, all having a merry time. The injustice of it... I rotted in a prison cell, everyone else indulged in frivolous fun.

Fury lashed my heart and dimmed the bliss of my escape.

Roth sat upon the throne, so beautiful it hurt to look upon him. I'd never seen him so dressed up. A white jacket fit him to perfection, molding to his muscles. Gold tassels lined the shoulders, and a golden sash slanted over his chest. A utility belt hung at his waist, sheathing daggers. Beige riding pants and knee-high black boots completed the look.

One suitress after another vied for his favor, hoping to win his hand in marriage. I couldn't blame them. The king looked good—really, *really* good—but he was stiff and uncomfortable, even sulky. Why? And why did I still yearn to be in his arms?

An orchestra played a lovely song, and one of the girls began a slow, sensual dance for Roth. She had delicate features, long black hair and pale skin with a hint of blue. A Grecian white gown with spaghetti straps that crisscrossed in back molded to an hourglass figure. Like Reese, she had scales on her arms.

A mermaid shape-shifter? The siren duchess Farrah had mentioned? A shape-shifting swan, perhaps? I'd studied all three in the annals Roth had given me, fascinated by the undersea culture. Did this girl live underwater?

Everyone but Roth watched her, enraptured. Including me! Did she possess some kind of enchantress magic?

Why didn't Roth succumb?

I pressed my tongue to the roof of my mouth, my ears twitching as a trio of girls held a whispered conversation.

"I hear she's cursed."

"I hear her voice makes men kill each other in a fit of jealous rage, so she hasn't spoken in years."

"It's not her voice, it's her song. When she sings, people are enthralled and battles erupt."

So. She *was* the siren, and she would be a wonderful ally to have…or a terrible enemy. I might risk her wrath to syphon some of her power.

Roth shifted to peer in the direction of my tower. Could he be…missing me?

I thrilled as I studied my new battleground. Armed guards were posted along the walls. Saxon stood at one side of the royal dais, and Vikander stalked through the crowd. Every avian wore a mask or headdress. A handful of the mer-folk wore one, as well. Though Noel and Ophelia had been dismissed, they were in attendance, too. They laughed loudly and danced with abandon.

"All right, my darklings," I said, stroking Phobia and Webster. "Follow me into the throne room and hide. When I give the signal, attack."

Twitters, chirps and hisses created a chorus of agreement.

I glanced at Farrah over my shoulder. "Don't worry, step-daughter, I'll show Roth the same kindness you showed me."

If looks could kill, I'd be bleeding out right now.

I laughed, the way Roth had once laughed at me. "You are adorable."

My flippancy pushed her over the edge. She bucked and strained, despite her fear of my critters.

"Calm yourself, or you'll miss the final stage of my plan." I waved a hand, giving myself the face, hair, and skin of a su-permodel I'd once seen in a magazine. Brown eyes, dark curly mane and bronze complexion. I took the disguise a step further, making the mask, gown and jewelry bloodred.

With the illusion in place, I didn't need the mask, but I derived comfort in its cover.

Farrah bucked with more force, struggling to no avail.

"Now you know how I've felt all these months," I said, and refocused on the mirror.

The party grinded on. Had Noel foreseen my attendance? Would she or Ophelia recognize me, despite the illusion? Probably. But I would proceed anyway.

Head high, shoulders back. Link with Farrah—still in place. Heart racing, I stepped forward, walking through the mirror. Warmth enveloped me, and I luxuriated. Different sounds erupted, some loud, some quiet. White lights exploded all around.

When I exited, I stood in front of the wall of mirrors, just behind the crowd. Animals and insects followed, racing to hide in the shadows as I'd commanded. No one noticed us, everyone too busy enjoying themselves.

I remained in place for a long while, soaking in the revelry, my captivity officially at an end. The scent of pine and cinnamon steeped the air, my drug of choice, overshadowing candle wax and sea salt. Roth was within reach and unaware I was about to upend his entire world.

After tonight, neither one of us would ever be the same.

Panic squeezed my heart and refused to let go. Should I reconsider this? If he compelled me, I'd lose. Game over.

No! I wouldn't fear his magic. I'd planned for it. As Roth had done after I'd compelled him, I would find a way around any and every order.

Showtime. Fighting to keep my nerves on a tight leash, I sauntered to the throne.

"Hey!" A guard noticed me and stalked over to clasp my arm. He bowed, telling Roth, "My apologies, great king. I am unsure how she bypassed us."

"Quite easily," I quipped, even my voice like the supermodel's.

"The dais is off-limits to guests." Roth spared me the barest glance and dismissed me with a flick of his wrist. "My guards will escort you somewhere, anywhere else."

I was the fairest of all, and he remained unimpressed by my obvious beauty? Unacceptable! *Let's kick things up a notch.*

I wrenched free of the guard, spun, and plopped onto Roth's lap, startling both males. "You're right. I should leave." Batting my lashes, I traced a fingertip along the collar of Roth's jacket. "Or I could stay, and we could discuss your favorite part of my body."

We stared at each other for several heartbeats of time, the heat in his eyes making me dizzy. Could he tell who I was?

No, no. He couldn't. He *didn't*. He relaxed into the throne, even draping an arm around my waist.

Guess he liked his girls bold and brash, after all.

When the guard grabbed my arm for the second time, Roth caught his wrist—*without* looking away from me. Shiver!

"Leave her," he said, giving the guy a push. He returned his muscular arm to my waist, spreading his fingers over my hip-bone to cover more ground. A possessive hold. With his free hand, he gently pinched my chin and angled my masked face into a beam of candlelight.

I trembled. *Must preserve the illusion.*

Drain him and go.

Not yet. So much more to do.

He leaned closer to me, and I sucked in a breath. Was he going to kiss me? I would stop him. Of course I would stop him. But the diabolical boy merely dragged his nose along the column of my neck and sniffed.

More shivers…more jealousy. In his mind, I was languishing in the tower. Yet here he was, flirting with a supermodel. Never mind that I was the supermodel in question.

He would pay for this.

"You smell like someone I know," he said, his voice all smoke and gravel.

Oh, crap! Because of Roth's scent, I could pick him out of a lineup while blindfolded. I should have realized he could do the same for me. Even the centaurs had claimed I smelled like "apple blossoms."

But Roth didn't toss me off his lap or call for reinforcements and a torque, or compel me to return to the tower. So, my true identity remained secret.

"Someone. A girl, I'd bet," I said. "Do you *like* her scent?"

"I do not. I *love* her scent."

I wanted to preen and claw his face to shreds. I compromised by wetting my lips and sinking my nails in his shoulders. His gaze tracked the glide of my tongue, and I nearly cried out with longing.

With his free hand, he motioned for Saxon.

I tensed as the avian approached the throne. He wore a mask the same shade of blue as his wings.

Roth spoke in a language I didn't understand. Avianish, I think. The other male stiffened, gave the king a clipped nod and strode away.

"Oooh. What did you say?" I asked, pretending I wasn't awash with nervousness.

"I asked him to check on my treasure," he replied, a strange gleam in his eyes. "Sometimes guests wander where they should not."

"Treasure?" What did this boy value above all else?

"Mmm-hmm." He said no more, dang him, and I couldn't push without rousing suspicions.

To get us back on track, I dragged my nose along the column of *his* neck, breathing him in. "I noticed your scent, too," I admitted. *Play the game.* "You smell like the happiest day of the year, the best present under the tree and every girl's downfall." Wait. Did they celebrate Christmas here? Had I just given myself away?

Smoldering with intensity, he reached up to sift a lock of my hair between his fingers. "You are not from the Azul Dynasty."

"Correct. But I have every right to be here. I'm related to royalty." Uh-oh. Resentment had seeped from my tone.

He gave a half smile. "Are you here to win my hand in marriage?"

I arched a brow. "You speak as if *you* are the prize, King Roth."

"Aren't I?"

"You are not. I am." I winked and extracted myself from his hold. "Parting is such sweet sorrow, that I shall say good night till it be morrow." Yes, I'd just quoted *Romeo and Juliet*. An impulse I should have ignored. Of all the plays, in all the world.

How would Roth respond?

I rose. He did the same, and embarrassingly enough, I swayed into him as I craned my head up to meet his gaze.

He brought my hand to his mouth and pressed a kiss into the center of my palm. Butterflies took flight in my stomach, and my knees knocked together, my tactile awareness of him deepening.

How would a proper Enchantian maiden respond to this?

"My lord." Saxon returned to the dais, saving me from a mistake.

Scratch marks littered his face, and a smear of blood stained the collar of his shirt. Stiff, he spoke in Avianish once more.

He must have confirmed the treasure remained undisturbed, whatever it was, because Roth expelled a relieved breath and dazzled me with a smile.

As I tried to breathe, the avian said something that made the smile vanish.

I gulped and asked, "Something wrong?"

Clipped nod. "A fae courtling was found unconscious, his fingers severed," Roth explained. "Our healers are working to reattach everything."

Sweet! No one had put two and two together! Relieve, I toyed with the ends of his silken hair. "Worry about the fae later. Entertain me now."

"Yes." He motioned Saxon away. "Will you honor me with a dance?"

How could I resist? "I will."

Satisfaction oozed from him as he took my hand and led me around servants who carried trays of wineglasses. We bypassed different cliques of royals. So much power, so many abilities, there for the taking. Good thing I hadn't severed my link with Farrah. Temptation was almost irresistible. But resist I did.

Most attendees watched us, some angry, some curious. Whispers arose. "Who is she?" "How did *she* gain the king's notice?" "He has ignored everyone else."

I smirked. If Roth heard the gossip, he gave no outward sign. The only hitch in his step came when Noel and Ophelia twirled directly into our path.

"Oracle. Witch," he grated in greeting. "Now isn't the time to pester me."

"Since I'm no longer on your payroll, I stopped caring about your personal timetable. I tease, I tease. I never cared." She patted his cheek. "Since my happily-ever-after is dependent on others, I need you to listen to me." Though she'd always presented herself as scatterbrained, I detected keen intellect in her gaze. "When the clock strikes rat o'clock, grab hold of your treasure and do *not* let go."

Another mention of his treasure. My curiosity doubled.

She winked at me before flouncing away. Ophelia leaned in to whisper, "Nice earrings," then trailed after her friend. Phobia and Webster hissed at her retreating back. The oracle and witch *did* see past my illusion, but they hadn't outed me. Guess they weren't *all* bad.

"Rat o'clock," Roth mumbled.

I understood the reference—the moment Bitsy and her crew came out of hiding—but nothing else.

Before I could rack my brain, the king swept me into his arms. "Shall we have our dance?"

I held on tight, barely managing to stifle a groan. "I haven't danced in years. If I make a mistake…the fault is yours."

He laughed. "I'll endeavor to lead you well, then." Something about his tone…as if his words had a deeper meaning.

Music drifted through the room, soft and decadent. Roth urged me into an elegant one-two-three rhythm. Wait. I knew this dance. Mom had already taught me.

That's right. When Hartly and I were little girls, Mom hadn't just read us bedtime stories; she'd played "princess" with us, hoping to prepare us for our return.

Do not think of Mom. I had to remain clearheaded. As clearheaded as possible anyway, considering the king made me stupid.

He glided me left, back and right. Again and again. Then he whirled me, catching me against his chest. I felt the erratic beat of his heart, a perfect mimic of mine.

We needed to stop before I melted against him and forgot the rest of my plan—before he got me addicted to his nearness, and I began to crave the life I could have led if the prophecy had never been spoken.

Resolve hardened my spine. "I'm going to leave now," I

rasped. I would give the signal and thrill as my army ruined the party and any chance of an alliance between Sevón and Azul.

Stay. Just a little longer…

"Why must you go?" His voice thickened. "I'm not ready to part with you."

Had he known my true identity, I would have loved hearing those words. Now? They just made me sad. "I must go because I must, and you must let me." If he fought to keep a strange girl here, when he hadn't fought to keep me *period*, I might just raze this palace to the ground!

He stiffened, nodded. "Come to the balcony with me. Please. Allow me to bid you a proper goodbye."

Did he hope to kiss me?

Did I want him to?

Kiss him. Excise him from your mind. Say goodbye. Mean it.

My stomach churned as I nodded.

Triumph brightened his irises. He rushed me off the dance floor.

The people from Azul bowed as we passed. Many whispered, "May the water wash you."

Approaching two guards stationed in back, Roth said, "No one else comes out here. Understood?"

Once we passed the double doors, both males extended a spear, crossing the ends crossing to create a block. Icy air stroked my exposed skin, but Roth radiated enough body heat to warm the Arctic. I remained wonderfully toasty.

He pivoted in my direction, golden moonlight haloing him. Panting, he took a step closer. I panted, too, but I took a step back, keeping distance between us. I needed a moment to get myself under control. The aches…the throbbing need… Neither lessened.

He crowded me against the wall. Sounding drugged, he said, "The things you make me feel…"

"Good things?"

"The best." Without preamble, he added, "I want to taste you."

How could a stranger rouse such strong desire in him?

Forget the kiss. Resist his allure. Reject him. The charade had become too dangerous.

Great! I was divided again.

When he brushed the tip of his nose against mine, his minty breath fanning over my face, the pro-kissing side won by a landslide.

I rose to my tiptoes as he pressed his lips to mine. With a moan, I met the thrust of his tongue with a thrust of my own, too keyed up for a simple get-to-know-you kiss. I already knew this boy; I liked him as much as I hated him.

The kiss quickly spun out of control, becoming wild, possessive, fierce. Territorial. We took and we gave. I demanded more, and he demanded all, everything.

Being still wasn't possible. I scraped my nails through his hair, caressed the stubble on his jaw and kneaded his shoulders, rejoicing when my body melted against his, creating a cradle for him. A cradle he accepted with a groan.

We rocked against each other, once, twice. At the same time, he did wicked things with his tongues. Expert flicks. Sucking. Stroking. Our fire raged hotter. Burning, aching, I clung to him.

"Love having your hands on me." He clasped my wrists and moved my palms to his chest, letting me feel his raging heart. "Never let go."

"Never." I curled my fingers, sinking my nails into him.

He grunted his approval, angled my head, and deepened the kiss. Our breathing became hectic. Thought became impossible. But I tried. Oh, I tried, needing to stop this before I lost myself.

He was the king I shouldn't want, and the boy I couldn't have and…and…in this moment of fiery passion, I tasted salvation and hope, absolution and rapture and…and…

He would never be mine, and I would never be his, but we had here, and we had now.

No, there would be no stopping this. The memory would warm me during the coldest, harshest nights.

"Can't get close enough to you," he growled against my lips.

"Keep trying." Nearly blissed out. More, I had to have more.

He rocked. He rubbed. Hot, so hot. Little snarls rumbled in his chest, driving me wild.

"Everly," he said and moaned. "Even better than I remembered."

In an instant, realization struck, dread pouring over me. He knew the truth. He'd always known.

I wrenched away, gasping for breath.

He was gasping, too. "Yes, I know it's you. I've known from the beginning. Can we end the pretense now? Show me your real face, beauty."

Beauty? "How did you know who I was? My scent?" I asked, letting the illusion fade. "There. Happy?"

As he looked me over, I expected the heat in his eyes to fade, as well. It didn't.

"I haven't been happy in months." Every inch a king, he removed my mask and tossed it aside, then flattened one hand onto the wall, then the other, caging me in. "I knew the moment you sat in my lap. You alone fit me like a puzzle piece."

I did, didn't I?

"I asked Saxon to check on Farrah," he said. "He says you left her alive and well in the tower. For that, I am grateful."

"Ah. I see. *She* is your treasure." I should have known. And I shouldn't care.

"No. Not her," he said with a hard shake of his head. "I planned ahead, just in case you escaped."

My brain had trouble computing facts; arousal had fried my circuits. "Noel warned you?"

"No. But I know you. My princess is smart, diabolical when necessary, and a survivor."

His princess? The claim affected me more than the compliments, blunting my anger. It almost—almost!—distracted me from my goals.

I severed my link with Farrah and started syphoning from Roth. Warmth. Tingles.

He sensed the loss of power, no doubt about it, and narrowed his eyes.

"Sorry, but I can't let you compel me again," I told him.

"I will not compel you ever again, Everly. You have my word. I learned my lesson."

Did I return the favor or protect myself? I couldn't do both. Once, Roth had tested me. Today, I would do the same to him.

"I won't compel you, either," I said, "as long as you mind your manners. And you don't have to worry about your precious sister. I wanted to kill her, but I didn't. Now, I will leave you with a warning. Do not come after me. Do not come after my family. If you do, I'll make you regret it. Let this be the end of our war."

"How about we make this the beginning of our alliance?"

He wanted to ally with me?

No. A trick! "Never," I said. I filched a dagger from his side and pressed the tip against his collarbone. "You locked me away. You don't get to be my friend."

No change in his expression. He nodded. "I did lock you away."

"You don't regret it."

"How can I regret doing what I thought was right?"

So calm, so collected. So irritating! "I should punish you," I snapped. "You deserve it."

Another nod. "I do."

Argh! I would rather deal with his fury than…this. Whatever this was.

"I have been in torment since I discovered your sorcerian heritage," he said, his composure beginning to fade. "I wanted the enemy. The girl who brought me to life."

My eyes went wide.

"Until you, I didn't know I was a dead man walking," he continued. "I went from day to day, moment to moment, with a single goal—protect what I love. Then you showed up and made me want more."

The rest of his composure faded, revealing all the torment he'd mentioned, plus an endless well of doubt, confusion and fury.

I couldn't do this. I couldn't look at him and want him and hurt for him—hurt for *us*. I needed to go. Now!

"Goodbye, Roth," I croaked. For once, *I* was the one to walk away from *him*.

I felt as if I'd been hit in the ribs with a baseball bat. Tearing my heart in two… *Tearing my heart in two…*

"I won't be leaving your side, Everly," Roth said, catching up to me.

Because he didn't trust me to leave his people alone, or because he couldn't bear to part with me?

Did it matter? I would be ditching him in a matter of moments.

Pang, pang. "Good luck with that." I shoved past the double doors, pushed past the two guards and their spears and glided into the ballroom. "Now," I shouted.

In seconds, sounds of panic rang out. Wails. Screams. Curses. Trays were dropped, and glass shattered. Rats, rats, everywhere. Spidorpions and lava ants crawled over the walls, infesting everything. Guests and guards charged toward the exits. Well, those who hadn't collapsed after being bitten. Chaos reigned.

Roth clasped my wrist, stopping me while scanning the room. "Rat o'clock," he said. "Must grab hold of my treasure."

I pressed the dagger I'd filched against his throat. "I told you I'm leaving, and I meant it. I will *not* go back to the tower."

I needed to sever my link with him, needed to syphon from someone else, anyone else, and use an illusion to move through the crowd and exit through a mirror. For too long I'd let my desire to spend time with him overrule my common sense. But no longer.

Do it! Sever.

Still I hesitated, hating myself.

"I will never put you in the tower again," he said. "You have my word."

"Liar!" I spat, pressing the dagger more forcefully. A bead of crimson welled, the sight almost my undoing. I'd injured him. I'd injured the boy I'd just kissed.

Monster! Tears gathered and fell unchecked.

He collected one of those tears, threw back his head and roared, as if he, too, had reached his limit. My chest tightened, wrenched.

We locked gazes, his eyes like wounds. "You had an opportunity to harm Farrah. You didn't take it. You've earned your freedom, Everly. I won't put you back in the tower," he reiterated, "but I won't part from you, either. Right now, you need me. The danger…"

"I—" Screamed. Agonizing pain sliced through my shoulder, a river of blood gushing down my torso. Someone had stabbed me from behind, the metal tip coming out the front. My knees quivered, threatening to buckle.

The incarnation of rage, Roth shoved me out of the way, taking the next blow himself. A slice from elbow to wrist.

As I panted, seeing stars, determined to defend myself against another attack, the King of Sevón ripped the sword from Stabby's grip, and tossed the male to the floor.

The guy tried to rise, but my spidorpions leaped onto him.

Phobia bit. Webster stung. Between one blink and the next, Stabby died, white foam seeping from his mouth.

My pets returned to my ears. I gulped back bile and tried to make sense of what just happened. Roth had risked his life to save mine. On purpose! But why?

The answer doesn't—can't—matter.

Roth was distracted. No better time to do my disappearing act. World spinning faster, faster still, I stumbled forward, heading for the mirror. *Hurry!* One wrong move, and I would fall and be stampeded.

Lava ants swarmed me, creating a barrier between me and the party goers. Anyone who touched me got zapped. Other insects, animals and rodents cleared a path for me, mowing down the guards. *Spinning...*

As soon as I reached the wall of mirrors, my knees gave out, no longer able to carry me, and I tumbled through the glass, uncertain where I would end up...

39

My wish, your command.
Your heart, my quicksand.

My wound screamed in protest as I breached the surface of the water and sucked in a ragged breath. I blinked cool droplets out of my eyes and took stock. The forest. I had emerged in the pond where Ophelia and the birds once doctored me. Familiar sounds—crickets, bees, locusts. Familiar scents—pine and honeysuckle.

Phobia and Webster made twittering noises, letting me know they were alive and well.

Relief left me dizzy. Well, *dizzier.* Or maybe blood loss was responsible. Whatever. I had done it! I had escaped Sevón.

I had come home.

When something tugged on my ankle, I kicked and performed a one-armed breaststroke, going nowhere fast. The shore seemed miles away, fatigue setting in quick. I began to sink, my dress weighing me down.

A stalk of ivy slithered over the water to wind around my wrist and pull me toward the shore. *Allura?*

Problem: the more the ivy tugged, the more the wound in my shoulder throbbed and burned. New rivers of blood spurted, and I screamed. The ivy retracted. *Too weak to swim…sinking again…*

Behind me, water splashed and someone else sucked in a breath. I'd been trailed through the mirror? I fought to stay afloat. Frantic, I glanced over my shoulder…

Half of me shouted, *No!* The other half of me purred with approval. Roth was here, bathed in a soft azure glow as he swam in a circle, his wild gaze scanning…

Spotting me, he heaved a relieved breath. The wildness dulled to concern.

"Go back, or I'll kill you," I said, panting. Only he had the power to ruin something *and* make it better.

"You are injured. I will help you recover."

"I'll recover just fine on my own, thanks."

—*He help friend.*— Phobia's voice pleaded with me. The darling worried. —*Let him. Please!*—

"You say you'll recover, yet your blood currently paints the water red." Roth swam closer. "Use me. Let me do the work and get you to shore." He unsheathed a dagger, cut the ivy from me, then snaked an arm around my waist. His entire body convulsed.

The mystical venom! My blood had touched his skin. "Let me go," I demanded. "My blood is poison to you." To everyone. "Every drop contains spidorpion venom."

He blinked, astonished. "I'm not letting go. What is a little pain when your life hangs the balance?" Still convulsing, he guided me to shore.

After gently lifting me and settling my limp body atop a carpet of dewy moss, he climbed out beside me, then stripped out of his soaked jacket and tunic and reached for me.

I regained my sanity long enough to slap his hands away, and realized there was something different about my arm…

What, what? No cuts. No bruises. But...

Realization. My ants had washed off. Which meant they were stuck in the water...drowning...

"We have to save them," I said, trying to sit up. "They can't swim. They'll die."

He frowned and skidded his gaze over the pond. "No one is in the water, sweetling."

"My ants," I said. *Don't cry. Don't you dare.* "My ants are in the water. They kept me warm. I owe them. Please, Roth!"

"Ants?"

"You have to help them." Desperate, I added, "I'll pay whatever tax you demand." I just wanted my babies saved, whatever the cost.

"Ants?" he repeated, glancing at my spidorpions as they walked down my arm to rest on my wrist. He shook his head. "Never mind. I will do this, free of charge."

"Hurry!"

He raced to gather twigs and logs, then anchored the pieces to the edge of the pond, stretched out over the surface of water. "Come to me, ants," he said, the magic in his voice eliciting chills. "Surface, exit and live."

I watched, jubilant, as hundreds of lava ants crawled over the wood to reach the shore.

Roth returned to my side. "Now, let me help *you*. Please." He attempted to remove my sodden dress.

Again, I slapped his hands away. "In your dreams. We are enemies. I would be a fool to trust you to help me." But I was growing weaker by the minute. *Hate weakness!* Especially in front of this particular boy. "Again and again, you have hurt me."

Familiar growls rumbled from his chest. "I didn't stab you, and I didn't command the soldier to stab you. In fact, I commanded every citizen of Sevón to leave you alone if ever you escaped. I'd made the consequences of such an action abundantly clear."

But that made no sense. "He *had* to stab me. I had a knife at his king's throat."

"You don't understand, so I will rephrase. The soldier disobeyed a direct order not to harm you if ever you escaped, *no matter what you said or did*. Upon my return, he will be imprisoned."

He'd planned for my escape, not to recapture me but to ensure I remained unscathed? I shook my head. "I don't believe you."

"I have never lied to you, Everly. I planned for everything." Mouth a thin line, he said, "Almost everything. How could I prepare for constantly wanting you? How could I guess you would—you *do*—come to mean more than the prophecy? That you would be the treasure I needed to grab or lose?"

No. More lies! Had to be lies. Me, an exception? A treasure to him? Please! But what if he'd actually fallen for me?

Inside, I soared... Until I crashed. Fury bubbled over and I snapped, "You want me, and I'm a treasure, yet you left me rotting in a tower. Gee, Roth. I'd hate to see what you do to people you *don't* like. And if you cared for me so much, why did you cave and agree to host the ball, letting fair maidens try to win your hand in marriage?"

He winced. "A mistake on my part. I desperately wanted to pick someone else. I thought the torment would end. But I couldn't do it. And tonight, when I realized you were the only one I wished to hold, I knew I was done fighting my feelings for you."

I couldn't breathe. I couldn't think. I couldn't not want his words to be true. *He isn't for me.*

"Whether you agree or not, I'm patching you up." He confiscated the dagger I'd stolen from him and very carefully, very gently cut away the top portion of my fancy dress, revealing my bra. Despite his best efforts, I was racked by searing pain.

"Sure. I'll let you patch me up." I brought out old faithful—my maniacal smile. "For a price. Your heart on a silver platter."

His expression softened. Softened! "I only own gold plat-
ters." He grazed his knuckles along my jawline. "Let me patch
you up without complaint, and I'll forfeit the healer tax you'll
owe." Grim, he added, "Your blood is venomous, and I cannot
sew the torn flesh together while conscious. I have to cauterize
the gash to stop the bleeding."

He wanted to press a white-hot blade against my precious
skin? "No! Absolutely not."

He ignored me, stacking rocks in a circle, then gathering twigs
and kindling, his every movement hurried. "I have a confession.
Before you showed up at the ball, I'd already decided to remain
alone if I couldn't have you."

He. Is. Not. For. Me. "You could have had me. Instead, you
left me in the tower," I snapped.

"I left you in a safe place. What if your predicted death *is* literal, as you first assumed? If something were to happen to you…"
He scoured a hand over his face. "I expected to panic when you
escaped, but I felt such profound relief. Such remorse. I'm sorry I
didn't trust you sooner. And I'm sorry I treated you like the sorcerer responsible for the death of my mother and brother…sorry
I treated you as my father's killer. I'm sorry for so many things."

If he meant these things, I was in trouble. But he didn't, so
I wasn't. "You're sorry I escaped and you're backpedaling. You
hate me. I'm a parasite!"

He paused for a moment, his head bowed. "I do not hate you,
and you are not a parasite. I was wrong to say such a terrible
thing." Spurred back into motion, he dumped the twigs inside
the stone circle and started a fire. Ribbons of smoke spiraled up,
carried away by a warm breeze.

"*Of course* I'm a parasite." I needed King Stubborn back. No
more Mr. Nice Guy. "I steal power from others. I just stole from
you. Remember?"

"You take what you need to survive, just as I take food from
the earth."

Gah! "I could drain and *kill* you in a matter of minutes."

"Nourishing you will be my privilege."

"Are you freaking kidding me?" I banged my head into moss. "You would grow to resent me, and we both know it."

"Resent you? Never again." Looking at me with stars in his eyes, he said, "I think...I love you."

Love. One word, four letters—together, they created a shiv and rammed it through my heart. "You don't love me. You can't. You're thinking with your...your penis, that's all." My cheeks heated white-hot, but I hurried on. "You don't hurt the people you love. And you hurt me worse than anyone ever has." Hadn't he? In my pained state, everything I should feel, did feel and wanted to feel was beginning to jumble together.

The regret in his eyes staggered me. "What I feel for you is like nothing I've felt before. Stronger. Deeper. Sharper."

"That sounds like a *you* problem."

"You got inside my heart and set up camp. Now I can't breathe without thinking about you or wanting you close."

The shiv got me again. Ram. Ram. *Stay strong.* "I might have believed you if you'd let me go. But you didn't, proving you will only ever think of me as a dirty sorceress, unworthy of—"

"No! No." He shook his head. "What I did speaks of my faults, not yours. You are...you... Every day I feel as if pieces of me have been dipped in fire and hammered into a sword, and you are the blacksmith. You are the best person I know. A fighter. Fear and pain do not slow you down. You take your hardships, and you create diamonds. I am unworthy of you. Because you're right. We protect our loved ones, no matter the cost to ourselves. I didn't protect you. But I will. From now on, I will."

Flayed alive, I shook my head harder. His words were potent and powerful; they destroyed me, but they remade me, too.

After he stoked the fire, he propped a dagger hilt on one of the rocks, the flames licking the blade. Forget his declarations for a moment. Or forever. Yeah, I liked forever better. The fire…the blade… I gagged, my vision winking in and out, my airways constricting.

"There has to be another way. You can compel me," I said, desperate. "This one time. Please, Roth. Please. You have to try."

"If I compel you now, after vowing never to compel you again, I will be without honor, and unworthy of your love."

"Extenuating circumstances," I insisted.

"That is another way of saying 'excuse,' and no excuse is ever good enough." He cut away the rest of my dress, pulling the sodden skirt away from me, leaving me in a bra and panties, with a sliver of glass anchored to my thigh. He sucked in a breath. "You *are* the one who watched me, even though you wore the torque."

"I had enchanted glass. Then you paid Ophelia to block me and ruined everything."

"I told myself it couldn't be you, even when I missed the mystery gaze."

Okay, he needed to shut up. Like, now. His confessions were messing with my already screwed-up mind.

I needed to think and figure out how to stop the bleeding.

—*Are you dying?*— Phobia demanded.

"No way. I'm not dying, baby. Promise." I smiled at him. "I'll fight, I'll survive."

Roth glared at the spidorpion as if jealous before beseeching me with his gaze. "I *need* you to heal, sweetling. My world is better with you in it."

Pretty words. Mean nothing. "Then compel me," I said. "Use your ability on me, the way you expect me to use my ability on you."

He jolted. Though guilt and shame darkened his expression, he didn't hesitate to say, "Everly Morrow, you will heal. Muscles and flesh and vessels will weave back together. Lost blood will replenish."

Magic caressed my skin. Beautiful, powerful…painful. My back arched, the regeneration of tissue sending javelins of fire through every inch of me.

As I healed, his shame and guilt melted away, awe taking their place, as if he finally had a reason to celebrate his gift. Roth clasped my hand, and smoothed hair from my damp brow.

"D-distract me," I begged. "Tell me more about your magic."

I expected refusal or hesitation. Willingly discuss his weaknesses with a sorceress? Never. But he confessed, "I cannot supersede another person's magic, or stop a poisoning after it has occurred. I cannot raise the dead or reverse time. I cannot compel multiple people at once. I cannot control the emotions others feel, and I cannot manipulate memory. The more black-and-white the command, the stronger the compulsion. Some people are naturally resistant, others more susceptible."

I listened, rapt.

"If you need more power," he said, his gaze blazing desperation at me, "I want you to take from me."

Had he sustained a knock to the head? "I will *never* take power from you again." I grudgingly added, "Unless I'm angry and need to make a point. Or I feel threatened. Or I'm dying."

His lips performed an almost-smile, the corners lifting and falling quickly. "I meant what I said. I've missed our link. And the thought of being what you need… It satisfies me in a way I've never before known."

I didn't… I wouldn't… might I couldn't deal with him, or the changes in him, or what they meant. Couldn't dare to hope we had a future with the prophecy hanging over our heads.

When my pain subsided to a dull ache, I tested my range of motion. Newly healed skin pulled taut and the muscle ached, but I had no doubt I would make a full recovery.

"Look," I said and sighed. "You don't need to worry about me. We're going to part ways. Instead of fighting each other, we'll fight fate. Hasn't the little bitch played with our lives long enough?"

Every time I'd annoyed, hurt or angered him, a muscle had ticked beneath his eye or in his jaw. Now was no different. *Tick, tick, tick.* Like the metronome I'd once found so pleasing. So what had I done this time? Annoyed, hurt or angered him? Perhaps a combination of all three?

"I deserve to be kicked out of your life," he said. Angered, definitely angered, though I suspected it was self-directed. "I am unworthy of your trust and your companionship. But I would like a chance to do—to be—better. Give me a chance to prove I can be good for you."

My heart tripped over my ribs, leaving *me* annoyed.

"If you will not," he said, "I will understand. But I will never stop trying to earn your forgiveness."

Stubborn to my core, I replied, "You should have proven yourself long before now."

"Yes." He bowed his head again, the shame back. "You are right."

Do not soften. Softness had another name—weakness. "As soon as I'm strong enough, I'm going to ditch you. Good luck finding me. This girl finally has the home court advantage."

Tick, tick, tick. Silent, he peeled off his clothes—everything but linen underwear—and hung our garments to dry in front of the fire.

Despite our state of undress, silken warmth settled over me. My eyelids grew heavy, drooping. *Can't let myself sleep. Can't entrust my life to Roth. My...boyfrenemy. Must protect myself.* But oh, I'd never been so tired... Should I use my earth magic to produce a mound of dirt around me?

The ability was so new, mostly untested. What if I buried myself?

The king settled beside me and gently smoothed a lock of hair from my cheek. "Sleep. I'll stand guard."

"Still don't trust you," I said, the words a bit slurred. But maybe I would rest for a minute. Only a minute! Then I would stomp away, like a halfway decent evil queen, and leave Roth in my dust.

"Tell me what I have to do for a chance to win your forgiveness, and I'll do it."

My too-heavy lids slid closed, remaining awake an impossibility. I managed to murmur, "Can't even think about forgiving you until my sisters are found."

I thought I heard him whisper, "I am up for this challenge. For *any* challenge, as long as you are the prize." Then darkness cloaked my mind, sleep overtaking me.

40

I welcome all...to my thrall.

I awoke in Roth's arms, still clad in my underwear and a boat-load of jewelry. Took a moment for my brain to switch from Power-save to On, memories surging. My escape. The ball. My stabbing. The king's tender aid.

He'd spent the night with me, and this time he'd stayed.

He thought he loved me.

My stomach bottomed out.

With one strong arm under my head acting as a pillow, and the other draped over my waist, with my back pressed against his chest, I *felt* loved. Cherished, even. But I'd meant what I'd said; I couldn't forgive him unless my sisters were found. If I couldn't forgive, I couldn't trust.

What would he do if—when—another portion of the fairy tale came to pass? Toss me in the tower again?

Also, I would never be first with King Roth. I would always come after Farrah.

My hands fisted. Sunlight filtered through the overhead canopy, twining with the forest's azure glow. Birds chirped. Crickets sang. A tabby cat with half an ear brushed against my knee.
Boomer! He purred happily. And there was Crouton, Cuddles
and Nutty, too. And Bitsy. And all the others! The whole gang
had arrived.

I extracted myself from Roth's hold, a task more difficult
than I'd anticipated, then skipped to my crew. My newly healed
shoulder offered a mild protest.

"Hello, everyone," I said, doling out kisses and pets.

Lava ants, bees and butterflies converged on me, tickling
my skin as they created an exquisite ball gown. I laughed, enchanted, then lavished praise on my army, thanking them for
their friendship and help.

A tree limb stretched toward me, offering a leafy bowl overflowing with cracked nuts and berries.

"Thank you, Allura," I said, patting the tree. "Why don't you
come out? I'd love to meet you face-to-face."

The only response was a gentle, rolling wind. I'd take that
as a *no, thanks*. Very well. I shared the bounty with my friends,
giggling when Phobia showed off his metal stinger to a spidorpion I hadn't yet met.

A muffled noise had me spinning around. Roth was awake
and peering at me with a strange look on his face. Dark locks
stuck out in spikes. The stubble on his jaw had thickened overnight. Still clad in his underwear, his tattoos and piercings were
on magnificent display. *Want to touch. Resist!*

"Good morning, Everly." His sleep-rich voice sent shivers
careening down my spine.

"Good morning, Roth." We'd never spoken after sleeping
together. What's more, this was the first time I'd been free of
my prison. A sense of vulnerability overtook me.

"The forest suits you," he said.

Do not preen.

Another tree limb stretched toward me, offering a pile of folded clothes—an outfit for each of us—toiletries on top.

Roth rubbed his eyes, frowned, then rubbed some more. "How?"

"Allura likes me. I think. She hasn't confirmed or denied it."

Astonishment and awe battled for supremacy in his emerald eyes. "Is there no one you cannot enchant?"

"Uh, only everyone?"

Tension settled over me as we bathed in our underwear, brushed our teeth and dressed. Allura had gifted Roth with a simple white tunic and leather pants, his usual attire. She'd gifted me with the exact same.

"Matching outfits, Allura? Really?" I said as I braided my hair. "I guess this will be our uniform. Go Team Evil."

Roth chuckled, the sound like music to my ears. "I think we are adorable."

I arched a brow, asking him, "Yeah, but who wears it better? And shouldn't you be heading home now?"

His amusement fled in an instant, leaving me with a staggering amount of guilt. I hated guilt! "You wear it better. Would I be a cad if I admit I prefer you *out* of the uniform?"

I snorted.

"...single file line, if you please." Noel's voice interrupted our conversation, and we stiffened.

In unison, we reached for a dagger. Leaves clapped together, and branches parted. Like a safari guide—even dressed like one—Noel marched into our camp, followed by Truly, Hartly, Thor, Warick, Nicolas and Ty, with Ophelia as the caboose.

"Hartly!" I dropped the dagger and sprinted to my sister. She sprinted to me, too, and we met in the middle, hugging, crying and hugging some more. Thor raced around us, yapping.

I pressed my forehead against hers. "Hisnow disno yisnou knisnow isni isnam hisnappisny? Bisnecisnause yisnou isnare hisnere." *How do you know I'm happy? Because you are here.*

She snort-laughed, then sniffled, her eyes welling with tears. "Whuuut uiuuuuku.i uuiiur umiuuilc? Fiunuciuniul miunuuuliunun." *What makes me smile? Facial muscles.*

"Are you okay? Were you hurt? I want to know everything!"

"I'm well. I met a troll, hated him, loved him, tamed him, and realized I'm kind of awesome. But what about you? When I heard about your imprisonment…"

"I'm well, too. I met a prince, liked him, then hated him, and now I'm trying to ditch him." We hugged again, clinging to each other. This girl was my lifeline. "I can't apologize enough about Mom. Nicolas was right. I'm responsible for her—"

"Hey, hey. Don't do this, Ever. I don't blame you. I *never* blamed you, and I hope you aren't blaming yourself. We knew nothing about magic."

Her announcement humbled, relieved and staggered me.

I heard Noel tell the others, "No fighting. Not with the fangless troll. Not with the gorgeous sorcerian." She blew Ty a kiss.

He glanced over his shoulder, clearly expecting someone else to be the recipient of her flirtation. Then he frowned.

Truly braved a step closer to me, hesitated, then braved another. "I'm so sorry, Everly. I never should have left you when you were poisoned. And I should have listened to you when you warned me about what would happen when the Charmaines learned about our connection. I should have done so many things differently."

I opened my arms. With a whimper, Truly hurled her body at me. We hugged. "I'm sorry, too," I told her. "I should have told you the truth right from the start, and I never should have asked you to choose between your girlfriend and your sister."

"You did what you thought was right. And while I'm happy you never had to deal with our father," she said, "I'm sad we missed seventeen years together."

"Agreed."

Beaming, Noel pressed a hand over her heart. "I just love a good reunion. I love being responsible for a good reunion even more. Aren't I the best mediocre friend of all time, Everly?"

"I do, and you are." At the moment, I could deny the oracle nothing, all forgiven. *You can forgive her, but not Roth?* "Am I strong enough now?" I asked her.

She patted my cheek. Before she could speak, Roth and Nicolas faced off, glaring death threats at each other.

I jumped between them to push them apart. "Roth, Nicolas isn't the one who abducted your family. He's just the smarmy POS who didn't help you out. You don't have to like him, but you aren't allowed to hurt him. Nicolas, if you taunt Roth, I will make you regret it."

As long as I maintained my link with Roth, no other sorcerer could syphon from him.

To reassure Roth I had his back, I pushed the barest stream of power his way, giving rather than taking. His entire body convulsed, and I feared I'd hurt him. Then his gaze shot to mine, his irises ablaze with...with...what *was* that? Primal possessiveness?

My eyes widened. He *did* like our connection.

To my world-rocking shock, he lifted his hands in a gesture of surrender and retreated without attacking Nicolas.

Thank you, I mouthed, and he nodded.

In theory, I should be able to protect our friends the same way, at the same time. Other sorcerers had no problem linking with multiple people.

To experiment, I reached out with a spiritual hand... Yes! Unlike before, when I'd tried this in the midst of battle, I had no trouble. I had strengthened.

I drew back without creating a link with anyone else. First, I would seek permission.

Wanting to avoid a conversation about what had just happened, I focused my full attention on my stepdad, giving him a hug. In typical Nicolas fashion, he awkwardly returned the gesture of affection.

When I pulled back, I searched his gaze for any glint of hatred, but found none. A reason to celebrate!

"You truly fare well?" he asked, chucking me under the chin. "You handled the new king when left on your own?"

"I do, and I did. How do *you* fare?"

"Better, now that we're all together again." Tone gruff, he added, "By the way, you and your sister have the worst taste in mates. A troll commander and the leader of Sevón. Really?"

Rather than correct his assumption about Roth and me, I hugged Ty. Because why the heck not? Roth stepped closer to me, white-knuckling the hilt of his dagger.

Jealous? I smiled at the green-eyed monster of a king, saying, "You aren't the only one who has other people vying for their hand in marriage, Majesty." Okay, so Ty and I had zero romantic interest in each other. Big deal. Let Roth think whatever he wanted to think.

"Being in the middle of a lovers' spat is *always* fun," Ty muttered, but his eyes twinkled.

Though stiff, Roth shook the sorcerer's hand, shocking me anew. "Thank you for saving my sorceress while I was trapped in another dimension."

Uh, had *I* entered another dimension?

"But," Roth continued, "your services are no longer required. I have signed on to Everly's roster."

He'd what? I sputtered for a minute, then managed to eke out, "Unfortunately, there are no open positions on my staff."

He presented me with an indulgent smile. "I have met the terms of our bargain, sweetling. I wanted a chance to prove myself. You wanted the safe return of Truly and the safe return of Hartly." He spread his arms, all *Behold!* "You got yours. Now, I get mine."

"This reunion happened without a contribution from you."

"The outcome mattered, not my involvement."

Well. He wasn't wrong. Great! I'd have to keep up my end of the bargain and think about the possibility of forgiving him.

Problem: as I dragged my gaze over our group, I couldn't help but wonder if fate had brought us together for a reason, arranging us like dominoes. One would fall, and the others would follow.

41

When all is lost, do not despair.
Dare to act, dare to care.

When Warick's army arrived, I sent my insects and animals away, including Phobia and Webster, my staunchest supporters. Just for a day, maybe two. If a troll warrior were to stomp on one…if a sorcerer were to eat one…if anyone were to hurt one in any way, intentionally or unintentionally, I would unleash hell. Better safe than sorry.

I'd been on my own so long, the sheer magnitude of the crowd left me uneasy, my sense of foreboding only growing stronger.

We set up camp there in the clearing, erecting tents Ophelia had conjured and constructing firepits. Working with a troll commander and a sorcerian overlord had to be hell on earth for Roth, but he never complained.

Over and over, he glanced in my direction, making certain I remained nearby. I always turned away, too afraid my heart would betray me. Tomorrow we would go our separate ways; I would put our fairy tale behind me, mourn the death of what could have been and kick off my new beginning.

Beaming with pride, Hartly introduced me to her boyfriend, "Everly, meet Warick, the most wonderful guy in all the worlds. Once upon a time, he wanted to kill you. Now, he's your biggest fan. Warick, meet Everly. The most wonderful sister and best friend."

Oh, how I envied their hard-won happiness.

He banged his fist against his chest and inclined his head. "I have...forgiven you for harming my youngest brother. Ha rtly told me of the many times you protected her from—quote unquote—'unscrupulous rogues.' I will be forever in your debt."

"I will *always* protect her," I said, and yes, the words were a warning.

"The very reason I let you live," he replied.

"Let me?" Ha! "I could drain you in minutes, and you couldn't stop me." I smiled sweetly, batted my lashes and added, "If you harm my sister, I'll prove it."

Hartly gave me a thumbs-up. "You're so fierce!" She rested her head against her boyfriend's chest and said, "Isn't she fierce, Warick?"

"The fiercest," he echoed, though he sounded unconvinced. "To drain me, you'd need your head, yes? I could take yours in *seconds*."

Hartly slapped his chest, saying, "We play nice or we get our toys taken away, remember?"

His shoulders rolled in, yet still he kissed her temple. "I don't want my toys taken away."

Hartly and I shared a toothy grin.

Truly watched the entire interaction, as envious as I was.

One of Warick's men called him over. He kissed Hartly's temple before stalking away, never addressing my threat—because he didn't see me as a threat.

"Isn't he wonderful?" Hartly asked as she sat before a roaring fire.

I plopped down at her side, and Truly did the same, Thor running circles around us. For once, he let me pet him *without* trying to bite off one of my fingers.

One hour after another passed as we talked about everything and nothing. We teased. We laughed. I only wished Foreverly could have stepped from a mirror to join us.

A mirror that continued to call to me. *Look. See.*

Resist! To see anything, I'd have to syphon more power from Roth or link with someone else. I'd already burned through the magic I'd derived and stored from the spidorpion bites.

The trolls remained on their best behavior at least. Well, all but one. A three-horned brute who eyed me like the last slab of meat at an all-you-can-eat buffet. He stopped only when Warick joined us at the fire, sitting behind Hartly, wrapping his muscular arms around her; she leaned back, propped against his chest, completely at ease.

Up close and personal, he was shockingly handsome, with thickly lashed bedroom eyes. He had an aquiline nose, and lips a lovely shade of rose. As sunlight filtered through the treetops, his dark skin developed a burnished copper tint, and the horns protruding from his scalp sharpened.

Warick and Hartly could have passed for "Beauty and the Beast." But Hartly wasn't the real Beauty and Warick wasn't the real Beast. Another couple had the...honor; they were somewhere in Enchantia, living their fairy tale. So were Cinderella, Sleeping Beauty and the Little Mermaid. How many others?

"I miss Farrah," Truly admitted.

I stiffened at the mention of her name.

Truly looked like she wanted to say more, but Roth was striding over, and she lapsed into silence. His gaze was on me as if there was nothing else in the world worth seeing. I couldn't bring myself to protest as he eased behind me, his legs bracketing mine, and wrapped an arm around me to pull me closer.

"I can't stay away from you." He brushed his stubbled cheek against my smooth one, his heat and Christmassy scent enveloping me.

My heart leaped, then crashed. "For now," I grumbled.

"For always," he said, and nipped my earlobe.

My breathing quickened. What had happened to my icy captor? I could resist him. I wanted him back.

Truly decided to forge ahead. Earnest, she peered at me and said, "I know Farrah did terrible things to you when grief overwhelmed her."

"She flayed the skin from my back. That goes beyond terrible. But, uh, she did terrible things to you, too, and trauma isn't a good enough excuse."

Hadn't *I* used trauma as an excuse?

Still Truly persisted. "She regretted it. Before my escape, we talked. If Noel hadn't told me you would need my help out here, I would have stayed put and worked things out with her."

I wanted my twin happy, no matter what. "You should escort Truly to the palace," I told Roth.

"We can certainly discuss it." He kissed my temple and said, "What a shocking turn of events. Never did I think I would aid three sorcerers and an army of trolls. Or see their commander place a female on a pedestal—and not just to peer up her skirt."

"Attention everyone," Noel called, moving to the center of the campsite. "I thought you'd like to know that we are about to be invaded."

What! Roth and I stiffened in unison, then jumped to our feet. Murmurs of shock sailed through the clearing.

Suddenly, armed soldiers stepped from the shadows, surrounding our camp.

I readied my hands, preparing to syphon. Roth palmed his

daggers—*my* daggers—giving one to me. I'd had no idea he'd kept and carried them.

I experienced the smallest, most trifling—not even worth mentioning, really—flare of tenderness for him. If Queen Violet hadn't stepped from the masses, resplendent in a pale pink gown, I would have given in to my impulse to kiss him. At the first sight of her, my insides went haywire: panicked mind, racing heart, shaking limbs.

"Mother?" Truly gasped out. "What are you doing here? How did you find us?"

Violet looked from Truly to me, her eyes narrowing. "Three days ago, the oracle and witch snuck into my palace to tell me I needed to be in this location, at this time, on this day, if ever I wanted to save my daughter. Now I find you cavorting with *her*."

Ignore the hurt. At least she hadn't beat me with wind.

"She is my sister. My true love." Truly raised her head as if proud—of me! "I will always cavort with her."

The declaration dulled the ache of yet another rejection.

Fury detonated in the queen's dark blue eyes. "*I* am the one who protected you throughout the years. Me! Yet you support her?"

Roth returned both of the daggers to the sheaths at his waist and wrapped an arm around my waist. An action of support and comfort, one Queen Violet didn't miss or like—an action I hadn't expected or known I needed.

"You are Snow White," Violet told Truly. "She is the Queen of Evil."

"No." Truly shook her head. "*She* is Snow White, and *I* am the Queen of Evil."

What the what?

My twin faced me, tears gathering in the corners of her eyes. "Think about it. Like the Queen of Evil, I betrayed you time and time again. The night I denied our connection, I all but strangled your heart with pain—as the queen strangled Snow

White with the corset. The comb symbolizes my poisonous thoughts about you the day I abandoned you in the palace. The apple symbolizes our new beginning."

Wow. She'd given this some thought. And what she'd said made sense…but it didn't gel with me. Deep down, I knew we were missing a very important puzzle piece.

"Truly sees what she wants to see," Violet said, glaring at me. "But you and I know the truth. She is all that is good and fair. You are all that is wicked and wrong."

Ignore. The. Hurt.

"Enough," Roth barked, surprising me. "You know nothing about her."

Surprising Violet, too. She jumped and scowled. "A little too interested in our stepmother, are we?"

"You can leave my camp now," I snapped. "Be sure to pick up your Mother of the Year award on your way out."

"If Truly stays," she snapped back, "I stay."

Nicolas blasted the queen with a dark, sardonic look. "Stephan would be so proud, Violet. You mimic him well."

She huffed and puffed like the big bad wolf. "I am *nothing* like him."

"I don't care if you are like Uncle Stephan or not. You don't get to hurt Everly and live to tell the tale." Hartly lifted her arms. A hundred different animals emerged from the shadows to face off with Violet's soldiers. Wolves. Dogs. Jaguars. Griffins. Tigers. Minotaurs. Centaurs. They stared at the queen, unimpressed as she withered. "My trolls want a crack at you, too. You'll taste bitter, I'm sure, but that's why we brought mustard."

My sweet, gentle sister had never threatened a fly, much less another person's life. Seeing her like this—unwilling to back down in the face of injustice—made me want to be Hartly Morrow when I grew up. The trials she'd endured hadn't broken her. She'd walked through fire and come out stronger. A diamond. A pruned tree. A butterfly.

Who could have guessed trolls would be the best thing to ever happen to her, or to me? But they were. They'd kept her safe when I couldn't. They were strong enough to keep her safe *always*.

Nothing mattered more than strength. Nothing.

"You will not harm Everly. Say it," Roth commanded. Compulsion crackled in his voice, stunning me.

I peered up at him, agog. He (usually) reviled his magic, yet he hadn't hesitated to use every weapon at his disposal to protect me.

"I will not harm Everly," she intoned, then blinked with astonishment.

"Good," he said. "Tell your men to lower their weapons."

"Lower your weapons," she commanded. As her soldiers obeyed, she frowned and shook her head, confused.

"No one will be harming anyone." Ophelia clapped her hands over her head. Power swept through the entire camp, the fine hairs on the back of my neck standing at attention. "Until the rise of the sun, anyone who lashes out at anyone else will experience the same pain, only doubled."

Once, the witch had told Farrah she had to make a sacrifice to cast a spell, so I assumed that was the reason she'd given this one a time limit.

"Yes, we will call a truce for one night," Noel announced. Everyone went still and quiet, the air crackling with tension, excitement and fear. The whites of her eyes had bled into her irises. "In the morning, all will be made clear. The hunt has begun. The flames are frozen. Friend is foe, and foe is friend. Venom destroys venom. Shackles fly, and trees bleed. The ocean falls, one drop at a time. The end is the beginning, and the beginning is the end."

Whispers rose from the crowd, and foreboding crashed into me.

Ophelia led the oracle away. Violet stalked to Truly, bypassing me without speaking or even glancing in my direction. Her men remained on the outskirts of camp, keeping watch.

Truly mouthed, *Forgive me*, as Violet dragged her away.

"I do not trust Queen Violet," Warick said.

"No one does." Roth traced his fingertips up and down the bumps of my spine, and all I wanted to do was curl against his strong body and bury my face in the hollow of his neck.

Even outside my cell, he was my chief source of comfort?

I faced him, my traitorous heart fluttering. Stupid firelight! A golden hue caressed his dark skin, making me want more than comfort from him. "You can spend the night in my tent—on your own pallet." Or next to me. I liked sleeping in his arms. "In the morning, I'll use a mirror to take you home." He had a kingdom to run, and I had a future to figure out—a future without him.

"I want you to return to Sevón with me." He cupped my face with his big calloused hands and brushed the rise of my cheeks with his thumbs. "I want you by my side, always."

I reeled, my entire world seeming to spin. Tone dry, I said, "Yes, let me trot myself right back to your tower and don my torque."

His emerald eyes blazed with a mix of shame and determination. "I'll burn the tower to ash and outlaw torques, *after* you've imprisoned me for the same amount of time."

I kind of believed he'd let me do it. *Can't wrap my mind around this change in him.* He was giving me exactly what I'd wanted—before. Now? I couldn't let it matter because I couldn't let myself trust him.

"I'll either live here in the forest with Allura," I said, "or move in with Hartly and the trolls."

Roth stiffened, but didn't push—yet. Judging by the stubborn set of his jaw, he would be pushing as soon as we were alone.

He pointed to somewhere over my shoulder. "I do not like the way that troll looks at you."

I turned, dreading who'd I see. Yep, Three Horns was scowling at me. "He won't attack. Not today, anyway."

Nicolas came over, and Roth stiffened further. The two men stared at each other, radiating intense dislike and distrust. I wasn't sure what to do...until Thor trotted over and peed on my stepfather's boot.

Nicolas snarled with displeasure. I stifled a laugh, and his narrowed gaze swung to me.

"I need to speak with you. Alone." He pulled me aside, out of Roth's arms, though Roth held on until the last possible second, rousing satisfaction in me. "I brought some things from home. This particular item, I thought *I* would need, not my stepdaughters."

"What are you—"

He slapped a condom in my palm. "Either he wraps it up, or he puts it up. We don't want little royals running around until the prophecy is settled, now, do we? Tomorrow, you should buy a contraception spell from Ophelia, even if it costs you a fortune."

I groaned, a blush spreading from my forehead to my toes.

Roth heard the groan, and hurried to step between Nicolas and me. "What's wrong? What did you do?"

Blush heating, I stuffed the foil packet in my pocket. "Nothing. Everything's fine." I pinned my stepfather with a look. *Don't you dare tell him.*

Nicolas grinned, a rare sight both beguiling and calculating. "Enjoy your night, Roth." With that, he stalked off.

Could this day get any more embarrassing? I scanned the camp, desperate for a distraction. No sign of Noel and Ophelia. Warick led Hartly inside their tent. His trolls circled it, standing guard. Violet led Truly to the tent next door. My twin paused at the entrance to search for...me? Yep. She smiled and waved me over.

Spend more time with the queen? I shuddered and shook my

head, then tempered my refusal with a smile. I had all the time in the world with Truly, but only a limited time with Roth. I might as well hash things out with him tonight, once and for all.

"Come on," I said, taking his hand and herding him into my tent. "We need to talk."

The second the flap closed behind us, he traced his heated gaze over me, the once-over as potent as a caress, battering my resolve to resist him. I shivered.

"Shall we get more comfortable first?" He pulled his shirt over his head and tossed the garment to the ground. "I do my best conversing naked. You?"

Okay, he didn't just batter my resolve; he annihilated it. His tattooed skin mesmerized me, every ridge of strength drawing me like a moth to a flame. "You're not playing fair," I whined.

"Because no outcome has ever mattered more."

Pang. "What is it you want from me?" Maybe I could give him something, the way Hartly had given her trust to Warick, ultimately winning him over.

Roth didn't miss a beat. "I want your forgiveness. A second chance. Your name on *my* roster. Your touch. Your heart."

Reeling again... "So, just the basics," I quipped.

The corners of his mouth curved up, sending electric pulses zipping along my skin. But his amusement didn't last long.

Intent, he said, "I want to give you everything, but I want to take everything, too."

As he waited for my response, he trembled. Trembled! I'd seen this boy in the heat of battle. Had witnessed his determination as he'd ended a friend. Had watched him rule a kingdom. Not once had he trembled. I affected him in ways nothing and no one else could.

Flutters in my belly, fire in my veins. A thrum of tension arched between us. Forget having a conversation. Maybe I would experience everything he offered, just for a night? You know, to say goodbye properly.

"I'll always be a sorceress," I reminded him.

He held his head high. "And I'll always be grateful. Helping power you has given me a sense of purpose and satisfaction I've never before known."

Uncertainty besieged me. He meant those words; I could tell. But I'd been hurt so many times, in so many ways, by so many people. If I forgave him and went all in to a relationship, and he changed his mind, I might not recover.

He said, "You are nothing like I once assumed, sweetling."

"You mean I'm not too bold or too brash? I'm not selfish and greedy? Devious and untrustworthy? Shameless?"

He withered at each new insult. "You are none of those things. Well, you are the perfect amount of bold and brash. But selfish, greedy? No. You were generous enough to share your power with me. Devious and untrustworthy? No again. You kept secrets when necessary, but never lied. Shameless?" He tweaked my earlobe. "You harbor too much shame, none of it deserved."

Argh! He kept saying beautiful things, and my uncertainty kept dimming. "I will never be sweetness and light, Roth."

"Do I look like someone who craves sweetness and light?"

He looked like someone on the edge, who'd seen and done terrible things. Anything to protect his loved ones. "I'm not right for you." Even though I had the ability to do what few others could: make him laugh.

"I like everything about you, sorceress." For the first time, he used the designation as an endearment rather than a curse, his yearning for me palpable. "I would change *nothing* about you."

Hope stirred, the uncertainty almost nonexistent now. *Careful.* "The prophecy... We are supposed to be enemies."

"A life without you, Everly Morrow, is a fate worse than death." He stalked to me, fisted my hair with one hand and gripped my waist with the other, but he didn't kiss me as I wanted—needed—to be kissed. "Whatever happens, I will never again consider you an enemy. You are the girl who looks as fragile as glass, yet you have the power to drop a king. The juxtaposition makes me crazed."

He saw me as strong? While I fought my attraction to him, simply to ward off future hurts?

I could have all the strength in the world, but it wouldn't matter if I didn't have bravery, too.

Could I be brave? Could I take a chance on him?

The aches in my body said, *Take a chance!*

I had to agree. The thought of being without him...

I didn't want to be without him.

"Roth," I said, his name a moan...a prayer.

We stared at each other, breathed for each other, pressure building between us. Building, building, until I could stand it no more.

With a needy cry, I rose up on my tiptoes. He bent his head. We kissed, his mouth slanting over mine. Our tongues dueled, tangled and rolled. But he did more than kiss me. He consumed and devoured, lighting a fire inside me. Every inch of me burned and ached.

As he drank down my ragged moans, I twined my arms around his neck and clung to his strong body. The aches only intensified. The fires burned hotter, my bones liquefying.

He clasped my lower back to lift me off my feet. I wound my legs around him, and he lowered us both to the ground, his muscled weight settling over me. The new position allowed me to explore new ground.

I kneaded his shoulders and biceps, the muscles flexing in welcome. When I sank the blunted tips of my nails into his hips, urging him into a slow grind against me, he uttered a growl of pleasure, emboldening me further.

"Strip me," I beseeched.

"Yes," he hissed. One by one, he stripped away my garments. Slowly. As if savoring the unwrapping of a present he'd wanted forever.

The sight of my nakedness must have frayed what remained of his control. The tone of our kiss changed, deepening, becoming fevered, wild. Hungry. I could not get enough of it, of him. He touched me in ways I'd never been touched, until the only words I remembered were *yes*, *please* and *more*. Then I couldn't speak at all, I could only whimper.

My skin pulled taut, the pressure building inside me now. Building and building. Any second I would explode into a thousand pieces—I *wanted* to explode.

With a groan, he wrenched his mouth from mine. I moaned a protest, until he began to strip, shucking his clothes, his boots.

He resettled on top of me and pressed our foreheads together. We panted, breathing each other's air again. "Are you sure about this? You want me this way?"

"Since coming to Enchantia, I've faced death again and again. I do not know what battles loom ahead, but I do know I want this night with you." I rolled my hips, grinding against his hardness. "I have...protection, in my pocket."

"Protection?" he asked, a bead of sweat trickling down his temple.

My cheeks heated as I explained. "You will be my first." My only. "I don't have any, uh, sexual diseases."

"I do not have any, either. And we do not need to worry about pregnancy until we are ready. Magic," he said, and tapped a wrist cuff, "The cuffs are enchanted to prevent both pregnancy and disease."

Could I trust someone else's magic?

"I do not want you worried about anything. I will wear the condom, too, yes?" he said, and I breathed a sigh of relief.

"Yes. Thank you."

He kissed me, then kissed me again before bending down to swipe up my discarded clothing. After withdrawing the foil packet, he studied it like an earthling would study an alien baby in a pod. "I've never seen anything like this. You'll have to help me with it."

Once we had figured out how to put it on, fumbling around, I expected everything to speed up. Instead, he settled over me once again, a wonderfully wicked gleam in his eyes, and kissed every inch of me. Kissed, sucked, licked. Touched, caressed. Kneaded, rubbed. His fingers played with me until I was gasping incoherently once more and writhing against him.

"Can't get enough of you," he rasped.

Our gazes met, held. Tension tightened his face. Sweat trickled from his temples. He *adored* me with his gaze, reflecting wonder and excitement. "Ready?"

"Beyond," I said, breathless.

Seconds later, I lost my virginity. And maybe my heart, too.

42

Death has come.
Who will succumb?

I lay draped over Roth's body, struggling to breathe as my heart continued to race. With my ear pressed against his pec, I got to hear *his* heart race in sync with mine. Such a sweet, soothing lullaby. I never wanted it to end.

Fatigue settled over me like a warm blanket, lulling my mind into darkness. I fought to remain awake. I wanted to savor this time with my king...who was busy finger-combing my hair.

When he finished with that, he traced the ridges of my spine and kneaded my backside. I only wanted more.

This boy had worshipped every inch of me, as promised. And, after being on the receiving end of his adoring gaze and reverent touch, I could hold on to my grudge no longer. I decided to let it go.

The past was the past. We'd both made mistakes. He'd hurt

me, and I'd hurt him. We'd both had our expectations and our prejudices, each born from experience and fear.

But we'd learned from those mistakes, and we'd grown together.

We were making better choices now. We would have a better future.

As I did it—as I let go—a crushing weight lifted from my chest, a weight I hadn't even known I carried. A smile bloomed.

"What is this?" Roth asked, tracing a fingertip over the edge of my lips.

"I'm happy." Was he? Though I wanted to whisper secrets to him and plan for that future, a worry began to niggle at me. Did he wish I would roll away and let him sleep?

I mean, he was utterly relaxed for the first time in our acquaintance, his cares gone. Or maybe his cares no longer mattered because he had something to look forward to—our relationship? But I didn't know how this afterglow thing worked. I only knew he'd been in a hurry to leave Annica soon after they'd done the deed.

So, I did it. I said, "Good night," and rolled away, just in case. My life story—just in case.

He rolled me back. He was frowning. "Talk to me. Tell me what's going on inside your head. Please."

Why not tell him the truth? "Before I came to Enchantia, I saw you in a vision. You were dressing after being intimate with Annica. She begged you to stay—at least, I'm assuming—but you were eager to leave."

His frown deepened. "And you think…what?"

"That you don't like clingers, and you don't want to stick around after getting busy."

The frown faded at last, and his tone gentled. "You are not Annica. You are Everly, my sweetling."

"So I'm an exception?" I asked, half scoffing, half pleading.

Okay, I might have forgiven him, but old fears remained. Noted.

"You are my...everything," he said, "so of course you are my exception. To be honest, you were my exception before we met. I didn't end things with Annica because of my engagement to Truly. I knew my sister loved Truly, knew I'd never be with her in a romantic sense. I ended things with Annica because of my dream about you. I'd begun to feel as if I were cheating on a girl I'd never met." He rolled me again. This time I ended up *underneath* him. "I want you to cling to me, sweetling, and never let go. Because I'll be doing the same to you."

I peered up at him, wide-eyed, feeling a bit shy for the first time in my life. With his dark hair tousled, his emerald eyes sparkling, his lips slightly swollen from our kisses, he stripped me of every last defense.

I remembered what he'd once told me. *I want to look at a girl and know she's mine alone. That I'm hers. That we belong to each other, body and soul. I want the world to stop when we're together. I want to dream about her at night and wake for her every morning. I want to put her first, and know she does the same for me. I want...everything.*

"Do you still dream of me?" I asked, tracing a heart over his, well, heart. "Does the world stop when we are together?"

He brushed the tip of his nose against mine. "I didn't know it until today, but my world had stopped long before I met you. You made it start again. And dream of you? I do. Every minute of every day."

Reeling again... "You still think you love me?" Fatigue got the better of me, and I yawned.

"I do not." Before I could pout, he added, "I *know* I love you."

I drifted off then, smiling and thinking, *So this is what contentment feels like.*

A scream woke me. My own? Panting, heart a jackhammer against my ribs, I leaped to unsteady legs. "Roth?"

He was gone. His clothes were gone, too. I dressed as quickly as possible, memories overwhelming me. The beauty of Roth's body. The sweetness of his taste. The pleasure derived from his hands. The perfect fit of our bodies, like two puzzle pieces had just clicked together. The sultry aftermath.

Behold. I am the Evil Queen, and I like to cuddle.

Did Roth regret what we'd done, and what he'd told me? Or had he truly accepted me just as I was? Were we a couple now, officially?

Gah! I needed to speak with him. Where had he gone?

Another scream echoed through the trees, and I sucked in a breath. Hartly?

Frantic and nearing panic, I sprinted from the tent—

And drew up short. Ice covered the entire camp, turning it into a veritable wasteland. Tree limbs drooped, weighed down by the ice. Animals and insects were frozen midaction. Trolls were frozen, too. Violet stood half in, half out of a tent, immobilized in the middle of a hasty exit.

I groaned. Nicolas and Ty—nowhere in sight. Noel and Ophelia—nowhere in sight.

Where was Hartly? Truly? Roth?

A strange melody floated through the air. A woman's hum? The sound chilled me to the bone.

Teeth chattering, I spun. Any leaves not iced now rippled like magic glass, as if in…warning? The firepit still blazed. Truly stood behind it, lighting the tips of her arrows before firing at a contingent of Sevón soldiers.

Fear for her, for them all, kindled. We were under attack.

The fire spread, melting sections of ice, but also charring sections of forest. A blessing and a curse. As trees went up in flames, dark smoke thickening the air, and I coughed.

The flash of sunlight on gleaming swords drew my attention to a group of trolls, and I whimpered with relief. They had formed a circle around Hartly and Thor, protecting the two as my sister lifted her arms to summon more animals to our defense.

Among the enemy soldiers were Vikander and Saxon. Why would they go to battle against Roth? Unless the king had bidden them here?

No, no. He wouldn't betray me. Something more was at play here. But what? And where was he? Growing queasy, I searched the terrain. Soldiers battled trolls with their customary brutality. No mercy. Metal slammed against metal, creating a macabre symphony. Whoosh, clang. Grunt. Groan. The scent of rusted copper tainted the icy breeze.

How could the world—my world—have changed so drastically, so quickly?

"Roth!" I shouted. If he'd been hurt, or worse...

Whack! Someone crashed into me, throwing me down. My head knocked into a rock, stars distorting my vision. Oblivion beckoned, but I fought, blinking until my sightline cleared.

Three Horns! He pinned me down and bared his teeth, and I nearly vomited.

"You killed my youngest brother, and your sister has ruined my older brother," he snarled. "Now I return the favor."

He swooped down to sink those fangs into my neck, but I punched him, breaking his nose. Cartilage snapped, and blood poured. Unfortunately, I'd only slowed him down. He dove back down, fangs piercing skin and muscle with brutal precision.

Fire flooded me, no part of me unscathed. The pain! Too late I recalled I still had a link to Roth. Though I hated weakening him, even for a moment, especially during battle, I syphoned a small stream of power and shouted, "Sleep! You will sleep!"

The troll shuddered atop me, his eyes closing. As he slumped forward, metal slicked through his throat—from behind, the blade slashing from one side to the other. His head slid off his neck, thudding to the ground before his body. A body about to land on me while spurting blood from its severed artery. Except, a booted foot kicked it away, saving me from a literal bloodbath.

Roth stepped into a beam of light, and I nearly sobbed with relief. He was alive, and seemingly unharmed.

Noticing the puncture wounds in my neck, he dropped to his knees at my side. Agony twisted his features.

"Sweetling," he croaked. "You were bitten. My magic cannot negate the toxin once it had been injected."

I lay there, muscles jerking as my level of pain magnified. This was it, then? My end. Journey over.

Losing track of the world around me, my life began and ended with Roth. Combating tears, I told him, "Do what needs doing, princeling. I understand." My survival instincts screamed protests, but I paid them no heed. I would not make this harder for Roth, and did not want him dealing with guilt forevermore.

Never had he looked more torn. "You're not supposed to die this way." Anguish had turned his voice to gravel.

"I know, but it's happening, anyway."

"No." He gave a violent shake of his head. "How am I supposed to go on without you?"

This boy really does love me. "You must."

Tremors rocked him. He raised his sword. The troll's blood still dripped from the metal. I braced, ready and not ready.

He roared and dropped his arm to his side. "I cannot do it. So you will heal, Everly. You will fight the troll venom. You will overcome it, and you will heal. You will not die. *Please.*"

My pain only escalated, weakness infiltrating my limbs, darkness peppering my thoughts, and I knew he was right the first time. He couldn't compel the poison away. In this, I would not be an exception.

"Heal, Everly." A hot tear dripped from his cheek and splashed onto mine.

"Save my sisters," I pleaded. "And Roth? I…" I frowned.

The pain and weakness were…dissipating, strength returning to me, bit by bit.

I didn't understand. I was healing?

Something Noel said last night prodded my mind. *Venom destroys venom.*

"Roth," I said, daring to hope. Once, he'd told me troll venom couldn't hurt animals. Arachnids must qualify, the spidorpion venom in my veins eradicating the troll taint.

"The black…it's fading," he said, shocked and jubilant, even as he turned and lifted his sword to block an incoming blow. Metal clanged against metal. He dodged the next strike, spun and delivered a deathblow.

The rest of the world came rushing back into focus. Someone still sang that haunting song—what *was* that? Trolls still battled soldiers. "Why are Sevón soldiers attacking you, their king?" I clambered to my feet.

When the soldiers broke through the first line of trolls, more trolls rushed our way to form a wide circle around us, preventing the soldiers from reaching us while I continued to heal.

"Magic. The siren's song." The song grew louder, and Roth's features contorted with pain. He pulled at hanks of his hair. "It rouses an urge to attack you specifically, and it's fierce, powerful…never experienced anything like it. Fighting it…"

Attack *me?* Why would a siren want me dead? I'd never hurt one…except the one I'd stopped Roth from choosing at the ball.

"I love you," he said. A vein throbbed in his forehead. "I will never harm you. I would rather die."

The song grew louder, louder still, until the sound scraped my ears. Like nails on a chalkboard. "That's right. You love me." I petted his face, trying to soothe him, relieved when he leaned into the touch. "Concentrate on me. Good, that's good." With danger all around, the future was more uncertain than ever, yet I had no defenses left. "I love you, too." Truth. I loved his strength. His wit. His intensity. Loved that we were both like pieces of the same puzzle and somehow fit together perfectly. Even when he'd hated me, he'd treated me well.

I craved a future with him.

His eyes flared with enough heat to singe my soul. "When this battle ends, tell me again."

Crisis averted. He'd regained control of his actions. "Have you seen Nicolas, Ty, Ophelia or Noel?"

"No. They were gone when I awoke."

On our own, then. "I'm going to syphon as many soldiers as possible. If black lines appear in my skin, do not touch me. Actually, no more touching me, period, just in case." Syphoning from Roth again would be foolish. He would weaken. But I *needed* to wield my illusion and earth magic ASAP. The soldiers were close to overcoming the trolls.

Where were Violet's men? Why weren't they helping us?

"Do not syphon from them," he said, slapping a dagger into my hand. "The soldiers are under the siren's spell, tasked with killing you. If you take from them, you might find yourself under her spell, as well." He picked up a fallen sword and handed it to me, too. "At first, she told me to leave you. I was helpless and unable to resist, until I heard you shout my name. Concern overrode everything else."

Concern…symbolic for true love's kiss?

Roth shouted, "You will stand down," but no one listened. His magic couldn't undo the song.

Amid grunts and groans, the bespelled soldiers finally succeeded, sweeping past the trolls.

"Do not leave my side," Roth commanded me, even as he struck at an opponent. Then another. And another. He should have fought to kill, thinning the herd, but always he did his best to only wound and immobilize the soldiers. Men he'd trained with and fought for.

The stakes had never been higher. I helped, fencing like a pro. In deference to Roth, I delivered injuries rather than death…

but my mercy came with a steep price. The injured got up and kept fighting, allowing more and more men to surround and attack us. How many cuts, slices, bruises and cracks I sustained, I didn't know. At least a constant flow of adrenaline helped dull each new flare of pain.

Vikander and Saxon cut through the trolls, heading our way, and they had no problem slaying their opponents.

"Stand down," Roth repeated. "That is an order from your king."

"We *can't*," Vikander shouted. "Your sister performed a ritual. The one Challen attempted with Everly, killing a siren and stealing her power. When Farrah sings, we obey."

This was Farrah's doing.

My rage ignited, my only source of warmth as a new wave of ice swept through the camp. Trolls froze midaction, and icicles grew from tree branches. Seconds later, Farrah crested the far hill, her arms spread wide as she sang. *Nails. Chalkboard.*

Wearing the same dress as before—now splattered with blood—she glided over the sea of ice. Her hair... She'd chopped off her hair to free herself, the chin-length bob framing her face.

The perfect Snow White, with an edge. Both regal and menacing, she ended her journey on the other side of the firepit.

"Farrah," Truly gasped out, lowering her bow. "You must stop this. Please! People are dying."

Longing passed over the princess's face, quickly erased by hatred. "I will stop," she sang, eerier and eerier, "when Everly is defeated. The sorceress has bewitched you. You are not in your right mind. But I will save you, even from yourself."

How could *I* be the one labeled "evil"? In this situation, I was more like Snow White.

The answer crystalized at last, all made clear in the light of the morning, and I sucked in a breath. The reason none of us had figured out the one character we were supposed to be was because...we weren't just one character. We had the potential to be any character we wanted to be. The sweet Snow White. The jealous Evil Queen. The conflicted Huntsman. The protective Dwarfs.

Every day, our choices decided who and what we would be. Here, now, Farrah acted the part of Evil Queen. When Violet had tried to kill me, she'd played the part of Evil Queen, too. When Roth had judged me for my parentage, *he* had been the Evil Queen. At some point or another, evil had worn each of our faces.

"Farrah." Roth spat out a mouthful of blood. "You have always striven to help our people. Now you seek their harm, just to hurt the girl who showed you mercy, despite the fact that you'd never done the same for her."

"You get no say in this. I am your sister, she is nothing, yet you chose her over me." She waved in his direction, unleashing a tsunami of magic.

From head to toe, ice sprouted over him.

Shock—yes. Fury—absolutely. The urge to murder this girl— off the charts! *Will* make *her fear me.* How dare she hurt the boy I loved. Her own brother. "I walked away, left you alive. I had no plans to attack. Now? You'll be lucky to crawl away."

All but spitting fire, she sang-shouted, "You, a sorceress, have taken *everything* from me. My father, my home. My brother. My one true love."

"That's right. I'm a sorceress." I linked with her, intending to drain her once and for all. Or tried to. Something stopped me; mystically, I bounced back.

Instinct told me another sorcerer had already linked with her.

She laughed, manic and gleeful, even crazed. Still singing, she said, "You think I learned nothing from my father's battle magic? I planned for every eventuality. You cannot syphon from me while I'm linked to another."

Who had linked with her? Nicolas and Tyler wouldn't betray me like this...would they?

As I floundered, desperate for answers, she waved toward *me*. I dove to the ground, passing the firepit, grabbing a flaming log as I shot to my feet. Excruciating pain left me gasping, blisters popping up all over my fingers.

I lobbed the entire piece of wood at her. *Contact.* With a scream, she reared back. Flames licked over her dress.

As she stopped, dropped and rolled to douse the embers, she sang, "Kill Everly. Kill them all, save for Truly. Leave the princess unharmed."

Ding, ding. Just like that, the battle resumed. Soldiers versus trolls and Truly's fiery arrows. More of Hartly's animals arrived—wolves, griffins and chimera. Even a unicorn. As they drove back the soldiers, I began to hope. We could win this!

Of course, that was when Farrah decided to spray her ice indiscriminately, blasting her soldiers, the trolls and animals all at once. Only Truly was safe.

"Kill the troll commander and his mate," the princess sang next. "Kill, kill."

Un-iced soldiers focused on Hartly and the remaining trolls surrounding her. I wouldn't let myself worry. The trolls would protect her; they would prevail. I needed to take out the source of the friction.

"Vikander, you will kill Everly," Farrah sang.

The fairy focused on me, his gaze all remorse and angst, and I gulped. If I killed Roth's friend... If I *didn't*...

"I'm sorry, Everly. You'll never know how much." That said, Vikander launched my way.

Truly launched an arrow at him, bellowing, "Run, Everly!"

He dodged. I reeled. Leave my loved ones behind? Never. I tightened my grip on the sword and braced, ready to defend myself. If I could knock out the fairy, great. Otherwise, I'd have to injure him so badly he couldn't stand, then try to heal him when the fighting ended.

Halfway upon me, Vikander lobbed a metal shard in my direction. Midair, the shard grew…and grew… I dove, but not quickly enough; the metal slapped against my ankles—grew *around* my ankles, becoming shackles. I landed without grace, eating dirt.

Comprehension: I now wore *iron* shackles while a fire raged hotter and hotter around me, jumping from tree to tree.

The fairy tale was unfolding right before my eyes.

We might decide the roles we played, but I was not the one who brought us to this point. My evil acts had incentivized Farrah, yes, but it was her decision to attack that brought us to this moment—the moment I would die or begin anew.

Vikander was almost upon me. *Hold, hold.* He raised his arm, a spear budding in his hand. *Now!* I linked with the fairy, syphoning a stream of his power, then waved my hand and hit him with a spray of dirt, burying him and buying myself a moment to take defensive measures.

I turned my focus to Hartly. Syphoning another stream of power from Vikander, I created a dirt wall around the trolls— a shield—forcing the soldiers to dig their way through and tire themselves.

A cool tide of relief. Hartly was safe—for now. How to end this? How to win?

To my left, a griffin pecked out a soldier's eyes. To my right, a chimera chewed through a soldier's throat.

An anguished cry echoed through the trees. "Stop me," Saxon pleaded. He circled the trolls from the air. No, no, no. If he dropped into the center of the circle…

"No!" I shouted.

He'd done it. He'd dropped into the circle I'd fortified with my dirt mound, giving him a straight shot at my sister.

Heart in my throat, I crawled toward Hartly. The shackle worked with the ice to trip me up. I continued to slip. *Please, let Hartly survive this!* I couldn't lose her. Not now, not ever.

Different animals fought to reach her, too. More soldiers

surged into the clearing, all focused on attacking me, forcing me to stop and defend myself.

From the corner of my eye, I saw Warick fall through the dirt wall, his chest soaked with blood. Instant panic. Hartly... without protection... Letting the soldiers take swings at me, I crawled toward the circle, faster and faster. Everything would be all right; I just had to get to Hartly.

Through sections of fallen dirt, I caught sight of Saxon. I paused to reach out—*click*. Using our link, I picked up his magical string and pulled, drawing from him. A rush of heat and strength for me, weakness for him.

He wobbled on his feet—but he still slashed his dagger in my sister's direction. She blocked. Go Hartly! But self-defense had never been her forte. How much longer could she hold him off?

I drew more power from him. He fell. Using his wings, he came up fast and—

"No!" I screamed. But he did it, anyway. He sank the blade into Hartly's side. Jab, jab.

My sister bellowed in pain, blood pouring from her wounds. Saxon struck again. Another jab, jab. I crawled, shouting curses and pleas until my voice broke. When I slipped, I righted myself. Almost there...

Someone latched onto my ankle and yanked me to a stop. I didn't take time to check the culprit's identity. I purposely cut my hand on my sword, then flung my blood at...a soldier. My venom zapped him, and he dropped, releasing me.

I kicked him in the face. As he stumbled back, I scrambled forward once again. Hartly had fallen. Her blood... So much blood. She remained motionless. Thor whimpered and licked her face.

She wasn't dead. Nope. She had fallen asleep. I could patch her up and revive her.

Saxon sprang into the air, but a mortally wounded Warick pulled himself into an upright position, caught the avian's foot and wrenched him back to the ground, where the two grappled. A savage battle, the combatants without mercy. The troll commander bit and clawed, enraged, but weaknesses slowed his reflexes…until Saxon managed to stab him in the neck before shooting away like a bullet.

Warick collapsed next to Hartly, the remaining trolls closing in around them once more, only to part when I arrived.

My beloved sister wheezed as she reached for Warick. See! I knew she was alive. But the light in her eyes was fading fast.

Warick wheezed as he reached right back. Thor sat between them, licking my sister's wrist.

"Come on, Hartly. Come on! You will heal." Syphoning another stream from Roth to borrow his ability, I commanded, "Hear my voice. You. Will. Heal."

Her gaze slid to me, and she smiled, destroying my heart. "Wisnorth isnit." The words were barely audible, yet they wrenched a full-on snot-sob out of me. Worth it—the trip to Enchantia, giving herself to Warick, saving me.

"You're not going to die," I told her.

With her dying breath, she whispered, "Love you." Then her body went lax, her head lolling to the side, her eyes staring at nothing.

A tear ran down Warick's cheek before he, too, went lax.

Thor howled at the sky. He knew she was gone. Gone and never coming back.

I shook my head in denial. *This isn't happening. You can't leave me.*

But she did leave me. She had no pulse.

No life.

No future.

No new beginning.

For Hartly, death had been literal.

Grief stabbed me and twisted the blade. I'd lost my mother,

my home and now my sister. I'd killed. I'd endured rejection after rejection and months of captivity, but this…

Nothing was worse than this.

An anguished wail ravaged my throat. Trembling uncontrollably, I caressed Hartly's soft but cold cheek. "How do you know I lived a good life? Because I lived it with you."

A troll helped me out, using his ax to sever the length of chain link between my legs. The shackles fell away.

I had a choice. Remain here with Hartly, and likely die with her, letting her killers escape unscathed, or get up and make them pay.

Rage boiled inside me, torching my grief, consuming me.

I couldn't let Farrah win. The one who'd overseen my sister's murder should not win *anything* but a death sentence.

Oh, yes. Farrah. Would. Pay. I would not rest until I'd buried her in every way.

For the first time, I wanted to be the Evil Queen.

I *chose* to be the Evil Queen.

Ears buzzing with a rush of blood, I climbed to my feet and walked forward. Dead bodies littered the clearing. Smoke billowed and ice gleamed. Without Hartly, the mythological creatures she'd summoned lost interest in the battle and fled. No matter. On the enemy's team, only Vikander, Saxon and a handful of soldiers remained standing, but they were outnumbered by trolls. Truly's fiery arrows had taken out a good portion of our foes.

Even as she sang and choked on sobs, casting her gaze to the fallen Hartly again and again, Farrah drew back her elbow, ready to pelt me with ice. It was then, that moment, that I noticed Nicolas. He stood behind her, his arms crossed over his chest, his narrowed gaze on me and filled with hate—more hate than before.

"You cannot defeat us both, Everly," he said.

"How can you aid her? She killed Hartly. *Why* do you aid her?"

You know why. I...did. Because he'd never forgiven me for Aubrey's death. Instead, he'd held on to his contempt, nursed it, fed and watered it, letting it grow from a seedling to an oak, until he was okay with murdering an innocent girl he'd once loved just to strike at me. Now branches of bitterness stretched through his mind, his heart, and his lungs, throwing shade on every thought, beat and breath.

Hate had poisoned him. The same might have happened to me, if I hadn't forgiven Roth.

Nicolas had given me the condom last night to ensure I remained distracted. Betrayal rocked me to the core.

"Why don't you fight me yourself, coward?" I spat at him.

"Fate says Farrah will kill you," he replied easily. "If that is how I get what I want, so be it. You murdered my Aubrey, and you will pay for it."

You will pay for it. Words I'd thought and uttered today, as well. The fact that I had something in common with this man... I shuddered. "How many wives, mothers and sisters have you murdered over the years, huh?" I demanded.

He scowled at me. I'd take that to mean "many."

"Don't," Truly shouted, aiming an arrow at her girlfriend's heart. "Don't make another move against Everly."

Nicolas had distracted me—again—to allow Farrah to reposition, preparing to nail me with ice. I shuddered. If not for Truly's outburst, I would have lost this war.

"I must do this," Farrah sang. "Don't you see? We cannot have our happily-ever-afters until she is vanquished."

All of this, for a happily-ever-after? *Then that is what I will take from her.*

"You're right." I smiled at Farrah and sauntered to Truly's side. "I *did* steal her away from you. Your brother, too. Haven't you heard? He's in love with me. Shhh, don't tell, but I think he's going to propose. Just think! I'll be your stepmother *and* your sister-in-law."

Farrah's cheeks mottled with rage.

I wasn't done. "The men in your family can't get enough of me, huh?"

That did it. That pushed her over the edge. With a war cry, she punched her hand in my direction. Ice daggers flew from her fingertips, hurling straight toward me. Expected. Like before, I unleashed dirt magic, stopping the daggers midway.

What I didn't expect: Nicolas had linked with someone who created water. He conjured a jet of water to wash away the dirt, giving the next set of daggers a clean pathway. Daggers Farrah did not hesitate to unleash.

I drew from Vikander, planning to craft a metal shield with my dagger.

But Truly threw her body into mine, knocking me down, stopping me. The daggers cut through *her*, slicing in one side and flying out the other.

Dizzy from impact, I scrambled to my knees. "Truly!"

My twin rolled to her back, gasping for breath. Blood gushed from multiple wounds on her torso.

I'm to lose her, too? I was supposed to watch my twin die? I clasped her hand, her grip limp. "You fool! Why did you do that?"

"Love you." Blood poured from the corners of her mouth, too. "Didn't get...enough time... My fault..."

Finally, Farrah stopped singing. She screamed and dropped to her knees.

"Shhh, shhh. Save your strength, love." Frantic, I scanned the crowd around us. Vikander and Saxon appeared shell-shocked. "Help me. Help me save her. Please!"

With tears streaming down her cheeks, Farrah crawled to her fallen ex, our war forgotten. "Truly, you have to be all right."

She patted my twin's cheek. "You have to heal. I never meant… You weren't supposed to…"

Act! Now! Tears streamed down *my* cheeks, blurring my vision, but I didn't care. My enemy had willing placed herself in striking distance. So I struck, sinking a dagger into her—

"No!" A spray of water had just whisked the weapon from my grip. Nicolas!

Farrah continued patting Truly's cheek. Truly tried to say more to me, but blood gurgled from the corners of her mouth, muting her voice. I could guess what she wanted to convey— *Do not hurt Farrah.*

I. Didn't. Care. I must. Farrah couldn't be allowed to live.

As I readied my sword, Saxon flew over, grabbed her and carried her away.

"No!" Allow her to live, even one more day? "Bring her back!"

Displaying superhuman strength, despite the power I'd boosted, Vikander lifted the frozen Roth, planning to carry him away.

My rage boiled over. "Stop him!"

A troll slammed into Vikander, tossing him to the ground empty-handed.

The fairy fought back, shouting, "Let me take Roth, Everly. I will help him."

"I'd rather die than let you have him," I roared.

Vikander took my words seriously. He raced away, shouting, "Retreat! Retreat!"

The remaining soldiers followed him, Nicolas among them. Why hadn't he struck at me again? Were his batteries running low?

Some of the trolls gave chase. Others remained behind to deal with the wounded, friend and enemy alike.

I turned back to Truly. Her watery eyes pleaded with me as she tried to speak. Blood still gurgled from her mouth.

Not knowing what else to do, I syphoned a little more from Roth, more, more, until my tongue tingled with readiness. *Careful, careful.* If I saved Truly only to kill Roth in the process...

I shouted, "You will heal, Truly. Now!"

43

The time has come to pick a side,
for you will never bridge the great divide.

Was I too late? Roth's compulsion magic couldn't bring back the dead. But life still glowed in Truly's eyes, a pulse thumping at the base of her neck. She *had* to heal. So I waited.

And waited.

I'd told Hartly to heal, too, and still she'd died.

Worry made me feel as if my skin was peeling away. I was raw and exposed, every whip of wind making me jerk with pain. "Come on, Truly. Heal!"

Her gaze found mine, an apology shining in her eyes. She gasped out a word I didn't understand just before her lids closed, and her head lolled to the side.

No! Bordering on hysterical, I dropped my sword and straddled her, preparing to administer CPR, careful not to let my poisoned blood drip on her skin. When I pressed my palms over her sternum, however, I encountered a beating heart. She was alive? I slumped over, tears spilling down my cheeks. Tears of relief, impotence and more rage.

As she mended, the trolls corralled the fallen soldiers who'd been too injured to retreat. Then, those trolls shouted, "For Warick and his bride!" and attacked.

I gaped. The violence, the savagery. The sheer malice...

Would I be next? Did the trolls know I'd killed Three Horns?

They approached me when they finished, one after the other, all soaked in blood. I gripped the sword hilt once again and geared for a fight, ready to defend my twin until I took my final breath, but each male bowed his head, slammed a fist over his heart and paid tribute to Hartly.

"We loved her."

"Your loss is our loss."

"She will be missed."

I sniffled. I cried. I thanked these warriors for caring for my sister all these months, and for aiding us today. Without them, Truly and I would be dead, too.

The army stalked from the clearing, leaving me alone with the carnage. I wanted to scream and never stop. Blood, char and ash coated the trees. Smoke billowed, thicker than before. Roth and Violet remained imprisoned in ice.

A crack appeared in Roth's ice, and I knew he was fighting from inside it.

I sent a stream of power across our link, infusing him with strength, then used the dagger to chisel from the outside. As soon as he was free, we needed to set out to search for Noel and Ophelia. I wouldn't waste my time looking for Tyler. No doubt he was working with Nicolas.

Betrayal cut through me, sharper than any blade. When would I learn? Trust *no one*.

Thor started barking up a storm, and I frowned. Was something wrong? He remained at Hartly's side and—

What was *that*? A bright green sprout had broken through the ground—through Hartly's *body*. I rushed over, shouting with shock and dismay.

The bud expanded, growing like Jack's magic beanstalk, quickly encompassing her entire body. And still growing. Soon, a massive tree towered in Hartly's place. Tall, strong, majestic, with black bark and white leaves, the limbs already heavy with white apples.

My sweet Hartly had become the apple, the one used by the Evil Queen. Maybe all *bonum et malum* became trees when they died, maybe not. I didn't really care, I just wanted Hartly back.

I beat my fists against the trunk. The bark scraped my hands raw, droplets of my blood splashing the leaves—leaves now withering. I didn't stop. Finally I understood "hurt so good." Every punch provided a slight release of the agonizing pressure teeming inside me.

I punched and screamed, punched and screamed, creating a chorus of heartbreak. Around me, animals wailed, mourning Hartly's death.

For most of my life, I'd had a single job: protect Hartly. I'd failed her today. I'd failed Aubrey, too.

Another scream, then another. My heart had been hollowed out, and only a shell remained.

Strong arms circled me, stopping me. Familiar heat and the scent of cinnamon fogged my head.

Roth! He'd gotten free. I turned and beat at his chest. I don't know why I did, or why he let me. But he did. He withstood my abuse and cooed words of comfort at me.

"I checked on Truly," he said. "She's healing nicely. Should awaken any minute."

When the last of my strength abandoned me, I collapsed against him and buried my face against his neck, sobbing violently.

"I'm sorry for your loss, love," he crooned over and over. "I'm so sorry."

Eventually, I quieted. My eyes were swollen, my nose stuffy. My hollowed-out heart filled up again, overflowing with my rage. I'd castigated Farrah for her choices, yet I'd made mistakes, too. If I had killed her when I'd had the chance, Hartly would still be alive. This was my fault. All of it.

According to Noel—who still hadn't showed—Hartly had been safe inside the troll dimension. *I've seen Hartly's future. As long as she remains in the troll dimension, she doesn't just survive. She thrives.*

My precious sister had exited to save me. Which meant she'd come to Enchantia to die. Which meant she would still be alive if I'd decided to stay home.

Oh, yes. This was my fault. But I could make it right.

My spine like steel, I drew back to peer at Roth. "I'm going to kill your sister," I stated baldly.

He evinced no surprise. He'd known I would want this. "You know the fairy tale. If you go after her, *she* will defeat *you*."

"No," I said, shaking my head. "Our choices decide which character we play. In this, we are both the Evil Queen. Only one of us has to die, and it's her." I *had* to be crowned the victor. "But even if you're right, even if I am the only Evil Queen in this scenario, I will not alter my course. I will punish her, whatever the cost, and at the moment I don't care if that makes me exactly like Nicolas. She killed Hartly. My sweet sister is just... gone. Saxon wielded the blade, but Farrah pulled his strings."

"Everly—"

"She betrayed you, too. Don't you dare defend her."

"I cannot defend her. What she did today... It's inexcusable. But that doesn't mean I've stopped loving her."

I admired his loyalty; I did, but I also resented it. He would do everything in his power to protect her...even betray me.

No. He loved me.

But he loved her more.

Did I understand his dilemma? Yes. Farrah was family, and I was the girl he'd banged a couple times last night. A former stepmother to boot. It was time to face facts. We were doomed from the start.

"If you try to prevent a showdown... Do not try to prevent a showdown, Roth." The iciness of my tone rivaled Farrah's magic, the need to hurt her *seething* inside me. I extracted from his embrace, saying, "Free Queen Violet. The animals and insects, as well."

"I will do this, and we will figure out our next move *together*." He picked up a sword, moved to Violet and chipped at her prison.

I remained in place, dividing into two different Everlys again. Half Evil Queen, half Snow White. My EQ side wanted to plow full steam ahead and murder Farrah as planned. My SW side wanted to comfort Roth the way he'd comforted me. After everything that had happened, he was hurting, too.

My conscience, instinct and ambition voted, and shockingly enough, EQ won.

Something was broken inside me now. My heart, yes. My trust, definitely. I had nothing left to give the king or anyone, no matter my desire to the contrary.

Thor remained seated in the shadows of Hartly's tree—a tree I both resented and treasured.

I returned to Truly. A rosy glow had returned to her cheeks.

"Hey, sis," I said, and kissed her brow.

Moaning, she blinked open her eyelids and eased up. I knew the exact moment memories invaded. Horror darkened her expression. With a sob, she threw her arms around me. "I'm sorry, so sorry. I wish... I wish... I'm so sorry."

You did nothing wrong. But Farrah... I'm going to make it right," I said.

She drew back, the horror intensifying. "What are you planning, Everly?"

Free at last, Violet dashed to Truly's side, saving me from having to admit the truth. To my surprise, she didn't rip the girl away from me.

As mother and daughter embraced, Violet's wide-eyed gaze remained glued to me. "I am sorry, Everly. You weren't—aren't—the Evil Queen. You saved Truly. You didn't hurt her." How shocked she sounded. "I never meant for this to happen. It wasn't supposed to end like this."

"What, you want to kiss and make up?" I sneered at her. "No, thanks. I'd rather eat my own entrails."

She flinched. Good! I hoped her regrets haunted her the rest of her life. "No, I just... I don't..."

"Everly." My name drifted on the wind, spoken in a voice I'd never heard before.

Frowning, I scanned the area until I spotted someone I could not possibly be seeing. But...

In Enchantia, nothing was impossible.

Air hissed between my teeth, my chest constricting. A shimmering version of Hartly stood beside the apple tree, crooking her finger in my direction. Was she real? An illusion? She had to be an illusion.

I didn't care. I would take her any way I could get her.

Almost in a trance, I straightened and walked, no, ran to her. I thought I heard Roth call my name, but I didn't slow.

Just before I reached her, the world around me changed. The forest disappeared, only Hartly and her tree remaining, a wealth of clouds surrounding us.

I threw my arms around—

Nothing. I ghosted through her mist-like body, my chest constricting with more force. I turned, gasping as her face changed again and again. From Aubrey, to Warick, to Reese, to Hartly again.

Though sadness glinted in her eyes, she smiled at me. "Hello, Everly."

"Who are you?" I demanded. "*What* are you?"

"I am Allura, and I have a proposition for you."

The nymph had decided to introduce herself *today*? Why? Had she watched Farrah's invasion? Could she have saved Hartly?

"Wear a different face. Now." Before I started screaming again.

In a blink, she morphed into a beautiful black woman with a shaved head, clad in a dress made of ivy.

"Why are you here?" I asked. "Why now?" Why not ten minutes earlier, when I'd desperately needed help?

The sad smile returned. "I can do many things, but I cannot override another's free will, or rewrite fate."

"This battle, these deaths, had nothing to do with fate and everything to do with an emotionally bankrupt princess." My rage boiled hotter.

"Would you like to pay her back?"

"Yes," I hissed.

"Become my replacement, and you can."

Her replacement? "I don't understand. Why do you need one? How does this help me?"

"For centuries, I have mined power from the dead, both good and evil. I have hoarded treasures, spied, loved and hated, aided and hurt. I am tired, so very tired, but I cannot rest. War is coming—to the kingdoms and to the forest, the beating heart of Enchantia. But I am not the one to weather it."

And I was? I gave another bitter laugh. When I recollected the endless well of power I'd sensed the two times I'd syphoned from Allura, I quieted. To have unlimited access to it...

I would have all the strength, power and security I'd ever wanted.

Oh, the temptation. And really, I'd always planned to open my own business. Why not Forest Inc.? "Why me?"

She smiled again, this one merry. "I have observed you. Every time you've made a mistake, you have learned from it. Every time you've fallen, you have fought to rise. When you love, you love hard. Like me, you are intimately acquainted with both good and evil."

"So are others." A lot of others. "What would be required of me?"

All elegance and grace, she glided a circle around me, saying, "*Everything*. Where much is given, much is required."

"That's a big ask."

"I know. Perhaps you need a taste of what you will receive in return."

In an instant, with no effort on my part, I linked to the forest. Undiluted power swamped me. Suddenly I had a keen awareness of every nook and cranny, secret hiding place, speck of dirt and every person and creature within the woodland border—including Hartly. I could feel her love for me emanating from her tree.

Who I could not feel? Nicolas. He seemed to have vanished without a trace. But I easily found Farrah, Vikander and Saxon, perched atop horses, galloping home.

Farrah sobbed for Truly, thinking the girl was dead. Saxon's wings were broken and hanging at odd angles. Vikander sat behind him, facing in the opposite direction. Holding a bag of metal shards, he created and threw spears, making barricades, slowing the trolls even now in pursuit.

I gnashed my teeth. My sister's blood splattered Saxon's face and chest—and Farrah's soul. If they reached Sevón, they could hole up, forever unscathed by today's events.

I couldn't let them reach Sevón.

"There is more," Allura said, waving her hand. A few feet away, a full-length mirror appeared.

Peering at me, Foreverly said, "Look. See."

Violet's image materialized. She wore a pink gown—the same

gown she'd worn yesterday. She led a contingent of her army through a full-length mirror of her own, using the ability she'd stolen from King Stephan. Then, she and those soldiers surrounded my camp.

My heart raced. I was seeing into the recent past?

The scene switched, the sun rising on the horizon, beams of light filtering through the treetops. Violet stood at the door of her tent, using her magic to create a tornado, gather Ty, Noel and Ophelia into the vortex, then blow the threesome into a quagmire of writhing vines, where they remained, trapped.

"There," she said to her companion. "It's done. I did it without harming Everly, circumventing the boy's compulsion."

Nicolas stepped from the shadows, entering a beam of golden sunlight. "Everly will not survive the coming battle. You know this, yes?"

"Know it?" Violet laughed. "I'm counting on it."

"My hatred for her makes sense," Nicolas said. "Yours does not."

I cringed.

The queen lifted her head, haughty and indignant. "All those years ago, you came to me. Do you remember? You said you would convince Stephan to let Truly live if I vowed to open Airaria's gates to the sorcerian upon the king's death."

Her "deal with a devil," no doubt. I should have known she'd meant Nicolas. What was his endgame?

"When I learned of your familial connection to Stephan, that you had journeyed to the mortal world and married Princess Aubrey, that you were raising Stephan's sorcerian daughter, I knew you would try to seize my crown upon your return. You played us both. You played us *all*."

"True." He shrugged, not the least repentant. "But that doesn't explain your feelings for Everly. She is your daughter as much as Stephan's."

Violet said, "The second I absorbed his magic, I got to see what he had seen, the reason he'd killed the witch and oracle, and wanted to kill the children One of them Everly doesn't just herald our doom. She *is* our doom."

How could they not see the truth? They'd doomed themselves.

Tears burned my eyes. The worst of their crimes had happened while I'd been busy coming apart in Roth's arms. Violet had acted as the Evil Queen *and* Snow White's protector. Not because she liked Farrah, but because she hated me. Nicolas had acted as a protector and the Evil Queen, as well. The evilest of us all.

Violet had to be Petal. Nicolas had to be Viper.

I'd suspected Roth was Crusty. Now I knew. He was.

Whatever. I didn't need or want any of them. "Can you free Noel, Ophelia and Ty from the muck?" I asked Allura.

"I can and I will. For you," she replied. "Let me show you what else I can do."

My clothes...just...dissolved, gone in a blink. A gown made of raven feathers appeared, molding to my curves. Fragments of crystal and glass began to grow over my arms, twined around my wrists, branching over the back of my hands, along every finger, and ending in detachable metal claws.

The better to cut you with, my dear.

Bloodred crystals grew from atop my head, forming a jagged crown, and Cuddles materialized, coiled around my neck. Phobia and Webster materialized next, hanging from my earlobes, the perfect accessory to any outfit.

"Accept your plum, and you will never again go without power," Allura said, as tempting as Eve with the original apple. "Vengeance will be yours...if you still wish to have it?"

Did I? I craved vengeance, but I knew Aubrey would not approve. Hartly might not approve, either, if she had lived.

If I did this, I would be making the same mistakes as Farrah and Violet. I would be killing in cold blood. I would lose Roth.

Hadn't I lost him anyway?

If I did this, I would wear the face of true evil, like Nicolas. Because I knew what was right—I knew fighting hate with hate never worked. But what else could I do? Farrah had forced me to wed her father, had flayed the skin from my back, had begged Roth to wed another girl, to forget me as I languished in the tower, had arranged Hartly's murder, tried to kill me and nearly killed Truly.

"What I offer is not vengeance against one," Allura said, "but *all* who wronged you."

All—like Violet, who had ordered her guards to kill me, had watched as they'd stabbed me, had sent centaurs after me, had betrayed me, helping Farrah, offering me like a lamb for slaughter.

Determination scorched my nerve endings until I felt numbed to the consequences. I would strike at Farrah as prophecy dictated. I would hurt her, no matter the cost to myself. I would make sure Violet had a front row seat.

"You can feel the forest's power," Allura said, still giving me the hard sell. "You can *control* the forest, and the curtains between dimensions. You can even revitalize this part of the forest, cleaning away the damage caused by today's war."

Could I? *Let's find out.* I waved my hands to unleash magic. Tree limbs swept the dead bodies away. New foliage matured, char vanishing. Flowers and fruit bloomed in seconds. I watched the miraculous transformation through the mist, flabbergasted.

"You are a natural at this," Allura praised.

I grinned and twirled a finger, saying, "Bring me Truly and Thor."

Outside the fog, limbs collected the pair, whisking them into my dimension. And yeah, okay, I could get used to this.

My twin picked up the melancholy dog and looked me over, her eyes widening with astonishment. "Everly? Where are we? Why do you look like...that?"

"You will stay here, where you are safe," I told her, ignoring her questions. No way I'd give her a chance to dissuade me from my current path. "I will return shortly."

"You're frightening me," she rasped.

"Don't worry. I'll be better in a bit." After I'd delivered my brand of vengeance.

Another twirl of a finger sent vines shooting out far, far away in the forest, capturing Farrah, Vikander and Saxon. Still no sign of Nicolas. Another twirl, and the trees carried the trio through interdimensional doorways, bringing them back to the clearing in a matter of minutes.

Mythological creatures followed the group, curious.

Another twirl. Vines caught Roth and Violet. I would give the king a chance to side with me. If he didn't...

He would join his sister.

"What's happening, Everly?" Truly asked, a tremor in her voice. "What are you planning?"

"I'm forging a better future for us," I said, my tone even colder than before and beyond creepy. Excellent. "And I'm having fun in the process."

Leaving the other realm and Truly behind, I stepped forward to confront my foes.

44

Mirror, mirror, on the wall.
Who will perish when I call?

"Well, well, well." Overcome by dark delight, I unveiled my coldest, wickedest smile. "Hello, my darklings."

Standing before me, bound by thorny vines, were my greatest enemies—Farrah, Roth and three of the seven dwarfs, or *protectors*, Saxon, Vikander and Violet. Above us, golden sunlight filtered through a canopy made of ivory leaves. Around us, majestic trees teemed with fruit and flowers.

The loveliest war zone I'd ever seen.

Radiating her patented mix of shock and fury, Farrah bucked and strained for freedom. I didn't want to brag, but I was the one who introduced her to that fury. Before me, she'd been all sunshine and roses. *You're welcome.*

One by one, the protectors bowed their heads, ashamed. *Too little, too late.* All the while, Roth held my gaze, unafraid of my wrath. But then, he was a warrior to his core, forged in fire, then honed and sharpened like a blade, one strike at a time.

Shivers careened down my spine as I breathed in the sugar and spice of his scent. *Focus.* "Dear, sweet Prince Charming. Mere hours ago, you wished to prove your love for me." Would he prevail at long last, or let me down once again? "Behold. This is your chance. Side with me, and lose her. Or, side with her, and lose me. What you cannot do? Side with us both."

Farrah had wounded me so deeply, so profoundly, I would never recover. But I could be comforted by him and only him— if he did as I asked.

The fact that he didn't respond right away...

I bit my tongue until I tasted blood. *Calm. Steady.* Whatever his decision, I would survive.

Finally, he said, "I love you, Everly, and I choose you." His ragged voice teased my ears. "I will *always* choose you."

Joy began to stir to life. I'd actually *won*?

Then he added, "But I will not let you kill her."

My lungs deflated, leaving me breathless and dizzy. "You love me, so you protect her? Good one. For your next trick, pull a rabbit out of your invisible hat."

He lifted his chin. "I will be your sword, and I will be your shield. I will protect you until I take my last breath...even when *you* are your own worst adversary."

A lie! No adversary was worse than his precious sister.

I longed to shout curses at him. But I couldn't reveal my true feelings without also revealing my vulnerabilities. Vulnerabilities could be exploited. So I blanked my expression. Or tried to. My muscles refused to obey my mind, my pain simply too great.

Very well. My illusion magic wasn't second nature, but I could wield it when needed, as long as I remained linked to someone else and syphoned enough of their power.

Since I had tapped into an amazing power source only minutes ago, I had this in the bag.

Streams of heat and energy flowed into my every cell, and I moaned. Had strength ever been this intoxicating? I wanted more, more, *more*. More strength meant I could safeguard who and what I loved.

A truth I'd learned: love without strength equaled misery. Strength equaled security.

Or maybe I should cut ties with those loved ones instead. No ties, no heartache. I would be bulletproof.

With a twirl of my finger, I unleashed a tendril of magic to craft an illusion of calm. Excellent. After faking a yawn, I buffed the metal claws that adorned my fingers. "Why am I not surprised you claim to want me while defending her? Oh, yes. Because you *always* defend her."

Eyes hauntingly beautiful as they filled with torment, he said, "Do you not see the irony, sweetling? You plan to commit the same crimes as the one you loathe."

How dare he! I would *never* be like Farrah. "This just in," I said, mimicking a prime-time anchorman. "Prince Charming could have enjoyed a happily-ever-after with the Evil Queen, the best thing to ever happen to him. Alas. The fool tossed her aside, and she moved on."

"*You* are the best thing to ever happen to him?" Farrah laughed. "Poor, poor Prince Charming."

Do not react. "Yes. Poor, poor Prince Charming. A supervillain in denial."

Without missing a beat, he said, "Every hero is a villain, and every villain is a hero. It just depends on who you ask."

He wasn't wrong. I was a villain to many and a hero to… myself. Roth and Farrah were heroes to the world, but villains to me.

I had a brand-new "no mercy" policy for my villians.

"She struck at you, and we *will* punish her for it—calmly, rationally," he added. "Otherwise, we merely perpetuate the cycle of violence."

My heart leaped. We would strike at his sister together? "Tell me how we'll punish her."

"We will lock her in the tower to suffer as you suffered."

I waited for him to elaborate, to mention the whipping I'd suffered, too. The forced marriage to an old man. The insults lobbed at me, and the common kindnesses I'd been denied. But he didn't. Of course he didn't.

"We both know you'll fill her cell with luxuries, then free her far too soon." *Not. Good. Enough.* I doubted any sentence but death would be good enough. "Face it. You are blind to her many, many, *many* faults."

"How can you...you can't..." Farrah peered at Roth, the fury melting from her countenance, leaving only raw despondency. "She killed our king and hopes to break our bond. You cannot support her."

"I can. I will." He held my stare, unwavering. "I will do *any-thing* for Everly—except help her destroy herself."

I thrilled, and then I cursed. *Enough!* If anyone had the power to sway me from the proper path, it was this boy and his black-magic voice. But I couldn't let him do it. Not this time. Pretty words meant nothing without consequent action.

"You have made your choice," I told him, "and I have made mine. Our course is set."

"That is true, though it will not end the way you hope." Farrah's fury returned in a flash, her gaze spitting fire at me. "Prophecy says I will come back to life and slay you. Prophecy is *never* wrong."

Prophecy was fairy tale, and fairy tale was prophecy. While some parts were literal, other parts were symbolic. Oh, how I prayed my death and her victory were symbolic.

"You will *not* harm Everly," Roth snapped, causing Farrah to flinch.

I kissed the tip of my middle finger and blew in her direction. Once, I'd admired this girl, and yes, okay, I'd envied her, too. Such strength! Now? Pure, unadulterated rage blistered me inside and out whenever I thought of her.

"Why don't we liven up this party?" I twirled my finger, unleashing another tendril of magic.

No need to look over my shoulder to know vines had grown together to construct a regal throne, different flowers blooming over the seat, creating a colorful bouquet.

Head high, I swished the tail of my gown aside and eased down.

Creatures hid in nearby shadows, watching as the prophecy unfolded. I welcomed our audience, calling, "Come one, come all. Look. See. Learn what happens when you betray the Queen of Evil…"

One by one, the creatures moved into sunlight, forming a circle around us. Trolls and chimera, unicorns and griffins, nymphs and centaurs. What a fearsome sight they made.

How much more fearsome was *I*?

Incalculably. I almost fluffed my hair.

As the creatures twittered with excitement, Farrah shrank back. Roth raised his chin higher, refusing to back down, no matter the odds stacked against him. Violet and Saxon struggled against their bonds, determined to aid their royal charges. Vikander merely watched as if satisfied.

Drumming metal claws against the arms of the throne, I announced, "Today I am your judge, jury and executioner. Spoiler alert. You're all guilty, and you're all going to die. But we shouldn't let the outcome taint our enjoyment. There's fun to be had—for me. Shall we begin?"

Stubborn to his core, Roth took a step in my direction. An action he surely regretted when the vines jerked him back in place, their sharp thorns cutting into his wrists, streams of his blood dripping to the ground. "This isn't you. Grief has hidden your joy, but we can find it again."

Hardly. "I was born to be the Evil Queen. The monster other

monsters fear. Selected by Fate, Joy is the carrot forever dangled out of my reach."

He shook his head, a lock of midnight hair falling over his forehead. "Fate might have predicted our course, and the corresponding outcomes, but we decide what parts of the fairy tale are literal and what parts are symbolic. We still have freedom of choice, and I am thankful for that. You are the one I crave more than breath, Everly."

Perhaps. *No ties.* "You may call me Your Majesty." A howling wind blew past us, leaves rattling and branches clapping, an eerie ballad I enjoyed. "Or Stepmother Dearest."

"I'm sorry you were forced to wed my father." Once again, he took a step forward. Once again, the vines stopped him. But all the while, his eyes implored me. "Words cannot adequately express my remorse."

Another gust of wind, the scent of cinnamon, nutmeg and cloves—*his* scent—filling my nose, stronger than before. Awareness heated my blood and fractured my defenses.

Well, why not? He was my most wicked fantasy come to startling life.

"Let me think about whether or not I care what you feel." I drummed my claws with more force. "Still thinking…no. I don't care."

He radiated abject disappointment. *Too bad, so sad.*

Determined, I returned my gaze to Fuxxxx, who regarded me with haughty disdain. "Come closer, child."

I made the vines push her forward. And okay, okay. Maybe I was showing off. But only a bit! I had a link to never-ending power; she did not.

"Let's forget the atrocities you've committed this day." *Do not choke on your hatred. Exhibit control.* "You are also accused of selfishness, greed and rampant stupidity. Opening argument?"

"*You* are guilty of being a plague upon humanity." She struggled for freedom, a little crazed. "One day, one day soon, I will burn you alive, just as our fairy tale suggests."

I canted my head and met Roth's gaze. "Any admonishments for *her*?"

"Right now, you are my primary concern." He searched my eyes. Hoping to find a hint of the optimistic girl he'd first met? "You have never enjoyed harming others. Don't start now."

"Don't do this. Don't do that," I mocked. Inside, I commanded, *Don't soften.* "You're no fun anymore."

But then, I wasn't fun anymore, either. Once, I'd been an innocent who'd thought I could have anything I wanted as long as I worked hard enough. Once, I'd chosen to believe the best of people. Once...but no longer. You could work yourself to death and gain nothing. And people, well, they would always put themselves first, no matter how many others got hurt in the process.

To survive, I had to do the same. I had to be tougher, smarter, stronger.

Everything always came back to strength.

Finally, one of the protectors decided to speak up. The one I hated almost as much as Farrah. "If you do this," she said, "if you step off this emotional cliff, you *will* fall."

"I guess you would know," I snapped. "All of you fail to comprehend a single glaring fact." I motioned to Farrah. "I will eagerly walk into a sword as long as I can impale her, too."

The members of my audience regarded me with horror and awe—the perfect combination.

I stood and sauntered toward Roth, the hem of my gown swishing at my feet. "Evil isn't born, it's made. One thought and action at a time." I paused for effect. "Take a good look at what you've made."

Farrah spit curses at me.

When I stopped a few feet away, Roth swept his gaze over

me, slowly, leisurely, devouring me one tasty bite at a time— and I liked it.

"I'm looking," he rasped. His irises flamed, every muscle in his body knotting with sudden tension. "Never want to stop."

New shivers almost knocked me down. *Hide your vulnerabilities. Grin.* Better. I traced a fingertip along the dark stubble that shadowed his jaw, then glided around him, scrutinizing him the way he'd so often scrutinized me. Could I truly destroy this beautiful warrior?

He turned with me, twisting the vines that bound him. *Fraying* the vines. Soon, he would gain his freedom.

"Want to know the difference between us?" I asked, unconcerned. "I admit I'm bad. You pretend you're good."

The vines fell away, and he walked me backward. Soon was now. Got it. My heart raced. Eventually, a tree trunk halted my retreat.

Roth reached up, bracketing my temples with his hands, caging me in. At six-foot-four, he loomed over me, his gloriously broad shoulders seeming to surround me...and I loved it.

When I inhaled, he exhaled and vice versa. We breathed for each other, agonizing awareness sizzling between us.

"Once, I hurt you when I should have safeguarded you. Something I will forever regret. But I have learned from my mistakes." He moved one of those big, calloused hands to my jaw and traced my cheekbone with his thumb. "Your happiness is *my* happiness."

Pull away. Pull away now! But my limbs had frozen and refused to obey my mind. I stood there, floundering, trapped by my own weaknesses. For him. For what he made me feel.

And he wasn't done! "Marry me, Everly. Become my wife. Let's make each other smile and laugh for eternity."

I gulped. Technically, I *could* wed him. My so-called husband was dead. But...

No! "You can't be serious," I said, my heart racing faster, thudding against my ribs.

"This madness must cease." Farrah yanked at her bonds. "Has she ensorcelled you?"

The protectors issued protests of their own, until my tree limbs stuffed their mouths full of leaves.

"Your thoughts and opinions are unwelcome," he told his sister. His gaze never released mine. Those exquisite eyes, framed by the longest, thickest black lashes, created a beautiful portrait of fierce adoration. "Say yes, Everly."

Must stay strong. If I weakened, the vulnerability he oh so easily cultivated would cost me everything—again. I'd lost too much already. "I say...no. My vengeance will not be denied."

I twirled my finger, new vines wrenching Roth back in line. Much better. I returned to my throne and sat with far less grace than before.

"Do I have your full attention?" I asked.

He remained unperturbed. "You've had my full attention since the moment we met."

Ignore the pleasure of his words. Forge ahead.

"I declare everyone is guilty as charged." I extended my arm to the side and slowly opened my fist. At the same time, a tree branch stretched out...out...to place a white apple in my palm. Prophecy proclaimed I would kill Farrah with poisoned fruit—for a time, at least—so I would. Only, hers would not be a restful sleep. "Now, for the sentencing portion of the trial."

Just as the Apple of New Beginnings had once granted me life, the Apple of Life and Death would grant me peace.

"One bite," I said, "and you will sleep for eternity."

Still not good enough. I raked my claws over my forearm. Skin tore, my venomous blood welling. I painted each claw crimson before I sank the metal tips into the apple.

In seconds, one-half of the fruit turned red.

Fear shook Farrah when I added, "You will willingly eat

this poisonous, poisonous apple, Princess, or you will watch me force-feed it to your friends. Decide."

Roth jerked as if I'd struck him.

Realization: yes, I could destroy him, as long as I destroyed Farrah, too. I might feel guilty for it, but I wouldn't be swayed from my course. Not again. *This is justified.*

She paled, her mouth floundering open and closed. "I won't... you can't..."

She would. I could.

Sounding resigned, Roth said, "This is what you need, Everly? This will help you heal from the damage we've caused?"

The questions surprised me.

"Without a doubt," I replied. Except, deep in my bones, I knew I *couldn't* heal. Some wounds were permanent.

"Very well. For you, my queen, I will do anything. Even this." Somehow, he freed himself a second time, shot across the distance in a blink, and snatched the apple from my grip.

No! "Don't you dare—" Too late.

With his gaze still locked on mine, he bit into the poisoned fruit.

45

The taste of vengeance is foul, not sweet.
If only you hadn't believed the deceit.

Roth had chosen to act as Snow White, to epitomize her character and take his sister's place. A true sacrifice. He'd given to me, expecting nothing in return. He'd trusted me to do the right thing.

As soon as he swallowed the bite of apple, time stood still—but he and I did not. I leaped to my feet, and he collapsed.

Blood rushed out of my head and dizziness rushed in.

Farrah screamed a denial. Vikander and Saxon shouted obscenities. Violet watched everything happen, tearful and shamed.

I dropped to Roth's side and patted his cheek. "Come on, you foolish boy. Wake up." We were still linked; I syphoned a small stream of power, let compulsion coat my tongue, and said, "You will wake up."

But the compulsion could not supersede another's magic,

which meant I couldn't compel him from this. Not now, not later. Not ever.

Every few seconds, the muscles in his jaw spasmed, indicating an influx of pain caused by the mystical venom in my blood.

"You had no right to do this, no right to take my vengeance from me," I croaked. I had to wake him up. I couldn't let him suffer endlessly for Farrah's crimes.

Desperate, I kissed him, even though there wasn't a kiss in the fairy tale, pressing my lips against his, willing him to respond. *Please, wake up. Please!*

No change.

"You." Glaring at Farrah, I bounded to my feet.

She stared at her brother's unconscious body, sobbing. I wanted to kill her more than ever, but I wouldn't. I wouldn't void his sacrifice. He'd been right. If I acted in anger and grief, I would be no different than her, the one I hated. I would be no different than Violet. It hadn't mattered before—or I hadn't *let* it matter—but it did now. Had I walked away this time, rather than striking, he would not be in this situation.

Every decision I'd made had backfired in some way, and I didn't have to wonder why. I'd based everything on my emotions. But Farrah had just taught me an invaluable lesson. Emotions were fleeting and always subject to change; they led you astray.

Despite my epiphany, I would not be letting Farrah go free. I've believed Snow White needed to spend quality time inside a glass coffin, so that was what I would give her.

There were little shards scattered throughout the forest, things people had dropped or broken. Not enough to do what needed doing. But there were thousands of diamonds.

"Bring me diamonds," I whispered, my voice carrying on the wind.

In the end, you, Everly Morrow, will sparkle.

Birds, squirrels and mice rushed to obey, laying diamond after diamond at my feet. A small pile accumulated. Using vines, I forced a shrieking Farrah to stretch out upon the grass. Those same vines crafted a diamond coffin around her.

I expected relief. It was done. Over.

I just felt sad.

When I freed Vikander and Saxon, they knelt at my feet, and bowed their heads.

"I'm sorry for what transpired here." Saxon dropped his head and cried for a moment. "I'm sorry for what I did to your sister. I'm sorry she hurt, sorry she died."

"I will never forgive myself," Vikander rasped.

I knew where to place blame. "Just go," I said, cold, so cold. "Leave my forest."

But they didn't.

"Roth pledged his life to you," Vikander said. "Now I do the same."

Saxon offered me the dagger sheathed at his side. "You are the chosen queen of my king. You are his family, and I will gladly give my life to save yours."

Looking at them was painful. I turned away—and came face-to-face with Allura.

"You will accept my offer now?" she asked, hopeful.

Would I? *For a price...* I gnashed my teeth, afraid to hope. "Can you save Roth?"

Vikander said, "I would do anything, but I do not know how."

Saxon said, "Nor I."

I scrubbed a hand down my face and grumbled, "Quiet. I wasn't speaking to either of you."

Both boys gave me a strange look. They couldn't see or hear Allura?

"I could save Roth, yes," she said. "But I won't. You'll have to do it...after you accept my offer."

"How?"

"Do you know what's more powerful than the truth you led him?"

"True love?"

"The antidote."

My mind whirled. The Forest of Good and Evil. Or maybe Schrödinger's Forest fit better. Here, you could both find yourself and get lost, find insects and herbs that killed and healed. You could be saved and damned. What Allura asked of me…it was both my salvation and my damnation.

She'd said I had to give up everything. *Sacrifice* everything. I'd have to say goodbye to Truly, though we'd only just reunited. I would save Roth and lose him. In essence, I would trade my future for his. Perhaps a fair trade. He hadn't rejected me today. With my enemy vanquished at last, and my grief-colored glasses momentarily lifted, I saw the truth. Roth *had* protected me— from myself. He'd put my well-being above his own.

Could I do any less for him?

And really, this opportunity offered the safety and security I craved for so long. I could protect myself and my twin, and my sister's tree. I could give the Evil Queen a good name, and overcome the stigma of her—my…our—fairy tale.

So why was I still hesitating?

"Why must I give up everything?" I demanded. "Why can't I keep my loved ones?"

"Either you are loyal to the forest, or you are loyal to another. You must choose."

"I need time."

Anger flared in her dark eyes, my link to the forest evaporating as quickly as it formed. "I'll give you an hour. If you cannot recognize the great honor I wish to bestow upon you, then you are not worthy to receive it, and I'll need to find someone else." A second later, she vanished.

Truly and Thor appeared in her place, the sight of them as welcome as it was agonizing.

Pale and trembling, she asked, "What happened?"

She hadn't gotten to watch through the mist? I wondered how she would view me when she heard what I'd done. But I wouldn't lie or hold back. I explained Roth's predicament, as well as Farrah's, and the part I'd played. The part *everyone* had played, even Queen Violet.

Truly hugged me, shocking me to the core. "I love you, Everly. Nothing will change that, I promise you. Thank you for showing mercy to Farrah." She kissed my cheek, and my heart punched my ribs. Then she crossed to Violet, who remained in a tangle of vines. Oops. My bad. I hadn't yet freed her. As she cut those vines, she demanded, "How could you do such vile things, Mother?"

"I hoped to stop Everly before she harmed you." A tear tracked down Violet's cheek. "I am sorry."

Too little, too late. To me, she would always be the Queen of Betrayals. Once, I'd gone to her full of dreams, and she'd crushed every single one. I'd forged a life without her. Now I had no place for her.

So why did I feel like I was breaking down all over again?

Would I forever be torn in two?

"Everly," she said, trying again. She stepped toward me.

Vikander and Saxon moved between us. To protect me?

Too little, too late, dang it. "You had your chance." I turned my gaze to my twin. "Will you be returning to Sevón with Vikander and Saxon, or going home to Airaria with the queen?" And what about Roth? If I accepted Allura's offer and got my hands on the antidote, would he want to stay with me in the forest or go home?

Could he stay with me? Just like his magic could not stop other people from negating his compulsion, I couldn't stop him from staying if he wanted to stay. But his people needed him. He had to go back, no matter what.

Wait. I hadn't sensed any kind of antidote when I'd been

linked to the forest. Had Allura hidden it from me? Or did it not exist?

"Airaria," Truly said. "I will escort the queen home and return here."

I...didn't know what to say.

At the edge of the campsite, tree limbs parted, revealing a scowling Ophelia. The witch stomped into the clearing, covered in muck. A scowling Noel and an infuriated Ty trailed her.

"I'm going to turn you into a toilet!" Ophelia bellowed, pointing at the ashen Violet.

"Forget her." I stepped between the witch and the queen, telling Ophelia, "I need a favor. Can you—will you?—enchant the diamond coffin? I want Princess Farrah to see her crimes, again and again. *And again.*"

"Yes. I can, I will." Satisfaction glowed in her eyes. For once, she didn't demand payment. She simply waved her hand toward the coffin, an azure mist shimmering over the diamonds, and said, "Let remorse cut her heart and make it bleed… Only then will the curse be broken, and Farrah freed."

Now, Farrah would live, as Roth had wanted, but she would suffer, as she deserved.

I expected my own rise of satisfaction. It was done, the war won. No satisfaction. Only more sadness. I'd gained much today, but I'd lost so much more.

When Noel took in the scene, namely, Hartly's tree she fell to her knees. "I saw so much, but not enough. I knew the trolls would protect her, but I didn't know Violet would work with Nicolas, or how violently Farrah would react when she learned of Roth's feeling for you. Now Nicolas will make a play to overtake Sevón, and Azul royals will help him. Farrah killed one of their favorite princes, and they seek revenge."

I couldn't castigate their choice. I'd sought the same only minutes ago.

Roth and Nicolas, at war. One would win, one would lose. Even die?

"What are we going to do, Everly?" she asked softly. "Months before you came to Enchantia, I saw you. So many visions. What happens when you do this, but not that. What happens when you do that, but not this. With you at his side, Roth can defeat Nicolas. But, if you do not control the forest, another will. You, at least, are the evil we know. I wish I had seen more, felt more, knew more. I wish I had seen the outcomes of the other fairy tales. They are occurring right now, in other kingdoms, and they will spill into ours. Now there's something wrong with my magic. Shhh." Her voice trembled. "Tell no one."

Ty came over and squeezed my shoulder. "Nicolas never searched for your sister. He created the perfect altilium instead. I tried to warn you, the day I visited the palace, but I had vowed to serve my overlord, and I could not betray him."

Pang. "Why are you telling me now, then?"

"Just before Queen Violet blew us away, Nicolas ordered me to tell you everything." He dropped his chin and said, "What you love, he plans to take. What you protect, he hopes to destroy."

I'd already pegged Nicolas as an Evil Queen, but I realized the analogy went deeper. He'd donned the disguise of a caring stepfather, a concerned uncle and a staunch ally. Like the foolish Snow White, I'd never suspected a thing.

I looked to Noel, to Ophelia. To Truly and Violet. To Saxon and Vikander. They all watched me expectantly.

I had to decide. No more waiting.

Take emotion out of the picture and... I couldn't leave Roth in his unconscious state. Not because I loved him—I did—but because he was a good man, with a pure heart, responsible for the lives of millions. I had to do whatever proved necessary to ensure he awakened and saved his kingdom from Nicolas. Decision made.

"All right, guys. It's time for you to leave," I announced. "Each and every one of you. I'm going to stay."

Truly set Thor down and walked over to hug me. "I meant what I said. I will return our mother to Airaria and come back. If Farrah is freed before then, please send me a message."

Truly still loved the girl and hoped they could be together, didn't she? I couldn't help but admire her unwavering devotion. And I guess I understood. What wouldn't I do for Roth? "I will," I promised.

"Would you mind if I took Thor with me?"

No. Yes. Maybe? "Whatever he wants."

Thor bounded over and sat next to me, surprising me.

"Come on, boy," she said, but he stayed put.

I petted him, and he let me.

She gave a little laugh. "Well. He prefers to stay."

Violet inclined her head in my direction, acknowledging my existence. "One day, I hope you'll forgive me," she whispered.

"I will," I said. Resentment would forever be poison. "That doesn't mean I will ever want a relationship with you."

Tears filled her eyes, but she nodded and led my twin away.

Tyler accompanied Noel and Ophelia. I heard him tell the oracle, "Earlier, you mentioned a desire to kiss me. Let's explore this."

"Changed my mind," she replied.

"We will go," Vikander told me, "but we will not go far."

"Shout if you need us," Saxon said.

They stalked past a line of trees, disappearing in the foliage.

As soon as I was alone with Roth and Thor, I rested my face in my upraised hands. Though I'd made my decision, doubts still plagued me. Could I really do this? Could I abandon Truly to save Roth? Should I have to? I'd endured tragedy after tragedy in Enchantia. I had strengthened, weakened, strengthened again, nearly died multiple times and overcome pain like I'd never known. I'd fallen in love, fought evil and both won and lost.

I was the Evil Queen. I'd accepted my role and lived my assigned fate. I shouldn't have to kowtow to anyone, even the mighty Enchantian Forest. And...I wouldn't.

Noel once said I would be happy if I strengthened. I realized now, as I lifted my head and peered at the sleeping Roth, that true strength sprang from love. *Love* was strength and power, which meant love was safety and security.

Love was everything.

I could have everything!

In the fairy tale, Prince Charming saved Snow White by knocking loose the bite of apple that had lodged in her throat. Here, now, I felt as if I'd just had good sense knocked into me.

I saw the truth so clearly now, a film of darkness peeled away from my mind. Time wasn't what healed all wounds—love was. Love mended broken hearts.

My eyes widened. Love welded the two parts of me together, creating one super Everly who loved her family, her boyfriend and even her life.

I'd fought to preserve this life. Why shouldn't I enjoy it?

I could never guarantee the happiness and well-being of the ones I loved, but I could make the most of the time we had together.

Still linked to Roth, I peered at Farrah's diamond prison and waved my hand to summon Foreverly.

She looked as ragged as I felt, her eyes rimmed red and swollen, her skin splotchy with patches of pink. Like me, she'd cried for Hartly. "We have come full circle," she said and sniffled. "From one loss to another."

One loss had kicked off this adventure, and the other had ended it. "I want to create a new fairy tale with Roth. The Enchanting Queen and Her Charming King, perhaps."

A new fairy tale, a new beginning.

"No one gets a happily-ever-after handed to them on a silver platter," she said. "They have to fight for it."

"So I will fight." Allura would not dictate the conditions of our agreement. As the president and CEO of Forest Inc.—no! Everly International—I alone had access to the supply of Everly currently in demand.

"Allura," I called, moving beside Foreverly. We were a team. "I have an answer for you."

The forest nymph appeared in a blink, all but vibrating with eagerness.

I wasted no time. "I must refuse your offer. If there's an antidote for Roth, I can find it. And I will. What I won't do is show loyalty to you or the forest, while being disloyal to everyone I love. You watched me," I continued without taking a breath. "You know how important family is to me. If I purposely cut Roth, Truly, Noel, Ophelia and Ty from my life, I will seriously suck." And yeah, okay, I could see that one day I might include Saxon and Vikander in this list. "If I suck, you shouldn't trust me to see to the forest's well-being."

I expected anger from her. Protests. Something! Instead, a slow grin curled the corners of her mouth. She brightened—literally!—sunlight seeming to seep from her pores. "Congratulations, Everly. You have passed another test."

"*Another* test?" I squeaked. "How many others have you given me?"

"Every minute of every day is a test. With your actions, you prove who you are," she said. "If you want it, the forest is yours. But I must warn you. The power will be limitless, but the responsibilities will be vast. I will remain—for a short time—to train you, and help you ease into your new life. But when I leave, you will face hardships. Do you still wish to rule the forest?"

Everyone faced hardships, whether they were rulers of forests or not. "I just want to be clear. I can accept your job offer without sacrificing my loved ones?"

"As long as you want them in your life, yes."

When would I ever not want them in my life? "Then I accept

your offer." Limitless power *and* loved ones—yes, yes, a thousand times yes. Sign me up.

Allura smiled, the link to the forest clicking into place once more. A second later, she was gone...

Aubrey and Hartly stood in her place, both wearing gowns made of butterflies and roses, their golden skin shimmering.

I sucked in a breath, not daring to hope. "Allura?"

"No. Harts," my sister corrected with a happy twinkle in her eyes.

"All hail the Queen of the Forest," Mom said with a grin. A grin I'd missed. "And now you learn a new truth. Those who ate of the Tree of New Beginnings—and those who were born after the consumption of an apple—come here after physical death."

They were *here*. They were here, and I would get to see them every day! Now I understood what Noel had meant when she'd said apple babies would be united forever.

With a groan, I darted over and threw my arms around them—only to ghost through them. We shared a laugh, though my humor didn't last long. "I failed you both," I said, "and I'm so sorry."

"If you could see what we see, you wouldn't be sorry, and you wouldn't feel you'd failed us." The wonder in Hartly's voice... "Oh, Ever. The magnificence!" Then her shoulders rolled in. "I wish Warick were here. Thor, too."

The little dog remained in place, watching me.

"I'm sorry I couldn't save Warick," I rasped. "Sorry I couldn't save *you*."

"My death isn't your fault. You fought your hardest. What more could I ask for?"

Tremors shook me. "I'll take good care of Thor."

"I know you will."

"Go on, my love," Mom said, her gaze adoring. "Go awaken your Roth. We will talk again soon. We have time now." She winked at me. "For now, just know that I've never been prouder of you."

My chest squeezed with a cluster of happiness and uncertainty. "*How* do I awaken Roth?"

She glided to my boyfriend and crouched at his side. I followed and crouched at his other side. I still hadn't severed our mystical link; I couldn't bear to lose my connection to him.

"Place your hand on his heart," she instructed.

I slipped my fingers beneath his shirt. The heat of his skin singed me. His heart thumped with life, wonderfully strong. *My* heart sang.

"The greatest sign of love...is giving," Mom said. "Giving your time. Your energy. Your attention. Your possessions. You are a sorceress, and so often you have taken. Occasionally you've given, too. So do it again. Give."

From Farrah's diamond prison, Foreverly said, "Yes! Give what you once valued most. Give, asking nothing in return."

"I love you, my darling," Mom said. With another heart-warming smile, she vanished.

Across the way, Hartly told me, "I love you, Everly. I'm never far. When you need me, you have only to call my name, and I'll come." Then she vanished, as well. But I knew they remained nearby, watching over me.

I could take, and I could give. Schrödinger's curse. That silly thought experiment had colored every step of my journey and proved the importance of choice.

What I'd most valued. strength. I could give Roth my strength.

I closed my eyes and focused on our link and pushed my power across the bond. Not just a minute amount, like before. I gave him so much, I weakened.

He sucked in a breath and jolted upright, his eyelids popping open.

Joy exploded inside me, propelling me against his body. I clung to him, amazed. In the fairy tale, Prince Charming awakened Snow White when he dropped her casket. Simple. Easy. This had been simple and easy, too.

The tension drained from him as he wrapped his arms around me and pulled me onto his lap. We held each other, clinging.

I heard cheering—barks, chirps, buzzes and hisses—and scanned our surroundings. Thor ran around us. My other pets had returned to encircle us.

"My sweetling," Roth said, shuddering against me. "I knew you'd find a way."

"I'm so sorry." Tears swam to the corners of my eyes. "I should have believed in you, in us. You were right about Nicolas. If I'm not strong enough to be the sorcerian overlord, I will be. Soon. I will not allow him to lead *anyone*."

"*I* am the one who's sorry," Roth said, squeezing me tighter. "I have done you so many wrongs. When I finally tried to do right, I only caused you more pain."

"I caused *myself* pain. And okay, yes, your sister caused me pain, too." Speaking of Farrah… "I need to tell you what happened after you ate the apple." Would he still want me when he learned about the curse I had bestowed upon Farrah?

"No need. I remained aware. And I am so *proud* of you, of the decisions you made and the actions you took. You are wise, sweetling. No wonder you won my heart. I love you."

"I love you, too. So much." I lifted my head and smiled, so happy I could burst. "Guess what? I'm going to help you defend your kingdom against Nicolas." And the wars Noel had promised? I would be here, running my forest empire and protecting my loved ones as I'd always wanted.

"*Our* kingdom, love." He kissed my lips, then my eyes, the tip of my nose and my jaw, his warm breath caressing my skin. "Half mine, half yours."

Remembering his marriage proposal, I said, "As much as I love you, and I do, I really, really do, I'm not ready to get married again." Not anytime soon, anyway.

"I understand. But that won't stop me from trying to win you over...and it won't negate the romance tax you owe me."

I laughed, and he joined in. "Romance tax, hmm?"

"For payment, you must declare your love for me every day for the rest of your life."

"Wow. Since when did you become so easy to please?"

"Since I met you and gained everything I've ever wanted."

I melted. This boy...oh, this boy!

He pressed another kiss onto my lips, and I sighed into his mouth, content. We had lived through the prophecy, and though another fight loomed, a happily-ever-after awaited us. Right?

Yes, yes. Of course. We had entered uncharted waters, that was all. I had no guidebook for the future, no idea what would happen next. But with Roth at my side, I knew we were going to have a wild ride.

I couldn't wait. I was ready. *Bring it on.*

After I'd gotten more of true love's kiss, of course.

★ ★ ★ ★ ★